MW00882536

ZOMBIE FALLOUT 17

THE LOST JOURNAL

MARK TUFO

DEVIL DOG PRESS

SWANVILLE, MAINE

MAC'S STORY

THE YEAR WAS 2036, but as far as Mac could tell, there wasn't any real reason to keep up with the Gregorian calendar; God had left the building decades ago. There were no appointments to keep, no flights to catch, no soccer camps to drop the kids off at. He figured he checked the calendar and kept his figurative watch wound merely out of habit, things that harkened back to the olden days, something that resembled normalcy. Though the world had been circling the drain for a while before the brain eaters—or beaters, as they were called—had shown up, that's what placed the final straw. He didn't mark time for nostalgia; his childhood had been for shit. Better forgotten. His parents had divorced before he'd even finished kindergarten. His mother was a junkie whose life revolved around her next high, although, to be fair, when she wasn't nodding off, she'd been an attentive mom. It just wasn't good enough, and the judge agreed. He frowned mightily on a woman who brought her kids to drug deals and then OD'ed on the product in a Greggs' parking lot. Mac, along with his sister Annie, had become the sole custody of their father, who, besides being a workaholic, was an alcoholic. He was a functioning one, for the most part, but as soon as Jack Daniels crossed his lips, he became an instant asshole. Not physically abusive, but there were more ways to scar a kid than by striking them. So, by default, their father's mother had done the bulk of their raising, and, through all of his travels, Mac had never met anyone less suited to the rearing of children than Grandma Caroline. She wasn't verbally abusive, like their father, she was just...*inattentive.* "Neglectful" would imply they weren't fed. They ate, but she doled out love like a dragon gives up gold from his horde, so, not at all. He figured she was incapable of the emotion.

Mac was ten, his sister six, when the beaters came. They'd been left home alone while Caroline had gone to get the newest flu shot; (because of her age, she was considered "high risk" and was one of the first in line). By the time she came home, she was complaining of feeling ill and was flush with a fever.

"I'm going to lie down; there's peanut butter in the kitchen," she said before walking past the television and down the hallway to her bedroom.

"Okay, Caroline," Mac said. The woman stiffened. She hated that he didn't call her some form of "grandmother," but she was too tired and ill to argue about it. Later she'd have his father teach him some manners.

The next morning, when their grandmother had still not risen, Mac made himself and his sister breakfast consisting of two bowls of cereal. There was only enough milk for one, so he ate his Cheerios dry. He'd tell Caroline when he got home from school that they needed milk.

"Come on, Annie. Dad's going to be here in five minutes, and I have to go catch my bus."

"I don't want to go to pre-school today. Timmy Collins bit me last week and said he was going to do it again this week."

"What did I tell you, Annie? You make a fist, and when he leans in to bite, you bop him as hard as you can on his nose. He won't bother you anymore."

"Mrs. Grendell says we'll get in trouble if we hit people."

"Yeah, well, stupid little Timmy Collins isn't biting her now, is he? You pop him!" Mac gently tapped her nose, she giggled. She ran down the hall and dressed in her favorite outfit, a Princess Peach skirt, striped socks, purple jelly shoes, and a Gryffindor sweater. "Again?"

"I like it." She frowned.

The horn beeped out front, their father was there. Mac opened the door for his sister and waved half-heartedly to his bleary-eyed dad.

"Love you, stinky face!" Annie said as she climbed into the car and strapped herself into her booster seat.

"You're the stinky face!" He stuck his tongue out at her. That was the last time he ever saw his sister. Not a day went by that he didn't berate himself for not telling her he loved her back.

When he got home after school, Caroline was either back in bed or had never left, it didn't matter much. He prepared some mac and cheese as he waited for his sister to get dropped off. When it got to seven o'clock, he wondered where she was, but his favorite show was on, and he didn't think about it too much. He assumed his father had just stopped at the local pub to start things off for the evening before dropping Annie off.

It was the smell he noticed first. It was a cross between burning marmite and moldy cheese, and it was wholly unpleasant. Then came the groans.

"Caroline?" Mac timidly got up off the couch. He noticed it was nine-thirty and still no Annie; that was unusual, especially on a work night. His father didn't give two shits about his kids' schooling, other than it got them out of the house, but on a work night, he made sure to quaff his liquor as quickly as possible to ensure he got a good night's sleep. He would ask Caroline to call her son. Worry had not quite settled in, but something wasn't sitting right. He couldn't explain it, but he was pretty sure he didn't like it.

"Caroline?" He tentatively walked down the hallway calling her name, the smell growing more fetid with each step. That didn't necessarily mean anything; his grandmother was known to use some of the more earthy and odiferous home remedies whenever she was feeling under the weather. She'd once told him that the worse the smell, the better the healing properties. He figured if that were the case, the stuff she was wearing now would peel years from her ancient frame. He wanted to smile at his funny thought, but the moaning was making that difficult.

"Caroline, Annie's not back." He was by the door. Instead of a grouchy answer or even a louder moan, there was a thump against the door. Startled, he let out a small cry and leapt back. "You...you need to call your son! It's Annie's bedtime."

Another thump. Curiosity won out over his better judgement. He turned the knob and lightly pushed the door into the bedroom. The smell that assailed him was a physical entity. His eyes teared and his nose crinkled as he placed a hand over his face and turned away. Another thump, and the door closed in his face. He wasn't so sure he wanted to open it again, and, if not for Annie, he wouldn't have. First, he went back down the hallway to the kitchen, grabbed a dish towel and wrapped it around his face to use as a makeshift mask. He wanted to clap himself on the shoulder for his excellent idea, until he opened the door again and realized it did absolutely nothing to hide the stench.

This time Caroline struck the door in a way that pushed it farther open. He stepped back. His grandmother emerged from the darkness of the room and into the light of the hallway. She didn't look right. Her eyes were opaque, her face was a pale blue color, crisscrossed with the darker blue of prominent veins. Her arms were half-extended in front, and she was shuffling towards him. To Mac, she was older than the rocks they were learning about in school, but she wasn't sliding-feet-forward-for-locomotion-old.

"Caroline?"

Her head perked up and she turned as if she were noticing him for the first time.

"Are…are you a zombie, Gramma?" He'd seen enough low-budget horror films to take a guess, and since she wasn't covered in white gauze, it was unlikely she was a mummy. "Do you have a gun? I'm gonna have to shoot you in the head." Caroline moved toward him. He ran back to the living room, putting the couch between himself and her advance. She stepped against the sofa and reached for him, trying to get closer. Much to Mac's surprise, she did not pursue him by going around. He knew zombies ate brains; he wondered if she'd started with her own. He heard a car approaching; he was worried it might be Annie. He moved closer to the front door, and Caroline followed. She tangled herself up on the end table and went down hard onto her face, sending two teeth spinning away across the wooden floor. She did not even attempt to brace her fall.

The car traveled on past. Mac headed to the kitchen to get something to use as a weapon. It took more than a minute before his grandmother could pick herself up off the floor, find him with her watery gaze, and advance. Mac's chest hurt with the force of his heart hammering out its beat. He'd never really liked Caroline; he knew she only took care of them because his father paid her to do so, but she'd never been mean. Whether she was a zombie, alien-controlled, or a bandage-less mummy, he didn't know how he could possibly feel okay stabbing her.

"Stop." His voice cracked and wavered, the knife he held out in front of him shook. He pulled over one of the kitchen chairs as she came closer. Like with the end table, her feet got tangled, and she went down. She held on to her remaining teeth this time, but her face was a mess. Blood dripped freely from her broken-open chin, forehead and from her mouth, where the teeth had been knocked loose the first time. Inspiration struck, and Mac pulled all the chairs away from the table and knocked them over. As far as he knew, he'd made the first-ever zombie obstacle course or maze, he wasn't quite sure which name fit better.

For a solid hour, Mac ran around the house, pulling over everything he could, splaying books, pillows, and knick-knacks across the floor. Caroline had tripped and fallen over nearly all of it. She kept struggling up, though her face looked worse than a second-rate boxer facing down the champ. Her nose was lying flat to the side, she'd knocked out at least another five teeth, he'd stopped counting. She had abrasions on both cheeks, a deep laceration on her chin, her hair was matted to her head from the various places her skull bled. He'd heard a loud snap, and from her pronounced limp, he was convinced she'd broken a hip but still, each time she fell, she stood, and the pursuit, such as it was, would continue. Mac heard the familiar warble of sirens in the distance and mistakenly believed they were coming to help; wishful thinking, since he hadn't called for help. When they came no closer, hope faded.

"Stupid," he said as he grabbed the cordless phone and dialed 999. The other end was busy. "NO!" He dialed again and again, each time yielded the same results. In frustration, he hurled the handset at Caroline; it struck her flush in the forehead, but she didn't even flinch from the contact. "Stop," he begged, she didn't listen. "I don't know what to do." He broke down and wailed. Tears streamed from his eyes, making his vision blurry. "Mom? Dad?" he asked, hoping that help would come from that most unlikely of sources.

Caroline kept coming, but with each subsequent fall, it was taking longer and longer for her to stand back up until, finally, she fell hard. She struck the side of her head against the marble coffee table and lay still. Mac watched her for long minutes; he suspected a ruse. Caroline perhaps only pretended to be dead so that, as always happened in the movies, when he finally went to check on her to see if she was gone, the monster, only pretending to be dead, would lurch one final time at the hero. Well, he would not fall for it. Not now, not ever. But still...he really wanted to know. He sat in her over-stuffed armchair, feet firmly planted, in case he had to run. Minutes became hours. He heard sporadic gunfire and more sirens, but still no one came, and he was growing tired, weary, really. His bedtime had passed long ago, and he wasn't sure how much longer he'd be able to keep his eyes open. He cried for a while; he was worried about his sister. He was scared, and he was lonely. When it became too much, he retreated to the bedroom he shared with Annie, never turning his back on Caroline. He closed the door and dragged the toy chest in front of it. He climbed into bed, pulled the covers entirely over his head, and fell into a deep sleep.

When he awoke, there was a brief moment of normalcy, until he looked over at Annie's bed and realized she wasn't there. He tossed the covers off and headed to the door but hesitated before moving the toy box. He imagined a blue, bloated, and bloodied Caroline on the other side of the door. She would be justifiably angry, and when she spoke, she would ask him why he had done this to her.

"Annie? Caroline?" he called out, there was no reply. Oh, how he'd hoped that his father had come back during the middle of the night. He had to urinate to the point he was close to dancing around like Annie. He had no choice; he had to go. He instantly forgot about his needs when he opened the door. The stench of death punched him square in the nose, forced his mouth open, drove a hand down his throat, and pulled strings of yellow bile back up to spill them on the floor. The stomach convulsions were enough to force the evacuations of his bladder. He cried again when he realized he'd wet himself like a baby.

After he cleaned himself and changed, he went cautiously

down the hall and stopped at the living room. From there he could see Caroline's body; she was in the same spot. He picked up the phone to dial emergency services, but this time he didn't even have a dial tone.

"You can't stay there," he told the lifeless body. "When Annie comes home, she'll have nightmares for weeks if she sees you. I need to move you." He still had an irrational fear that she would jump up at him when he got close, but he'd never seen a movie where the "dead" monster had waited an entire night.

Caroline had been a slight woman in life, and in death, she was even more diminished, but Mac was only ten and still a few years removed from any testosterone-induced muscles.

"Maybe I should just cover you up with a rug or a blanket." That sounded like perfect reasoning to him, out of sight, out of mind, but he didn't think they owned enough air freshener to cover the stink. "Shit." Mac looked around after he swore, expecting to be punished for his transgression. When nothing happened, he felt emboldened. "Err...fuck!" He moved around the couch, grabbed a vase off the side table and threw it at the body. It struck her cheek, and still nothing. He moved closer to her feet, bent down, and grabbed her ankles. He jumped back. "So cold." He looked at his fingers like he could catch death by contact. He washed his hands furiously then grabbed some oven mitts. He grabbed Caroline's ankles again and pulled backward, straining with all his might. For all his effort, he was rewarded with a solid six inches of a slide. A half-hour later, Caroline's body was on the front lawn, and Mac was soaked in sweat. If nothing else, he figured the body would bring help. He'd never been more wrong in his life.

He spent the next hour cleaning up the blood trail and splatters, sweeping up all the broken bits of glass and debris and again washing up and changing. He wanted the place to be as clean as possible for when his sister came in. It was when he sat down to watch television and every channel was static that part of him doubted she was ever coming back. He spent the better part of the morning staring out the window until he noticed a large man with a strange gait had stopped suddenly on the street and turned to look at him. The dark suit he wore did not hide his face, which looked much like Caroline's had as she lay on the floor. He ambled onto the lawn and did not even glance at the body as he passed. Mac was terrified and frozen in place as the stranger came closer. The loud blatting of a horn drew his attention away; an old white pick-up truck was cruising down the roadway, and two men in the back were holding upraised cricket bats.

The thing in the lawn seemed curious. It turned to walk toward the truck as the vehicle jumped the curb, drove over the sidewalk, and onto Caroline's property. Mac knew if she weren't so dead, she would have been royally pissed off. He wanted to turn, felt like he needed to turn away, but he couldn't. What happened next was the most horrifying thing Mac had ever seen, worse by far than the *Friday Night Frightfest* he sometimes stayed up to watch. First, the truck ran over Caroline's midsection, making her sit up. Mac's mouth opened, but his voice was jammed. A silent scream ensued as the first of the men swung his bat at the businessman-thing's head. Mac thought at first it was a "hair rug," as his father called them, that flew off; a few seconds later he realized it was the top of the man's skull. His brain glistened wetly as he fell over face first. The truck circled to make sure they had completed the job, then they parked directly in front of the window. Mac just stared.

A young woman rolled down her window. "Hey, kid! You all right?"

All he could think to do was nod.

"Is there anyone in there with you?"

He shook his head from side to side.

"Is anyone going to be?" She looked concerned.

9

"I...I don't think so."

"You can come with us. The world's gone to hell...I mean, heck."

"Zombies?" Mac asked.

"Smart kid. It looks that way." She smiled. "My name's Posey. The two brutus's in the back are my brothers, Parker and Peter." They nodded sternly. "Come on, we've got a safe place to go."

Mac was told never to go anywhere with strangers, but it didn't look like any of the people that told him that were around any longer. He grabbed a jacket and headed out.

That was several lifetimes ago. Peter had been the first to die, Parker was right behind him as he attempted to avenge his brother's death. Posey, at that point, had given up, relegated herself to an ugly ending. Six months after the zombies came, Mac again found himself on his own. He stayed in the basement of the now deceased siblings for close to a year, slowly going through the stores of food and water that they'd gathered in those first few chaotic days. Stuff that he'd helped carry to the hidden and fortified place.

He was sad when he left; he'd felt safe there. For the next few years, he hid in Sherwood Forest, of all places, though there were no rich to steal from, nor poor to give to. And out there, gold meant nothing anyway; food ruled all. The first few weeks, he was on the brink of starvation; finally he came upon a small cabin with fishing gear. The first fish he caught he ate while it was still alive; he couldn't help but compare himself to the zombies he was trying to elude. Most of the next day he spent unintentionally cleansing his bowels, often and forcefully. Lesson learned, he cooked the next fish and all that followed. As he grew stronger, he began to forage, lay traps, and create an early warning system around the cabin with twine and suspended pots. Life was trying and lonely, but he thrived. He went into Edwinstowe a few times, looking for canned goods and a bow. He figured if he was going to live in the same woods as Robin Hood, he might as well start acting like him. If he lived to be a hundred, he didn't think he'd ever be as good as the fabled character, but in time he was able to adequately feed himself.

Over the years he called the place home, he'd only seen and dealt with a handful of zombies, and, in all that time, he'd only seen one person, an older man whom, for some reason Mac couldn't identify as friend or foe. Mac had decided to not show himself; he told himself there wasn't enough food to share, but it could have been that the man looked a bit like his father, and he wanted nothing to do with the cunt. By the time he turned twenty-one, he was certain he was the last inhabitant on the planet, and on that day, he decided to venture out. He wasn't exactly certain what he expected to come across, but it was not the scene that lay before him. The world, though it had, for the most part, stopped for him, had continued to march on outside the protective cocoon of his forest—and not for the better.

"Well, that's a matter of perspective, I suppose." He was standing outside the remains of Edwinstowe, hands on his hips. The village was unrecognizable. What hadn't burned or crumbled was covered in vines; the street had heaved up in various places as nature took hold and began to shake off the shackles of humanity. In the few buildings he dared go inside, he came across zombies in various states of rest. Most he left undisturbed, but if he could find an ignition source and a safe getaway route, he had no problem burning the infestation to the ground.

He joined two groups during the next decade of his life. The first claimed to be a peaceful sect doing their best to live in quiet harmony with what nature provided. At first he sensed they were too good to be true, that there had to be something insidious lurking under the surface, and that he would witness it in all its ugly vulgarity soon enough. But six years passed, and he lived what he considered his best life ever.

He even had his first girlfriend, whom he loved deeply. Being surrounded by these good people made the ache of missing his little sister hurt less, and he finally began to feel like life could go on, happily. The negative undercurrent he'd suspected never did appear. At least, not in the way he imagined. Late one night, Mac's life crashed down around him once again.

. THEY CALLED THEMSELVES "THE WANDERING WOLVES," after the soccer team, of all things. They were an evil, small-minded clan that wanted nothing more than to conquer and rule what little of humanity still existed. The gold-and-black painted warriors attacked in the middle of the night, slaughtering all they encountered. Mac fought savagely, killing six of the invaders before the flat of a sword caught him in the side of the head and knocked him out cold. The wielder, believing him to be dead, had moved on to the next murder. The following morning, Mac awakened to discover his ankles had been chained and his hands tied behind his back. The side of his face was covered in blood, and his skull ached, but all he could think about was Gwen. He looked around wildly for her amongst the thirty prisoners. Each member of his group wore a haunted expression of pain, fear and confusion. Tears and blood streaked their faces, and every single one among them had lost someone they loved and cared for, Mac included. For the next year, Mac and the other survivors of his group would be treated inhumanely, made to sleep outside in the dirt and mud, fed only the merest of scraps to be kept alive, and forced to do all the labor in the camp deemed beneath their masters.

Most of those he'd been taken with died that first year; those that didn't were pressed into raiding parties, forced to steal and sometimes even kill. Because Mac had shown an innate ability to kill, his captors gave him training, and he rose within their ranks until they finally accepted that he was no longer a slave or a forced mercenary but a full-fledged member. He'd willingly been branded with the wolf logo, knowing that it would one day give him the freedom he needed to do what he'd intended from the morning he awoke to the knowledge that they'd murdered his Gwendolyn. He'd made up his mind that he would kill Commander McGowan, the man responsible for the group of thugs and miscreants. McGowan was a stumpy mountain of a man who appeared to have been hewn from granite. He boasted that he'd once played for the Wolverhampton Wanderers, and there was no reason to doubt him. He kept his head shaved close to the scalp but let his red beard run wild; that, coupled with his dark, beady eyes and cruel, jagged toothed smile gave him the look of one who had gone mad and was perfectly satisfied with that fact.

It was nearly three months after he'd been branded that Mac was aware of an opportunity to exact his revenge. Getting near McGowan was no easy feat, and he would have to take the chance when it presented itself, no matter the ultimate outcome. He didn't care if he lived because he was already dead inside; if he was killed, it would merely be an extension of that. Long-range scouts had reported finding a large settlement some twenty miles to the south and McGowan had called a war council with all his captains, and Mac's captain had invited him along for his insight.

McGowan's office was in a small municipal building which Mac thought was ironic, given the man's inflated self-worth. Mac figured he would have found a mayor's office, a mansion, or better still, why not one of the many castles that dotted the landscape? For as pompous as the prick was, that was something Mac had never been able to reconcile about him, McGowan's ambition seemed to drop off past killing or enslaving every surviving human.

Mac listened with half an ear; it was the same old fear-based rhetoric that drove others to attack. The other group threatened their very existence, would usurp their limited resources, we should attack before being attacked...that sort of thing. None of the captains were brave enough to question McGowan to ask why they killed everything in sight. He hoped that once he got rid of the megalomaniac that someone would step into the vacuum of power and rule with a kinder hand, or at least a more rational one, although he wasn't hopeful. Sometimes it was easier to do a thing because it had always been done that way, and people could be openly hostile to change. It wouldn't matter much to him; by then he was most likely going to be dead, and he'd be able to pass away secure in the knowledge that he had done all he could to make the world a better place, at least at the end.

Mac noted that their leader was a good orator; there certainly was an air of charisma about him, and he supposed most narcissistic psychotics were good at this. Caroline used to call his mother by one wordy insult or another all the time, and he'd looked them up, so he knew what they meant. It had hurt at the time because he'd loved his mother, even if she loved chasing her dragons more than seeing her kids. As much as he hated to admit it, Caroline had been right all along.

For over an hour, the group huddled around the table and talked about the best way to attack, to maximize kills while minimizing losses. On the periphery, Mac had listened, sidling as close as he could to the leader without him noticing. Getting past the two men that constantly flanked him was going to be tricky, but he only needed one good strike with his blade, and he'd been sharpening it, especially for this event. Leaping on the table and diving for McGowan had merit, and if no other opening presented itself, that was precisely what he was going to do. He briefly wondered how they would kill him once the assassination was complete. He hoped it would be swift, but the Wolves were not above prolonged, drawn-out torture. It had happened to Del Gentry. The man had attempted to leave the group, he'd grabbed a few days' worth of supplies but had the great misfortune of walking straight into the arms of a forward observation post.

Del had been tied down to a recreated Medieval torture device called the rack. His ankles were secured to the bottom, his arms pulled up over his head then handcuffed to the top. A crank was spun one complete revolution every day, slowly pulling the man apart. The noises his body made as his ligaments tore and bones pulled from their sockets were disturbing, but they paled in comparison to his constant shrieks of pain and cries for mercy which eventually became bare whimpers and mumbled prayers. Mac wanted to kill him, not out of pity, but rather so he could get a quiet night of sleep. He was deeply ashamed he felt that way, but the moron had chosen his fate and then had poorly executed it.

Mac had just got next to the burlier of the two bodyguards, a man aptly named Grugg, when the meeting was adjourned. The attendants had begun to file out, and his captain had called for him to follow. He had reluctantly started to when he heard McGowan tell his bodyguards he could bloody well shit without them watching.

"I'll be right back, sir; I think it's time to drop the kids off at the pool," Mac told his captain, who got a good laugh and clapped him on the shoulder before going back to rejoin his squadron. He headed for the latrine, noticing McGowan up ahead as the man entered the middle of the three small stalls. Mac picked up the pace and went to the one immediately to the left. He wasn't sure what he was going to do. The wood was thick, and by the time he could kick through it, McGowan would know what was going on, and the guards would be all over him. He finally came upon a viable plan. He would wait for the commander to finish and attack as he left the stall. He pulled his knife free from its sheath; he'd not been expecting the slight knock on the side of the booth.

"Who's there?" McGowan asked.

"Uh, it's a Rager, sir. First Class. Staders, sir."

"You know who I am?" McGowan asked.

"I saw you go in, sir."

"Very well. I need something from you, Staders."

"Okay, sir." Mac grabbed some toilet paper, a commodity that was quickly becoming worth its weight in gold, figuring the commander was in need of a wipe. When a small metal disc was pushed up, and an erect penis slid through the opening, Mac was at a loss as to what to do. Of course, he'd known about the glory holes, he'd just never seen one used.

"I can count on your discretion, correct?" McGowan asked. To say otherwise or not perform would mean Mac wouldn't make it through the night alive.

"Of course, sir," Mac said as he dropped the wadded-up paper. He stood and firmly grabbed the head of McGowan's penis.

"Easy, soldier, it's a cock, not a rifle."

Mac yanked harder, pulling the man tight against the stall wall. "This is for Gwendolyn," he said as he dragged the blade across the shaft, as close to the base as he could manage. Blood ejaculated from the wound, Mac dropped the severed member, quickly exited the latrine, and moved as far from the scene as possible while attempting to stay undetected. He'd made it a street away before McGowan was able to overcome his initial shock and pain and began to scream for help. Soon after, the hand-cranked air raid alarm sounded, though it hadn't been used for its original intent for decades. It did, however, muster the entire encampment. Mac knew he had to disappear soon or he'd be found, and he was certain that after what he did, that Gentry, by comparison, had gotten off easy. He moved in close to a small home when he heard the footsteps of a person running. It would be one man from a two-person guard station, sent to find out what was going on.

"Shit, Mac, you scared the hell out of me!" It was Sam

Tellings, Mac's friend and squad-mate. Sam was a decent person, as far as murdering pricks went.

"Yeah, sorry about that. I was coming out to tell you what's going on," he said, thinking fast.

Telling's eyebrows furrowed in confusion. "Protocol is for someone to go up to the command area."

"Yeah, yeah, I know, but they want to spread the info quicker. They sent runners out to each of the stations."

"Yeah, that makes sense. But why is your knife out? Is that...does that have blood on it?"

"Fuck, Sam." Mac lunged, driving the entire blade into Tellings' midsection. Sam's look of betrayal and pain would be something that haunted Mac's dreams for the rest of his life and probably afterlife—if Caroline's ravings about the subject had any legitimacy. Mac covered Sam's mouth and lowered him to the ground softly, then sliced the man's throat open to prevent him from yelling and partially to ease his suffering. He ran until he could no longer hear the siren then took a quick break before resuming his escape. By the time he was spent, he figured he had covered in the vicinity of twenty-five kilometers; his legs felt leaden and jelly-like. He stepped through the broken-out doorway of an apartment building, picked his way through the debris to the topmost floor on the third level, and looked for a door that had not been broken in, hoping that would mean an apartment not already ravaged. Much like the toilet paper, finding something with those attributes was akin to stumbling upon the Holy Grail in the bargain bin at ASDA. He spent the next few minutes looking for the one least destroyed and not inhabited by wildlife. The apartment he settled on still smelled like stale piss and fresh vomit, but it was the best of the lot. He settled down onto an old recliner and was almost asleep before he could even prop his twitching legs upon the moldy ottoman.

Mac awoke early the following day. His body was nearly fully recovered from his escape, but he knew he was going to need some water soon. He could go long stretches without food; the Wolves had taught him that much. He stood and, more out of habit than worry, moved cautiously toward the window; the remnants of tattered, sheer white curtains fluttered in a small breeze. He moved one slightly to the side and peered out, catching movement to his left.

"Shit." He ducked back. Two of the Wolves were checking the dwellings along their route, and soon enough they would be to the apartment building. The patrol meant that McGowan was most likely alive. He would have been mad enough to order his personnel to walk off the edge of the earth to find the villain responsible for his injury, but Mac wasn't so sure the successor would have been in such a turmoil over finding the person who made their ascension to power a reality. Or maybe they would, just to cement in the fact that they were as big an asshole as McGowan, and just as much to be feared. Either way, Mac knew he couldn't afford to be caught. Not alive, anyway.

He was quickly debating his next course of action. He could lie in wait; odds were good that, with the element of surprise, he could kill them both, which would buy him days on a lead. He didn't know how long the patrol was scheduled to be out, but eventually it would be noticed that they hadn't checked in. Of course, there was also no guarantee he could overpower them without sustaining some sort of injury. He could make a run for it, but they were close, and he might end up having to run forever. Stand and fight: risk injury, death or recapture; hide: hope they pass by; run: be caught now or eventually. Mac was weighing all the risk and reward factors when his hand was forced. The answer came in the form of a young girl.

"Annie?" he asked, confused. He knew it couldn't be possible; the girl was too young. She didn't look much older than his sister had been when the zombies came, not nearly old enough to account for all the time that passed. But oh how his heart ached. Her size and shape were so much like he remembered Annie's, even the long brunette hair that hung in front of her eyes. She was far enough away that he couldn't make out the sharper details; he realized she might, up close, look very different from his Annie, but his heart was overriding any argument his brain could come up with.

One of the Wolves, Mac knew him as the aptly named Hunter, had his hand wrapped around the girl's upper arm and was dragging her into the middle of the street. She was kicking and scratching at him, and as she leaned in to bite, he gave her a backhand that sent her thumping to the ground on her ass. Mac almost shouted to him to cut that shit out, or he was going to kill him, but, as it was, he gripped the hilt of his knife so tightly his hand began to throb.

"Little bitch!" Hunter was dabbing at the blood that had welled up on his forearm. "Probably have fucking rabies now."

"Shit," Mac muttered as he saw the second man. It was Tellings' guard mate, Junker. He didn't know much about the perimeter guards, but he did know that they were generally pretty tight, having to spend long hours together. Which meant this was personal to Junker, and unfortunately, the man was famous for being unstable, which was why he was generally relegated to duty away from the rest of the group.

"Hunter, you need to shut up," Junker said. "We're trying to find the traitor, not see if there are any sleepers around."

"What do I do with this one?" Hunter raised a backhand, and the girl, who had been looking at him defiantly, shied away. It broke Mac's heart; he couldn't help thinking that this had probably happened to his sister.

"Normally, I'd say tie her up and we'll take her back with us, but I'm not going back until I cut Mac's balls off."

"The boss said he wants his head, not his balls."

"The balls are for me, dipshit."

19

Hunter laughed. "That so? What are you going to do with them?"

"Tellings was my friend, asshole. He didn't deserve to be gutted, and for sure not by somebody who was supposed to be one of us. I'm taking Mac's balls, I'm going to force him to eat them, then I'll kill him and take his head back to the boss. Happy now?"

"Yeah, yeah, I am." Hunter grinned.

The girl looked as if she'd swallowed a hummingbird in midflight.

"So what do I do about the girl then?"

"You're going to have to kill her."

The girl wasn't a fool. She had survived in a harsh world by grabbing opportunities and reacting swiftly. As soon as Junker said he needed to kill her, she was up and running.

"Stop!" Hunter said.

"Seriously?" Junker asked. "Do you think someone you've just said you're about to kill is going to stop because you told them to?"

"It could happen."

"Go get her and finish it. I want to get moving."

Hunter went after her.

Mac willed the girl to run in his direction. He wasn't sure what divine intervention was at work, but the girl looked up, and his heart nearly froze. Even close up, he held on to the illusion of his Annie. Mac frantically motioned for her to come toward him. He wasn't sure if she would heed his advice or not, but when her course veered slightly, Mac headed out of the room and bounded down the stairs to meet her at the entrance. He stayed to the side of the door as the girl raced in.

"Third floor," he told her. She spared him a glance before taking the steps two at a time.

Hunter had been close and moving fast. "Gonna catch you, little girl!" The only thing he caught was a glint of metal, but was far too slow to react; he'd not been expecting an attack. Mac drove the blade deep into the side of his neck and withdrew it. Hunter threw a hand up to the gushing wound, his hip struck a railing, and he careened off and into the wall on the other side of the hallway before his legs collapsed, and he fell to the floor. Mac turned and looked to the first landing; the girl was watching him. She was wary. Just because he had helped her didn't necessarily make him a friend, or even a good person. Mac placed a finger to his mouth in a shushing gesture.

After five minutes, Junker called out, "Hunter, man, stop fucking around. Kill the little bitch and let's go!" When he got no reply he became suspicious. He pulled a knife from a scabbard that looked more like a short sword.

"Run. Get as far from here as you can. They're looking for me, not you, and I don't know if I'm going to be able to stop him," Mac told the girl. Wordlessly she turned and ran. "You're welcome," he told her, but she was long gone. He retreated up four stairs, enough to give himself the high ground, though he wasn't sure what that would accomplish, as Junker had the reach with his longer blade.

Junker's shadow approached first, then a boot; he paused when he saw the body of Hunter crumpled up against the wall. "You surrender yourself now Mac, and I'll make this quick."

"So, no ball swallowing then?"

"You heard that huh? Tellings was my best friend. In a world as shitty as this one, populated by even shittier people, he was one of the few that I enjoyed hanging out with, and you took that from me. You're going to have to pay. The balls thing...well, that's not the worst I can do. If you had just taken McGowan's knob, I'd probably have brought you a bottle of vodka and sent you on your way. Can't stand that asswipe. The Wolves have needed a new leader for a couple of years now, and there's no way he's not going to be challenged for leadership now, considering he's a eunuch, thanks to you. Shit, once I take your head back, maybe I'll throw my hat in the ring. But you didn't stop there, so that's not where we're at."

"Yeah, Tellings was an unfortunate casualty, but it came down to him or me, and I chose me."

"Looks like you're getting chosen again." Junker came through the door, the blade held out in front of him. Mac backed up a step.

"What the fuck is this?" Junker asked, pointing past Mac.

"Not turning."

A razor-sharp arrow tip breezed past Mac's face, the feathered end barely caressed his cheek. Junker let out a grunting exhalation as the arrow penetrated deep enough to break through his chest plate and deflate his left lung. He grabbed the shaft and tried to pull it out, screaming as he did so before falling to his knees then face forward, pushing the arrow even deeper.

"Go on back down the stairs, mister, or the next one goes in you," the girl said.

Mac held his hands high and did as she said.

"Stop," she told him as he got to the doorway. "Why did you help?"

Mac's shoulders sloped some. "You look like my sister."

"She's dead?"

"Most likely," Mac told her. "I haven't seen her in close to twenty years."

"How old was she when you last saw her?"

"Six."

"Do I even remotely look twenty-six?"

"Not at all."

"So you helped a person just because they looked like her from twenty years ago? Do you have the dumbs?"

"I don't think so."

"One minute to tell me why you're a Wolf and why they're hunting you. Or you're going to end up like him." She nodded to Junker.

"I *was* a Wolf because they killed most of the clan I belonged to. For a good long while, I was a slave, until they realized I was good for something more than digging latrines."

"And what was that?" she asked.

"Killing. They conscripted me into their army. When I got the chance, I tried to kill the leader."

"McGowan? You tried to kill him?"

"How do you know him?"

"Not your concern. Did you try to kill him or not?"

"I did."

"What happened?"

"How old are you?" Mac asked.

"What's that matter to you?"

"What I did is more for an adult ear."

"I've seen a lot of death, and you're down to about twenty seconds left, and I still haven't heard any reason to save you."

"I cut off his wiener. Asshole didn't have the good grace to die from it."

"*You what now?*"

"I'm not saying it again, not in front of you."

"I have so many questions." She snorted. "Why was his cock out? Were you targeting it? Was it hard to find?"

"If you're going to kill me, do it. Otherwise I would like to put as much distance as I can from here before these two are missed."

"Where will you go?"

"Are you letting me go?"

"You're the first person to put a smile on my face in three years; I think that merits a pass."

Mac took another step.

"Whoa, mister, I asked you a question you haven't answered."

"I'm thinking about heading up into Scotland."

"Scotland? What for? That's on the whole other side of the country."

"First off, I can't imagine McGowan would ever travel that far and second, I've always wanted to see it."

"Hold on, I'm going to grab my stuff."

"Why?"

"Because I'm going with you."

"I don't want you to."

"That's not a very gracious way to say thank you for saving your life."

"I saved your life first."

"From that tall wanker? I could have killed him twice before he realized it," she said. "Do not move, or I will hunt you down."

Mac walked outside. "What in the fuck have I got myself into? Caroline always said you shouldn't help people. What was that phrase?" He walked around in a tight circle. "Right, right, no good deed goes unpunished. Sometimes that old sod hit things right on the head."

"Ready!" she said, coming out of the apartment. She had a sword in a sheath, the bow slung behind her back, and knives strapped to various places on her body. The dark green backpack looked to be filled with supplies. "Where's your gear?"

"I didn't really have time to pack."

"That's right, the whole…" she dragged her pointer finger across her thumb then folded her thumb in. "I've got to imagine that hurt."

"I would think."

"What's your name?" she asked.

"Mac, yours?"

"Not going to tell you. There's a lot of power in names, you know, and to willy-nilly hand it over like that can be dangerous." She laughed again. "Psych. You should see your face. Wilkes. My name is Wilkes."

"That your first or last?"

"Only, and before you ask again, I'm thirteen, I've been on

my own for the last four years. My dad died when I was seven; he was on a supply run and had the misfortune of walking into a hive. My mother got sick; at first we didn't think it was much more than a cold, then she had a fever that wouldn't break, her breathing got shallow, and, well, that was it." Wilkes got somber. "I haven't hung out with any group; it's just too hard to trust anyone."

Mac didn't tell her he was sorry. There was no reason to. He hadn't done anything to her, and there wasn't anyone around anymore who didn't have a story of incredible loss. Telling someone you were sorry was tantamount to an insult.

"Enough about me." She wiped her nose with the back of her sleeve. "What was your sister's name?"

"Annie."

"You were close then," she said like she knew.

"Even before the beaters came, we were all each other had."

"How'd she die?"

"Don't know," he shrugged. "She was with my dad, and I never saw either again."

Wilkes didn't offer the typical, "maybe they're still alive" bullshit, and for that, Mac was appreciative. Very few people survived those first couple of years, and the odds of more than one member of a family doing so, were the equivalent of winning the lottery while being struck by lightning.

"Where'd you learn the bow?" Mac asked as they walked.

"Mum taught me the basics. I honed my skills when I realized the only way I was going to be able to eat was if I could hit what I aimed for."

"How good are you?"

"A squirrel at twenty meters good."

Mac didn't question her on it. That was a hell of a skill set to have, and all of a sudden, he was happy to have her along. "I tried; best I could do was a deer at that distance. I'm much better with a sword." He held up the blade he'd grabbed from Junker.

"Water?" she asked, lightly hitting his arm with a green plastic canteen.

"Thanks." He spun the top off and took a swig.

"So, these Wolves you belonged to."

"Owned by," he clarified.

She shrugged. "How long are they going to come after you?"

"Having doubts about your choice of company?"

"Not yet, no. But you give me a reason to, and I will cut your throat long before they can get you back," she told him in a matter-of-fact way.

"I can see why you've been alone so long." She laughed. When she kept looking at him, he responded, "I don't know. McGowan is usually too busy focusing on how he's going to rule the world than any individual facet, but, well, he's never had his…junk sliced off, so there's a chance he never lets it go."

"His willy or the vendetta?"

"Wilkes!"

"Embarrassed?"

"About what I did? No. Talking about it with a teenage girl, yeah."

"Young woman."

"Okay, young woman. Yes, very much so. Like I said, though, he may chase me to the ends of the earth; it's not safe being around me."

She frowned.

"Okay, it's even *less* safe, being around me."

"Give me a timeline of when I should become more concerned."

Mac sighed. "It's tough to tell, after the, umm, deed, I ran for over twenty kilometers, got about five or six hours of sleep, and two scouts were already on me. They should have never been able to catch up to me that quickly. I'm going to have to chalk it up to incredible luck, on their part, for now. My guess is they're supposed to report back within three days. Which means by the time they're figured missing, I should have seventy or more kilometers of a lead."

"Cool. I should have a week to decide what I want to do. It's getting late; we should begin looking for a place to get some rest."

"Like you said, Wilkes, it's hard to trust people, so why me? Why are you coming with me?"

"The eyes, Mac. The eyes never lie, and yours, while having a depth of sadness within them, also have pools of kindness. Plus I'm sick of having conversations with myself."

"Ah, the real reason revealed at last."

The sun was low on the horizon when they came to the outskirts of a village.

"Stone buildings, these were old before I was born." Mac dragged his hand along the rough surface as they headed to the front.

"Oy." Wilkes waved a hand in front of her face as she went to the opening. "Stinks."

Mac noticed that the roof had long ago collapsed, and the inside was wilder than the overgrown yard. "On to the next," he told her. As he started back down the road, he turned to notice her going into the home she'd just complained about. "What are you doing? There's got to be something better down this way."

She came out quickly, holding a worn and beaten green camouflage backpack. She dumped the contents onto the ground. A brown plastic pack fell out first, followed by two small bottles that contained a clear liquid and, finally, notebooks encased in a plastic bag.

"Don't open that," Mac said as the girl had grabbed her knife and was about to puncture the bloated brown bag.

"What is it?" she asked, not necessarily going to do as he'd said.

Mac looked at her, confused. There were large black letters printed on the package labeling it as an MRE, a Meal Ready to Eat. In this case, it was ham medley. "It was food—a long time ago," he told her, once he understood that it was very likely she couldn't read. "It's puffed up like that because it has gone bad."

She poked it, even after his warning. He jumped back as an eruption of grayish pink slime blew out from the hole. Even from ten feet away and outside, the smell was like being smacked in the nose by a dirty diaper. Wilkes tossed the bag and retched a couple of times.

"I told you." Mac had backed up further and was smiling. "You wanted to make sure I wasn't lying and just wanted it for myself, right?"

"I'll be more likely to listen next time." The bag continued to sputter and spew, but the worst of the odor had begun to dissipate. "Cured my hunger pains for a while. What are these?" she asked, holding the bottles.

Mac approached and took the one she offered. He read the label and twisted the cap off to take a sniff. "Hand sanitizer, I think. It's still good."

"What's it for?" she asked, taking the bottle back and smelling the lid. "Ooof."

"Kills germs."

"Be better if it killed Wolves." She put the two bottles in her pack.

"Agreed. Ready to go?" Mac asked.

"What about this?" She stripped a bag away, and a small stack of blue-colored binders fell out.

"Looks like notebooks."

Wilkes opened one up; each page was crammed with words. "What's it say?" She handed it over.

Mac turned it back to the first page and read for a few minutes. "Looks like a journal."

"A what?" Wilkes asked somewhat impatiently.

"Umm, like this guy's personal thoughts."

"Like a story then?"

"Yeah, I guess like a story."

"My mum used to read me stories. That was before my dad died; she didn't after. It was the last time I remember being happy." She stopped talking suddenly when she realized she was confiding in a near stranger.

Mac could tell she was feeling awkward and attempted to diffuse it. "You should feel lucky; my mum never read me anything."

"Yeah, well, they're both gone now, so what does it matter." Wilkes turned to again wipe the back of her sleeve across her eyes, presumably from dust. Mac continued to read as he followed Wilkes to the next stone-built home, which had weathered the passing of time in admirable fashion. The roof had stayed weathertight, and, except for a couple of broken-out windows, the inside was in decent shape.

"Do you want to get some firewood?" Wilkes asked.

"Yeah, sure, go ahead," Mac told her as he sat down on the stone hearth and continued to read.

"I meant the both of us."

Mac looked up. "Oh right, sorry."

"Is it good? The journal-thing, I mean."

"Looks like a Yank wrote it."

"A Yank?"

Mac realized as he watched Wilkes just how much knowledge would be lost in the next few years. It wouldn't be long until they'd regressed fully into another dark ages.

"Why are you looking at me that way?"

"Sorry, sorry." Mac snapped out of it. "Umm, a Yank was someone that lived across the ocean, in a country called America.

It was a colony of ours a long time ago, and, well, they hated tea, I guess, and England kept sending it to them, they got so pissed off they started a war against us and we finally just gave them their independence." He wasn't quite sure if he was remembering correctly or if she even understood half of it, but he figured it didn't matter. He was far from qualified in teaching History, or any subject, having not even made it through Year Six.

"There was a war over tea?"

"That's my understanding."

"Humans really will fight over anything."

Mac could only nod.

"The journal."

"Oh right. Um, so it looks like it's from this guy named Talbot, which is a British enough sounding name, by the way. It's during the time of the beaters; they're on a ship."

"I'm going to round us up some rabbits. Can you get a fire going?"

"As soon as the sun goes down." Mac was looking at the fireplace, which was in need of some cleaning. It appeared to have been some animal's roost.

"After we umm, eat... umm," for the first time since Mac had met her, Wilkes seemed hesitant about something, "...could you, you know, maybe read me the journal? I mean, if you don't want to, that's completely fine."

"No, no, of course. It'll give us something to pass the time."

She smiled gratefully as she headed out. Mac weighed continuing to read or getting the fire ready. Duty won out over curiosity.

As promised, Wilkes returned with a clutch of fat rabbits. She tossed them on the table. "Okay, you're up."

"I'm up?" Mac asked.

"I caught 'em, you clean 'em."

"I hate this part, I never really got good at it."

"How do you eat?"

"When I was a kid, we just had food, and later, when the beaters came, there was still plenty of food in bags and cans. When I lived in the woods, I ate a lot of fish; they were easy enough. The deer were a bit trickier. Then when I was taken prisoner, they just tossed stuff at me, and when I became a soldier, that same food that was tossed at me was handed over."

"Seriously?"

"Yeah, Wilkes. I'm just as likely to destroy this meat with my knife skills as I am to ensure we eat some meat."

"Okay, but you're going to watch me and learn, and then I'm going to want something in return."

"Sure."

"Can you teach me how to read?"

"Maybe?"

"*Maybe?*" she echoed.

"I know how to read, okay? I'm just not sure I know how to tell somehow how to do it. But I'm willing to try, if you can be patient with me."

"Deal."

After seeing and doing all he'd done, Mac was surprised at how queasy he felt as Wilkes gutted and skinned the small animals. None of that, however, stopped his mouth from watering once they were on the flames. After they ate, Wilkes was nearly bouncing on her toes as she waited for Mac to begin.

"Okay, let me know if I read a word you don't understand." Mac cleared his throat. "Prologue."

"That one."

PROLOGUE

I REALIZE in my last journal I had sworn off writing down any more of my nightmarish memoirs, that putting my thoughts to paper was too painful. Want to know what I found out? Keeping them bottled up was even worse. My goal now is to find some semblance of peace from this exercise. I once read (or saw it in a movie or heard someone say something about it, I don't know, doesn't matter), something that said the way to get over the ending of a relationship was to gather up all the things that remind you of that person and do a sort of ritual-istic burning, ridding yourself of that baggage, physically and symbolically. In this case, the relationship I am trying to exor-cise myself from are the demons lodged in my head. The best thing I could think to do was to once again write down my travels and travails, maybe trials is more accurate. Don't know if that makes sense, I just like the sound of the words together, and since I'm going to dump it into the ocean upon comple-tion, what does it matter? It's unlikely I'm going to have a dolphin give me shit for it. So I'll hold on to my sixteenth journal as the *final* installment and add anything if it becomes relevant. These new ones, though, they are merely a band-aid for an open wound that will not heal and only seems to fester.

2

MIKE JOURNAL ENTRY 1

I STOOD upon the deck of the great ship, the sun shining bright, the wind flowing past my body. Behind me, personnel were busy doing a multitude of tasks. We'd been at sea for two months, and still, I refused to go much deeper into the ship than the top two levels, having no desire to revisit the ghosts created down in the bowels. No matter how many cleaning crews went down there, I was convinced my olfactory senses would dredge up the memory of the stink and, at every turn there would be a missed reaver, griever, or even a garden variety speeder, just waiting to grab a quick bite to eat. No, it was much better closer to the surface. Fewer things could be buried up here, or so I told myself.

In one hand, I held a Cuban cigar, I couldn't even remember where it was procured from. I'd take a puff from time to time, savoring the richness of the tobacco. In the other, I had a half-full bottle of beer. I'd been fearful that the boredom of safety would begin to erode my threadbare hold on sanity, but, to my surprise and probably everyone's around me, I'd begun to rebound. The funny thing about a dropped ball is when it hits the ground and bounces back up, it never quite reaches the previous height. I knew this but was happy for the reprieve, nonetheless.

"You know people talk when they see you out and about in your boxers." BT tapped my shoulder with another beer.

"Hey, thanks," I told him, finishing the one I was holding in one large draught. I looked over to him as I took the bottle. "BT, if we were to take a vote, which do you think the people aboard would be less scarred by? Me in my boxers, or you in that ridiculous Speedo?"

"This is how I assert my dominance without having to say a word." He stuck out his barrel-sized chest. He merely needed to be in the same room with you to assert his dominance. I think he just got a kick out of folks' reactions when they watched him in that get-up.

I had to smile; here was a sight everyone should see once in their lifetime: BT, in a gold banana hammock, green canoe-sized flip flops, and a canary yellow terry cloth bathrobe. Or maybe no one should ever be exposed to it, and maybe the word *exposed* is more description than I need here.

"We should be coming up on the Cliffs of Dover in the next couple of days," he offered.

I knew we were going to make landfall soon; I'd chosen not to think about it. My hand tremors had finally stopped, and I could usually go about four minutes before I needed to check over my shoulder to see if anything was sneaking up to kill me. We'd continued to train, harder than we had when we were in the thick of it because to lose our edge meant we'd lose our lives. Resupplying along the way had always been a given of this new missive. The part I wasn't too keen on was our broadcasting our approach in the hopes of picking up rogue survivors. We were all survivors; it was how they'd managed to stay alive that concerned me. Was there a UK version of Deneaux waiting to board us and work her way toward supreme commander? We were finally rid of the hag; I could not imagine seeking out another to replace her. Or what if we run into another Durgan? The boat's not big enough for that much hostility or ego. This ship, while it wasn't the Garden of Eden, was, for the most part, harmonious. Yeah, there were the occasional lovers' spats, and a fight or two would break out from time to time. But no one had been killed since we'd been out here, and that's saying something. Humans, seemingly by their very nature, aren't disinclined to killing each other. In fact, we seem relatively okay with that perversion in our essence. Since we were already bucking the trends of our predecessors, I had no desire to muddy the waters by adding in unknown variables. It was difficult to voice my concern without sounding like a selfish asshole, and after my initial protest and subsequent dressing down, I'd stayed silent.

"Getting any sleep?" I asked BT in regard to his new baby.

"It's five am, and I'm on the deck with you, drinking a beer. That a good enough answer for you?"

"It's five am?"

"How long have you been out here?"

"I don't really know. I got out of bed and came here; it was still dark out."

"Nightmares?"

"I had to piss."

"I thought the major told you he wanted you to stop going over the side?"

"The major and I have an understanding. He tells me shit he'd like for me to do, and I actively ignore him." We clinked our bottles together.

"You think we'll find anybody in England?" he asked after a few moments while we stared out to sea.

"Tough to say. We had all that access to firearms, and we barely made it. Can you imagine fighting a horde with a shotgun or worse, a pitchfork?"

"Lot of people in London carrying pitchforks back in the day?" BT asked.

"Well, yeah. For storming castles. Who knows what Brits do? Traveling around in their lorries, going to the loo, riding in the lift while they eat crisps; they're about as strange as women," I said, making sure to look over my shoulder before finishing that sentence.

"You know, if you took a moment to get to understand them, they're not so strange."

"Women or the British?"

"Women, dipshit. You know, talk to them, ask things."

"What is this dark magic you speak of? Don't make me have you convicted of being a witch, heretic."

"Just how many beers have you had?"

"Five am, carry the eleven, divide by pi...seven or eight tops. Speaking of which, I have to go," I told him as I moved closer to the edge.

"It's broad daylight; there are people everywhere. You can't just piss into the wind."

"Hang around for a sec; I assure you I can."

"Training is at eight. Try not to be too drunk when you show up." BT was shaking his head as he made his hasty retreat.

WE ROTATED who would lead training each day; just so happened that today of all days was BT's, and either he was angry he'd been kept awake all night or that I'd sloshed my way to the formation, both, probably. By the time he was done, I was drenched in sweat and stank of stale beer. My humble squad consisted of Rose, my demo expert, and we had Kirby, BT's punching bag, - Harmon, Grimm, Stenzel, Winters, my brother, Tommy, and Dallas, and we'd gained

Reed and Walde, the only surviving members of the SEAL team. On occasion, Major Dylan and Sergeant Sorrens joined our exercises. Both must have got the memo that BT was on the warpath because neither showed up today.

More than once, Gary had raised his hand to ask if he could move away from me, and each time BT had told him to shut up then made him drop and do twenty push-ups, and because the kid could not learn, Kirby would invariably laugh and say he was thankful it wasn't him, which, well, you know, would lead to BT telling him to do the same.

"Dismissed!" BT had finally ordered after three hours of exercises and hell.

When we were done, I told him to fuck off, but he didn't hear me because my head was hanging down, and the words were directed to the deck. There were the groans and moans of the stiff-legged as they ambled away. I had to aid Gary, as his arms weren't working well enough to push himself up.

"Feel free to help in any way," I told him as I grabbed his hand and was hauling backward on his limp form.

"I might just stay here for a while," he replied.

Stenzel grabbed his other hand, and we finally had Lazarus standing, albeit wobbly.

"Holy shit, sir." Stenzel placed her hand up by her mouth and nose.

"Yeah, sorry about that," I told her.

She helped Gary get below decks. I had a feeling the next time BT came up in rotation, we were going to have a lot of people at sickbay.

"What the hell was that about?" I asked him, making sure I got close enough and downwind that he couldn't help but waft in my presence. Somehow, he didn't seem to notice.

"Your sister." He hesitated before speaking anymore.

"What, man? Are you having problems? You can talk to me." I was concerned; there was genuine pain on his face. Although, asking me for advice usually opened someone up to my infantile humor; I learned long ago that the only thing I was good at was alleviating tension.

"She said she was making a huge breakfast today."

I was confused for a second; I blamed it on dehydration and possible heatstroke.

"Breakfast, Mike!" he said, his eyes pleading with me for understanding. "The *most* important meal of the day!"

"Oh! I get it. She realizes there's a galley, right?"

"She volunteered at the galley." Resignation in his voice.

"*What?!* Who authorized that! We're going to have mass casualties! Exodus! Defection! Defecation!" I was looking to the bridge, wondering if it was too late to sound a general alarm.

"I was hoping that if we did PT long enough, breakfast would be over."

"You know she's going to save you some, right? And the only thing worse than my sister's food warm is when it's cold and congealed." I shuddered, thinking about it, my mouth somehow able to pull enough moisture from the rest of my arid body to give me the sweet water effect.

"Captain Talbot, to the bridge," it was Master Sergeant Wassau coming over the PA system. I waved up, though I couldn't see him. He'd been an MP at Etna station, and the duty had followed him aboard the aircraft carrier. What he was doing up in the con tower I couldn't guess. Maybe someone had reported my urination habits to him, and the major was going to give me another stern talking to. I thought about taking a shower first, but if I went up there smelling like I did, it was likely they'd get me out of there quickly.

"I've got to go. Good luck," I told him. I patted his back; he was muttering incoherently as I left. When I got upstairs, I took a moment to look down; he was still standing there.

"Captain." Wassau nodded at me when I came through the door.

"No leg irons, I'll take that as a good sign. What's going on?"

"Major Eastman wants to see you."

"Am I in trouble?"

"No." He let out a small laugh. "I came up here to get some coffee; it would appear that Mrs. Tynes is in the chow hall."

"Wow, the reach of that woman's cooking is famous."

"Yeah, more like infamous."

"What is that smell?" Eastman asked as he came out of the commander's office.

"Might be in trouble after all," Wassau said as he headed out the door.

"Is that *you*, Captain Talbot? I had a roommate in college who had no idea how to pick up after himself. I remember throwing out weeks' old, half-empty moldy beer cans; they smelled similar to you, only at least the memories they held made them tolerable, now you're bringing it all rushing back. I'll make this quick, out of necessity."

"I'm starting to get a little self-conscious here." I began to lift my arm to get a pit test.

"For the love of all that is holy, do not do that." He backed up a step.

"Maybe just tell me what you need to."

"As you know, our original plan had been to pull up alongside Hastings once we got past Dover and have two teams scout out the area. We've altered that and are going to drop anchor outside of Wales, near Cardiff, a place called Swansea."

"Okay." Again I was confused, shouldn't be a shocker. "That next to Hastings?" I shrugged my shoulders.

"Are you being serious right now?" the major asked.

"Major, the only places I went outside of the US were when I was sent by the Marines Corps to go and kill people, and the last time we had a shooting war with England was over two hundred years ago, and even if I had gone there, I wouldn't have stopped to ask for directions."

"It's basic geography, Talbot."

"We going to discuss the details of how poorly I did in grade school, or are you going to tell me the new mission parameters and how they affect my team? I'll let you know which one is more pertinent."

"Fair enough, my apologies."

"I'll allow it."

"If I were to say that's magnanimous of you, would you understand?"

"Even if I didn't get that big word, I'd for sure understand the sarcastic tone."

"Swansea would be on the other side of the country. Here." He pointed to a map.

"This anywhere near Stonehenge? I always wanted to see that in person."

He gave me a steely gaze; he wanted to say something more, to his credit, he held it in check. "Nowhere near it, unfortunately."

"Why the sudden change? Did you get warned off our initial target?" Once again I was about to offer him my thoughts on the whole "We come in peace" message.

"No, nothing of the sort. We've not heard a word from any quarter, which is alarming in its own right, but that's a different discussion."

"Says you," I said under my breath, but considering we were four feet from each other, it wasn't like he didn't hear it.

"You know, Captain, if I didn't think it would start a mutiny aboard my ship, I'd demote you to civilian."

"I don't think you understand quite how willing I would be to take you up on your offer. But unfortunately for both of us, sir, you need me. You can't kick me out, and I can't leave. Match made in purgatory. Can we get on with this before my workout clothes have to be cut free from my skin? Already starting to stick with some serious adhesion."

"The zombies here, they're acting...strangely, different from anything we've seen thus far. I've got some video you're going to wish you hadn't seen."

"If it's zombie porn, I'll just leave now."

"After this, you might wish that was all it was."

"Shit," I said as he opened his laptop. When the major tapped on the screen to open a file, I didn't even know what I was looking at. Like some overt foreshadowing out of a black and white horror movie set in the 1700s, my words to BT just hours previously would prove shockingly prophetic, although this was a very twisted version of them. Hundreds of zombies were racing across an open field, chasing a drove of wild boars. The sheer number of zees was unsettling on its own, but there was so much more. "Are they holding *weapons?*" Fundamentally, I knew they were, as the resolution of the feed could have been 4k, but my astonishment warranted speaking aloud. The zombies were corralling the giant feral pigs, herding them into a tight u-shaped formation as more zombies raced from the top of the screen to shut the door on the horseshoe.

"Bats, pitchforks, shovels... there may be a rifle or two in there, but, as of yet, we've not seen a muzzle flash," Eastman said.

"And we're sure they're zombies?" I asked. They moved so fluidly, and it was a coordinated attack using implements on a wide scale, he'd understated when he said: "strange." Speaking for myself, this was something I could have gone a lot longer without being exposed to, preferably never-length longer.

"Keep watching, then you tell me."

Once the zombies from the top had blocked off the last escape route, the entire ring around the pigs began to draw closed like a department store shopping bag having its string pulled. The boars ran from edge to edge of the sprung trap looking for a way out. I knew from experience they could be a nasty, dangerous animal, but in this instance, I could feel their rising panic within my chest. As absurd as it sounded, I was thankful Rasher wasn't watching this. When the circle was as tight as it could get, the zombies began to poke, prod, or smash at the pigs until they were stunned or wounded into submission, and then the zombies really flew their freak flag as they descended, mouth first, in many cases, onto the pigs and began to rip chunks of bacon free. Thankfully, there was no audio.

"I still…I'm still having a hard time believing what I'm seeing," I told the major as I closed the lid to the laptop.

"Even if it wasn't zombies, we'd still have a problem, right? Those people, live or dead are as feral as the prey they're hunting."

"And this was around where we were going to make first landing?"

"We've been seeing something like this across most of the country, many sightings are…worse." He had a far-off look in his eyes. Didn't take an advanced degree to realize that the zombies were using the same methods on people. I was relieved he had spared me that sight.

"How long have you known?" I was suspicious that maybe this wasn't new news to him. The likelihood that I, as part of the landing crew, was just now finding out was sitting as well as my sister's breakfast would, if I dared to try it.

"About a week." He continued quickly before I could give him an earful, "We've spent most of that time looking for a safer place; Wales appears to be the only choice."

"How about we skip the continent altogether? I know we've got some things to resupply, but nothing urgent."

Eastman said nothing, which said a lot.

"Ah. There's more."

"Ever heard of the Babraham Institute?"

"Don't try and cover up this shitshow with my ignorance. Tell me what's going on."

"The institute is a laboratory, research, and science facility."

"Great, more eggheads. That went so well in New York." Pretty sure I rolled my eyes, if I didn't, I meant to. "Lost a lot of good people there."

Eastman ignored me. "They are, or were, involved in biomedical research, including molecular biology." I knew where this was going, I was merely waiting for Eastman to get there. "And we heard from them."

"Major, I realize I'm a lowly grunt captain, but it's not like there's a bunch of officers running around anymore. You explicitly told me that you were going to keep me in the loop with major developments, especially since you are now treading in my wheelhouse."

"Considering I was in New York as well, I know all too well your less-than-fondness for scientists. This is different."

"Wow, I just got it. Fuck me for being so slow. I guess *people*, meaning *me*, don't want to believe that those in power don't have our best interests at heart. Which, by the way, makes no sense. History is fraught with countless examples of higher-ups shitting on the heads of the lower echelons. Picking any one example is unnecessary."

"What are you talking about?"

"My daughter, Major."

"What about her?"

"I'm getting to it, just ruminating. Nicole, in her teenage years, was a world-class teller of lies. Seriously, she could have gone pro. She was so good at lying I think she believed herself, which is no easy feat."

"Your point?"

"My point is you're nowhere near her league. I was just beginning to get the hang of spotting her tells when she finally, and, thankfully, by the way, grew the fuck up and out of that particular phase. You, sir, have lied to me since the moment I boarded this tub, probably before, and your big tell is that your lips start moving and sound comes out. This coordinated hunting? That's the reason we're going to the UK. We shouldn't be in a rush to get anywhere, Major. I seem to remember that being on land equates to danger, and that's the reason for all this." I spread my arms out.

"Bennington knew about the facility; he was feeding them data on Avalyn. They've had a breakthrough."

"Shit." This was huge news. Yeah, I was pissed I'd not known, I'm not a fan of surprises, but a potential cure? The chance to have the planet back? "What kind of break-through?" I was trying to temper my potential runaway angry thoughts. "And why now? I mean, we've been steaming around for a long time."

"A potential vaccine, not a cure, and we were just notified a few days ago."

"Potential?" That was all I could focus on.

"They've been somewhat vague."

"What have the scientists aboard this ship said about it?"

"Babraham hasn't forwarded much."

"Oh, that's rich. They want to make sure we come and pick them up before they share their discovery."

"Can you blame them? What's to say we don't take their research and stay safe and sound right where we're at?"

"So I risk my squad's lives for these non-trusting souls? Yeah, I know it's for the greater good, or, so they say, guess we have to believe these people we don't know, but still, you realize that the greater good for some means the lesser good for others, right? There's a scale, a balance; can't have too much of either. Okay, I see a big flaw in that argument already; the world is one giant burning dumpster right now."

"We need them, Captain. Just the chance that what they're saying is possible makes the mission worthwhile."

"I…" I opened my mouth then quickly closed it. He was

right; he was one hundred percent right. Anything I said would just reveal how friggen scared I was to head back into it. My protective shell had nearly cracked the last time. Yeah, I'd slapped on some decent duct tape, but if I started stressing the adhesion, it was sure to break, or even worse, the tape would retain the shape of the shell, but everything inside would have crumbled away. "How far is Swansea from this facility?" I asked. The resignation in my voice was loud and clear, no matter how hard I tried to hide it.

"Close to two hundred and forty miles."

"Are you insane?"

"I was going to ask you to give me a minute before you went that route."

"Two hundred and forty miles? How are we supposed to do that? You want us to hike in and out? It would take weeks in what is all enemy-occupied territory. And if you say horses, I'm going to resign my commission." I didn't necessarily hate horses as much as I hated ham, but it was close.

"We came up with a plan."

"Who's we? Forget it, doesn't matter. What is this fantastical plan?"

"Train."

I was wracking my brain. "Trains use diesel, don't they?"

"Most."

"Okay, so we know fuel was nearly down the shitter before we came out to sea; what's changed? Are the scientists making fuel? Are they going to take a train from Babraham to Swansea?"

"Not quite. The train is in Swansea."

"How are they going to get us the fuel then?" I wasn't trying to be difficult; none of this was making any sense to me.

"Can I finish?"

"I wish you would," I told him.

He sighed. "I liked when the military made sense and superiors were listened to."

"I'm still here; I'll listen. Might not necessarily act on it, but I'm listening."

"There's a train called the Flying Scotsman. It's in Swansea right now."

Stenzel came onto the bridge. "Have you told him yet, sir?" she asked.

"I'm trying, but getting a story told without questions and obstinacy from the captain is a difficult maneuver."

"Stenzel? You're in on this?"

"Sir, you're going to think it's crazy, and you're going to give all sorts of reasons why it can't work and the dangers involved, but in the end, we all know you're still going to go through with it, so I figured I'd get a leg up," she replied.

"A leg up?"

"Maybe you should tell him, Sergeant. I can't seem to go more than a sentence without an interruption."

I turned to Stenzel.

"How far along are we, sir?" she asked Eastman.

"Babraham, Swansea and the Flying Scotsman," he told her.

"I was hoping you'd be farther along, and I could come in after most of the yelling had stopped, sir."

"Me too."

"Captain, the Flying Scotsman is a steam-powered engine."

A clean sheet of paper and my face shared the same look. (Blank, if that wasn't clear.)

"It uses coal or wood tossed into a firebox to produce steam."

The jumbled pieces of the puzzle began to click into place. "Nope."

"That's it? Just a nope, Captain?" Eastman asked.

"Standard operating procedure. I just want to have a protest on record."

"Duly noted," the major said.

"Go on, Stenzel," I prompted.

"Satellite imagery shows great stores of combustible fuel at Swansea and water towers to fill her tanks."

"The water towers, are we sure they have water? I've got to imagine pissing into the engine like an overheated radiator isn't going to work."

"Thermal imaging shows the tanks are cooler than the surrounding ambient air temperature," Eastman responded.

"One word answer, sir," I told him.

"Yes. Though none seem to be full."

"How fast is this train?" I asked.

"It made a world record at a hundred miles per hour, but for this journey, forty or fifty might be for the best," Stenzel said. "We could be outside the research facility in four or five hours."

The room fell silent.

"Okay, great, this is where it gets fun, right?" I watched as a look passed between Stenzel and Eastman.

"It's the return trip. Whereas we will have plenty of fuel, water is going to be an issue. But we should still be able to make close to four hundred miles."

"Four hundred is less than four hundred and eighty."

Eastman's face appeared to have something condescending to say, but he held it back when the look on my face said I would rip his off if he went there.

"How many passengers are we picking up?"

"Five."

"Eighty-four miles, hostile territory...won't be able to travel much quicker than two or three miles in an hour, unmolested. That's four days with our asses flapping in the breeze, taking into account the ridiculous rest time scientists seem to need."

"Unless we stop for more water," Stenzel said.

"Gonna go out on a limb and say that train is a lot louder than, say, a Tesla. Zombies for miles are going to be headed for that noise. Once we run out of juice, they're gonna catch up."

"A few towers or fire hydrants, sir. We could pump water in. We could do somewhere between five hundred to a thousand gallons a minute, so we would only need to be stopped for ten or fifteen minutes for set-up and to load enough water to get us back."

"That sounds optimistic. And we have a conductor, now? When did we pick up John Henry? Who on this ship is qualified to drive a train?" I asked, hoping to have found a hard-stop to this insanity. Another look between Stenzel and Eastman. "Traitor," I told her.

"I've been studying, and they have a mock set-up where I've been practicing." She shrugged.

"How do I not know this?"

"It's below decks," she offered. Made sense. They could have hidden Godzilla down there, and I'd never know, and now I wondered how much beer they'd stowed out of my reach.

"And you're confident you can run this train?"

"I am, sir, I wouldn't be here backing up the major if I didn't know I could do it."

"And if something breaks on this train?"

"We can be as prepared as possible, Captain, but there are some things we're going to need to trust to Providence," Major Eastman said.

"Yeah, because that's been working out so well. How much of a shit do you think Providence gives?"

"The train is a hundred years old, but it was restored less than a decade ago. Until recently, besides a faulty braking issue, it has been running flawlessly, sir," Stenzel continued.

"This braking issue, it's been repaired? Or is this a fore-shadowing?"

"They were working on it when the z-poc began, and by

all indications they were done or close to it, but we can't confirm due to obvious reasons," Eastman said.

"You two work on this routine for a while? Toss me a line, then reel it in quickly?"

"Captain, I will assign another squad this mission if you do not wish to go."

"Bring it, Major. Blow some smoke up my ass. I like the way it tickles my balls."

Stenzel quickly covered her nose and mouth as a short snort escaped.

"Captain, you and I rarely see eye to eye, and I am exasperated nearly every time we talk. You have an unorthodox approach to the military and how you perform your duty, but the results, they speak for themselves. I'm on my figurative knees here, Captain; you quite literally could be our only hope."

"Stenzel, did he pull that from *Star Wars?*"

"Close, sir." She made sure to keep her hand up, but the lines on the sides of her eyes showed she was still smiling.

"That wasn't half bad, Major. My stomach got all butterfly-like as you sang my praises, but you also knew that by getting Stenzel involved, there was no way in fucking hell I was going to allow one of my people to go out on a dangerous mission without the rest of my squad around her."

It was the major's turn to smile. I was surprised that he didn't say "Checkmate."

3

MAC & WILKES

WILKES HAD STOPPED Mac's narrative a few times initially but finally allowed herself to be pulled into the story as his soothing voice read. For the most part, she was able to figure out the meaning of some of the longer words or, if not, slide past them. She yawned. It had been a long day, her stomach was full, and she was as contented as she had been in a great while.

"You want me to stop for the night?" The handwritten words on the page were not the neatest; he had to struggle to make sense of them, and with the dying down of the fire and his own exhaustion, he wasn't sure if he could continue, even if Wilkes wanted him to.

"The story, is it real? Or made up?"

"I think it's real; it reads as real. Or best I can tell, it's real to this Talbot guy."

"He's funny."

Mac saw that, on the surface, it could be construed that Talbot was funny, but that wasn't all. His words clearly showed a troubled man, someone who was doing their best to hold on when everything around them was falling apart. He looked over to Wilkes, her eyes were shut, and he was pretty sure she was asleep.

"Good night," he said softly, not wanting to disturb her. He turned over, got as comfortable as he could upon the wooden floor, and closed his eyes.

Wilkes opened her eyes to watch him. She had her knife in her hand, and she didn't relax until she could tell beyond doubt he'd fallen asleep.

THE FOLLOWING morning when Mac awoke, he saw that Wilkes wasn't there. She'd left sometime during the night or early morning, and it didn't look like she was coming back—if the missing journal was any indication. This saddened him more than he realized. She very much did look like an older version of his sister, or an imagined version anyway; he had begun to forget what Annie truly looked like. That and the journal, he had been curious and very much wished to continue his trek into Talbot's world, to be pulled away from his own for a while. He could sympathize with a man who may have had it rougher than he had. He grabbed up his meager belongings and headed out the door. A smile broadened his face when he saw Wilkes leaning against a tree, the open journal in her lap. As he approached, he could hear her.

"Standard operating procedure. I just want to have a protest on—" She looked up.

"I thought you said you couldn't read?"

"I can't. I also can't forget anything."

"What? Are you reciting that from memory? How is that possible?"

She shrugged.

"Anything making sense?" He sat next to her.

She shrugged again.

"Okay, start over; we'll sound the words out."

For two hours, they went over the first chapter. Wilkes' mind was sharp, and she was eager to learn. By the time her stomach growled, signifying lunchtime, she had a basic grasp. She came back an hour later with another rabbit and a squirrel. In contrast, Mac's cleaning skills seemed to have taken a turn for the worse.

"Quick question," Wilkes started.

"Yeah, go ahead." Mac had his tongue firmly grasped in his teeth as he cut.

"After your incident with McGowan, how were you planning on eating once you were out on the run?"

Mac paused. "You know, I never really even thought about it. It kind of didn't matter, because I wasn't expecting to survive this long. I just knew he needed to pay for what he'd done, and if I could make it so he never did it again, all the better. My life was a sacrifice I was prepared and willing to make."

"Give me the knife before you make this inedible. You need to watch."

Mac could have easily gone until the night or even the next before he had to eat again. Two meals in two days was a luxury he was unaccustomed to. He was not thrilled with lighting a fire when the smoke could be visible for miles, but he reasoned he would keep it small, and besides, there was no sense in wasting the meal Wilkes had provided. As soon as the food was cooked, Mac quickly doused the flames with dirt; his anxiety increased as he watched a large plume of smoke rise into the air.

"It's fine. They're not close enough to see it; I patrolled before I hunted," she told him as she tore off a portion of meat.

"McGowan's not the only thing we need to worry about out here. Beaters sometimes show up when they see smoke."

"I haven't seen one of them in over four hundred days. There might not be any more of them."

Without broaching the subject, they both decided to stay another night. Adequate shelter was not something to be taken lightly, and small game was abundant. Mac thought that, if given the time, he could get fat here, a malady that didn't trouble much of humanity anymore.

As soon as the sun began to set, they went inside and Mac started another fire. This time when he started to read, Wilkes sat next to him. She'd asked him to place a finger under each word as he read so that she could follow along. Her mouth was moving, though she made no sound. He knew in a couple of days it was likely she'd be reading at a better level than he was. He wasn't so sure he would be nearly as proficient with cleaning the wild game, but her genuine interest in improving her skills was inspiring; he was going to try.

She held on for as long as she could before her eyes drooped down and her head gently nestled against Mac's shoulder. He'd had what he could call *friends* since the fateful day; he'd even cared for people that had cared for him back. But this was something different, something more meaningful and deeper. He figured he was merely replacing the lost love of his sister with someone similar, but he didn't care. As far as he was concerned, Wilkes was his family now, and he would do everything he could to make sure she stayed safe, even if she might be better suited to survival than he was. A smile pulled up the corner of his lips as he fell asleep. He had to rouse Wilkes the next morning.

"What the hell?" he chided her as she groggily sat up.

"What?" she asked.

"Look at my arm. It's soaked in drool."

She stretched. "Sorry." She smiled. "It's been a long time since I slept that soundly."

"As much as I like it here, I think we should get moving."

Wilkes didn't argue. They gathered up their belongings and began their trek.

"The ship they're on, do you know how big it is?" Wilkes asked.

"Warships could be huge; I've seen some in movies." He had to explain to her what those were, although he wasn't sure if she believed him when he said that movies were like books but with moving pictures. "They used to say that they were as big as small cities." He could see she was about to ask what that was. "Umm, bigger than the building we met at. Like, *a lot* bigger."

"No way!" Her eyes grew huge. "No beaters? No enemies?"

"Doesn't seem like it."

"Why would they ever leave?"

Mac shrugged and shook his head.

4

MIKE JOURNAL ENTRY 2

"Shit, it's beautiful," I said as Tracy and I looked upon the coastline of Cardiff.

"God, I would love to go over there and look around."

I thought about telling her I'd trade, but it sounded slightly mean-spirited in my head, even if I wouldn't have meant it that way.

"Is it worth it?" she asked, turning away from the view and at me.

"Eastman thinks so."

"I'm concerned about your opinion, not his." She held me with her unwavering gaze.

"I don't know, woman. Apparently, there's the chance of a vaccine."

"A chance?"

"I have my doubts; these scientists are up against it. In severely hostile territory, probably low on supplies.... They might say anything to get us to come and save them."

"Pretty cynical."

"Have you met me?" I got her to smile, which always makes me smile in turn. "It's difficult to weigh the promise of the unknown against the obvious, inherent dangers. If what they're saying is true, it could be world changing. But saving five nameless, faceless people while risking those I love…" I let that dangle there; it didn't need any clarifying descriptors.

"I wish you wouldn't do it."

"I wish that, too," I told her as I wrapped her up in a hug. "Someone's going to do it."

She let go far too soon; I'm gonna go out on a limb and bet she was going to say something along the lines of *why is it always you?* but she just let her unsaid words form a sad smile.

Maybe it was some twisted hero complex. In no way, shape, or form was it because I wanted accolades. I'd read a few stories about war heroes awarded Iron Crosses or Medals of Honors that would then turn around and toss the hardware away because they didn't want anything that reminded them of the shit storm they'd been through or of the people that had fallen along the way. When I was younger and read that, I was always like, what the hell, you earned this incredible award and just tossed it? It didn't make any sense to my inexperienced and sadly naïve mind. Now it was as clear as the sky above me.

I was going because people's lives were going to be at risk, whether I stayed or not. And if I stayed behind and people died…well, let's just say living with myself was already a chore; I did not need it to move into the nightmare realm. Not again.

"Mike," BT said softly as he approached.

I turned back; he was all geared up.

"Hi, Tracy." He waved, giving her a sheepish smile. I'm sure he'd just been through his own complicated explanation to my sister.

Tracy sighed, and a deep sadness settled into her features. I hated seeing her this way, especially since I was the one causing it. It was one thing to be out and about and in the thick of it, but it was also another version of hell waiting and worrying, having no idea what was happening and no way to help if things went sideways. *If…*funny I even used that word. No way to help *when* things went sideways.

"I love you," I told her.

"Duh," she responded before pulling my head down for a kiss. "I expect you home soon. BT." She nodded at him as she walked away.

"What a view!" I yelled at her; she threw a bird over her shoulder.

"How'd that go?" he asked.

"Well, if your face is any indication, it went better than your goodbye."

"She sent me with muffins."

"Fuck man! Just how pissed is she?"

TEN MINUTES LATER, after some serious soul-searching, I found myself at the boat launch. All our gear was loaded into one Zodiac along with Kirby and Grimm. The rest of my squad, plus the remnants of the SEALS, were in another. It was a mile to shore, generally a pretty quick transport hop; this was not like that. There were four sailors on the supply boat manning oars.

"Do your thing." I smacked BT's shoulder.

"What?"

"You're the bad guy. Do your thing." I pointed to the other boat; Kirby and Grimm were kicking back, looking like they were about to go on a pleasure cruise.

"Grabs oars, you malingering bastards!" BT yelled.

Kirby was so startled I thought he might fall out.

"I blame this on you!" BT pointed at me. "You're too soft on them!"

"I uh, what?" My only recourse was to get away from him and into the boat. The rowing was a welcome distraction from the folly we were in the midst of performing. Eastman had assured me, and I'd seen the images for myself, that it looked relatively calm where we were headed. That didn't mean it couldn't change in a heartbeat. But at least it wasn't going to be anything like landing in Normandy on D-Day. Where I figured it would get iffy was when we got to the Bay of Cardiff, then we'd be taking the River Taff upstream, where the train tracks bridged over the river a mile farther up. The depot with our ride could be found there.

The chatter was down to only what was necessary as we entered the mouth of the river, and even that was in hushed tones. Our success lay in the ability to make it to our destination unseen. And even then, in terms of all the problems we could face today, staying hidden was low on the list of potential issues. According to Stenzel, it could take up to six hours to get the steam engine up to heat. She thought she could do it in four, but that was still a ton of time to be sitting there. And there was no way this was a quiet procedure.

We rowed the inflatable boats right up onto a rocky shore. The trestle to our right was awash with weathered graffiti, and it seemed that Kilroy had been there, albeit a while ago. Ahead of us stood our ride, wasn't entirely sure what I was expecting, I suppose one of those old steam engines from the eighteen-hundreds, target for payroll bandits. It was for sure a dated train, but it was not the fossil I had in my mind's eye.

We quickly unloaded our gear. "Radios on and count off for testing." I pointed to Gary, who started. When I was certain all our comms were working, I put Kirby, Grimm, Dallas, Harmon, and my brother on perimeter patrol. "Keep close," I told them before sending them off. "Reed, Walde, I'd like you to check the train and clear it if need be. Once that's done, if you could keep an eye on the engine, I would appreciate it."

"On it," Walde said, smacking Reed in the chest.

"Sir, we'll anchor offshore until you get underway," Corporal Gratsnik said as he pushed his boat away.

"Thank you." I turned to see Stenzel, Winters, and Rose boarding the train's engine. "Okay, you two, let's get this gear up there," I said to Tommy and BT. "And by let's, I mean you two."

"What are you going to do?" BT asked as he hefted a large canvas bag.

"I'm going to protect you."

He grunted as we followed the pack-mulish Tommy. The kid had to have been carrying three hundred pounds of stuff and still seemed unencumbered. They continued on to the passenger cars where we were going to set up shop. I poked my head into the engine. There were dials, knobs, copper tubes and gauges everywhere; the setup looked like something out of a World War II submarine. Stenzel was at work going over all the equipment and checking her notes. Winters was shoveling coal into a small port that fed the furnace.

"Sir, the tender is low; we're going to have to top it off," Rose told me as she was doing her best to stay out of the way.

"Tender?"

"Coal car," she explained.

"You realize you could have just said that instead of whipping out the train jargon and making me look dumb."

"Yes sir." She smiled.

"Come on, show me what needs to be done then I'll order BT and Tommy to work on it."

BT came out of the train, rifle in hand. He nodded to me. "Check-ins are clean." He was referring to the patrols. "What's going on?" he asked as he saw me looking up.

"Our first problem," I told him. "The coal car."

"Tender."

"Seriously? You know what that is too?"

"What? If you paid a modicum of attention during the briefings, you'd know."

"Fine, the tender is low."

"We figured that would be the case, not a problem. We'll just fill it with that raised box thingy."

"Raised box thingy? Was that in the briefing, too?"

"Kiss my ass. Your nephew has too much Talbot in him; kept me up last night."

"Okay, well, the raised box thingy is empty."

"You're sure?"

I led him to the other side of the train, where a large pile of coal sat upon the ground directly under the thingy.

"Shit," was his reply.

"We're going to have to do this manually."

"Are you including yourself in this *we*?"

"Leadership by example, I always say, and by leadership, I mean directing. Come on, we're going to need to find a few things and then see who we can pull for shit duty."

"Mike, this is all shit duty."

I gave him a fist bump. Found a couple of shovels, a wheelbarrow, and a ladder easily enough, but finding something to transport the coal up onto the top ended up being the most difficult. Tommy came to the rescue with burlap bags. The distance from the spilled contents to the tender wasn't far, slightly over sixty yards, but I knew after a thousand round trips that was going to seem like circumnavigating the globe.

"Reed, going to need your help," I said, going up to the engine.

"Sucks to be you," Walde told him as she saw what we were about to do.

"Dallas, Kirby, report to the engine," I said over the radio.

Within a few minutes, we had our line set. I was shoveling coal into Walde and Kirby's wheelbarrows then they'd walk the distance to where BT was and drop their loads. Dallas would shovel it into the burlap bag BT was holding, the big man would then climb halfway up the ladder where Tommy would lean down, snag it and dump the coal into the box. It was back-breaking work, and I was enjoying it immensely. There's something to be said about menial work; it's honest, and you work the body so hard the mind doesn't have a chance to wander, and in my case, that was a blessing. The day wasn't overly warm, but I'd stripped down to my t-shirt and was soaked through with sweat, as was everyone on the detail. The shoveling, the wheelbarrows, brought me back to my much younger days when I did road construction for my dad's business. God, I missed him.

It was past noon. We'd been at it for close to four hours. Periodically, a loud blast of steam would come from the engine; I internally winced each time, and sometimes externally. Finally, what we figured was going to happen, did.

"Sir, it's Grimm. Contact to our six o'clock, three speeders coming fast."

"Grimm, Gary, pull back to the train. Tommy, how's the box?"

"Three-quarters full."

"Stenzel, what's our ETA?"

"Sir, I know I initially said I could do this in four hours, but I'm going to need another hour, maybe two."

"Walde, I want those zombies taken out as quietly as possible. Grimm, Gary, you back her up. The work detail is on break; stay close or on the train." I climbed the ladder to be with Tommy and also for the view it afforded. The zombies were a quarter mile away and running fast. Three wasn't bad, but they were like cockroaches; if you saw one out in the open, that meant hundreds were lurking in the shadows. I did a slow three-sixty looking for any others that might be trying to sneak up on us while we were distracted. Nothing so far. The trio were a scouting party; it was anybody's guess how much time we would have before the main force would come when they didn't report in.

Luckily, we'd been outfitted with the diminishing supply of tainted bullets. Walde was a hell of a shot, much better than I, but she wasn't Stenzel, who was a freak of nature with a firearm. If getting the engine started wasn't the most crucial task of the day, I would have pulled her off it to deal with our infestation. Walde, despite my thoughts, plugged the first straight through the brain bucket from two hundred yards. Its head canted to the left, its body to the right as it spiraled to the ground, kicking up a small eddy of dust.

"Damn," Kirby said, watching what we all had.

"No noise," BT warned. Walde didn't need the distraction in her ear, although, as a professional, it was unlikely to bother her.

Tommy tapped my shoulder; I'd been so fixated on the kill I'd missed the real drama. Unlike almost every encounter we had with the zombies, this one was different. The two partner zombies stopped when their fellow runner was dropped. They quickly checked him over, and, when they realized he'd been killed, they split up. One went to the side for cover, the other kept advancing. Walde quickly put it down.

"Sir, I think that one's going back to tell others," Walde said.

"Stenzel?"

"Forty-five minutes or never," came her clipped response. She was in the middle of something; I didn't press her on it. I had no idea how far away the zombie conclave was, and I wasn't going to risk sending a fire team out into the unknown.

"Gratsnik, this is Talbot. How's everything out there?"

"Quiet, sir."

"Okay, good. Be ready to move toward shore."

"Will do, sir."

I could hear Stenzel swearing, even though she'd shut off her radio.

"Keep filling the hopper?" Tommy asked.

"No, if we need to, we'll do it when we get water."

If anyone had eyes on me, they would have thought I was part bird with the way my head bobbed constantly. I was continually alternating looking down at my watch and checking for predators. It was impossible not to believe we were rushing for a climax, and suffice it to say it wasn't the good kind. I resisted the urge to check in with Stenzel; it wasn't like she would withhold that information from me. At thirty-two minutes and fourteen seconds since I'd last talked to my engineer, we got another sighting of zombies, this from my river crew.

"Got a problem, sir," Gratsnik said calmly.

"Listening," I told him.

"Multiple zombies splashing into the river upstream. If you're going to want an evac it's going to have to happen within the next three minutes, otherwise we're going to have to leave before we're overrun."

"Rose, how's it going down there?"

"She's pissed, sir."

"I don't need to know her disposition, just if this is going to work or not."

"Well, she just asked me if I had enough explosives to blow this piece of shit up."

"Rose, I need something more definitive."

"Harley, Cap wants to know if we can expect to go for a ride."

"Do I look like a wizard? Do you see a pointy hat decorated with moons and stars? Wait. Where did I put my wand? Did I already shove it up the Capt—"

I could hear her clearly enough over Rose's pick-up.

"Ten minutes," Rose said.

"She didn't say that," I told her.

"She flipped me double eagles five times."

"Comforting. So you two have developed your own language."

"Mike?" BT asked.

Our window to retreat to the carrier was closing quickly. If this mission went belly up and we did go back, the powers that be were going to come up with a plan B, and it was a guarantee it was going to be worse than this clusterfuck and Eastman would make sure I was heading that mission as well. I had a theory that grew stronger with each one. There weren't even scientists at this institute, he was just doing his best to keep me off the ship.

"We're staying," I said as I ran through the options. "Gratsnik, pull anchor and get out of here."

"Sir, you sure?"

"No. Go anyway."

"Yes, sir." I watched as the navy personnel, not content to let the river drift them down and away, paddled furiously. A minute later, I saw why. A gross of zombies were swimming toward them. Figured that was a good a word as any to describe a group of the disgusting beings and anyway a preliminary count had revealed there were a hundred and forty-four of them, more or less. None of the swimmers were ever going to compete for a gold medal at the Olympics, but watching them swim as well as I can was unsettling.

"Gratsnik, one more thing."

"Yes, sir."

"Let them stay as close to you as you safely can for a while."

"Roger that, sir."

I hated using them as bait, but once the zombies realized their prey was out of range, they would head to the shore and then us, and the longer it took for them to realize that, the better.

"Back of the train," Grimm said.

I spun and was looking back, into the enormous, covered train hub. It was bathed in shadows. With the sun just about overhead, I couldn't see much within, but enough to realize the zombies were rallying there, and in numbers.

"Everyone in the cars. Close the doors. Rose, close up the engine."

"This ought to be fun; it's already a furnace in here, like, literally."

"Rose."

"On it, sir."

I don't know what specifically the zombies had been waiting for, but somewhere around eight minutes later, they began their charge.

"They're coming back from the river, too," Tommy said.

"Choo-choo motherfucker!" Stenzel was back on the line. "Hold on, we're going for a ride." The train whistle blasted three long times. I'm not sure that was the best move; we already had a plethora of zombies, there was no need to invite more from neighboring communities. But that was her victory cry, and I couldn't blame her entirely. Tommy grabbed me as the train lurched forward. I'd had minimal experience with the giant transport machines, but I expected us to get underway a little quicker; a snail on Quaaludes could have outpaced us. The zombies were up to the third car of our seven-car train. Some were hopping aboard like undead hobos, but most were going for the meat-filled cans.

"We've got boarders," I warned those inside. I had no idea if they could manipulate the doors, but the safe bet was on the yes side of that. "We need to get someplace safer," I told Tommy. Watching James Bond run around on the top of a train made for a good movie scene, but, believe me, it was terrifying in real life. The train couldn't have been going more than five miles an hour as Tommy and I descended the ladder attached to the coal car, but one slip up and the tons of metal would be completely unforgiving. BT opened the door to the car and helped us in, realizing the same thing I was.

"Is there drink service on this line?" I asked.

"Nice to see you, too."

Zombies were running next to us, looking in, some moving past and toward the engine.

"Rose, you're going to have company real soon," I said.

"I see them. Permission to engage."

"By 'engage' if you don't mean explosives, sure. Odds are you toss a boom out there you'll derail us," I told her.

"Blow up one mountain, and all of a sudden you're labeled as heavy-handed."

The zombies fired first, not that we cared about any court of law, but they went on the offensive, tossing rocks at the windows. I stepped back when one the size of a baseball starred the glass in front of me.

"Son of a bitch. Stenzel, any time you want to make this thing a Ferrari and not a Yugo would be fantastic." I watched with extreme satisfaction as the rock thrower tripped over a bent sign. It tried to get up, but its lower leg was snapped, making it look like it was made from rubber. It was disgusting; I watched as it fell over again. I gave it the finger, though it wasn't watching. We were beginning to outpace them, and in haste, they were trying to find handholds or get in between the cars. I slid the window down to watch. Also disgusting but immensely entertaining, I watched more than a few become chum as the wheels diced them up. I was telling myself I was looking because I needed to assess how many zombies were going to be on the train with us, maybe there was a nugget of truth there, but the bulk of it was I couldn't turn away. I'd seen my share of gruesome events, even before the apocalypse, but this was a whole other level. I was deriving some sort of sick satisfaction from their vicious, violent, visceral deaths.

"Fuck 'em," I said as I finally pulled my head back in.

"What's that?" BT asked.

I shook my head.

"Contact," Reed said. I saw his muzzle flash from the other car, never heard the pop of the rifle. "Shit, pulling back."

Tommy moved to help. He'd no sooner opened the door between train cars when a zombie barreled into him. If he wasn't so strong he would have fallen over, the hit so sudden and forceful. Tommy wrapped one hand around his zombie's throat; Kirby shot the next one through. I couldn't see where all the damn things were coming from. Tommy dragged the one he had somewhat subdued further into the car. He crushed the windpipe and neck bones, his hand closed so tightly it looked like he was making a fist. Blood exploded through the gaps in his fingers and the zombie's head lolled to the side. I put a 45 into its skull from less than an inch away. The sound would have been deafening if not for the fact that our comms had built-in sound suppression. Tommy's teeth were gritted together as he watched the zombie sink into the dark depths of a second death before he let it drop to the floor with a wet thud. I'm under the belief if he had not let go, the head would have popped free as there was very little tissue left hanging to hold it in place.

"Any time you guys want to come help is fine with me!" Reed yelled over the pops of his rifle. "Walde, where you at?"

"Last car," she whispered, "stuck in the loo."

When in Rome, I thought sourly.

"How many fucking zombies can there be aboard?" I flipped the safety on my rifle to full auto, stupider than shit in such tight quarters and with steel as a backdrop, still, I moved Kirby to the side and sprayed the entry. When that was clear, I popped in a new magazine and cleared away the five still waiting patiently for their turn. Reed had his back to me; he had retreated nearly as far as he could. A quick estimate on my part put twelve zombies in there with him. I had to dodge a thrown elbow as I opened the door to his car and grabbed his shoulder to pull him out.

He nodded when he realized it was me. "Walde?" he asked.

He must not have heard her reply through his own battle. "Safe but pinned down. We'll get her. For now, let's get out here." Superfluous words as we were already leaving when I said them. I'd no sooner closed the door when zombies slammed up against it. BT had an arm out and wrenched Reed into our car. I stayed for an extra second on the small ledge, a zombie's head tilted to the side as it looked at me. Its dark eyes burned with hatred, its teeth gritted in a snarl, drool fell from the side. Greasy hair matted down upon its head. The clothes, weirdly, looked as if they'd just been lifted from a drycleaners; did not at all fit with what I was looking at. I found picturing a zombie changing into fresh duds unsettling. The amount of thought and coordination, not to mention the desire, to perform the act would be leaps and bounds above what an old-school shuffler would have been able to accomplish.

"Anyone know if they had the lethal bullets here?" I asked once I was back in our car.

No one answered because no one knew. We thought we'd traced the sharp increase in intelligence to our tinkering with the bullets, so what was the reasoning here? The well-dressed zombie did not approach; he was peering intently through the window and into our car, though. He was assessing the risk and reward factors. A direct assault now, with us alert and waiting and armed, was not a recipe for a successful venture. More zombies streamed in to where he was, a couple dozen, easily.

"Walde?" I asked.

"Still here."

"What's your status?"

"Shitty."

"Potty humor, I'm a fan. Can you give me anything else?"

"The door is about as solid as one on a plane, so, not at all. I lost my rifle in a struggle; I do have a pistol and thirty-two rounds. Last I saw before I hid, there were eight zombies in the car with me. I can't tell now if there's more or less. What are the chances you're making your way toward me?"

"We're a bit bottled up at the moment and we'll need to

go on the offensive. Sit tight don't go for another ten minutes. Maybe read a magazine."

"You're funny, sir."

"Got a problem," Rose said. My ears hurt when Stenzel's yell of frustration came through.

"We're slowing down," Tommy said.

"Hit me with it, seems like the right time," I told Rose.

"Coal feed's not working," she replied.

Tommy stuck his head out the window; he didn't even need to say anything when he came back in. The zombies that had been running after us had never stopped, and even now, they would be gaining.

"I am not sure how much more fun I can handle today." I sighed. "Okay, Walde is our priority."

"I appreciate that, sir," she whispered.

"Rose, do we have an estimate on repairs?"

"I'm not asking her."

I raised my face into the air in an exasperated way. "Stenzel?"

"*What Goddamit!?*" she yelled. "Sir," she added as if that made it all better.

"Do you need help up there?" I asked.

"A fucking sledgehammer would be great, barring that, an industrial-sized air conditioner. If neither of those, Rose has what I need."

"Rose, you know not to give her anything, right?" I asked.

"Sir, if something were to fall out of my bag, I wouldn't have control of that. Plus, she's mean right now, and I'm a little scared of her. I'm not telling her no."

"Winters, any chance you can get the feed working again?"

"Working on it," he replied.

"Need help?"

"Should be good to go. We know what to do, just being able to do it and the train agreeing seems to be the issue."

"ETA?"

"Maybe a half-hour."

"Okay, keep us informed. Tommy, Reed, you two are going up top to do some train hopping. Just keep the trailing zombies from getting too close. Kirby and myself are going to do a frontal assault. The rest, outside to the left. We'll clear the car with a crossfire once Tommy and Reed are far enough away. Then we'll hit Walde's car the same way. Stay away from the rear of the car, though, that's where the bathroom is."

"I'd appreciate that," Walde said.

"We're clear," Tommy said.

The train was moving slow enough now a bad-kneed vagabond with a three-legged dog could have hopped aboard. "Let's move. Kirby, you stay behind me until we're in."

We gave the boy shit, but he was actually a good soldier. A little hot-headed, maybe, but what young Marine wasn't? He nodded. "Ready, sir." Determination on his face. I don't think he was the least bit afraid... not always the greatest quality. Fear kept you honest, sometimes kept you alive.

The smartly dressed zombie had watched as Tommy and Reed jumped above him, then he watched as my people filed out and took up places outside. The last thing he saw was my muzzle flash as I put one through his skull. We stayed in between cars as the firing line went to work. The explosion of glass, the tearing up of seats, bits of fabric floating around like a lazy day of snowing in mid-December. Zombies were flailing about as they were hit multiple times. Standard fare in these times. I wondered what the best song would be to overlay the scene in a movie. The Stones and Creedence Clearwater Revival had the Vietnam War genre sewn up. The original brat pack could stake a claim to mobster flicks. Ah, got it, Chevelle, *The Red* would work. Angry, grungy song; it fit perfectly.

"Seeing red again!" I shouted as I opened the door and

finished off the three remaining zombies that had somehow miraculously escaped the maelstrom.

"Sir?" Kirby asked as I replaced the magazine.

"Might be before your time. Top, we're clear here, meet you at the last car," I told BT. Could hear the pops of shots further down; Reed and Tommy were working on the trailing horde. If they were close enough to shoot, that meant the rest of my team was in danger.

"Winters, we may get cut off from you," I told him as Kirby and I quickly picked our way through the bloody car, and that wasn't a British euphemism.

"Nothing's getting in here." He grunted the words out as he wrestled with whatever was jamming up the feed.

"Everyone on the train now!" BT ordered.

Kirby and I were still two cars from Walde when he said that. It could only mean the zombies were here.

"Reed, how many?" I asked.

"All of them," he said and kept shooting.

"Rear car clear. We've got Walde, but we're not going anywhere," BT said.

Zombies began to blaze past our location. "Kirby, the door." I directed him back the way we came. "See if you can jam it."

"It has a lock."

"Really? Well, hot damn," I said as I looked at it. "Needs a key; is there one up there?"

"Nope." He was struggling with the door. We'd been seen, and a zombie decided it wanted in.

"Kirby, you're about as useless as a sausage at a vegetarian convention," BT chimed in.

"If he tells you to drop down and give him twenty, I'm countermanding that order," I told him.

"By vegetarian, do you mean lesbian?" Rose chimed in.

"What?" Kirby asked.

Yeah, the situation we were in was absolutely horrible, but

seeing his face turn a crimson red, I had to figure was going to be the highlight of my day.

"What's this?" Winters asked. "Sir, the lock, what's it look like?"

"Square hole, looks like a gas shut-off type of lock," I told him.

"There's a key up here hanging on a hook, looks like it might work."

"That's about as helpful as Kirby's sausage," I said. The boy somehow turned redder, and Rose snorted. I don't know what that said about us, that we could literally laugh in the face of extreme peril; we were either that confident in our abilities to extract ourselves from the situation or that psychotic.

"I'm coming, there's nothing by the engine yet."

I was about to tell him the folly of the idea when Stenzel told us he was on the move. The zombie in front of me was a petite female. Dark hair was matted to her face; I want to say it was with dirt, but it wasn't. I just wanted to say that, otherwise, I had to think of her as eating the colon of some unlucky soul, and I wasn't ready for that. She had one hand on the handle and was attempting to twist it from side to side. With her free hand, she was tapping her fingernails against the glass, off-tempo, I might add, like a jazz musician. I wanted to kill her for that alone. The noise was grating. Our car was surrounded, easily over a hundred zombies looking for a way in.

"Shit," was all I could think to say as one bent down to grab a rock. Not all the synapses were working up to speed with this one as the rock more fell forward out of its hand than was tossed, but like a good monkey that showed all the other ones how to dip a wet stick into a termite mound to get some juicy protein, others took up the rock tossing craze. Most were of the small, trestle type stone, they made for a racket but weren't overly dangerous. Eventually I think insanity would set in from the constant barrage and the inability to get sleep, especially since we couldn't leave the doors untended, but that was definitely the long-game. I didn't see the asshole who found a brick, but the hit was louder than anything thus far. Luckily, the zombie had missed a window but realizing the better weapon he'd found, he went to retrieve it. I tried to swing my rifle around and get a shot, but the angle wasn't there, and I wasn't overly keen on taking out a window.

"Sir?" Kirby asked as we both watched the pitcher wannabe wind up and throw. It sailed high.

I was about to tell the tosser he sucked, heckle him like those people do in a dunk tank, that was when Winters spoke.

"That was close."

Like meerkats sensing danger from above, all the zombies' heads pivoted in that direction. Though, in this scenario, they were the predator looking to knock the prey from the sky. We really hadn't thought this one out, sort of my specialty, although I wasn't going to take the brunt of the blame on this one. Winters began the mission before we could even talk about it. I caught a quick glimpse of him as he popped his head down to take a look at our situation.

"Motherfucker." I'm assuming by his grunt a rock had found its mark. "Doesn't look like you're going to be able to open a window; going to have to shoot one out, Cap."

"Yeah, do it and get the hell out of here before you get a concussion," I told him. If that was all he got, he could count himself lucky.

There were so many rocks flying the light in the car dimmed. Most missed, the vast majority in fact, but even one percent of a thousand is ten. The window exploded in, the key quickly followed.

"Winters, you okay?" I asked.

"Some superficial wounds, stings like a bastard. I'm going to lay low until you get secured."

I wanted to tell him to head back, it was too dangerous,

but I had the majority of my squad in the same situation, two cars down.

"How are we going to get that, sir?" Kirby asked as we both looked at the keys.

In a stroke of sort of shitty luck, Winters had tossed them toward me, had struck the back of a chair, and rebounded to about midway across the car on the floor.

"Perfect." The two options, as I saw them, were I let go and Kirby covered me or vice versa. Kirby was a decent marksman, but there was no way on this clusterfuck of a forsaken world God had created I was going to be downrange of him.

"You're going to make me get them, aren't you sir?" His head sagged as he sighed the words out.

"And Top says you're too thick to learn new things."

"He is," BT replied. "Now hurry up!"

"I'd like to request Mast," Kirby said.

"Is he serious right now?!" BT bellowed over the radio.

Requesting Mast was a military person's right to speak with a higher-ranking commanding officer or enlisted personnel if he or she felt the order they had been given was unjust, unfair, or unlawful. Theoretically, a military person could go all the way to the commander in chief, though, in most instances it didn't go past a boot lieutenant who would then make the lowly, enlisted malcontent pay for their idiotic belief that they could get out of complying with an order given by a senior NCO by telling mommy.

"Kirby, you realize I'm the highest-ranking officer here, and I'm the one that gave the order."

"I'll wait."

"Sweetums, get the keys, or I'll never do that thing you like, ever again," Rose told him. "You know…wiggle, wiggle."

I'd seen the shade of red displayed on his face only once before in my entire lifetime, and that had been on a brand new freshly painted fire engine. On the truck, it was awesome, on Kirby, not so much. I was under the impression every blood vessel in his face had spontaneously burst. He dashed for those keys like he'd been shot out of a t-shirt cannon. I'd just got my rifle up a moment before he reached them.

"Go back, over the seats!" I yelled, needing the aisle clear as the zombie by the door was already entering. Kirby dove to his left; my first round hit dangerously close to the bottom of his boot as he crashed into the side of the train. "My bad!" I shouted when he looked up. In my defense, I was shooting one handed and from the hip. Blew a nice-sized hole straight through the seat.

My next round was better, although still a miss. The third hit the lead zombie in the knee, its leg gave out, and he caved to the side. He'd be dead soon enough, or anyway, unable to catch a train. The next one stepped over her dying brethren; her I hit in the midsection. Blood that looked more like tar seeped out. Her expression changed when she realized that the less-than-lethal wound was, in fact, deadly. Surprise, confusion, tough to tell, and honestly, I didn't give a fuck. Kirby was worming his way over the seats. He'd joined the fight out of necessity as, once they spotted him, he was fair game. It was easy enough keeping them from getting to him, the difficult part was going to be able to get the door clear for him to shut it. The area jammed up with both living people and dead zombies.

"Winters, going to need your help!" I told him through the sounds of the battle.

"What can I do?"

He was already in danger with the hurling rocks, although that had subsided somewhat now that the dining car was open.

"You've got to try and keep the zombies off the juncture while Kirby clears some bodies away."

"Can do."

We could hear him shifting around on the top of the car.

The rifle blasts as he fired straight down into the turmoil were welcome.

"Start moving the bodies, and if you request Mast again, I'm going to get clarification from Rose what 'wiggle wiggle' means."

He didn't hesitate. Jumped down into the aisle and slid bodies away like he was clearing his quarterback from a team-sack. He was doing his best to try and send them all the way down the car to me as payback, but the rubber flooring was causing too much friction, even with the pooling blood. In less than a minute he was able to close the door, then the frantic search for the key began. I would have facepalmed if I'd had a free hand. He finally found it down by his feet, it was coated in gore, but that didn't stop him as he slid it in and turned. When he pulled on the door, and it didn't budge, we both gave a strained chuckle of relief.

"All right, come on, get mine locked."

He didn't move.

"Rose, I've got a question," I said.

Kirby catapulted over the bodies, getting to me as fast as he could.

"I'm listening, sir."

I waited until his outstretched, key-laden hand opened. "All good, sorry to bother you. Mast my ass," I said as I swiped the key away and quickly locked my door.

"Winters, we're ready for the handoff."

"Zombies seem to be stocking up on projectiles again, wouldn't mind a little clearing," he said as he scooted back our way.

The pelting started back up. As soon as I let my window down, I caught a rock in the shoulder. More surprised than hurt, but I made sure that ass was the first one I took down.

"I'm ready," Winters said. This time, instead of ducking his head down, he reached blindly with his hand. I was reaching up when a half brick smashed into the back of my hand. Fortunately, I felt one of the bones snap—that was the only reason my hand hadn't reflexively opened up and dropped the key. I pulled my lucky hand in. Had to pry my fingers back to pull the key free. I muttered a litany of swears as I did so.

"Going again," I told Winters. More rocks, no connections. This handoff went without a hitch.

"You all right, sir?" Kirby looked over his shoulder.

"Yeah." I winced, flexing my hand, trying to get the bone to snap, more or less, back into place.

"Fuck," that from Winters. "I'm good, I'm good," he assured us.

The transfer went much better in BT's car with more personnel. In less than a minute, Winters was heading back, and half a minute later, we got the all-clear. I let out a breath I'd not known I was holding, or more accurately, I was able to take a full intake of air without the pressing weight of the added stress upon my chest. We shot some of the zombies, but it was a supply and demand issue, I demanded that they be killed, but our supply of bullets was not inexhaustible, and we'd not even started our journey. I gave the ceasefire order.

"Let's just hunker down until such time as Stenzel gets us moving again. Stenzel?"

"Headset is off again, lot of swearing. I'm writing some of them down, sir, as I've never heard them before," Rose said.

"Winters, any chance I can get a more on topic update?" I asked.

"Well, sir, she does seem to be using either truly outdated profanity or on-the-fly expletives."

My squad had lost their collective minds. I'd no sooner had the thought when I ended up with a shower of glass chunks on my head and shoulders. I wondered what kind of shampoo corrected that malady.

"She's fairly certain she can get us up and running," Winters said.

"You didn't add, 'in no time.' You realize that's the standard expectation to that sentence, right?" I asked.

He was silent. The good thing was the zombies could only break out so much glass, but they could ring the bell housing forever, and that had been old a minute after they'd started.

"Sir, this is Harmon; Major Eastman is on channel two."

"Fantastic." I switched over.

"This is Captain Talbot."

"Captain, satellite imagery shows you're not moving. Is there a problem?"

Oh boy, the shit I had lined up for that one. "No sir, just doing a bit of sightseeing," or "no sir, the cars aren't quite full; we figured we could pack on a few more," or maybe "no sir, we have a running bet on who can shoot off more zombie genitalia." None were great, and maybe that was my reason for telling him the truth instead of just calling him a fucking idiot.

"We're having some train issues."

"You need to get moving."

If I had a handset, I would have tossed it across the car. "I suppose we could get out and push, sir." I did my best to pull the derision out of that last word, mixed results at best.

"I'm sorry, Captain, sometimes I'm so focused on the end result I don't take into account all the other variables. Being a military operations commander is a lot different from being a pilot."

I was damn near speechless. Hearing a superior officer apologize was almost as rare as my wife saying I was right and she was wrong.

"Do you have an ETA when you may get underway?"

"Right now, sir, there's a bigger chance we may need an extraction."

If he had less military decorum, this might be when he tossed his radio. I don't know if he'd do it; we'd need somewhere near a company of a hundred to two hundred to get us out of this mess. That was far too many resources to jeopardize for one squad.

He was honest, even if it was not what I wanted to hear. What he didn't say was clearly spoken: "Let's hope it doesn't come to that," he said.

If we didn't get ourselves out of here, we were a lost cause. He would have to use a portion of the fighting men he had left to complete the mission. Maybe our loved ones would get a nice memorial serving tray engraved with all our names.

"I'll keep you updated," I told him before switching back to the squad frequency.

"Umm, sir," it was Rose. "Stenzel is sitting cross-legged in the middle of the compartment doing some sort of yoga shit."

"It's meditation for Zen, you heathen," I heard Stenzel say in the background.

I pinched the bridge of my nose, head down, eyes closed. I could have used a little Zen right then, but two hundred rock strikes a minute was beginning to fray my nerves.

"Rose, let me know when Stenzel reaches cosmic stillness. Fuck," I said at the end when no one except Kirby could hear me.

"Hungry?" He was digging into an MRE he had stuffed in one of his pockets. He was chowing down on squeeze cheese and crackers. I almost didn't have the heart to tell him, did it anyway.

"I hate to crash on your fine dining experience, but what are you planning on washing down that wet cement covered cardboard with?"

There was a genuine look of panic in his eyes as he felt around for a canteen he wasn't carrying. If it were a bit quieter, I would have been able to hear the food he was eating sucking the moisture from his body, would have sounded a lot like two pieces of sandpaper scraping together. His mouth was drying up like a bagel left out in a Saharan dust storm.

"Fupid MREef." He was having difficulty talking as the cheese began to solidify.

"What the fuck?" BT said. "What is that?"

I stood up and was almost rewarded with a rock to the forehead, which wouldn't have been nearly as cool as a gold star my kindergarten teacher used to adhere when something good was done. I mistakenly figured zombies were making impromptu ladders with themselves to come in the windows; that circus trick would have been preferable.

"Mike, *you seeing this?*" he asked.

From my angle, that was not possible, and sticking my head out the window frame was not a good idea.

"What's going on?" was all I could offer.

"I...I don't know what I'm seeing; some of the zombies have four arms, some..." He paused to collect himself or maybe force down the gorge that had been rising, I mean, that's what I did when I first saw them. "Some are *impossibly tall.*"

It seemed that England had its own version of mutating zombies, and they were coming to join the party.

"What fresh hell is this?" I asked as the first mutant came into view.

Kirby didn't even bother to ask. He plugged the thing with three bullets, dropping it immediately to the ground, and for that I was grateful.

My brain could not reconcile what I was seeing. Some sort of conjoined twins, but that wasn't right... one looked of Latin descent, the other Asian. The heads were tightly packed, stuck, congealed together, so much so that one of the four eyes was pushed back into the skull and was useless. It had four arms, and for something with four randomly attached legs, it moved with surprising grace. After Kirby killed the thing, he didn't look at it again, but I did. What do they call it when you're inside the train wreck and can't stop looking out at the world? I was doing everything I could to make sense of the insensible.

Shooting was coming in earnest from the last car.

"Top?" I asked.

"The melders, the tall ones, they're trying to come in!" he shouted to be heard.

"Melders." The word gunked up inside my mouth, sort of like Kirby's cheese and cracker meal.

"Get off the seats!" BT roared.

Our rock tossing assholes had finally relented from their salvo, good in one regard, but there were only bad reasons as to why they would ceasefire.

Kirby coughed up something that could have been used for deep-sea welding when the first of the tall melders came into view. It was a good thing he wasn't choking on it because there would have been no way to dislodge the consolidated mass.

The one that showed looked like a science experiment gone wrong. An older woman, early sixties, maybe, was carrying a man, half her age and double her size, in the traditional piggy-back mode. I guess *carrying* isn't the right word because she was never going to put him down. To the great misfortune of us all, the duo were naked. The man's calves were adhered, melded, to her breasts, his twig and berries neatly glued to the back of her neck; this I was witness to as they strode over. It was nearly impossible to tell where his thighs ended and the woman's shoulders began. There were no seams, no way to differentiate between them, like marshmallow humans left out under the blaze of a nuclear detonation.

"How is she carrying him?" Kirby asked. For as fast as he'd killed the four-armed abomination, he seemed too shell-shocked to deal with this one.

My rifle was wavering as I fired; ended up putting one in the man's ass cheek. Because everything wasn't already strange

enough, it got weirder. Like they were still two separate entities, the piggyback rider fell backward as much as he could,
dead. His ride appeared to be fine, although she was having
some difficulty adjusting to the new center of gravity as he
flopped bonelessly around. She was heading straight for us; I
let her. A mistake on my part, as she was now below the
windowsill and the dead shoulder-sitter's head thumped
repeatedly into the side of the train and sometimes into the
car itself.

"I didn't think that one through," I said to no one in
particular. And fuck it all if I was going to approach now and
finish her off. Again, Kirby to the rescue. He just went farther
down the car, stuck his rifle out, and dropped her like a sack
of potatoes carrying a larger sack of potatoes.

"I probably would have thought of that eventually," I
told him.

"I know, sir."

"I'll give you a promotion if you don't say anything."

"I'd rather you got us out of this mess."

"Fair enough."

"Rose, we have new players on the field. I need something
besides a downward dog or a child's pose or whatever the fuck
is going on up there from our chief engineer."

"She got up a couple of minutes ago, sir. Looked like she
had the spark of an idea in her eye."

"Stoke that spark, Rose; we need a flame soon."

"Roger that, sir."

The gunfire intensified behind us. I was about to ask BT
what was happening when the window toward the front
exploded in. A zombie, holding what looked like a metallic
ball, had a shit-eating grin plastered on its face when it realized it could reach inside. It was feeling around for a locking
mechanism, which should not have been part of its standard
operating procedure. When it didn't feel anything, it looked in
and grabbed the handle, trying to open the door that way.

They were adapting their hunting tactics for the diminishing source. This one I took care of, but there was no lack of contestants. By tiny degrees, they were passing the information that there was no way to open the door; I knew this because they again changed tactics, trying to climb in. A few ambitious souls attempted to dive in headfirst.

It was easy enough to keep the interlopers at bay—at first. Then they decided to do the same thing on the other end. It was getting a little trickier; they weren't coming at us in vast numbers, but it was constant. We had decent ammo stores with us, but not unlimited. And if we were somehow able to keep them away, there was that pesky interruption called sleep, but if it got to that point, we'd have to go up top and make our way to the engine or just stay there until dehydration finished its insidious job. I love when I have choices; just a damn shame they all sucked the ass of a hippo with fiery explosive diarrhea.

Then, because we hadn't ramped up the fun factor enough, we got the next contestant on *The Nightmare is Real* to come on down! The extra tall zombies were coming; I couldn't fathom how it had happened. The first was stuck flush to the back of another, knees at the host's shoulders, feet dangling loosely by its ass. How the zombie doing the running wasn't falling backward, I'm not sure. More were coming, mashed up in various other ways. A few talented go-getters even stood atop shoulders like Cirque Du Soleil performers, though these ones were never going to do an impressive dismount.

"Sir?" Kirby asked. I know he wanted some sort of rational explanation; he might as well have asked me how cold fusion worked, or hot fusion, for that matter, didn't understand either of them.

I was thinking it was some adaptation, like giraffes getting longer necks so they could reach food higher up in trees. Made sense. But some even stranger mutations began to reveal themselves. A thin man was attached to a huge man, but instead of in any useful way, the skinny one was adhered to the back of the other upside down, his chest stuck to the small of the back so that his head was…well, you get the picture. I couldn't imagine any scenario where that benefited the zombie. Looking at the shit caked on the rider-zombie's head was stomach turning. Then it got worse. Two women were stuck together in the traditional sixty-nine fashion, though neither seemed to be enjoying it. Both had gaping bite wounds all along their lower regions. The zombies were unable to contain themselves when food was shoved in their face. Eating each other out had taken on a whole new meaning, and not in a good way.

I shot the worst abominations first; they were assailing my senses in such a way that made it difficult to concentrate on anything else. My primitive reptilian brain was threatening to go to war with the instinct to run from something so radically strange and different from anything ever cataloged before. The taller, more functioning zombies were beginning to climb through windows. There were too many avenues of approach, and we didn't have the manpower to stop all of them. More than once, Kirby had swept his rifle past me, yeah, he had trigger control and discipline, still wasn't my favorite thing happening that day.

"Ha, ha, fucker!" came over my headset, it was Stenzel. Either she'd gone completely insane, or she had a breakthrough; no reason to think either, or both, wasn't valid.

"Talbot?" BT asked.

"Busy," I told him.

"How bad?"

"As busy as you, but with only two people."

"Shit."

"Reloading!" Kirby called out. "Four mags left!" He withdrew closer to the center of the car. A zombie at his door had made it all the way through, falling to the floor before pushing up and getting immediately to its feet. I don't know what it is about the kid zombies that make it so much creepier. Maybe it's the fact that you can picture adults being evil, but a kid's loss of innocence strikes deeper, going against everything we think about our future. Adults often become what we abhor, whereas there is hope our children will become what we adore.

"Move!"

"I've got him, I've got him," he was saying as he again pulled on his charging handle. Either he had a jam, or his magazine wasn't seated properly. I felt a hand tug on my rifle strap, pulling me backward. I watched in horror as the zombie child lunged at Kirby. I'd finally wrestled myself free, but ended up dragging my attacker into the car. I tossed an elbow, caught it flush in the Adam's apple, don't think it hurt it any but it caused the head to come forward and gave me enough time to butt stroke it, then I turned my rifle and gave it something up close and personal. I whipped my head back when I heard Kirby's rifle fire three times in rapid succession.

"That was pretty stupid of me." He had a lopsided grin. "Forgot to pop the bottom of the magazine."

"Are you alright?" My eyes widened when I saw blood pouring from his calf and the zombie kid lying by his feet. "Fuck." I think I said it out loud or tried to; it may have gotten stuck inside my constricted throat. It would be horrible losing him, and add to that, what would I tell Rose?

"Feeling a little woozy."

I wanted to help him, needed to help him, but the nearly impossible task of keeping the zombies at bay between the two of us had been halved.

"Keep pressure on it!" I yelled as I began firing like our lives depended on it.

"What's going on!?" Rose was privy to everything that was happening, as were the rest of the team.

"*Snuggle-ums?*" The word came out in such a panicked tone

there was nothing endearing about it. Kirby had sat down on the floor. He was fashioning his sling into a tourniquet.

"Sir, tell me what is going on!" I'd never had an order so compelling to answer except from my wife.

"Kirby's wounded." I was not going to elaborate that his wound would be fatal in a couple of hours and that I would be the one delivering the final blow.

"How wounded?!" she shouted so loudly her voice was static-laced, like she'd damaged her pick-up.

"Sir, do you need me there?" Winters asked.

If I told him *no* outright, Rose would know precisely why.

"Too dangerous. He's applying a tourniquet right now." Nearly every word was punctuated with a bullet.

"He can keep it on for two hours." Winters' medical advice was useless and everyone knew it; the odds we survived for two hours were pretty slim.

I almost told him he was hilarious, but there was no type of humor to be extracted here except within the very dark realm, and none would appreciate it.

"Sir, can you, the both of you, hold on for another hour?" Stenzel asked. Concern in her voice.

"Roger that." Kirby grimaced. Easy enough to tell he was in a lot of pain, but he put himself back in the fight. He didn't stand up; he just swiveled from threat to threat. I kept an eye on his back as that was not something he could easily take care of.

When the windows weren't completely blotted out by the enemy, I took disheartened note that there were now more zombies than when we'd started our defense. We were not going to be able to shoot our way out of this particular situation.

"Fire in the hole!" Rose shouted.

I heard a whoosh in stereo, through the headset, then outside. I barely had time to react as an explosion struck in a dense pile of zombies off to my left. It was only twenty feet away, but the zombies were clustered so heavily there wasn't much danger of getting hit by shrapnel. The boom was unexpected, the damage ferocious, but in terms of true devastation to the enemy, it was about as effective as taking a magnifying glass to some ants running around their hill. She didn't bother with a warning the next three times.

"Winters, what the hell is going on?" I asked. The zombies attacking had taken a break from our car as they investigated the new boom-y things.

"Your demo expert is popping grenades through her M320."

"That's an option?" Gary beat me to the punch.

"How!" (boom) "Dare!" (boom) "You!" (boom) "Hurt!" (boom) My! (boom) "Snuggle-ums!" This was followed by two cracks in quick succession.

Not sure how someone would narrate this event, possibly with explosive noises.

"She loves me." Kirby was smiling.

I was having a lot of trouble with the level of insanity; was I the only one facing certain death here? Maybe this was how others felt when they dealt with me. See, there was hope: I could at least be empathetic. With the break in the action, I moved quickly over to Kirby. The lower part of his left leg was a bloody mess. I pulled my knife free and cut the material to get a better look, my heart beat with a dull thudding that was resonating throughout my entire body; my hands trembled as I ripped the bottom part of his pants. I looked up at Kirby, expecting to see an ashen face full of fear; he was grinning like the village idiot that knew something the town elders didn't. Again, it was like having a nightmare in which the other characters weren't responding correctly to the monsters. My mind was so confident of what I was going to see, I could not make sense of what was actually there.

"First two rounds blew into the kid's skull, the third into

my leg!" He laughed; how could he laugh? Didn't make sense, "Bet you thought I was a zombie goner for sure!"

Marines have a fucked-up sense of humor, comes with the territory. You either make fun of everything, or you become unhinged...on second thought, that might not quite fit. Marines tend to be unhinged already, that's why everything's so fucking funny. I wonder if I'm on to something. Does the Marines Corps make people crazy, or are they already leaning in that direction when they join? Chicken or the egg scenario for sure. Right now, I didn't care. I was so happy I could have kissed him. Then came another explosion from Rose, and that was one person I didn't want to make jealous. I took a gander outside. The zombies, still numbering in the hundreds, had begun to pull back. The casualties they were suffering, with absolutely no reward to show for, had them rethinking their strategy.

"Holy shit, Rose! It's working," I told her. "BT, what's your status?"

"We're in good shape," he replied.

"Kirby and I are heading for the engine."

"We are?" he asked as I helped him up.

"Are you, er, sure, sir?" Winters asked.

"I am. The malingerer shot himself, classic ploy to get out of his duty. The only problem is he did it *after* we were deployed." I couldn't count the number of relieved sighs and chuckles I heard. As mad as I was for him making me sweat this out, it disappeared when I realized it was a bullet wound. It looked fairly serious, but not fatal. "You could have told me," I said once I got him in a rough approximation of standing.

He motioned for me to shut my headset off, as he did the same. "Didn't know for sure, sir. I suspected, but I wasn't in any rush to check."

"Fair enough, put your comms back on, it's time to let your girlfriend deal with you."

"Might be safer here, sir."

"For you, maybe. I'll be fine." I dragged him toward the front door.

"You're going to want to get a move on, I'm down to my last six!" Rose informed us.

"Hold on to the seat for a sec. I want to make sure there's nothing waiting on the other side." I poked my head through; nothing tried to rip my face off, so I took that as a good sign. Always pleasant when nothing wants to chew on you. I tried the door much like a person during a power outage will try the lights in the bathroom—same results. I knocked out what little glass remained in the frame of the window and climbed through. That got the attention of some of the zombies, but in a stroke of fortuitous luck, Rose's next grenade took care of the looky-loos. Got Kirby through, doing my best not to make the wound any worse.

"This fucking hurts."

"Why are you trying to take Gary's mantle for 'most often hurt' away from him?" I asked.

"Hey!" Gary interjected.

We made good time through the next couple of cars, although there was a contingent of zombies that monitored our progress. I wanted to flip them off; it didn't seem prudent.

"You woozy at all?" I asked as blood was running down his leg and soaking his boot.

"Mostly hungry."

Another thing about Marines, they can generally sleep anywhere with only a moment's notice and are always hungry. Lunacy burns a shit ton of calories. Have you ever seen a genuinely deranged fat person?

Rose had just shot her last grenade round as Winters let us into the engine. It was hotter and more humid than Florida in the dead of summer. My entire body shot out sweat like I was being squeezed for it.

"Fuck," was all I could manage to say as I pulled my shirt

away from my body. Winters more than once had to push Rose away as he began to work on Kirby's injury. It was disgusting and cramped in there, but finally being able to take a breather helped. I was concerned for all those still in the last car, but for right now, that was as safe a place as any on this rolling steel coffin.

"Just in time," Stenzel said as she began an elaborate choreography of lever pulling, dial turning, and encouraging word spewing. It somehow got hotter. The small coal viewing window was difficult to look at with unshielded eyes, it was burning so bright. She yanked a cord to let out a series of whistles. I wanted to question her lack of sound discipline, but who was I kidding? We'd been waging war for hours. What was a whistle in all of that? Plus, she looked like a pretty happy camper, and I wouldn't deny her that even if we had been successfully stealthy.

I waited until we were under total steam, or whatever it's called when a train is moving, before I opened the door. The zombies kept pace for about a mile (or one and a half-ish kilometers, I guess, considering where we were). Europeans always had to be different. And they say Americans are egocentric. By this time, Kirby had been disinfected, sewn up, and even had a merry little shot of morphine to give him a reprieve from the pain.

I squeezed Rose's shoulder as she sat next to him. She looked up, her eyes shiny with unfallen tears.

"That's one tough Marine," I told her.

"You'd think that, sir. He's actually a big baby." The smallest of sobs broke through. "I thought I lost him." She'd broken eye contact with me, maybe fearful that if she began to cry, she wouldn't be able to stop.

"Thank you, Rose. You saved both our lives back there."

She bobbed her head in an affirmation but said nothing; I imagine her throat was closed off to words.

"Winters, can I have the key? I'm going to head back see how the rest of the squad is doing."

"Need company?"

"Stenzel, you need him up here?"

I had to shake her shoulder, she was staring out the front windows, possibly humming. I think besides shooting rifles, she'd found her next great love. Not sure how many trains she was going to be able to conduct going forward, but living in the present had been an admirable trait when the world was more normal, now it was damn near a prerequisite.

"Sir?"

"Do you need Winters up here for anything?"

"Should be fine," she told me.

"Like 'true fine' or the 'fine' my wife would use when I came home from work three hours late and smelling like a brewery?"

"All good." She was almost dismissive as she turned her attention back to the enormous machine.

"Track hypnosis?" I asked Winters, he shrugged in return.

He paused as we went through the battle car.

"Any thoughts on the mutations?" I asked as we looked down on one of the aberrations. "Not necessarily the why of it but the how?"

"The scientists onboard the ship might want a sample of this, but my guess is something that happens in statis."

"A mistake of some sort?" I was thinking. "That goo maybe breaking down their skin?"

"Possibly. We'd have to get it to a place with equipment for analysis. Good chance that we're only seeing the zombies that were capable of locomotion after the melding took place."

"You think there's a chance of one enormous stuck together blob of them?" It was disgusting to think about, but if that were the case, they weren't going anywhere, or, nowhere fast, anyway, and that was good news. What was potentially going on here that would make a stasis pile fail?

And would it be something we could exploit? Some sort of chemical reaction that maybe we could help along in other stacks? "We're going to need to find out where these zombies came from," I said as we made it to the end of the car.

"That would be the most helpful sample. But I think the zombies might be upset with our intrusion."

"We'll bring some wine, they'll get over it."

"It should probably be a red."

I laughed as we reached BT's car. "Room service. You need towels?"

"Very funny. Still glad to see you," he said as I handed him the key. "Everyone good?" he asked as he opened the door.

"Kirby's enjoying a drug-induced sleep, Rose is hovering over him, and Stenzel is approaching train-zen

"Train-zen?" he asked.

Winters nodded. "Anyone in need of medical attention?"

"I'll take what Kirby's having," Grimm offered.

MAC & WILKES

THE DAY WAS GOING SMOOTHLY, the temperature was cool, and the clouds were intermittent. Wilkes continually asked questions about the journal and Mac fielded them to the best of his ability. Try as he may, he could not attain the exuberance his traveling companion displayed. Something was off; he could sense danger. There were eyes upon them, and no matter how casually and cautiously he tried to discover the source of his unease, he came up wanting. The sun was high overhead when they came to a small stream, and they decided to rehydrate and take a break.

"I was thinking about doing some hunting; I've seen a lot of scat signs." Wilkes was looking at Mac as the other slowly gazed around. "In fact, I thought I'd shoot us a nice fat camel."

"Mm."

"Okay, so you're not the most talkative person in the world, but today has been exceptionally slow. What gives?"

"I can't shake the feeling we're being watched." He looked down at the dirt between his feet as he drew a map of the area they found themselves in.

"I haven't seen anything."

"Neither have I, and I find that even more troubling."

"Are you maybe being paranoid? I mean, I would if I had a whole army after me."

"You do realize that by being with me, that they are also after you?"

She pondered that as if, for the first time, she were putting the problem together.

"Here's where we're at." Mac drew an x in the dirt next to the small stream. "There's nowhere to hide here." He circled the clearing off to their right. "Off to our left, however..." He pointed at the squares in the dirt. "These houses, someone could be there, but it seems too far away. It has to be here." He circled the area behind them that contained a copse. "Those trees, it has to be. I swear I can feel their eyes dragging across my skin."

"That's kind of gross."

"You know what I mean. If we head to the houses, there's no way whoever is following us will be able to cross over that field without us seeing them, or they're going to have to go all the way around and risk losing us."

"I haven't felt anything before now." She rubbed her upper arms. "Plonker."

"I'm not doing it on purpose, it's just one of the things that made me an effective soldier. A live one, anyway."

"Real valuable. The ability to creep out your fellow soldiers."

"You're funny. No it was that, without fail, I could tell when the enemy was close."

"Yeah, okay, the houses then, definitely the houses. I really want to look back," she said as they got to the edge of the field.

"Worst thing you could do."

"The worst?"

Mac had to reach out and grab her shoulder to keep her from spinning around.

"Once they know they've been spotted, they'll attack, and we're not in a good position for that."

"I wonder if I should have shot you with an arrow when I had the chance."

"I'd like to say this will be the only time you'll think that, but I know myself well enough...you'll probably revisit that thought, often."

"And I didn't do it. Why oh why?"

"Because of Talbot and his journals?"

"I'm sure I could have found someone else to read it to me."

"If I wasn't worried about our lives right now, my feelings might be hurt."

Despite how she was feeling, Wilkes laughed. The closer they got to the row of houses, the faster they moved, as if there were a magnetic attraction that pulled harder as they neared. Mac could not fathom why his heart was pounding as furiously as it was. Then the realization hit that he wasn't so worried about himself as he was Wilkes. This was a feeling he was going to need to become reacquainted with. Not since Annie and Gwen had he felt the duty to protect someone to this degree. It was both welcome and unwelcome, and at this moment, he had no idea how he could reconcile his desire to keep her close to him with his need to keep her safe.

He spent a brief moment surveying the interior of the home before entering and moving toward a glassless window where he could glance out. Wilkes came in behind him and silently headed up the steep stairs.

"I can see something," she said from the top of the steps so she wouldn't have to shout. He raced up as she retreated into the bedroom she'd been in. The wooden floor looked like a rough sea frozen in place. Water damage over the years had warped the planked flooring, causing it to ripple, Mac wasn't sure if it was even safe to be walking upon it.

"Look, right at the edge of the field, the same way we

came." She was just peeking her head around the window frame.

Mac ducked down underneath and came up the other side. At first, he couldn't see anything out of place. Nothing was moving.

"I think it's a kid that's got you all worked up." Wilkes was smiling.

"I still don't…oh, there he is. What's he doing? He's not moving."

"I don't think he's much over eight. He doesn't look all that intimidating."

"Besides yourself, Wilkes, how many eight-year-olds you know that can make it in the wild on their own? You see anyone else?"

"I don't, but Mac, if he was with people, why would they send a kid?"

"All sorts of reasons, and none of them good. For one, we'd hardly feel threatened by a kid, especially one as scrawny as that one, so we'd be more likely to go to help him. And as soon as we did something like that, *bam!* the rest of the group grabs us."

"So, he's a trap?"

"Sort of, he's more the bait inside the trap."

"Sneaky buggers." She squinted, looking for the cage around the boy. "But…"

"But.." Mac echoed.

"What if he is alone? What if his parents like, *just* died? That would explain why he looks so bad."

"Dammit, Wilkes."

"What?" she asked innocently enough.

"You survive out there by *not* doing stupid crap, by not sticking your neck out for others."

"The only way people are going to survive is by doing exactly that. Have you looked around? My mum told me that there used to be so many people walking around in London you couldn't toss a pebble up in the air without it coming down and knocking one of the poor wankers on the head. Can you imagine?"

"Yep. That's true. Other cities, like New York and Paris, were even worse. I once saw a place called Time Squared; it was an area about as big as this group of houses. They had this big celebration for New Years, and there were thousands and thousands of people packed together all having a party in just that small area."

Wilkes looked sideways then sighed. "What I'm saying is that it's not like that anymore, and maybe it won't ever be again, but we need to help each other."

Mac didn't say anything, but speaking from personal experience, he wasn't so sure he wanted there to be that many people ever again. Most of them he'd ever encountered were for shit. He noticed Wilkes looking over intently at him.

"What?"

"I figured after what I'd just said that you'd want to go and check it out," Wilkes said.

"Not really. You sure you don't want to?"

"I'm only thirteen, and…and a girl," she tossed in.

"Convenient. Do you believe in ghosts?"

Wilkes shuddered and gulped. "I do."

"You'd better hope I don't get killed then," he told her as he headed down the stairs.

"That's a pretty messed up thing to say to a kid!" she replied.

At the doorway, Mac looked around for any sign this was anything other than what it appeared. None of it seemed normal, and what he was doing wasn't sane. Wilkes could have been correct that the kid was recently orphaned, but that wasn't sitting right in his gut, and his gut hadn't steered him wrong in quite some time.

"Bloody hell," he muttered as he stepped through the door frame, knife in hand.

"You're going to scare him," Wilkes called down when she saw the knife.

"Good, that makes us even," he told her. The kid's head pivoted when he saw the movement. He didn't say anything before he began walking toward Mac.

They were fifty meters away from each other when Wilkes shouted. "More!"

"More what?" he asked, looking around wildly. As soon as Mac took his gaze from the kid, he began to run at him.

"Mac, run!"

He stopped trying to figure out what was going on and heeded her advice. He ran back into the house and closed the door. He wanted to lock it, but the door had been kicked in at some point, and the jamb was destroyed.

"Beaters!" she cried out when he made it inside.

"How many?" He was leaning against the door.

"Six, seven. The kid beater is almost here. He's not stopping."

Mac braced, hands against the door, feet pressed to the floor. A loud thump forced the door back a couple of inches before Mac's weight pushed it back.

"He hit it with his head, dead on. I think he's unconscious."

"Not dead?" Mac asked.

"Twitching. I don't think you're going to be able to hold the door, a couple of the ones coming are a lot bigger than you."

"This a bad time to tell you I told you so?" Mac asked.

"Might as well do it now, if you stay there, you won't get another chance."

"Wilkes, if you were a little older, I'd have a bunch of curse words for you." Mac dragged over a weathered, tattered couch that may have been leather at some point in its existence. He pushed it tight against the door then berated himself for bothering to waste the time. He headed for the stairs at the exact moment the door was crashed into. The couch was pushed with such force that it slid halfway across the floor until one of the legs caught the edge of a warped board, and it flipped completely over. The hinges held on admirably, until the door slammed against the inside of the house. The hardware handed in its walking papers, and the oak slab surrendered and fell heavily.

Wilkes was standing at the top of the stairs, an arrow notched on her drawn bow. She moved to the side as Mac rushed up and past. He thought she was covering his withdrawal as he went into the bedroom. When he realized she hadn't followed, he went back. She let loose the arrow; he saw it slide into the right eye of the most enormous zombie Mac had ever seen. Black ichor flowed from the ruptured eyeball. The zombie vibrated spasmodically, as if it were being electrocuted.

"We gotta go," Wilkes said as she turned from her handiwork.

Mac was under the impression that the natural chokepoint the stairway offered was the perfect place to make a stand, but Wilkes was the only one with a ranged weapon, and she only had three arrows left. He'd momentarily thought about retrieving the one buried halfway in the zombie but gave that notion up when another ran it down in its haste to get upstairs.

"How are you at climbing?" Wilkes asked as she was halfway out the bedroom window. She turned to grab a lip on the roof. Before he could answer, she'd pulled herself up and was out of sight.

"And if I couldn't?" he muttered.

He popped his head out and twisted to see her sitting on the angled roof; it wasn't a steep pitch, and for that, he was grateful. He pulled himself up alongside her.

"Now what?" he asked.

"Now we wait until night, climb down, and get out of

here." She moved toward the chimney where a depression in the roof had created a somewhat flat spot.

"Move over. Not how I intended on spending the day." He was looking up at the sky and the clouds passing by.

"Crap." She sat upright quickly. "I left my backpack on the bed!"

"We'll find you a new one." Mac had closed his eyes.

"It has the journals in it."

"Doesn't matter, now. They're gone. Right?" he asked when she didn't respond. He finally turned and looked. "Right?"

"I have to know what happens to them."

"You're going to risk your life to find out what happened to some strangers almost twenty years ago?"

"It's a story, Mac! Best one I've ever heard...though I guess that's not saying much. Anyway, of course, I want to know what happens! How long ago the events took place doesn't matter. We're not going anywhere until night; maybe by then they'll have left, and I can pop in and grab it."

"Pretty optimistic view considering our current predicament. Beaters don't tend to leave a spot where they've seen food unless they're tempted by something better."

"I'm getting that backpack." She left no room for doubt or further discussion. Again he was amazed at how much like his sister she was.

"Fine. I'm going to get some sleep. Wake me if they find a way up here or if it looks like I'm going to roll off." He closed his eyes.

"If I didn't think I was going to need your help, I might push you off. There's not enough room up here for both of us."

"I'm comfortable," Mac told her before closing his eyes for the second time. He'd not been expecting to actually sleep, and certainly not so soundly. When Wilkes shook him awake, he found himself staring up at the stars.

"Remember you're on a roof," she told him.

"I know that."

"I wouldn't think so, considering how out of it you were."

"What?" he asked.

"The beaters were going crazy, tearing up the room looking for you. If they destroyed those journals, there's going to be a price to pay." She smacked a small fist into her open hand, her bottom lip clenched ferociously between her teeth in a display of anger.

Mac held his laughter. "When's the last time you heard anything?"

"Not that long ago."

He wondered if she had any concept of time in the way people used to. He knew his grasp of it was slipping; an hour meant far less to him than how much sunlight he had left. His father used to say it was five o'clock somewhere before invariably opening a bottle of liquor. Five, one, twelve...those numbers meant nothing. They were arbitrarily assigned by humanity in its quest to produce an ordered civilization. Now that schedules, and, indeed, civilization was no longer a problem, what did it matter?

"Can you be more specific?" Mac asked.

She tilted her head as if searching for a way to clarify. "Before I woke you up."

"That'll have to do. Listen, I'm going to go and get your backpack." He'd expected some pushback from her, something like, *Why? because I'm a kid?* He didn't know what to think when she said nothing. "I'm about to risk my life for your dumb story, and you've got nothing to say?"

"Um... Thanks? Good luck?"

"It might be nicer if you made it a statement and not a question."

"I really want those journals, Mac, but the beaters, they scare me so bad."

"You? *You're* scared?" When he looked at her, he saw how

vulnerable she was at that moment, she looked years younger than her age.

"I stayed up the whole time you slept, trying to find the courage to go and do this myself."

"Hey, hey, forget it. I've got this." He had to bite his tongue from adding "Annie" at the end.

"Be careful." She again bit her lip, but this was pensive.

"I can't believe I'm doing this," he mumbled as he headed down the slope. As a soldier, he'd risked his life plenty of times, but that was when it was necessary. He hadn't stayed alive by taking needless chances with his existence. That was a surefire way to a long dirt nap. He wanted to peer into the room first and get an idea of what he was dealing with, but with the slope of the roof and how far it overhung from the window, at the point he would be in a position to see inside, it was likely he'd slide headfirst to the ground some seven meters below. That'd be nearly as bad as going feet first into the mouth of a waiting zombie.

Mac grabbed the lip and swung down, using his momentum to send his legs through the window. He was trying to be as quiet as he could. His feet landed softly onto the floor, though he had to pinwheel his arms to keep from falling forward into the beater that was directly in front of him. Thankfully the fucker had its back to him. As he reached for his knife, the beater began to turn; either it had heard him or smelled him, didn't matter how, it was aware of his presence now. Mac could just make out Wilkes' backpack which lay on the floor next to the overturned, threadbare bed. He was debating making a grab at it and escaping quietly when the beater forced the issue and grabbed him roughly with hands the size of his head.

Mac had been completely focused on the backpack, and the room was shrouded in enough darkness that he was caught entirely by surprise. He could not pull free. The beater was digging its fingers into the material of his jacket deep enough to bruise the skin underneath.

"Fucking." Mac pushed. "Wanker." The beater pulled. He did the only thing he could think to do, and that was to stab the side of the thing. He got it high up on the rib cage, and he could feel as the blade scraped against bone. He knew it was hardly above an irritant for the monster, but he couldn't get his arm up past the beater's own to aim and stab it in the head. Mac jerked his head to the side as jaws snapped closed just where his nose had been a split second before. If he didn't break free soon, the beater was going to dine tonight. He dragged the blade across the ribs and stomach, slicing through inches of thick fat. The stink was incomprehensible as globules of gelatinous goop splattered to the floor. The beater finally took notice that it was taking damage and shoved Mac away. The man was sent reeling into the wall, the wind knocked from him.

"*Mac?*" Wilkes called down after hearing the commotion. She sounded scared, but he didn't have the air available to answer and appease her fears. And it wouldn't matter even if he could talk, he was in trouble. More beaters were coming, and now the gigantic, leaking beater was between him and his only escape route.

"Might as well," he whispered hoarsely as he ran toward the bed and slipped the backpack on. This way, he reasoned, when Wilkes found his body, she'd know that at least he'd died trying. The beater had grabbed its intestines and was attempting to stuff them back inside, although in the strangest way possible. As it couldn't help gnawing on the slimy tissue. If Mac hadn't been fighting for his life, he would have tossed up everything he'd eaten in the last month. He thought he might have an opening to get past the thing and was halfway to his destination when he felt himself being lifted from the floor and tossed to the side like a sack of beans. He'd thankfully landed on a rug; it wasn't much in the way of cushioning but beat the hardwood flooring. The beater squared off, facing him directly. This was it, then. He climbed and stood upon the bed frame, knife ready to inflict as much damage as he could, when, inexplicably, he saw an arrowhead protruding from its cavernous mouth.

"Come on!" Wilkes shouted from inside, behind him. Her eyes wide, she looked to the hallway.

Mac was positive he didn't need a written invitation to heed her words. She was out the window again and out of sight almost before he could get off the bed. If the next beater hadn't momentarily gotten stuck within the doorframe, he didn't believe he would have made it. As it was, the monstrosity had broken out most of the door and the surrounding plaster and had lightly smacked at Mac's boot in an attempt to pull him back in. He clambered up the roof and dropped down next to Wilkes.

"Whoa," was all she offered.

"Yeah," he answered once his chest stopped aching.

By the time he'd sufficiently calmed, the sun was high overhead. Mac was sitting with his back against the chimney. His stomach grumbled. Beaters inside the house were milling about, and that wasn't the worst of it. A few were patrolling the grounds outside. He'd taken a peek; he didn't get the feeling they knew the humans were on the roof, but, somehow they were still aware that they were somewhere close by and were reluctant to leave.

"Good news, bad news."

"I'm listening."

"You're supposed to say which one you want first."

"When you say, 'first,' that implies you're going to tell me both regardless of which one I want now, correct?"

"Well, I mean, yeah," he answered, scratching the top of his head.

"Then what difference does it make what order you tell them? Don't announce it, just say what you have to, and I'll decide which is bad and which is good. That can be very subjective, by the way."

"Um, what?" Mac asked.

"Just because you believe something is good or bad doesn't necessarily mean I'll feel the same way about it."

"But one is good, and one is bad."

"You've made that clear, and I truly think you believe that, and I can respect your opinion on the subject."

"I..." Mac didn't know what to say, so he spilled out the news he had. "I found a way we can climb down on the outside of the house, but there are beaters down there, so we're going to have to wait for the cover of night."

"Great," Wilkes told him.

"What? Did you not hear me? We're going to have to sit up here all day before we can leave."

"Sounds perfect. Gives you plenty of time to read to me."

"Are you kidding me right now?" he asked.

She patted the roof next to her.

6

MIKE JOURNAL ENTRY 3

THE TRAIN WAS capable of much higher speeds, but Stenzel kept it down below fifty miles an hour as an abundance of caution and even slower as we approached any sort of span, as we had no idea what the infrastructure was like. After only a couple of years with no upkeep, the tracks should still be fine, but I'd seen enough train disaster flicks to realize I didn't want to be in one. The trip was going to take somewhere in the neighborhood of six hours. After the adrenaline from the battle wore off, I told everyone to grab a bite to eat and get some sleep. It was like telling kids to play with their toys on Christmas morning. Soldiers knew the drill—you did the essentials whenever you had a minute because you might not get another chance for days, sometimes never.

BT and I went all the way forward again. I wanted to get Kirby into a more comfortable car, and if something again happened with the train, Stenzel would appreciate the extra space to work, scream obscenities, pace around or do yoga. Rose stayed with him, I called for Winters to rejoin Stenzel upfront.

"Is this because I wouldn't give you any morphine?" he asked.

"What do you think?" I told him.

Most of the squad stayed where they were, not wanting to traverse the blood bath zombie car. I wondered if it would be possible just to pull the pin and let the tail end of the train go; the only other option was to clean out the car.

"Kirby better get up soon," I told BT.

"What?"

"That car isn't going to clean itself," I said. "Screw it. Want to help me toss some bodies out?"

"No," he told me in no uncertain terms.

But he followed me as I headed over. The car was never going to be clean enough for me to eat off the floor, which is a stupid analogy anyway; there was no floor anywhere that I would ever eat off of, but that's not the point here. The zombie carcasses were gone, Tommy was sitting on one of the seats, a familiar foil packet in his hand.

"Thank you," I told him.

"They were starting to stink. Want some?" He offered up his Pop-Tart. He always got a kick out of my reaction.

I sighed. "What flavor now?"

"Lamb and Hollandaise sauce."

What's that say about me that after seeing melted together zombies, it was his disgusting ingredient combinations that made me want to get sick?

BT didn't even bother investigating further, he just turned around and went back the way we'd come.

"How have you been?" I found one of the few seats not soaked in drying gore or wholly crusted over with it. "Seems like it has been a while since we've talked."

"I miss my sister sometimes," he said so quickly it had caught me off guard. "More the idea of who she could have been, I suppose, than who she actually was. That make sense?"

"Perfectly." It was strange for me to think that if Tommy and Eliza's lives had followed a typical trajectory, they would have died centuries ago and not even been a footnote in history. There was zero chance I would have had a reason to realize they'd ever existed. More innocent lives forfeited to a cruel world.

"I can see those days as vividly as I can this one. All of my days."

"That sounds like a terrible burden," I told him, I was serious. It was nice to have memories, but I'm not so sure about the heartache of being able to pull things up in perfect detail along with the feelings and emotions at the time. To watch your own history in high definition and be able to do nothing to change it? The mistakes, the deaths caused, the loss. The absolute bittersweetness of seeing a loved one that was no longer with you would be an open wound that would never close.

"More than you can imagine." He looked wistful. "This is why most vampires don't make it past the five-hundred-year mark."

A pit formed in my stomach. I did not want to even conceive of what my life would look like in far less time than that. I wanted out of the car. Sitting down to talk to him was not doing me any favors.

"I'm sorry," he said when he looked over to me, I would imagine he saw the angst in my eyes. "It's not all bad. I met you and your family."

"If that's the highlight of your time on earth, I think I feel worse," I told him, trying to make light of the situation. "I'm going to check on the rest of the squad." As good a lie as any. I would have got a root canal right then without Novocain to get the fuck out of that situation.

He may have apologized again, but I was too busy opening the door to show my way out to hear it.

When I got to the last car, most everyone was sleeping or attempting to. Sergeant Walde and my brother were quietly picking up the mountains of expended brass on the floor.

"Sir," Walde said when she saw me. I nodded. It was a good idea to get rid of the bullet casings as they could become a slipping hazard, which would be bad enough, but if it happened during a battle, it could be exponentially worse. I gave everything the once over, then headed back out, wondering how dangerous it would be to go back across the roof. I needn't have worried, as Tommy had at some point left. What was odd was, he wasn't in any of the lead cars either. I thought about asking Stenzel if he was in the engine. I had a feeling had I decided on going up, I would have encountered him; the awkwardness then would have been ten-fold. *Hey, fancy meeting you here!*

I had my fill of something that was labeled as food and was sick of thinking. I did my best to get comfortable on a seat not designed for comfort, certainly not in any rational sleeping position, and summarily fell asleep. The clickety clacking of the traveling train serenaded me into the slumber realms. It was Stenzel that shook me awake seemingly minutes later.

I awoke with a start. "Aren't you supposed to be driving this thing?" I asked in alarm, sitting upright quickly.

"It's okay, it's not like it can leave the tracks. That's not exactly true, but we're fine. Winters is watching the helm."

I relaxed a bit. "What's going on?" I rubbed my eyes.

"We're a half-hour out."

"That's it? No pressing emergency?"

"I thought you'd want to know."

"I did. I do. I also want to know nothing's wrong."

"Nothing's—"

"Stenzel, get the cap and come up here; something's wrong!" Winters shouted.

"Premonition?" I asked Stenzel's back as we headed up.

More than once, I had to reach out and grab a handhold as Winters was heavy-handedly slowing the train down. I could see the heat wavering from the top of Stenzel's head as anger burned.

"He screws up my train, and I'm going to stick him in the furnace."

I did not think she was kidding.

Getting up there was no easy feat. The train was bucking around like a wild horse being broken. I don't know that from experience because I don't like getting on the animals unless they are a few weeks away from the glue factory. Was that still a thing before the z-poc?

"Move!" Stenzel shoved Winters out of the way with a hip check.

We were traveling through an immense grassy plain. An enormous sweeping curve was up ahead crossing a glistening ribbon of water; tall stalks waved lazily in a cooling breeze. It was damn near an idyllic picture, everything except the hastily erected barricade on the far end of the bridge.

"Stenzel, can you stop this thing before we get on the bridge?" I asked.

"If ham-hands over there hasn't screwed anything up, it should take about a mile to get us to a stop, so yeah, plenty of time."

"Ham-hands?" Winters looked at me, then down at his insulted appendages.

I closed my eyes, pursed my lips, and shook my head at him to not say anything. I breathed a sigh of relief; it was difficult accurately gauging long distances in the open like this, but I'd say we had three miles, maybe more. What we were going to do after we stopped would be the next question. The blockade didn't seem to be the work of zombies because the placement made no sense. On a trestle, their avenues of approach would be limited, whereas if it were a human trap, they would have us bottled up. I couldn't make out any obvious ambush places. Sure, they could hide in the tall grass, but in terms of cover, the greenery wasn't going to stop return fire.

"Rose, what do you have in your bag in terms of incendiary devices?" I asked. If someone wanted to start a firefight, I was going to take it literally.

"I have four white phosphorous grenades for my launcher," she replied quickly.

I winced; getting hit with one of those was a horrible way to go. "Okay, be prepared. This is what's going on. We have a roadblock or track block a few miles up. My guess is of human design. Stenzel is stopping us short of it, and we'll take a wait-and-see approach. Rose, Tommy, Dallas, and Walde, I want you in the car closest to the engine. Top, everyone else with you in the back."

"This a black thing?"

I appreciated him giving me shit, made things almost seem normal. He had Harmon, Grimm, Gary, and Reed with him. Whatever they hit us with, what we had, would have to be enough.

"Not at all BT! I need your bulk to anchor us in case we hit the barricade and we get derailed. I would imagine you'll be able to keep us on the rails."

"I suppose that's better than it being a black thing," he replied.

"Just be safe back there."

"Same," he told me.

"Stenzel, I feel like the mile has come and gone." I saw that her hands were moving quickly on the levers, and she was watching a couple of gauges with great interest.

"Something's wrong." Her eyebrows were furrowed.

"I did what you told me to do," Winters replied.

"It's not you," Stenzel answered absently.

"It's me." I couldn't help myself as I finished the most generalized break-up statement ever.

"Sir?" Stenzel paused what she was doing to look at me.

"Don't listen to him," BT said from a few hundred feet away.

Another mile clicked off. We were down around twenty-

113

two miles an hour. It wasn't the speed keeping us chugging along; it was the mass of the train that was going to be the bitch.

"When's a good speed to jump?" I asked.

"Off a moving train?" I nodded in response to Winters's question. "Zero."

"We're looking at a derailment."

"Hate to be the bearer of bad news," Rose chimed in. "But if people did this, there's a good chance that bridge is wired to blow. We meet their demands or, well, kablooey."

That had not even crossed my mind.

"I will not abandon my train," Stenzel said, working feverishly.

"You will if I order you."

She had to bite back the words, *the fuck I will*, I could see it in her face.

"I'll get her stopped."

I could smell smoke and not the good fireplace burning in the middle of winter smoke but that of superheated metals and other toxic crap melting.

We were hovering around ten miles an hour, the trestle was a few hundred yards away, it was now or never if I wanted my squad to jump. We were moving relatively slowly, but there was no way we were all going to come away unscathed from this.

"What's the distance to our target?" I asked.

"That's the River Cam, five or six miles, maybe a little more," Stenzel said.

That was a decent distance to hoof it even if we weren't carrying any wounded, and Kirby was already on the list. That and the sound of a train crash would bring everything living and or deadish our way.

"Stop this train. That's an order," I told her.

I got a "whew" from Gary; he didn't fare very well when he jumped from things.

We arrived at the edge of the bridge, and rolled on to it, trucking along at a pedestrian three miles an hour.

"Brace for impact," Stenzel warned.

By the time we crossed, we were going so slow, I felt like I was watching two turtles fuck when we hit the first part of the blockage, it was framed and reinforced with railroad ties. Unlike Winters and probably everyone else on the damn train, I was too effen busy watching to brace myself, almost got to taste glass. I was just able to catch myself before I face-planted. The railroad ties broke away like matchsticks to a sugar-fueled kid pushing a Tonka truck. That is, when they were still made of metal and were basically a wheeled weapon for an adolescent. The initial noise had been bad enough, but when a piece of the pitch-covered tie got hung up and was scraping against the rails, it was this high-pitched squeal that felt as if someone was dragging a toothpick across my eardrum—it physically hurt. Thankfully that stopped when we hit the first of three pick-up trucks. Three brand new pick-ups, I might add. This I knew from the stickers on the windows.

I kept expecting us to just stop. It was hard to comprehend how much weight was being pushed forward, making that close to an impossibility. The train was shaking as the trucks bounced around in front.

"We in any danger of coming off the tracks?" I asked. I wasn't quite as worried about a derailment as I had been, but without the train, that was a whole other set of problems with no easy solution. The furthest truck had hopped off the tracks just in time for us to hit the first of five concrete barriers. By this time, frozen syrup could move faster than we were. And still, we kept going, hard enough to crack two of the barriers apart. The remaining three were strong enough to do the job before we ran into the finale: a cement truck which, upon further examination, had been full of hardened concrete. That right there would have been the one that did us in, had we been going faster. Whoever had constructed this meant serious business.

"Cap, I've got a question," Winters said.

"Staff Sergeant, I'll take Captain or Sir or even Talbot, in less stressful environments, but that Cap crap makes me feel like we should be in a Marvel movie, and I don't see Black Widow here."

"Sorry, sir. The trucks."

"Yeah?"

"How are they sideways on the trestle? Couldn't drive them like that."

Now that he mentioned it.... What were the other options? Crane? Doubtful, they would have just left that on the tracks. Worthy enough question, but we had other things to be concerned about.

"Top, anything back there?" I asked.

"All quiet."

"Tommy?"

"Nothing."

"Kirby, you up for a patrol?" I asked.

"I'll give it a try," he answered.

"I was kidding, don't you move." The very tip of the train was off the bridge, the bulk of us still on. I was kind of waiting for an explosion to send us plummeting into the river, but what would that accomplish? Zombies didn't pour out of the grass, no rifle fire, just the sounds of the train.

"The longer we stay here, sir, the sooner we're going to have a water issue," Stenzel said, referring to the storage tank, which was showing close to three-quarters empty.

"This day blows," I said to no one in particular. "Okay, everyone in the car behind the engine, besides Kirby, I need you outside on track clearing duty. Top, I need you to watch our ass."

"Got it," he replied.

I was heading for the door.

"Sir, you realize this train isn't the *Enterprise*, right?" Stenzel asked.

"Sorry?" I was so focused on the task at hand the words she spoke sounded foreign.

"Star Trek. The *Enterprise*? Captain Kirk always went out on missions he had no business being out on."

"I appreciate the concern," I told her. "But much like him, I wouldn't risk another's life for my own."

"And yet someone on his crew died on nearly every mission."

"There's a reason none of us are wearing red," I told her. I doubt it did even the slightest bit of appeasement, but that was what I left on. The train was hissing and popping, great bouts of steam rising high up into the air, giving the equivalent of a Native American smoke signal announcing dinner time. If there was a way for her to shut that down, I would have done it in a heartbeat. Tommy and Dallas pushed the first truck off without much of a hitch. Tommy about lifted the rear end off the ground to get the tires high enough to clear the rail. Gravity did the rest, pulling it down a grassy slope and over the bank to plunge into the river below. He was moving toward the second truck when Reed stepped in, not to be outdone.

"I've got this one," he said as Rose sidled up to him. What Tommy had made look effortless, Reed and Rose were struggling with.

"I could always blow it up."

I don't know how many "Nos" came over the headset, but enough that she got the point.

"I can help," Tommy offered, but, Reed, being the Type A personality he was, took that as an insult and became even more determined to get the job done. I was a heartbeat away from ordering Tommy in when they finally got the truck up and over the rail, and this is where it turned disastrous. Gravity again did its thing, but Reed got a little more than he bargained for as he caught his camo blouse up under the bumper. With a heaving push, Rose let go, he did as well; unfortunately, the truck didn't. Tommy, moving only as he could, dove for the man, ended up coming short. Reed went over the edge with the truck with Tommy so close behind it was like he'd been stuck too.

They'd already hit the water before I could even get to the edge to see what was happening. I caught the tail end of the truck going under, dragging Reed. Tommy was reaching for him, then nothing except a bunch of bubbles.

"What do we do?" Dallas asked.

"We wait," I told her, if any more of us dove in, we'd only be compounding the problem.

"Mike, what's going on?" BT asked.

"Reed went in with the truck, Tommy is trying to fish him out."

Walde shot out of the train so fast I thought she was going to go right over the edge too. She was running toward us. I thought I would have to restrain her from going in, but she was well aware of the dangers another swimmer posed to the rescue mission already at hand.

A steady stream of bubbles was still rising to the surface, but as of yet, neither man had shown. As fifteen elapsed seconds rolled into thirty, I was pretty concerned, but Tommy was Tommy, and Reed was a Navy SEAL. I couldn't think there were too many people on the planet more prepared to be submerged. However, as the minute mark hit, I was heading more into the *oh fuck* mode. Personally, the idea of being underwater for that long filled me with panic.

"How long, Walde," I asked, not referring to the elapsed time but rather his survival time, and she knew.

"He's been clocked just under three minutes. And Tommy?"

Valid question because if he came up soon, she had to be prepared to continue the rescue effort; if he didn't, she *was* the rescue effort. I hadn't the foggiest idea how long Tommy could stay submerged, no doubt it was longer than Reed, but I didn't say that.

"Couple of minutes," I told her.

She began to take her gear off, then her outer camouflage blouse before finally taking off her boots. She stood close to the edge, ready to dive in, once she was tagged by the sight of Tommy. At a minute thirty of feeling completely helpless, we finally saw something coming up. Tommy's head broke the surface. Walde was poised to springboard off the bridge; I held her back as Tommy pulled his arm up, and attached to it was Reed. I could feel the tension physically drain out of Walde because it was exactly what happened to me.

As soon as the SEAL broke the surface, he took in a big chunk of air and then began to laugh his ass off. What was even stranger was Walde joined him.

"Nice one, B.U.B!" she called down.

"What is going on?" Dallas asked.

"She just called him a 'barely useful body,'" Rose told her and, well, me, because I'd never heard it either.

"But why are they laughing?" she asked.

That one I knew the answer to. "Because otherwise, they'd be crying."

I don't know if she fully grasped what I was saying, but she was young; unfortunately, there would be a point where she would get it, through hard-fought experience. The two men swam to shore, Reed may have been laughing when he came out, maybe an expression of relief or bravado, but he was exhausted as he pulled himself out. He lay down on the bank, staring straight up, spitting gunk, his chest heaving. Tommy hovered nearby. It was not easy to walk away from someone you just saved; there's a feeling of overwhelming responsibility at that point.

Walde began to get her clothes and gear back on, muttering swears the whole time. That was her way of dealing with almost losing another team member. With everything returning to more-or-less normal, my focus shifted to the cement truck. Five Tommy's weren't going to be able to lift that thing off the tracks. I climbed into the cab; the keys were still in the ignition. It didn't start, didn't even pretend to start. No dim overhead light came on, no clicking of a dying battery trying to turn the starter. This had to have been driven here at one point, at a minimum that meant months ago. That's probably why whatever ambush had been set up had long ago been abandoned. There's only so long you can wait to spring a trap.

Driving meant people, so my estimate of months ago was light; this may have been done within the first few days of the z-poc, but for what purpose? Were trains transporting refugees and some left behind wanted on? Certainly no need for resources that early on. Unless it was carrying weapons and ammunition, none of it made clear sense. Whoever had done it for whatever reason, we were no longer in danger from them, but that in no way made us safe.

"Fuck." I lightly tapped the steering wheel. Got down to see BT checking out the wheels.

"Pushing this is out of the question."

"You don't think we'd all be able to do it?"

"Maybe at one point, but the axle has been welded." He had me look underneath to a very professional-looking bead of solder attaching the axle to the transfer case.

"Who does that?" I asked when I stood up.

"Not zombies."

I walked over to the engine. Much like BT, Stenzel was looking at wheels, but of the train instead. "Hey, can this thing go backward?" I asked her.

"Shouldn't be a problem, but we have other issues."

I wanted to close my eyes and pinch the bridge of my nose, I refrained.

"Feel free to tell me at any time."

"I was waiting to see if you were going to have a mini-meltdown first." The look I gave her must have been enough to show her I wasn't much in a verbal jousting mood. "The brakes are screwed up. I don't think the repair job they'd been working on before was complete, or if it was, the work was from incompetent contractors, or Winters' hatchet job of driving, did it in."

"Hey!" he called out.

"Whose got the map?" I asked. We were immediately heading into Plan B territory, where B stands for Bad, very bad, horrible even.

Harmon came over, unfolding it.

I placed it on the ground, a small stone on each corner to keep it from fluttering about in the slight breeze. Reed and Tommy were coming back onto the tracks.

"Next time, let go," BT chided him.

"I'll keep that in mind," Reed answered.

"Good to have you back," I told him.

"Fuck it," Walde said as she went in for a full hug. Even given the circumstances, it seemed a little bit longer than the norm.

"Good for them," I said under my breath. I clapped him on the shoulder. "Top, I need you over here; we're going to have to set up an extraction team."

"Sir, there's also the problem of the water. I thought we would have been able to get some at the end of the trip, but, considering we can't get to the end...." Stenzel left the rest unsaid.

"All right, if anyone else has some shittastic news they'd like to lay out, now would be the time because I've passed the acceptable threshold, and everything else is just going to fall off the shelf." Crickets, if they had been chirping, would have been the loudest thing.

"I've got something," Grimm said. "Looks like a reaver with a rider."

I don't know who handed me binoculars, but I had them

in my hand and was looking towards where he was pointing. It was far enough away that it was difficult figuring out exactly what I was staring at. It could have been two people playing at horseback riding. That would have been fine, but two naked individuals playing games out in the open wasn't a good idea before the zombies.

"Safe to assume we've been spotted. Not sure how much time we have until the scout reports us in and backup comes, so we're going to have to move fast." I was back at the map. Straight line traveling had us about six miles from the institute. At a good, safe-ish clip, that was an hour and a half of overground traveling.

"Walde, get on the horn, let Eastman know our status, and make sure the yahoos we're going to pick up don't shoot at us when we show. Stenzel, is there anywhere you can get water if you backtrack? I saw at least a couple of towers."

"Someone thought shooting them would be fun, I can't imagine the ones close enough would have enough water to fill her. There should be fire hydrants we could find, but the issue will be a hose. We could find a fire station and get all we need there."

There were so many variables. And now we were splitting our already small force. The only decent thing to salvage was that when the train left, it would likely take the zombies with it. The problem would be when it came back to pick us up, the zombies would be along to welcome us all.

Walde came over with the radio.

"This is Talbot," I said, grabbing the mic.

"Captain, this is Major Eastman. I got the specifics from Walde; is there anything I can do to help?"

"Airstrike would be awesome, followed up by a few helos for extraction. Barring that, if you could pull up the sat pics and find us a fire station near the train line, along with a fire hydrant, that would be great."

"I'll get on that right now."

"And Major, when we get back, drinks are on you for the entire team, indefinitely."

"Fuck, yeah." Reed was sitting down with his head hanging low but gave a thumbs up and verbal confirmation that he liked my request.

"I can do that too," Eastman said.

I had twelve people. Stenzel and the injured Kirby had to stay with the train, Reed and Walde had the most extensive training and were well versed with hot zone incursions, but Reed was wiped, he looked like a drowned rat, I couldn't risk his exhaustion. This was horrible, like I was the only person picking teams in an awkward gym class as we got ready for a game of dodgeball. Under normal circumstances, I would have stacked the living shit out of my team and, on the other, placed the kid who was always more interested in mining nuggets out of his nose and possibly the emo girl who only ever stood with her arms crossed and sighed at the forced societal things the rest of us followers did. Perpetual wedgie kid was always going to go on the other team; it wasn't that he was given said wedgies, but rather that he pulled up his shorts so high to cover his nipples so that they wouldn't chaff as they scraped against his shirt. Yeah, that kid, other side.

Dodgeball, by its very nature, was a violent game, and not only did I want to win, but I also didn't want to get smacked in the face by a ball hurled by the likes of an individual named BT. Can you even imagine? I bet the ball would pop upon impact, the force behind it so great. The problem, as I could see it, was this was a game in which both sides had to win— needed to win. Divvying up the diminishing assets was done on the fly as I tried to figure out who would be a better fit for each task at hand. Winters was going to stay with the injured, plus he was potential back-up for Stenzel. Rose and her heavy-handed explosive responses were staying with the valuable asset, and then my brother stayed, only because I had a bad feeling we were about to do a lot of running.

With me, I debated leaving BT on the train as the next in command but, in truth, everybody but Kirby, Grimm, Harmon, and possibly Dallas, were capable of running the show. Walde and her expertise were with me, and rounding it off with arguably the three least experienced, Grimm, Harmon, and Dallas. This left Tommy as the odd man out. He was so valuable I wasn't sure which side I should tip the scales in favor of. He must have sensed my indecision as I was looking at him.

"Fuck," I muttered. As much as I wanted him to come with me, Kirby and Stenzel were off the board in terms of defense, for differing reasons. He would be needed there more if something happened. I think *IF* should be the new *F* word.

"You're on the train, and in charge," I told him. "Reed, Rose, Winters, Gary, go." I pointed to the train. "The rest with me." We were moving at a light trot; I wanted to get away from the giant noisemaker. "Okay," I said after we'd covered a half-mile or so. "Adjust your gear accordingly." This was something that always had to be done. The constant movement had a way of loosening what needed to be tight and tightening what needed to be loose. I had the map. "Okay, we're right about here." I was pointing to the middle of a large green area. "I want to cut across and pick up the M11 highway," I pointed out into the real world and then the map, "skirting Cambridge completely. We'll cut across on Church Road and pick up Babraham Way."

"The highway?" BT asked.

"Yeah, I'm not thrilled about it either, but it's the fastest route not going through a city."

We were just finishing up with our breather when our ride got underway, leaving us behind. A pit formed in my stomach and a hollowness in my chest. The distinction of countries as such didn't matter much anymore, but still, here we were on foreign soil, cut off from all help. It felt, at minimum, like abandonment. *All this maudlin without any of the drinking.* I thought. "Everyone ready to move? Harmon, you're on point. Walde, you have our six."

"What pace, sir?" Harmon asked.

"Double time until we hit the road, I'll decide after that."

"You sure?" BT mouthed the words as Harmon got to the front of the column.

I nodded. She needed the experience and the boost of confidence. She already doubted everything she did. I felt that giving her a measure of responsibility would help her develop assurance, plus, she was only about ten feet ahead in a wide-open space, so anything she saw, we'd all see, and anything that happened to her happened to us. Maybe in an urban setting with limited sightlines, I would have rethought my strategy, but right then, it was all a bonus—except for the fact we were there in the first place.

"Sir, we're being watched." We'd been running for a half-mile, and Walde sounded like she was sitting down on a couch drinking a cup of coffee. "Our three o'clock behind a hedgerow."

"Sorry, I missed it," Harmon said.

I couldn't blame her at all, Walde was telling me where to look, and I could barely make anything out.

"Okay, everyone, stop for a second; we need to check out our surroundings."

As a little kid, my sister had a game called *Masterpiece;* she would always rope me into playing, even when I just wanted to crash my Matchbox cars. I don't remember the specifics, you bid on paintings and tried to stay away from forgeries, I think that was the basics. I know, riveting! Way better than smash-up derby or doing jumps across the kitchen sink. Anyway, there was a painting with a farmer holding a pitch-fork, and what, at the time, I thought was his wife. *American Gothic* was the name of the picture. Anyway, my sister, who loved to tease the shit out of me, said they looked so severe in the painting because the man had just killed his daughter with said pitchfork. Yeah, she was a peach. I hated that painting, it scared the shit out of me, and I'd never bid on it, which I think she was counting on. Where the fuck was I going with this? Right, right, the zombie in the bushes could have been the original inspiration from which Grant Wood created his classic, replete with a pitchfork.

"Shoot it?" Grimm asked.

That it was hiding behind bushes didn't necessarily make it a zombie or an unfriendly human, for that matter. Hell, I would have been hiding if six fully armed military-looking personnel were taking a leisurely jog through my neighborhood.

"Everyone stay evenly spaced. Dallas with me. Ahoy!" I yelled over.

"Ahoy?" BT asked.

"Like chips or matey?" Grimm asked.

"I'm speaking the native language," I told them.

"I don't think they speak asshole," BT said. I took my hand off my rifle for the briefest of moments so that I could shoot a bird over my shoulder.

"Listen, I need you to say something. I can see you." Grimm and I were approaching, rifles up and ready to live fire. "We're not here to hurt anyone, I just can't leave any unfriendlies behind. So if you're a person, we'll be on our way."

"Persssson," It hissed.

Grimm's steps faltered as we registered what it had said. It was about as much a person as the weapon it wielded.

"Come out from behind the bushes," I told it, holding up where I was.

"Nooohohh." It was long and drawn out, like it didn't know the correct way to say it. The long o sound was turning into a moan of sorts.

"We need to shoot it," Grimm said.

I needed to be a hundred percent sure. A scary speech

impediment didn't make it hostile, creepy, but not necessarily dangerous. Shooting an innocent was something I didn't want to add to my personal history, but this thing was tempting its fate.

"BT, I need the .22." I was referring to the suppressed Ruger semi-automatic pistol. The thing wasn't much louder than an escaping fart, and I wanted to keep this kill as quiet as possible. It was doubtful the abomination was alone. Probably a scout, and as long as we didn't give it an opportunity to report back in, we'd make this journey that much safer.

"Last chance," BT said as he came over and lined up the shot.

The zombie moved quickly. The pitchfork came down ten feet from us; he'd thrown it like a spear. If not for the vegetation in his way, it would have been a lot closer but even as it was, I wasn't too thrilled. BT put two bullets center mass. It fell over into the hedges, propped up for a moment until a stalk snapped, then fell to the ground.

"It won't be long," BT said as the three of us looked down at it. The speech had freaked me out, but he was referring to the more pertinent fact that it was carrying a weapon, and it knew how to use it. It only made sense it would graduate from medieval armature to gun powder-based soon enough. I could not wrap my mind around the fact that gun battles with zombies were on the horizon.

"Let's get going." We were on the highway, for good or bad, now. I forgot how much fun it was to run on pavement in combat boots. There wasn't any part of my body that didn't feel the jarring impact with each footfall. Would it kill the government to throw in some Dr. Scholl's, for fuck's sake?

Saw the sign for our turnoff, it was 2 km up the road, so a little more than a mile, then another couple once off the roadway. I was just thinking about how much I hated the metric system with no justifiable reason when Walde cut into my reverie.

"Got a tail."

I half expected to see two dozen *Mad Max* fashioned cars, spikes sticking out at strange angles, chains dragging behind. Machineguns mounted on hoods...that type of thing. As cool as that would have been to see, I wouldn't have wanted to be the object they were hunting. Didn't matter, either way, it was zombies, six, but more coming to join in the hunt.

"Harmon, pick up the pace." We were going to have to run those last three miles as fast as our slowest person. That was probably Grimm. Always too busy working on his physique rather than his cardio, no matter how many times I told him muscle wouldn't stop teeth, but running legs would. "Grimm, you're in the lead." He groaned, much as the earlier zombie had.

We were somewhere in the seven-minute-mile range, reasonably decent for running in boots and packed out. The zombies weren't burdened with extra gear or the need for rest. They still had the limitations of the bodies they inhabited— a seventy-year-old woman wasn't going to break any land speed records—but anyone that was young and fit before they became a monster was running much faster than we were, and before the second mile clicked off, they would be in our midst. My headset was filled with heavy breathing from the strenuous exertion of my unit. Grimm could not keep the lead no matter how much Harmon urged him on. He was falling back. We were maybe a third of the way there, the lead zombies weren't more than a couple of soccer field lengths away. (Maybe the metric system doesn't work for me, but sports analogies are universal; I'm adaptable like that. I suppose I should have just called it "football" then, but that would have really confused my estimations.) Anyway, I was more worried about other things. I wrapped my arm under Grimm's and was pulling him along.

"Suppose....listen....you," he got out. "Next...time."

"You think?"

"Need help?" BT pulled up alongside.

"How...?" Grimm asked, referring to BT's bulk and effort-less stride.

"He's had years carrying all that mass; you're just trying to create show-off muscles to impress the girls."

"Engaging," Walde warned. I heard two quick percus-sions. "Two targets dropped." She quickly pulled back up to the group. "Four minutes until next engagement." She was speaking calmly enough she could have been talking about a train schedule. "By that point it might be a group effort."

"How many?" I asked.

"Twenty-seven total on last check, four leading the way."

SEALs were thorough, if nothing else.

We hit the ramp.

"Distance?" Grimm asked. He was still running, but he was nearing the end of his gas. Harmon was looking a little winded herself, but I was under the impression she could make it the rest of the way. I couldn't say the same for Grimm.

"Three miles." Honesty might not have been the best response in that instance; he sagged some as the wind went out of his sails. He had more in him, just not necessarily that many miles' worth. In hindsight, I could have got more out of him if I'd been vague; 'a little further' could mean about anything, and he would have adjusted accordingly. You can get more out of a lemon if you give it small, controlled squeezes rather than one giant juicing crush.

"Setting up," Walde said from the top of the off-ramp. This time there were six evenly spaced shots. Either she'd missed twice, which was doubtful, or two more than she'd initially estimated had caught up to the lead chase pack. "Thirty-six now and four minutes until next engagement. Should be able to handle it on my own."

"No heroics, Walde, you need help, ask. Harmon, find a defendable position." There was no way we were going to be able to run full tilt the rest of the way, it wasn't happening. I wasn't going to try to fight at the end, heaving for air. Hauxton Road turned into Addenbrookes Road, then we took a right onto the A1301. Walde was having a one-person war.

"Harmon, I meant sooner rather than later." Grimm wasn't exactly stumbling, but he was leaning a lot more on me.

She was looking around wildly; there were plenty of places, but calling them defendable was like looking at a trailer park and believing that a good place to ride out a tornado. She then took a hard right, easily hurtling a waist-high fence. I know if I tried that same maneuver, I would have torn my quad and shredded my calves, my muscles entirely too tight. Grimm and I ended up going through the less than impressive small wooden gate, ripped the thing right off the hinges. He grunted as he took the brunt of it. It was a big, tan brick home that ended up being the Shelford Lodge. There were two large sets of street-facing windows, not more than a foot off the ground. Those were definitely the weak spots. It wasn't the ideal place, but it beat being out in the open.

"Walde, we're in the tan brick lodge on your left. Look for the gate Grimm broke," I said, he might have given me the finger if he wasn't on a couch stretched out, trying to catch his breath and keep the charley horses at bay.

"I'm going to lead them past and circle around."

My mouth opened; I was going to order her to come in, and we'd deal with them as they came, but she'd made the right call. We didn't have the munitions for a drawn-out fight, and we were most definitely on a timer. If and when Stenzel found water, she couldn't stay in one spot just waiting for us to show. If she did, she'd be in a prolonged fight she couldn't win because we'd spent so much of our resources on the first one. Her only choice would be to keep moving, and where did that leave us?

Walde gave us a quick thumbs-up as she shot past. "Keep eyes on her," I said as I heard footsteps running up the stairs to get to a side window.

She had a lead, about eleven seconds' worth. Just as I saw the first trailing zombies, Dallas notified me that Walde had cut into a yard at the end of the street. I was keeping count; it was up past thirty when Dallas interrupted.

"Sir, some of the zombies are cutting through yards. If she comes back, they'll be in front of her."

"Walde?"

"I heard." I could hear the strain in her voice. She'd been running flat out for miles now, and it would seem that she had more to go. "Shit," was the next thing I heard, followed by a quick series of shots, then nothing.

"Walde?" I asked, nothing.

"Dallas?"

"Don't see her, sir."

"Walde?" I was about to grab two people and find her when the second wave of zombies passed by. There were too many, and they were moving too fast to get a count, but fifty was a safe enough guess. "Get away from the windows," I ordered as the zombies began to slow and spread out. It wasn't quite in a uniform line, and some had groups of two or more, but they were covering the entirety of the street from what I could see. A small child, no older than six, was in the street directly across from the inn. He was slowly turning in place as he looked over his area of responsibility. I ducked down before he could see me.

"What are they doing?" BT was crab walking over so low to the ground he looked like he was in the middle of doing some weird version of the limbo.

"Looks like they're setting up a search grid," I told him. I took a quick peek. "Shit. Anyone on the first floor find cover." I pushed BT toward the reception counter. "There's a trio coming." The zombies weren't content waiting for their meal, they were going to actively seek it out. BT and I slid behind the counter just as the door opened. I could hear one of the zombies come in, its bare feet sticking and smacking on the tiled floor. Then came the sound of a quick sampling of the air by way of sniffing. My squad knew enough to not use any sort of cleansing product with fragrance in it, but that didn't mean we didn't reek of sweat and other human-ness. The point zombie was wandering around the not overly spacious foyer. We weren't talking much more than the size of a large master bedroom. If he did anything but the most basic of patrols, he was going to find us.

It wasn't so much the idea of it finding us, although, that had the blood pumping at a good clip but rather the ensuing fight. I had been sitting with my back to the counter but slowly shifted as we heard the zombie approach. Then we got a scene right from a movie that I always called bullshit at. I saw the toes of the zombie as it placed a foot down, ready to make the turn. It had no toenails, which I found disturbing enough, but the small field of black mushrooms that were growing in their place turned my stomach. My rifle up, I was two, maybe three, rapid heartbeats away from putting one in its face and getting the Shelford Lodge battle underway, when a far-off shot followed by a loud gong sound made the zombie hesitate, turn away and make a sprint for the door. I eased up the pressure on my trigger and took a breath.

"Walde?"

"All good, sir. I was hiding under an overturned canoe, had zombies all around, couldn't talk."

"And now?" I asked.

"I'm in the house directly across the street. I saw the zombies going in, and thought you might need some help from a different angle."

"You realize we're the ones supposed to be helping you, right?"

"I'm a SEAL; wouldn't have it any other way, sir."

"They're going to find you," I told her.

"Not likely. I shot out a back window and hit a piece of steel. Got a good number heading that way."

"Anyone have eyes on the street?" I asked. I wasn't ready to move yet, as the door was still wide open.

"The creepy little zombie boy is still out there, but the next closest is almost a block away," Dallas said.

The zombies may have been learning tactics, but they were undisciplined. For now, anyway. That was bound to change; why not? Everything else had. I made my way to the stairs and joined Dallas on the second floor to get a better look at the kid. He looked like a Dickens orphan, old, ripped clothes, caked dirt, a brown derby. He would occasionally spin around, but other than that, he was not moving from his post. Ten minutes turned into a half-hour, which succumbed to an hour. The kid was still enough he could have been a sundial. Groups of zombies were still milling about but far enough away that Walde could have rejoined the squad, and we could have snuck off.

"We can't stay here forever." BT had come upstairs.

"You come up with that all on your own?" I asked.

"You getting bitchy with me?"

"Maybe," I told him. "This sitting around bullshit is pissing me off."

"Can't we just kill it and make a run for it, sir?" Grimm asked.

"We could, but it's still miles to Babraham, and now there are zombies all around us. We'd be fighting a circle of them in the open. A crossbow would be nice right now. Or a Stenzel. Who thinks they can make a fifty-yard shot with a .22 pistol?" I asked.

"I could," Walde offered.

"Great. Come on over, grab the gun, head back, finish off the zombie, and then we'll rejoin and have a go at getting to the institute," I told her.

"Not every response needs to be a smartass one," BT admonished.

"If I'm not mistaken, Walde started it."

"True," she replied.

"Don't defend him," BT told her.

"I'm pretty sure I can make that shot," Dallas said. "I used to bullseye swamp rats with my M16 back home."

I gave her the side-eye. "Did you just bastardize a *Star Wars* quote? Getting a lot of those lately."

"I may have; doesn't mean I can't make that shot."

The Dickens kid was a small target. It didn't need to be a headshot, but this was no gimme. I nodded at BT to give her the pistol. She did a couple of breathing exercises to regulate. While she was doing that, I slowly opened the window. It sounded like we were torturing a mouse. It wasn't overly loud, but in a world that had reverted to the sounds of nature, I was fearful the zombie would pick it up. I could only hope that the layers of dirt on his skin also applied to the insides of his ear canals. Assuming it was the same depth of filth, we could have a Dixieland jazz band happening up here, and he wouldn't hear it.

She slowly got into position, resting the small barrel on the windowsill. She sighted up, her hand as steady as I'd ever seen anyone holding a firearm. When she pulled the trigger, there was a slight click, then nothing. I knew the suppressor took most of the decibels away, but this was a misfire.

"Shit," Dallas said as she quickly withdrew from the window. "He turned."

"Did he see you?" BT asked.

"Don't think so," she shrugged.

"We'll know soon enough," I said. I wanted to check if he was busy warning the others, there would be nothing I could do about that, but if he wasn't, I needed to make sure he turned his attention elsewhere.

"All clear," Walde said.

Dallas cleared out the bullet. The primer was neatly dented on the outer rim of the cartridge, as it should be; it had just decided not to fire, not an unheard of thing with rimfire rounds.

"Going to try it again."

She was as steady as she had been the first time. The pistol fired, a sound like a semi-deflated balloon had popped, followed by the tinkle of the brass as it struck the side of the windowsill then fell to the ground.

"Shit," she repeated.

"Foot wide," Walde, her impromptu spotter, notified us.

"Did he notice?" I asked.

"Doesn't seem so. The bullet struck the lawn in front of the house, hardly made more than a puff."

"Dallas, maybe instead of the highly aimed crackshot, just litter the area," I told her.

"I've got this." Her tongue firmly grasped between her teeth.

"He's turning your way." Walde's tone picked up some intensity. I stood up. If Dallas missed, this time, I was going to put half a dozen hastily aimed shots downrange. The movement caught his attention just as his head caught a small caliber round. His knees sagged and he fell to the ground like he was exhausted from lack of gruel.

"Target down," Walde intoned.

"Nice shot," I told her, tapping her shoulder.

"What if I told you I wasn't ready to take the shot?"

"I'd tell you it doesn't matter. I'm more results-driven than goal-orientated. Walde, can you make it over here?"

"Shouldn't be a problem."

"The rest of you slackers, we're moving in five."

"You always know the best way to motivate your people," BT told me.

"Okay, people." Once Walde came back, I addressed everyone. We were assembled by the back door. "How're everyone's legs? Yeah, I'm looking at you, Grimm."

"I'm good. I'm good to go, sir."

"Great news because you're in front again."

"Where's Kirby when you need him?" he asked aloud.

"Not for nothing, Grimm; Kirby might be a pain in the ass, but he could run circles around you right now," BT told him.

"Yeah, and I'm the good one at motivating people." I had the map on a small table. "It's just around three miles to Babraham Institute, and the majority of it is fields, overgrown fields. Great for cover and concealment for us—and them. We need to be vigilant when we're going through. This detour has cost us some precious time, and as much as I'd like to take a careful, cautious approach, we're going to go damn near pedal to the metal. Drink some water, get yourself as hydrated as you can without puking after some sprinting."

I filled out a *How Did We Do?* courtesy card while they drank. *Lacking amenities. Appears they'll let anyone into their establishment. Do not recommend unless they give drink vouchers.*

"The fuck is wrong with you?" BT asked when he pulled the card out of my hand before I could deposit it in the box.

"People have a right to know what they're getting into when they spend their hard-earned money on holiday."

"Holiday?"

"That's what the Brits call it; they're weird about that stuff."

"You realize your relatives came from here...oh wait, that explains it."

"You ready to go?"

"Not really. I've got a blister bigger than your head on my heel; running another three miles is going to make me mean."

"That's what's going to make you mean? What the hell have you been all the rest of the time?"

He smiled. "Let's go get the eggheads," he said as he shoved Grimm out the door.

7

MIKE JOURNAL ENTRY 4

"I DON'T LIKE THIS," Stenzel said, her head sticking out the window in the door as she did her best to watch the track up ahead. The six cars in front of her made it difficult at times.

"I'll let you know if I see anything," Tommy told her from what was now the lead car.

"Not the same thing. What if you fall asleep or look away for some reason?"

"I will do my best not to take a nap in the next couple of hours," he told her. "If you want, I could get Rose to cover for me."

"God, no. She'd just blow up whatever was in the way and then run back to see how Kirby was doing."

"Hey!" Rose shouted.

"You heard that?" Stenzel asked.

"Open line, remember?"

"Apparently not." Stenzel was smiling. The wind was blowing her hair back. *Where's Jack when you need him?* She was thinking of the famous scene in the Titanic movie as the star-crossed lovers stood upon the prow of the ship.

"Finally get to England, and I'm stuck in a train." Gary was looking out at the countryside. "Want to know a secret?"

he asked Reed, who was sitting across from him watching the other side.

"Not particularly. I'm not big on revelations. I never know what to say. I had a cousin that came out to me, told me she was gay. I guess it was a pretty big deal for her, she said she'd been building up the nerve for a year. She got pretty pissed at me when all I said in return was 'okay.'"

"You realize she was looking for your support," Gary told him.

"What do I give a shit who she's attracted to? That changes nothing. She's still my cousin, and I love her dearly."

"It wasn't a shock or anything?"

"The year before I was on leave, I went to the bar her folks said she'd gone to. I wanted to surprise her. Ended up I was the one surprised. She was in the corner making out with Emily Frenchkin. I let her be. I didn't think she'd want me to catch her snogging a chick. The worst part about this was I had a thing for Emily; that's the part I'm mad about." Reed was smiling. "Hold on." He sat up straighter. "Company to the north."

"I see them," Stenzel said. She wished she hadn't. Her mind had no capability to understand what she was seeing. Three zombies had melded together, forming one grotesquely humped beast with six legs. The arms were reaching up from the back so that, from a distance, it looked like a crown. It was moving with much more speed than something with that much disfigurement should be able to muster. The six legs, though, they were from three different zombies and were moving in perfect unison like they were winning a ludicrous sack race.

"That thing has to be moving at close to thirty miles an hour," Reed said as he watched in fascination.

Stenzel pulled her head in to look at her instrument panel. The train was moving slightly over fifty miles per hour, plenty fast enough to outdistance the aberration, but they'd be stopped for water for more than enough time for it to catch back up, and it wasn't like they could hide anywhere; they were leaving a sun glittering trail.

"Winters, can you come up to the engine?" she asked.

"You going to try and shoot it?" he asked.

"Without a doubt."

"On my way."

"Fucking zombie spiders." Stenzel shivered, thinking about it.

"Technically, it'd be an ant," Tommy replied.

"I'm more scared of spiders," she retorted. *Come on, come on*, she silently urged Winters to hurry up. The zombie spider seemed somehow privy to their conversation, or possibly psychic or just lucky, as it began to drift further away. What had already been a challenging shot was becoming more so with each passing second. When they came upon a small village, the zombie-thing was lost behind homes and businesses.

"Forget it," she said sourly.

"Sorry, I got held up, Kirby popped a stitch."

"I'll pop something of his."

"Hey!" Rose defended her boyfriend.

Stenzel merely grumbled. She kept searching for a while, but when it didn't appear it was going to resurface, she let it go.

"We're at the marker you told me to look out for," Tommy said.

They were three miles from the outskirts of Cambridge and the fire department they would raid for fire hoses. It would take her that far to stop, provided the brakes held. Otherwise, they might coast all the way back to Wales.

If the zombie-spider continued to follow, it would be upon them in ten minutes, or, worse yet, it would attack the hose retrieval party. The already divided rescue team was once again about to go through mitosis, only there would be no cloning replication, only halving. Stenzel wondered if there was some biological term for that, not that it mattered. Rose, Reed, and Tommy were going, leaving only herself, an injured Kirby, the medic, and the captain's brother to defend the ship. All of them had proven to be capable fighters, but even the Three Hundred had eventually succumbed to the superior numbers of the Persians, who were rumored to number above a million. Sure, treachery had been involved, but still, such a small contingent could only hold back the might of their enemy for so long.

Stenzel was pampering the brakes, going as light on them as she could. She couldn't be certain, but something felt off, a vibration that shouldn't have been there, a strange high-pitched squeal that was out of place. "Hold it together, old girl." She rubbed her free hand against the iron of the housing. "Two more stops, and I'll let you rest in peace." She was saddened to think that, in all likelihood, this would be the train's final voyage. Wherever she stopped, it would be forever. The majestic old-timer would wither away with each passing season, flakes of rust forming, falling off, and blowing into the wind like the world's heaviest snowfall.

"We're coming up on our stop," Tommy told her. What was implied was that she was going too fast, and every foot she traveled past was one more that the hose retrieval team had to make.

She feathered the controls ever so slightly, the resultant vibrations traveling up into her forearm. "Yeah, that's definitely not right." She could watch her hand flutter at high speed. "Not going to be able to make the mark."

"Can't be going much more than five miles an hour."

"Four, actually," she told Tommy.

"Team, prepare yourselves to jump," Tommy told them.

"From a moving train?" Winters protested only because he would have to fix anyone injured.

"Cool," was Rose's response.

"We're already telling every zombie in the area we're out here. Putting a little distance between ourselves and this train is not a bad idea. We jump in thirty seconds. Gary, you're on standby if anyone gets hurt."

"What if the standby stand-in gets hurt?" Gary asked.

Tommy didn't answer. Jumping from a train was more dangerous than jumping from a plane, which hadn't ended well for Gary.

"Three, two, one." This was followed by some grunts and a few choice swears. "Check in?" Tommy called as he ran back toward the front of the train. Stenzel gave him a thumbs-up as she slowly passed. Reed was wiping the bottom of his pants where he'd landed hard. Rose was eating a granola bar.

"What?" she asked Tommy. "I was eating it before I jumped. I didn't want to waste it."

"You good?" he asked the SEAL.

"Bruised pride, other than that good to go."

"Let's get out of here while the getting is good. Rose you up for point?" Tommy asked.

"Ah, so now I know why my boyfriend shot himself in the leg. Can do, Staff Sergeant. Pace?"

"As comfortable as you feel like giving."

Rose started slowly but picked up her pace as she loosened up and got into a rhythm.

"Was this such a good idea?" Reed asked.

"You know we need those hoses," Tommy told him.

"Oh, not that part. Putting the PT junkie in front was what I meant."

They'd gone a quarter mile, the train still shuddering along until it finally came to an incredibly loud screeching and grinding halt. Even the normal hisses and pops of the steam engine traveled excessively far. Tommy was about to tell Rose to go even faster when she brought the team to a grinding halt with her hand motions. A half-raised fist followed immediately by a downward motion with an open palm. "All the way down," she said softly, to which they immediately complied. Rose was less than ten yards in front of him, yet Tommy had not seen or heard anything that would have necessitated the dirt-eating action. It wasn't long before he heard running footsteps.

"Stenzel, you're going to have company soon." The words were so soft, the ant rushing past his face carrying the leg of a beetle in its front pinchers didn't feel the push of the airwaves.

Dozens of zombies ran past. If not in such a rush to check out the canned foods aisle, they would have most likely discovered the fresh food section at their feet.

"Time to go," Rose informed them. She was up quickly and running faster than she had before. He knew why; it was likely more zombies were going to go for the train, and she wanted to make sure she was back as soon as possible to help.

It was not particularly usual for Tommy to have doubts, but the odds of this mission being successful were extremely long. It wasn't just a matter of getting hoses, it was managing to get enough hoses to stretch between a fire hydrant they hadn't found yet and the water tank on the train. The longer odds were trying to do all of this riding a train with failing brakes while being attacked on all sides by ravenous zombies. The degree of difficulty made making the trek back by foot seem like a better or, at minimum, a more viable option. If they encountered too many more obstacles, the plan would have to be to wait it out at Babraham while the carrier sailed around the country to the nearest port. Much better to fight through fifty miles of enemy-occupied territory than two hundred and fifty. Twice more, they had to stop and lay low as another group of zombies ran past.

"I don't mean to be a nag," Stenzel started, "but we're going to be in trouble soon, so maybe hurry up."

Tommy grunted an acknowledgment. He was very much used to being an integral part of a team, and now a family, but leading was not his area of expertise, and he was questioning himself every step of the way. Once he heard the faraway report of a rifle, he knew his opportunity to tell them to abandon the train had passed. It was one choice off the table, even if it added a more significant problem. All he could do was hold up his end of the plan and hope the others could as well.

8

STENZEL

"THEY'RE OFF AND RUNNING," Gary informed her. She had been too busy watching the water gauge pass below the quarter-full threshold.

"An hour, two at the most, *if* I can get this thing completely stopped and keep her idling." The thought spoken.

"Zombies," Kirby said.

"Aren't you supposed to be resting?" Stenzel reprimanded him. Winters and Gary had brought him back a couple of cars so that he could stretch out and get somewhat comfortable, seemingly another age ago.

"I'd love to be, and the drugs Winters gave me are kicking like a mule, but if you look off to the side, pretty sure we're going to need all the help we can get."

"Shit." Stenzel popped her head out the window. "Staff Sergeant Winters, as soon as I can get us to a complete stop, meet me in the car Kirby's in. I want us all in the engine. No way we're going to be able to keep them off the train. That means you as well, Staff Sergeant Talbot."

"Moving," Gary told her. "What about the supplies?" She could hear a train door being opened in the background.

"We'll get what we can once he's secure."

"Great, I love being deadweight," Kirby replied.

"Figured you'd be used to it by now," Stenzel told him as she grimaced, forcing to a stop the injured train quicker than she would have liked.

"Oh Sergeant, if I didn't consider you a sister and I wasn't floating around in the clouds, I might say something you'd regret."

"I'll think something up to humor myself." She quickly exited the engine and was heading back— or forward, in this case. When she got two cars down, Winters had a propped-up hopping Kirby on one arm and an ammo can in the other.

Kirby's head was lolling about. Even with the meds, he was in a great deal of pain, and Winters' herky-jerky movements weren't helping any. The aisle was too tight for Stenzel to get on the other side, she took the ammo cans from Gary's outstretched arms, so he could help Winters, then hurried back.

"I would have rather she took you, you're heavy," Winters grunted, doing his best to manhandle the injured Marine.

"Yeah, because this is fun for me."

By the time Stenzel came back, they were through the next car. "We have to hurry! The zombies are going to be here in about two minutes."

"Fuck this. I'd rather hop. Just make sure I don't fall on my ass or my face."

"Do not let him fall. Something tells me I'm not going to have the time to sew him back up."

Winters and Gary stayed close to Kirby, the latter waddling like a catcher waiting for an errant throw to the plate. Stenzel kept a hand wrapped around his jersey; they moved together as best they could.

"We are leaving a lot of stuff behind," Gary said once they were close to the engine compartment.

"You've got a minute, no longer," she told him, he moved quickly.

"Fuck, I was hoping it was the injury that made me think it was so hot in here." Stenzel got Kirby down onto a small stool, his injured leg sticking straight out.

"Just wait until I close the door. It's a makeshift sauna without the steam and umbrella-laden drinks."

"Having a hard time picturing you with one of those."

"Where are you, Gary?" Stenzel was standing on the small catwalk. The zombies were close; she'd be surprised if he had another minute.

"Coming."

She could hear the burden in Gary's voice. "Drop what we don't absolutely need, you need to get up here."

"Almost there."

"So are the zombies, hurry!"

"Sorry, I was busy practicing the Mambo."

"Ah, there's where the cap gets it from." Kirby was smiling, but that may have had more to do with his drug-addled mind than Gary's sardonic reply.

Stenzel glanced over at Gary, who looked like a poor, overburdened husband following his wife around on the most expensive shopping spree ever, as she saddled him with every bag and box imaginable. He was close, but not close enough. She dashed out and grabbed the nearest thing she could and pulled, he lurched forward, teetered on the brink of falling before righting himself, and stumbled inside. He missed dropping a fifty-pound box on Kirby's leg by inches.

"That would have been bad," Winters said just as Stenzel closed and locked the door. A hand slammed up against the glass less than a second later.

"Whoa," Kirby said about the box and the zombie.

9

MIKE JOURNAL ENTRY 5

"This sucks," I said as I pushed tall stalks of grass and weeds away from my face.

"You're worried about ticks, aren't you?" BT asked.

"Of course I am. Aren't you?"

"All the things we're dealing with, and it's a blood-sucking arachnid that's doing you in?"

"Better than thinking of all the other shit that might be in here with us. Don't they have a lot of snakes here?"

"You son of a bitch," he replied.

"Different story when I find something you don't like. Grimm, pick up the pace. A toddler on a soda could outpace you."

"To be fair, sir, I've seen a great number of my hopped-up cousins, and none of my aunts or uncles could keep up with them," he replied.

"Stop stalling and pick up your feet."

"Finally," Grimm said breathlessly as he pulled up in front of a sprawling brick building.

"That does not look like an institute so much as an institution," BT said.

I had to agree with him. It looked like something straight

out of a Batman movie, *Arkham Insane Asylum,* if I'm remembering correctly. "Always wanted to meet the Joker," I told him.

"Personal hero of yours?" BT asked.

"Marine Corps detachment, this is Special Agent Matthew Hammer. I have you in sight. You are clear to proceed." The voice had come across the agreed upon frequency.

"Does he sound like a dick to you?" I asked BT, but only after I'd shut off my pick-up.

"What part of that rubbed you wrong?"

"The words were fine, but the tone was a bit sketchy."

"You are high maintenance. Do you think we could get out from the open and go and get them now?"

"I mean sure, as long as he doesn't say anything mean."

"My captain is a seven-year-old. Grimm, hurry your ass up and get us there. Stay in front in case this special agent guy gets a happy trigger finger and decides to shoot something."

"I have rights," Grimm said as he started jogging.

"Not now you don't," BT told him.

"That's close enough," Matthew said as our group got to the somehow well-manicured lawn.

"*Close enough?* What the hell does that mean? You either let us in right now or go fuck yourself," I told him.

"I have to make sure you weren't followed."

"And if we were? What are you going to do, leave us out here to die?"

Without directly answering my question, he answered the question. "The assets within these walls are under my care, and as such, I will do nothing that jeopardizes their lives. You, as military personnel, should realize you are all expendable."

"I love when they roll out the welcome wagon like this. Always makes me feel so special, like we're truly making a difference."

"Mike."

"Don't even bother trying to talk me down from this one, I'm ready to unload."

"Fuck." BT buried his face in his hand.

"Special agent? More like a special kind of agent. Whatever badge you're wearing, I bet it came with a really cool plastic duty belt and that little flimsy billy club that bends in half when you try to hit something with it...but no, wait...I'm thinking you have other uses for that. A little hand lotion and some imagination…"

"Jesus Mike, just stop," BT pleaded.

"Ride 'em, cowboy!" I shouted. "Do you shoot your little cap gun in the air while you're doing it? Look at that double entendre, and I didn't even mean it. Hammer, I'm going to say this once and once only. I don't give one damn fuck about you or the precious little sheep you're herding. All I care about is the men and women that have undertaken this evacuation with me. Let us in now, or we're leaving, and you can, I don't know, mow the fucking lawn again, I guess, after you're done with your private rodeo, that is."

"I was a sniper in Afghanistan, Captain," Matthew started, "and I don't think I've ever wanted to shoot anyone more than I do you right now."

"He gets that a lot," BT said.

"Don't," I told BT, pointing a finger at him. He raised his hands and backed up a step. I was angry, and I didn't want him trying to smooth things over. "Listen, you bureaucratic little shitstain, I'm sure you've been pretty busy in there, filling out forms in triplicate and making sure they're filed in some arcane way that makes your job a necessary evil, but we're out here risking our lives. I've got injured personnel, some of which are doing wildly dangerous things right now, all in an effort to ensure that we get your precious scientists out alive. Oh, and just so we're on the same page, I don't think any of the geeks inside that building can do half of what my command believes they can. I think they got tired of warm, flat beer and conjured up a way out of their predicament by concocting a story or falsifying data, whatever. Gonna let you in on a little secret: if your royal douchiness finally decrees that we can come inside and we somehow, against all odds, make it back to the ship, if I find out that those lab techs inside don't deliver on their promises, I am personally going to ensure that they become chum for exposing my squad to unnecessary danger. So let me know now and save us all the headache."

"Captain Talbot, is it?" It was a distinctive, refined English accent. "My name is Doctor Timothy Bolt."

I had an involuntary shudder as he mentioned his name; for the life of me, I couldn't figure out why.

"Yeah, what's up, doc? That never gets old," I said aside to BT.

"I can assure you that everything that has been reported to your Major Eastman is, in fact, true. We are very close to creating a vaccine. It will not cure those already infected, but it could prevent others from turning into zombies."

"You're about two years too late," I told him sourly. There wasn't much a vaccine was going to do to stop a horde from tearing the unlucky person apart one chunk of flesh at a time.

There was a long pause on his end. "Yes, I realize that the existing zombies are less inclined to propagate their species so much as to feed. There are other benefits; the vaccine acts as a repellant, and will also kill a zombie, should it ingest a vacci-nated subject."

I wasn't sure how grateful the person being eaten would be, knowing that they took down their attacker with them, but at a minimum, their death would be avenged, for whatever that was worth.

"Repellant? Like dog collar for fleas and ticks repellant?"

"Something along those lines; I won't go into the scientific specifics of it."

"Why not? Because you don't think I could understand it?" I hadn't let go of all my anger yet.

"I...I," he sputtered. "I was not attempting to weigh your intelligence, Captain."

BT shut off his radio. "Mike, let the guy off the hook. If he said one word about molecule-this or reaction-that you would have tuned out."

"Fuck." I rubbed my face with my hand. I was suddenly tired. "Okay, doc. Will this make a difference, this wonder shot of yours?"

"I can't be certain, Captain. It may very well be that we have missed the boat, so to speak, as a species. Perhaps the tipping point for the extinction of man has already been passed. But by no means does that imply that we should just roll over and give up. There have been many points throughout humanity's history that have resulted in extreme population decimation, and we are still here. The data, although it has since been challenged, was that after the eruption of Mount Toba, some seventy-four thousand years ago, we had been reduced to fewer than ten thousand mating pairs; that's just twenty thousand people on the entire planet able to procreate, give or take a few thousand who are genetically or physically incapable of reproduction. That number is well below the estimated minimum for a species to survive; yet I have to believe there are more of us now, even after all of this."

What I didn't point out to him was that, while early humans had to deal with the volcano and the disruption that it caused, it eventually cleared up. Zombies weren't going anywhere. How would humanity have survived if there were constant eruptions? Safe to say, a very intelligent cockroach would be writing this journal by now, or not, wouldn't have to. Pretty sure they wouldn't be stupid enough to create zombie cockroaches. There's a thought to keep you up when you head to the kitchen in the middle of the night for a glass of milk, provided you have electricity. And a cow. Not super likely, but someone probably does. You've somehow managed to secure some scarce resources, all you want is a nice glass of milk, and you end up being undone by a zombified cockroach. Ain't that just a bitch?

"You may approach," Matt said.

"This guy." I was looking at BT but pointing to the building. We walked as a group. The door swung open, and a man I figured was Matthew stepped out. He was wearing camouflage, like we were, though he had on a blue bulletproof vest. He had close-cropped dirty blond hair and a well-trimmed beard. His face seemed affable enough, but his eyes were cold like maybe he'd seen too much, although there were very few people alive today that hadn't.

"Who the fuck wears a bulletproof vest to a zombie apocalypse? That's like wearing a cup to a face slapping competition," I told him when we were face to face.

He didn't say anything, just moved to the side so we could go in. We were met by what I figured were the scientists, if I went by the white lab coats they were wearing.

Timothy, who preferred Tim, by the way, was the first to greet us and shook each of our hands in turn. He was not what I was expecting, just going by his voice, anyway. His hair was unruly, he had a bushy beard, and his open lab coat revealed a t-shirt adorned with Chopper from the Star Wars universe; I liked him immediately. He then introduced his wife, Doctor Jackie Marie. He was punching above his weight class, good for him. Her long raven locks framed her heart-shaped face and piercing eyes.

"Hi." She smiled. "I'm the den mother, I guess. If I didn't feed them, I think they'd forget to eat."

"It's true; I think I was eight stone when we got married." He playfully grabbed his stomach. While none could claim to have very many extra pounds anymore, he was at least a healthy weight.

"Thank you for this." The next woman came up and shook my hand. Her name was Lina Aleksandrovna. Out of them all, she looked less like a scientist and more like a…

"She's a Russian spy," Matt said, completing my thought.

"Was." She gave him a stern look; it appeared to be an ongoing argument. "There is no more Russia, no more countries. I am here now doing what I can to help."

Then there was David Ferreira. He had his back to us and was working furiously on his computer. He gave a quick wave over his shoulder but never turned around.

"Your gratitude shows no bounds!" I yelled over to him.

"I've been told that." He didn't miss a beat.

"Forgive him," Jackie said. "We have another colleague, Chris Wren, who has been trapped in another facility some hundred and fifty kilometers away. He's tried to make it here twice but was turned back both times. He's alone, been alone. We try to stay in constant communication with him, though. He's been an invaluable asset in a lot of our research." I knew what she was doing, fishing to see if I would bite at the lure she was tossing out there.

"Jackie, or do you prefer Doctor?"

"Jackie is fine."

"I do not have the supplies, personnel, or, more importantly, the time to retrieve him. It will be a minor miracle if we make it. And that's something you all need to be abundantly aware of." I told them of all we had encountered thus far, what we were likely to come across on the way back, and the very real possibility that we would not have a ride once we got there. I gave them a few minutes to talk it over amongst themselves.

While they got into a group huddle, I pulled BT aside. "So, Lina. She's a spy, right?"

"So they say."

"What about Jackie?"

"What about her?"

"Take a second, look at her then her husband."

He peered over my shoulder. "I don't know, Mike, these brainiac types are really into brilliant minds."

"Hey, Jackie!" I called over.

She looked past Matt. "Yes?"

"Are you a spy too?"

"Zero fucking filter." BT walked away.

She merely smiled, but I took note she did not answer the question. Tim looked over his shoulder at me, then at his wife. Yup, I was the asshole that planted that seed in his head. The debate was taking much longer than I would have thought, considering they were the ones that had called us here in the first place.

I was getting impatient. "I hate to break up the party, but there are lives hanging in the balance, and every minute spent here is one more I can't help."

"There is something you are not understanding here, Captain," David said. "We are low on basic supplies; we are down to under a thousand calories a day. And, even with tight rationing that number will drop to five hundred by the end of the month. It becomes increasingly difficult to do highly technical work when the brain is malnourished."

"Not seeing the debate then; there's plenty of food on the carrier," I told him.

"The work that we are doing here is bigger than any one of us. It is truly a chance to save the entire human race, even if some of us believe we're not worth saving." He looked directly at Matt when he said that. There was one thing me and the special agent agreed on.

"What my brilliant friend is trying to say," Jackie cleared her throat from the knot of emotion that had got tied up there, "is that we're not sure we can risk it."

I was shell-shocked. I may have taken a step backward as if I'd been punched. "Are you shitting me? We've risked our lives to save yours, and now you're thinking maybe you're not going to come? Have you lost your minds?"

"You've already expressed that you can't save our friend and colleague Doctor Wren, and we'd expected that the rescue attempt would be less fraught with danger," Doctor Bolt said. I was going with his last name because every time I thought of the name Tim, I got some weird sensation along the base of my skull, and it was a highly unpleasant one.

"Well shit, Doc. I'm sorry about our less than satisfactory rescue, but our fucking limo broke down on the way. I sure do hope we can work this out, so you don't give us a negative review on Yelp. 'I give Captain Talbot and his people one star: the transportation was atrocious, lots of screaming, half the team died on us, I even had to suffer through rifle fire. Would not recommend.' You fucking people. So what? You're saying you plan on staying here and starving to death while you work on the cure?"

"That's exactly what we're saying," David replied.

Matt looked like he wanted to chew through some nails. Whatever the docs were cooking up, he was not on board with it.

"I've got a question," BT posed. "How long can you survive on the food at hand?"

"To maintain a somewhat balanced nutritional diet to keep us working at near optimal parameters, twenty-eight days," David replied.

"Next question. In your estimation, when do you believe you will have a final product you would feel confident administering to humans?"

"At the very minimum four months, but more likely six. We're close but not quite there yet," Doc Bolt replied confidently.

My mouth dropped open; none of them except Matt saw the flaw in their plan. Well, and obviously BT because he brought it to our collective attention.

"Umm, you want to let them in on the little joke, or should I?" I asked him. "Holy fuck, BT." I fist-bumped him.

"Oh." Doc Ferreira was the first to let it sink in. "We'll go and pack our things."

"Just like that?" I asked no one in particular as I watched them walk away.

"You have no idea how difficult it is living with people who can understand quantum physics but can't see a bloody tree for the forest," Matt said.

"I bet," I told him, falsely thinking that with the common ground, we would be making inroads into our tenuous rapport.

"These scientists are my responsibility, Captain, so when we get outside, I will be in command of your unit."

I laughed. I knew he wasn't joking, but my mind was so stunned it pretended that was how he meant it. No one ever said I was great at dealing with awkward and stressful social situations. What's that say about me, that I was vastly better in a scenario where I was killing shit as opposed to talking to it?

"Umm, how about you go fuck yourself?" I told him casually, but if he couldn't sense how tense I was, he had other issues besides being a jackass.

"Something wrong, Captain?" BT had come over. That he'd called me Captain showed that he was presenting a unified front, an enormous, unified front.

"The very special agent, Hammer, here, is wishing to get into a pissing contest. I was hoping you could check out his equipment to make sure he realizes what he's getting into."

"What?" BT stopped glaring at the man to give me a confused look. "I'm not doing whatever it is you're insinuating."

"Yeah, sorry, not sure where I was going with that. Just so we're clear, Hammer, not a chance."

"I have jurisdiction."

"You're just grasping at straws now. You didn't even have

that when the world was normal. An FBI agent on foreign soil?"

"I don't believe that you can ensure the safety of this group."

"I don't give a shit what you believe."

"My friend," BT started, "my captain here might be the rudest, most egotistical person incapable of cognitive thought when it comes to a plan..."

"Umm." I wanted to halt BT.

"...I'd even go so far as to say he might not even know the definition of a plan...."

"Umm, BT?"

"Yeah, I'm getting there." He dismissed me. "But."

"Finally," I said.

"Trying to give you a compliment, here. Don't screw this up."

"It had better be good," I told him.

"There is not one person on this entire planet more willing to go to the ends of the earth to ensure the safety of the people he's tasked with protecting."

"That's not bad," I said quietly.

"I would do the same for these people," Matthew said.

"You're a federal agent," BT stated. "Prior service in the Gulf?"

Matt nodded.

"Then you're all too aware of the chain of command. There cannot be two people in charge. And in case that doesn't sink in, Special Agent, these people here with him have followed him through hell and back, and they will not follow any order you give them unless the captain here told them to, including me. So we do this his way, or you can stay here."

"Fuck, I like having an advocate." I'm sure Matt saw the logic of what my Top was saying, but whether he would adopt the new paradigm was open for debate.

"You'd let these people starve?"

"The scientists? Oh no, they're coming with us. I'm saying you can stay." BT pointed a finger at the man.

"And if I say they aren't?" He placed a hand on the sidearm in its holster.

I'd not known the rest of the squad had even been paying attention, but Matt found himself rather quickly at the wrong end of four rifle barrels. He slowly raised his hands.

"Fine, we'll play his way for now," he said.

"I don't think you get it. This isn't a game, and we're not looking for another set of rules. You come with us, you do what the captain says, when he says it, no questions asked. If you can't do that, there is an alternative for you."

I wanted to say something to BT as to why *he* never took my orders without asking questions but right now didn't seem like a good time for an aside. The juvenile part of me wanted to run up to Matt and stick a finger in his face and yell, *Yeah, what he said!* I refrained with great restraint.

"We good?" BT asked.

Matt still hadn't answered. It was clear BT wasn't going to move until he got an answer, and it was beginning to get awkward. Walde, Grimm, Harmon, and Dallas still had their rifles on him. If there was ever an example of a coerced response, we were living it.

He made sure to look at each of us in turn before he briefly nodded. The rifles were put up as quickly as they'd appeared. If I hadn't have known better, I would have thought it was choreographed. BT grabbed my shoulder and pulled me away.

"What gives?" I asked him.

"He acquiesced, and I could tell you were just itching to say something. The battle has been won, no need to salt the earth."

"I like salting," I told him. "Life isn't interesting until it's properly seasoned."

"Mike."

"Fine, and thank you."

"I meant what I said."

"Which part?"

"All of it." He smiled. "Come on, let's top off our water."

"Ass."

BT and I were outside, right by the front door, looking out the way we came, when Dallas found us.

"We've got a problem," she said.

I figured it was Matt, that maybe he'd strapped a bomb to himself until he got what he wanted. The bomb would have been preferable. "What in the fuck?" I asked as I looked at the scientists and ten enormous green plastic trunks.

"This is the research and lab equipment needed to finish our work," David replied.

"Umm, doctors, how many valets, Sherpas, porters, or any other type of person or beast tasked with carrying baggage do you see here?" I asked.

"Surely we can take them with us; there's only ten," Doc Bolt said. "And the R2."

"The what now?" I asked.

"A project of ours, we made a full sized fully functional R2-D2," Doc Bolt said.

I may have staggered.

"You okay?" BT asked.

"They...they have an R2 unit."

"Oh right, forgot you were a Doctor Who nerd or something. We can't bring it, I saw the thing, gotta be close to a hundred pounds."

"You saw it?" It was then that Doc Dave used a remote control to bring out the glorious astromech. I fawned over that thing like women will a newborn. I would have gladly left any of the crates to make sure he came with us. "I'll miss you most of all," I told him as I caressed his shiny dome. I resisted the urge to kiss it. Before I walked away I looked over to Matt.

"I've got it. Doctor Bolt, we can't take all of this." Matt grabbed the handle of one of the trunks. "This has to weigh forty kilos. It's a two-person lift. We'd need twenty people to do this."

"There's a possibility if we repacked tighter, we could get it down to five trunks; they'd be heavier, but then we'd have enough people," the doctor replied, thinking he'd found a valid solution.

Matt held up his hand to me before I could speak. "Doctor Bolt."

I found it somewhat surprising that after all this time, he still used formal instead of familiar wording. He'd somehow never lost his professionalism, I didn't know if that made me like him a little more or a little less.

"If everyone is carrying gear, no one will be able to defend us should trouble arise," Matt finished.

"And, no, Doc, one person isn't enough," I cut him off, "to defend the caravan."

"I may lack some of the more basic common sense, only because I am generally lost in my work, but I've thought this through. Have you, special agent?" The doc was smiling.

"Got them all hitched up," Lina said.

When she said, "hitched up," I thought she was referring to a team of horses. Again, that would have been preferable.

"The Segways? Brilliant," Matt said.

"The what now?" I asked.

Jackie came tooling in on one of the obnoxious two-wheeled vehicles, favored transportation of Silicon Valley asshats for years. Though I'd never seen a Segway towing a trailer.

"No," I said without prompting. I was thinking of all my painful failed attempts to ride some of the less common wheeled vehicles, skateboards, and scooters (yeah, and that Big Wheels once, but that time had involved booze and an enormous set of stairs descending from a church).

"Captain, where exactly will we be rendezvousing with the train?" Matt asked.

Dallas handed me the map. I'd yet to take my eyes off the row of Segways that were now parked in front of me.

"Don't just stand around, help them load up," BT ordered.

"We need to secure these." Lina was handing out bungee cords and ratcheting straps.

"Shit. Hey, Doc." Four people looked back at me. "Umm, okay, I'm going to need to think of a better way to address you all. You need to get into a group huddle and decide which of those crates are the most important."

"They're all important," Doc Ferreira answered.

"Okay, I get that, but from a one to a ten, one being the most important, they need to be labeled like that, just in case something happens and we need to jettison one."

He looked at me like he had caught me kicking his puppy while simultaneously screwing his wife. Rage, I'm going with unbridled rage here.

David looked to Matt for back-up. Matt just nodded. It was weird being on the same page as him, didn't think that was going to happen until our first firefight, provided he survived.

Hammer came over and I showed him on the map where, in theory, the train should be. "That's about eleven miles of road. The Segways should be able to do that in less than two hours."

"Range?" I asked.

"Typically forty miles, under load, maybe a bit more than a quarter."

"That's cutting it pretty close."

"You want to carry this shit over the English countryside? Because they're not going to leave without it."

"Dammit."

"You don't like Segways?" It would have been impossible not to see me constantly glancing over at the machines.

"I have the balance of a toddler that's been sipping on mom's forgotten wine glass when it comes to those types of things."

"Come on, we'll do a quick lesson. It's fairly easy, just remember scientists aren't known for their coordination, and they all do fine."

"Great, I can't wait to give my Top something else to give me shit about."

After a five-minute lesson where I didn't kill myself, I stepped down, somewhat pleased.

"We need to talk." Not that Matt hadn't been serious already, but now he seemed to add more gravity to the situation.

"I'm listening," I told him.

"I'm not going with you. Not all the way, anyway."

"What? Does this have something to do with the ultimatum? Don't throw your life away over a pissing contest. I mean, sure, I won and you lost, but still."

"It's Doctor Wren. I know you can't get him; jeopardizing your team and the scientists here, it doesn't make sense. But I can't leave him."

"You're one person. How are you possibly going to do that? Are you trying to guilt me into this? I grew up Catholic, I know all about that shit."

"Is it working?" he asked.

"You already answered for yourself."

"I know, just sometimes morality intersects with survivability. Want to know what sucks about the whole thing?"

"Besides the obvious?"

"He can't stand me. The reason he's where he's at was because he volunteered to go and retrieve some stuff just to get away from me. He got trapped just as the zombies came in force."

"He's alone?"

Matt nodded. "He is now. I want to say there were a couple of people at the depot in the beginning, but I don't know what has happened to them since. Left to be with their families is my hope."

"A scientist alone...I'm assuming no weapons, this being the UK and all. How has he made it?"

"Surprisingly well. He's stuck in a depot. More food than he could eat in ten lifetimes. Solar power, equipment; the one thing he's lacking is companionship, although, knowing the man as I do, I don't think that's as big a drawback as it is for some."

"Provided you can even get to him, are you so sure he's going to want to leave?"

"Yeah, I radioed him. He told me after all I'd done to him that I owed him a rescue."

"What exactly did you do? Push him into his locker? Wedgie?"

"Nothing quite so juvenile. I broke his nose."

"That seems a little excessive."

"He kept hitting on Lina."

"The spy?"

"I was very frank with him the first time. For as smart as he is, he couldn't think past his custard launcher."

"Um. A lot of us get hung up there. The thing is like a giant roadblock to higher functioning."

"When he did it again, I told him there would be consequences if he continued."

"Oh! I get it now; you have a thing for Natasha Fatale over there. Makes sense, but wouldn't she be going for the scientists? What would you have to offer her superiors besides a shiny badge and a closet of cheap polyester suits?"

"You really are an arse, aren't you?"

I shrugged.

"She's not that *kind* of spy. She didn't need to sleep with

163

anyone to gain secrets; she is legitimately brilliant. Her credentials got her on the team. I was just an added bonus."

"Pretty full of yourself. Are you sure you didn't find her out and then blackmail her?"

"That would make more sense. No, we became an item, then she confessed."

"As a point of note, was it before or after the zombies?"

"What difference does that make?"

"All the difference, actually."

"You're a bloody tosser."

"Meh, I've been called worse. So continue. And by the way I think you've been hanging with the Brits too long." I was referring to his vernacular.

"Maybe and Doctor Wren was getting more persistent. He would wait until she was alone and repeatedly hit on her, even though he knew. I'd had a shitty day, lost my partner. We were out on patrol looking for some supplies that the doctors needed, and we got trapped by a small group of the fast zombies. We fought our way through but not before she got bit. At the time, we weren't exactly sure what we were dealing with. Figured out as soon as she turned."

"I'm sorry."

"I'd known her for three years. She was a good partner; wasn't too many others I would trust to have my back the way she did."

"You put her down?" I could see the pain in his eyes.

"I owed her that much. Anyway, I come back from burying her and I catch Wren practically humping up against Lina's leg like a randy dog, and I lost my shit. Grabbed his shoulder, pulled him away, and laid his nose against the side of his face. If it wasn't for the fact we now had an outside enemy, I would have been reprimanded and sent back to the States. Good bet I would have lost my job. By then, communication was getting spotty, and my superiors had a lot more going on than dealing with a broken lovers' triangle. In a strange twist,

Lina set his nose before he volunteered to get what the team needed. He grabbed a van and headed out. Stupid twat coasted into the facility on fumes. No gas and not a chance in hell of coming back, as the zombies were now tearing through everything."

"Not to state the obvious, well, I guess I am, but it seems like you would have had plenty of opportunities to go and get him at some point."

"I did once, didn't tell him I was coming. Thought maybe I could smooth things over. He threatened me with a microscope, of all things. Told me in a variety of very British ways to go fuck myself. When he finally got to 'gormless,' I'd felt as if I'd done my due diligence. Still thought about forcing him into the car at gunpoint; in hindsight, I should have."

"Gormless?"

"Idiot or something along those lines; I had to ask when I got back. She didn't say anything, but Lina seemed relieved I hadn't brought him back. I left it at that."

"It's a good bet you're decent with that weapon, Matt, and anyone that has the last name Hammer should be in a military unit. We sure could use you. This is already a precarious mission, and saying it's resting on the head of a pin is giving too much width to the implement."

"I'll be going about halfway before I have to get off the highway."

"And if he doesn't want to go with you?"

"Maybe I'll just shoot him for being a pain in the ass."

"I can try and wait once we get to the train, but that thing is basically an enormous cowboy dinner bell. And if the train isn't there, we're going to have to press on."

"I have no illusions."

"Matt, you've got a woman that's clearly out of your league and an opportunity to live out a relatively full life. Why are you going to risk all of that?"

"Duty."

"Fuck, I hate that word. Been there before."

BT eyed Matt up and down as he came over, I suppose checking to see how the two of us were behaving without adult supervision. "Docs are all loaded up, and you're going to want to see what else they're bringing."

"Electron microscope? Hadron collider? Lyophilizers?"

"Phyllis who?"

"It's science-y gear."

"*I* know what it is, I'm surprised you do."

"I don't really. Saw a checklist, just parroting."

"And *he's* the special agent. Come on." BT motioned.

When we went outside, I saw David standing, looking down at an intricate controller and a drone some ten feet away on the lawn.

"Talk to me," I said to BT. The thing looked impressive, and the chance to have an eye in the sky could be invaluable.

"It's a DJI Mavic 2," he said, for whatever that means. Then he started throwing technical jargon at me like he was reading a spec sheet. "The basics are it has a camera, including thermal capabilities that feed to a handheld display. It also has a half-hour flight time and a range of nearly six miles."

"Six miles? Thing must have cost a fortune."

"That's what you're stuck on?"

"Just making conversation. A half-hour should be fine, provided our trip is only two hours, and Stenzel is where we hope she is, but just in case."

"He can charge it back up; the equipment is in one of the bins. It's solar, so recharge will take a while. He's going to take a look around before we head out."

"Think he'd let me try it?"

"Mike, you couldn't fly a balloon. If he knew you better, I don't think he'd let you be in the general vicinity."

"Pull!" I shouted as the drone lifted off.

David turned, gave me a look that would have withered a willow.

"You're not nearly as funny as you think you are. Come on, let's take a look at what he's seeing." BT smacked my arm.

The controller looked pretty advanced, but I couldn't generally run anything more complicated than a toaster, so there's that, actually, probably anything more complex than a paddle ball would be a stretch. The display, at six by nine, wasn't the largest, but the image was crystal clear. Got more than a few heavy sighs from David as I about crawled into his pocket to get a better view. The drone was so high up I'd lost sight of it, but as I said, the image was incredible. He was flying it over our projected route, lots of fields, some houses, a town or two but nothing moving. Not on the ground, anyway. Few birds.

"Whoa, whoa, turn it back around. I think I saw steam." The urge to reach for the controller was acute, but even I knew that was a bad idea.

We were looking at a column of what I hoped was steam and not smoke, far off in the distance.

"Can you zoom in?"

He fiddled with some controls; it got marginally bigger.

"More."

"It's a camera, not a telescope," he said flatly.

"Is it moving?" If I got any closer to the screen, my nose was going to leave an imprint on the glass.

"I do not believe so."

"Shit. Walde, how long have we been out and about?"

"Four hours, forty-two minutes," she said as she looked at her watch. "What's going on?"

"The train isn't back where it belongs, and it's not moving either. Top, we have to make a call, muster the squad."

Didn't take long, there weren't many of us. I spun our limited options around to no conclusion.

"Here's the situation. The scientists here are trying to

167

move an entire building a fleet of Segways with just enough juice to get us to our desired rendezvous point. Unfortunately, the drone shows the train some distance away from that point and not moving. My immediate and knee-jerk reaction is to leave the docs here and drive the Segways as fast as we can to help the train crew. I need you folks to either talk me off the ledge or hurry me along."

"We can't leave them; it was hard enough getting here," BT said.

"And if we get to the bridge and the train isn't there, what do we do with them? Out in the open like that, they're sitting ducks, and we're babysitting sitting ducks."

"I say bring them. The odds they get another chance to leave are not in their favor," Matt, who had come over for the discussion, replied.

"Hey, could you all please come over here?" I motioned to the group that was going over the gear lists, checking and double-checking that they got all the vital materials. After I laid out the potential problems we were facing, they were still a go. Where it got dicey was when I told them that if the train didn't show, the trunks were going to have to be left behind.

"I think I speak for the group, Captain. If the trunks don't make it, then neither do we," Doc Bolt said.

I was going to let him have this verbal victory. If the shit was really sluicing down the side of the mountain and the train was out of play, I didn't give a damn if I had to zip tie their hands and force march them to someplace safe until we could secure an alternate means of transportation, whatever that would entail. I nodded and told him, "Sure." He seemed satisfied with that like we'd signed a contract. Fairly certain this verbal confirmation wouldn't hold up in a court of law. At least it better not; the weird UK courtrooms with the wigs and all freaked me out. I wasn't even sure if that still happened or I just had a warped sense of reality due to television.

10

MAC & WILKES

Mac's voice was raspy, his throat raw, he needed water to quench the burn. He'd never once read aloud for so long. Wilkes had been insatiable. Every time he'd stopped for a break, she had relentlessly chided him to start up again. He was thankful for the setting of the sun and the chance to run from beaters, it would be less demanding.

"That's it?" Wilkes asked.

"Are you serious?" The words felt strangled as he spoke them.

"I have to hear more about BT! He's my favorite, although I do feel bad for that Kirby guy. Michael Talbot, is he supposed to be a good guy? He says some mean things."

"Sarcasm."

"And that is?"

"Umm, when you say something mean but don't mean it. I think."

"Why say it then?" Wilkes asked.

"Good question, I don't have any idea."

"And do you think we could take a train for our trip?"

"I never even drove an auto. There's no way I'd be able to drive a train, and when's the last time you've seen something working from the old world?" He swallowed hard, hoping he didn't get a sore throat. "Can we maybe go now?"

"I guess." She was disappointed. "My mum used to say the old world would be considered magical now. Flying machines, highways that stretched as far as the eye could see. Giant buildings full of food.... I can't even imagine that."

"True enough." He placed a hand on his throat. "You're reading aloud next time."

"But…but I don't know how," she replied.

"That's crap and you know it. I saw your lips moving in time with the words on the pages."

"But you do voices! You make the characters come off the pages; they, like, come alive. I can picture them so well in my head when you read."

"Laying it on a little thick," Mac growled.

"Is it working?"

"Let's get down from here, find some water, and if I can get some proper rest, I'll think about it."

Wilkes clapped her hands together silently.

11

TOMMY

THE TRIO WERE across the street from the small firehouse. They'd not encountered any zombies, but the stench was something they could not ignore.

"We all know they're in there, right?" Rose asked as she stuck a primer inside a block of C-4.

"We need the hoses first," Tommy told her. "Then boom."

Reed laid an armbar against Tommy's chest as he went to rise. "I saw movement in the second-floor window, looked like a person—a regular person."

"Not again," Rose moaned.

"Guard or a hostage?" Tommy asked as he looked up but didn't see anything. Tommy knew *hostage* wasn't the right word, but he couldn't bring himself to call them "stock."

"I hate that you have to ask that, and I don't know. I only saw a shadow," Reed replied.

"Can't stay here; we need to get back. I'll grab the hoses. Reed, you cover my retreat, and Rose, you bring this place down."

"And if they're human up top?" Rose asked.

"Then they'll thank me," Tommy replied. "Let's move."

Rose could only shake her head. "Sure do wish we

171

brought gas masks." She was putting the final touches on her explosive party favors.

The smell was a physical, brutish entity as they crossed the street. Thicker, pungent, almost to the point it could be tasted upon the air. Tears involuntary fell from their eyes as they tried to clear away the foreign substance.

"At what point does this become poisonous?" Rose had pulled her shirt and camo top over her nose, and the rest followed suit. It did little to filter out the funk.

Tommy motioned for Reed to get the door and cover him. He moved quickly, his rifle at the ready. The handle turned noiselessly, and the door swung open effortlessly. The private was about to thank God for small favors until he looked inside. The small amount of food he had in his stomach, which had been more or less settled, instantly became upgorge, he had to work at keeping down. He couldn't help it as he turned away before forcing himself to remember that they were on a mission, and it was imperative that he keep it together and do his part. Tommy went through the door, hesitating ever so slightly as he did so.

"Fuck me," Rose said as she waited until the Staff sergeant cleared the area so she could place her charges. "I am happily going to blow this place to hell. I bet they try to get rid of whatever this is, too." The words spoken were quiet, but she could have talked in a conversational tone and not be heard. It was a stasis of sorts, but unlike anything any of them had seen before—a grotesquery of a bastardized orgy. The look was one of the thickly congealed fat sitting atop a canned ham, but that was the only familiarity. The zombies weren't stacked like cordwood, but rather were haphazardly writhing onto and over each other. The squishing, squealing, squeaky sounds were disturbing enough to be maddening. As bodies slithered, some began to conjoin even as Rose watched. A forearm stuck to a forehead, a calf became one with a hand. Then as quickly as the parts began to fuse, they would pull apart with a disgusting squelch until they found a more satisfactory merging.

Tommy had made it to the far side of the empty equipment building; the trucks had either been used on one final emergency response or to hasten a potential get away. He had less than a foot of space between the spare hoses hanging up and the side of the gel encapsulated zombies. A bloated, misshapen face with four eyes swiveled in his direction.

"Be ready," Tommy said, moving slowly as he lifted the heavy hoses off their hooks. The gel began to ripple slowly, then the vibrations picked up speed, great chunks of the viscous material sloshed to the floor. Tommy quickly made his way to the door as an arm reached out and grabbed hold of the trailing hose. He wrenched his body, ripping a distorted amalgamation of body parts free. A thigh where a neck should be, an arm protruding from a stomach, genitalia united in perpetual fornication.

"Rose, move!" Tommy was ten feet from the door. "Reed, kill anything that follows!"

They were halfway across the street when the first of the zombies made it to the doorway.

"Blow it, Rosester," Reed urged.

"Gonna be close." She trailed a few more feet of wire out as the rest took care of the first few.

"How much did you use?" Tommy asked.

"Enough. Fire in the hole." They all turned away as Rose depressed the plunger. A super-heated concussion of air blew past them, followed immediately by all manner of flying debris. Glass, wood, plastics and brick rained down, then came the blackened and burned zombie parts. Tommy had led them to a small porch across the street where they waited out the pelting skyfall.

The building was on fire. Part of the front wall had blown out, the side collapsed. Chunks of burning debris had set fire to over a half dozen nearby establishments.

"Shit, maybe the captain was right. I do use too much."

"Don't worry about it now. There was nothing living around here, not with that den. Let's move," Tommy advised. "This whole town is going to go up."

Reed looked back as they ran. It was likely the town had been uninhabited, but they couldn't be sure, and destroying an entire village to further their cause did not seem justifiable.

"There's no one to help." Tommy cut the other man off at the knees.

"We just lit an entire area on fire."

"And if we're lucky, it will bring every zombie for miles around to come and check it out."

"So as long as we're fine, everything is good?"

"Why are you getting so upset about hypothetical people?" Tommy had slowed. "Zombies go into stasis once they have drained the local food supply. And even if someone wandered into that town, as soon as they smelled that firehouse or saw what was inside, they weren't going to stick around."

"We…we destroyed a place that's been there for hundreds of years. It's gone. It'll never be back."

"We don't know that for sure. Maybe the fire doesn't take complete hold, or maybe the scientists we're trying to save will actually have a cure, and some day this place can get rebuilt. There's already too much loss to be upset by one more small piece of the old world." Tommy wasn't sure if that was the right approach, but there were always more depths to be plunged into when suffering, like it was a bottomless well. Both men knew there was no easy answer, and that, above all, their mission, followed by survival was utmost. Reed merely nodded and soldiered on. He'd heard Tommy's words, and he'd accepted them as truth, and not as some half-baked wisdom.

12

STENZEL, TOMMY ET AL

Gary had been staring out the window, not that the view was great; milling about zombies were never something anybody wanted to peruse. It was the chance to be outside in an atmosphere that wasn't reminiscent of a fireplace. To be anywhere else that wasn't a few degrees below combustion.

"How much water do we have?" Winters asked, wiping his mouth.

"A gulp less than we had the last time you asked." Stenzel had stripped down as far as she felt comfortable with, which was much more than Gary had been. That had also been part of the reason he was looking where he was.

"Damn."

"What's going on?" Stenzel asked. Gary moved out of the way as she came up next to him. "Am I making you nervous?" She wondered; Gary was busy staring at the ceiling.

"Just trying to be polite, chivalrous even."

"Too hot to be modest."

"Are you saying you're too hot to be modest?" Kirby asked.

"The engine compartment, ass." She wiped the side of her

neck with the shirt she was holding, Gary turned a brighter shade of red.

"Whoa," she said as she saw licks of flame and a billowing plume of smoke. "I'd say that looks an awful lot like Rose's handiwork."

"She alright?" Kirby was pushing himself up off the floor to get a better look.

"Nothing to see, stay where you're at."

He didn't listen as he crowded her out of the way.

"Why are Marines so pig-headed?" she asked.

"You're a Marine." Kirby's words were muffled, his face was mashed up against the window as he tried to get a better angle.

"I'm obviously not included in that statement."

"Some of the zombies see it."

Stenzel was leaning over by the front windshield. More than a few had turned to the flame and were gawking, some even deciding to go and investigate, drawn like moths. Not nearly enough had left to make a go of getting rid of the stragglers and getting some needed airflow, though.

"Stenzel, this is Tommy."

"Reading you clear," she replied.

"We're on our way back, no injuries, and we have what we came for."

"And the explosion?"

"A nightmare that needed to be put to rest," he told her in a clipped tone that suggested he didn't want to talk about it any further. "What's your status?"

"We have somewhere north of fifty zombies outside of the train, unknown number aboard. We're all safe but sweltering inside the engine compartment."

"Any news from the captain?" Tommy asked.

"Nothing."

"One problem at a time. We'll be in the area in the next

hour. I'll let you know what we come up with when we get there."

"Roger that," Stenzel told him.

"You should tell them to bring some Otter Pops; I could go for about a dozen of those."

"Sure thing, Kirbs. I'll make sure the Mr. Softee truck makes a stop here on its way past," she told him.

"You're the best, no matter what Rose says about you."

She blew a short raspberry before talking. "If only you knew what she says about you."

"What?" He turned quickly. "What's she say about me?"

"Don't listen to her, she's just trying to rile you up," Rose replied, it was clear she was running.

"Is it always this easy?" Stenzel asked.

"You have no idea," Rose responded.

"Let's keep the chatter to a minimum," Winters warned.

"Aye, Staff Sergeant," Stenzel said.

"Did Tommy sound off to you?" Gary asked after fumbling with the controls to his headset. Stenzel nodded.

"Fuck, if I could peel off my skin to get cool, I'd do it."

"You're not planning on taking off more clothes, are you? I'm not sure how many more corners I can find in here," Gary told her.

"They're doing the rock thing again." Kirby reflexively backed away from the window.

"The glass here is heavier duty than on the passenger cars; we should be fine," Stenzel told him.

"Is that a, 'we'll be fine because I know what I'm talking about,' or is it more like, 'we'll be fine because I said so?'" he asked.

"Sure," she told him.

The first rocks to strike were smaller than golf balls, loud but ineffective. Then the zombies began to venture, looking around for larger and heavier things to toss.

"This is just awesome. Why now, though? We've been sitting here for hours, why are they now deciding to attack?" She stepped back when a small boulder starred the windshield.

"Maybe the fire got them agitated? Kind of like Frankenstein's monster?" Gary offered.

"As likely an explanation as we're ever going to get." The boulder thrower recovered his glass breaker and heaved it again. He came up short but was quick to go and get his new favorite toy. "I'm saving a bullet for you, buddy." Stenzel pointed at him with her rifle. He jutted his face forward and bared his teeth at her gesture.

Winters was watching the exchange. "Safe to say he didn't like that."

Another star appeared a foot away from the original. By the time Tommy radioed that they were back, the windshield, while it was still holding up, was battered to the point that the tiny fractures had merged. It was no longer viable as a port for viewing, and the integrity was very much in question.

"Stenzel, we're looking at more than a hundred. Too many to handle," Tommy told her.

"I'm listening."

"We'll travel further down the line, find a hydrant in range of the hose, then I'll let you know."

"I don't think that's going to work. I've got a zombie that's about to break through my windshield." As if to punctuate the point, another loud cracking came.

"I see him." Shooting him had to happen, but as soon as the bullet exited its chamber, it would be a foot race. "How much range you have left?"

Stenzel looked over her gauges. "Fifteen miles, not much more than that."

"Okay, head back, we'll follow with mop-up duty."

"Dammit." Rose sighed. "I can feel a blister forming."

Tommy reached down into one of his pockets and pulled out a pair of socks.

"You always carry an extra pair around with you?" she asked as she gratefully accepted them.

"I keep them in the same place I keep my Pop-Tarts," he told her.

"I've been meaning to ask you about that." She sat and untied her boots. Stenzel was getting the train underway, the zombies began to follow.

"You want me to spell you on those for a bit?" Reed asked, referring to the two-hundred-foot sections of fire hose.

"I've got it for now. Let's go and get rid of some zombies." Tommy stepped out from where they'd been hiding and onto the track.

The nearest zombies to them were a hundred yards away and looking in the opposite direction. Reed lined up a shot and hit the first in the small of the back. It fell face forward, smashing against the rail; no others noted the loss of one of their own. Stenzel was going slow enough that the fastest of the pursuit group could keep up but was increasingly leaving stragglers behind. At first, they were solo zombies, most had suffered previous injuries that kept them from running at full speed and were dispatched of quickly. Then came groups of two and three that physiologically could not keep up, older or shorter legs, or a strange melding that made any sort of coordinated locomotion unlikely.

The day was unseasonably warm, and even Tommy found himself flagging under the weight of the hoses. They'd killed over two dozen zombies in the hunt from behind before a group of ten had figured out what was happening and turned back. Reed moved to the side to get a better angle and not hit anyone with the expended brass; the toe of his boot hit the lip of the rail and he fell awkwardly over.

"Fuck!" he shouted, immediately grabbing his ankle.

Rose had got down onto one knee near him to steady her shots. "You alright?" She spared him the briefest glance before shooting.

"Can you stand?" Tommy got to the other side of the man. Reed had his hands wrapped around the top of his boot. His teeth clenched as a bead of sweat popped on his forehead. Rose was covering them, shooting much quicker than she had been.

"Doubtful," Reed responded.

"Could use a little help here," Rose called out as she switched out an empty magazine. Eight zombies were quickly advancing. Tommy let the hoses fall from his arm before joining in. Rose lightly touched Reed's chest before rising and shooting. They quickly got the attackers down to two before they peeled off.

"Stay with him," Tommy said as he took off after the zombies.

"What are you doing?" Rose asked.

"We're going to have to leave him behind; we can't have any witnesses to that fact," Tommy told her.

She was about to protest, but they still had to get the train cleared of zombies and water into the tank. She appeased herself with the fact that they weren't going to leave him behind permanently, even if there was a dark recess of her mind that thought differently.

"I've got you," Rose told him.

Tommy caught up to the first of the zombies, the monster had still been running away. He pulled his knife free so as not to spook the second one. He felt confident that no one could see him as he moved with his enhanced speed and sliced so forcibly with the blade that he decapitated the zombie.

Rose swallowed hard as she watched it all through her scope. "That's not possible."

"What's that?" Reed was looking for other threats.

Tommy's head spun when she spoke. His angered face was emblazoned upon the entirety of her optics. She let it down quickly; she was certain he was far enough away he shouldn't have been able to tell exactly what she was looking at, but his expression had spoken volumes. Tommy continued; she was startled when she heard two quick shots.

"You alright?" Reed was looking at the confused expression on Rose's face.

"Ah, yeah," was all she could think to say.

Tommy jogged back and helped Reed get into the best hidden place possible. The culvert wasn't going to be comfortable, but something would literally have to stumble into him before he'd be spotted, plus they wouldn't be too far. Tommy avoided Rose like she'd caught him doing something much less deadly but far more embarrassing.

"Would you rather stay with Reed?" Tommy asked before they headed out.

"Reed probably does need more help than you do."

The perpetual private flipped her off.

"You ready then?" Tommy asked.

"Good luck." Rose reached down and grabbed Reed's hand, he nodded.

"Can we talk as we run?" she asked when she stood.

"I'd prefer it if we didn't, but if you want, then…" He shut his radio off, she followed suit.

"I know you're strong, Staff Sergeant, just running around with over two hundred pounds of firehose proves that. But a Ka-Bar decap without some serious sawing motion shouldn't be possible, yet you popped that thing off like a dandelion head."

"How much truth do you want? And I seriously need you to think about that before you answer."

They jogged in silence for a few hundred yards. "I'm human, Staff Sergeant, and you phrased a question in such a way that would pique my curiosity even further. I would like to know—if you're willing to tell."

"You probably aren't going to believe me, and whether you do or not, this stays between us."

"Been watching you for a while now, not sure you could surprise me."

"Got all sorts of theories, do you?" He gave her a sidelong glance. "What's the one you think has the most validity?"

"I'm stuck on cyborg or super soldier, another government experiment, although this one actually worked."

"Got me pegged as Jason Bourne?"

"I figure those Pop-Tarts you're always eating contain the meds that keep your system from spiraling out of control."

"That's actually a blood sugar thing."

"Are you stalling?"

He didn't answer for a bit. "I am. What if I told you I was a super soldier?"

"Well, now I don't believe you."

"I'm a vampire."

Rose pulled up short, Tommy a half dozen steps after.

"If you didn't want to tell me, why did you offer?" She was getting angry.

"Just because the truth is not something you believe in does not make it any less the truth. There is no such thing as a lighter truth. It either is, or it isn't."

"A vampire? Like in the books? Last one I read, they sparkled. I've never seen you sparkle."

"When I prove to you what I am, will you still look at me the same way?"

"I'm sufficiently freaked out right now, but you're still Tommy, still Staff Sergeant Van Goth. We've fought a lot of battles together; there's no reason to think how I feel will change."

Tommy came back to her. To Rose's credit, she did not flinch when he placed his hands on her upper arms and lifted her so that they were face to face. When he opened his mouth and his canines elongated, she gasped.

"Are those real? Or some sort of super cool prosthetic?" She reached a hand to touch one.

"Are you mad?" he asked as he put her down quickly.

"I play with explosives."

"Can we continue now?"

"I suppose."

"That's it? You're not going to flip out and try to get away from me?"

"Are you planning on trying to bite me?"

"I would never."

"Good." She placed the pin back in the grenade she'd been holding in her hand.

Tommy laughed. "You are a unique individual, Rose."

"I've been told that before. Lead on, Lestat."

"…reading me?" Stenzel asked when Tommy turned his headset back on.

"Sorry, technical difficulties," he told her.

"How's it going back there? I can still see a bunch chasing."

"We've taken down a few dozen."

"I'm running low on water. I'm going to have to start back in another few miles. Going to need a refill, or it'll be time to abandon ship."

Tommy looked over to the left. A small village was a half-mile up, as close to the railway as they could hope for.

"Going to look now."

"You haven't found anything yet? Sorry, I realize how that sounded."

"Got some more zip in you?" Tommy asked, pointing toward the town.

"I was wondering when you were going to pick up the pace." Rose passed him by.

"This is more than two hundred feet." Rose was looking from the pipe sticking out of the ground to the tracks.

"Two fifty would be my guess." Tommy had locked the buckle onto the pipe and pulled out the opening tool.

"Um."

"It's not a garden hose; we should be able to shoot water for about sixty feet."

"Um."

He stopped what he was doing to stand. "I'm listening."

"So, we're going to stand here with a high-pressure hose trying to drain three-point shots from half-court?"

"Basketball reference? I never really liked the sport. More into jousting. Come on, help me roll this thing out."

"There's going to be zombies," Rose said once they were done.

"Looking forward to it," he told her as he lifted the end.

"Oh, right, we've got a water cannon now. Are we going to be able to hold that?"

"I was on a bucket brigade in Kansas once while a house was burning down during the Dust Bowl. That's the most experience I have in firefighting."

"The Dust Bowl? How old are you?"

"Train's almost here, you should turn the water on."

"We're not through here," she told him as she jogged off. The hose bucked in his hands, becoming heavy and rigid when she opened the valve.

Tommy flipped the large brass lever to let water flow, he moved his left leg back to brace himself as he got familiar with the forces. He held it at a forty-five-degree angle and was pleased as the water sailed over the tracks.

"Rose!" he called back as he closed the end.

"Yeah." He was surprised she'd been able to come upon him completely unnoticed.

"I'm not going to be able to do anything else. Once I start filling the train, you're, going to have to watch our backs."

"Wouldn't have it any other way," she told him as she pulled off her backpack and placed four claymore mines around them.

"Do you ever leave home not prepared to destroy a city?"

"With what Captain Talbot gets us into? It'd be silly not to."

"Good point."

"I can see you," Stenzel said. "I was hoping you'd be closer."

"This'll work," Tommy assured her.

"Beginning to brake, we stopped early to thin them out, you're still looking at somewhere close to thirty on foot."

"We'll be fine, Rose laid out the welcome mat."

"Be there soon, out," she said.

"Did you know I was going to be a beautician?" Rose told Tommy as she ran her lines.

"I have a hard time seeing you perming hair."

"I was going to do nails, actually. It was the smell of the chemicals that turned me off. That and one of the people that came to the school for a freebie had a rampant case of toenail fungus."

"What?" Tommy asked as he helped her set up.

"Older guy, mid-forties, wanted a mani-pedi. Handsome enough, dressed to the nines in traditional women's clothing; he had these high heels on that I don't think I could have afforded after a year of working. God, I wanted those shoes, not the size, though. Looked like a pair of patent leather canoes. How he got a women's shoe in a man-sized fourteen is beyond me. And plus the toenail fungus."

"Rose, we should maybe get this done, then you can regale me with your story."

"I'm all set." She flipped a switch on a small panel she had, there were four green buttons illuminated. "So, as I was saying. He takes off his shoes, I couldn't have worn them if I'd stuffed a sweater in them."

Tommy sighed.

"I was busy looking at the shoes when I caught a whiff. Now I'd been exposed to a few feet with some odor. It's not pleasant, but you can work around it, especially with the mask on. But this, this was different, it smelled like old beer and damp mushrooms. His big toenail was raised almost a quarter inch from his toe, this brown thick sludge stuff was running down the sides like he was trying to press a lid down on an overflowing pot full of bad beef stew."

"Rose."

"I'm almost done. That was it, that was when I decided I wasn't going to be a beautician, went down to the Marines Corps recruiter and told him I wanted a job where I blew stuff up. He obliged."

"Stenzel, you can't overshoot this mark," Tommy said.

"Trying, these brakes are spongey as hell. How big is my window?"

"Like stopping a speed boat on a dime," Rose offered.

"Staff Sergeant, can you clarify Rose's answer?"

"Any more than twenty feet past me, and it's going to be difficult if not impossible."

"Shit, she wasn't kidding." The squealing from the train was wince-worthy, Tommy and Rose both turned their heads away from the noise. The stuttering shudder came next as the train bounced on the tracks, the vibrational sound rocketed down the rails.

"That doesn't sound good." Rose had her rifle trained on the zombies closely following the train. She was going to wait until they were much easier targets. She was an accomplished marksman, but she was not on the upper echelons. Rose would rely on her strengths. She smiled as she looked down at the box by her feet. "We'll play later."

"What?" Tommy asked.

"What," she replied.

Stenzel was a hundred feet from her desired stopping

point, the train traveling two miles an hour. Kirby was moaning in agony from the spine shattering tremors. Gary was afraid his fillings were going to pop free from his teeth.

Rose took her first shot. The bullet ripped through the ball socket of the zombie's ankle, dropping it to the ground where it thrashed about for a moment before lying still. Tommy looked over at her.

"It's dead, isn't it?" she said defiantly.

The group of zombies focused their attention on the fresh meal as opposed to the canned one. Gary came out onto the small catwalk to help, but he was too busy holding on to offer any assistance.

"Stenzel," Tommy warned.

"I'm trying!" She had to yell to be heard over the commotion.

"I don't think I'm going to be able to hold them!" Rose shouted over her shoulder.

With better-placed shots, he thought she could do it, but that would mean she wouldn't be able to use the Claymore, and that was like telling a kid that got a bike for Christmas that they couldn't go ride it on the ice-packed streets. Rose switched out her spent magazine and placed another in before letting the rifle down onto its tactical harness.

"This is going to be loud," she told Tommy with a gleam in her eye.

If she looks at Kirby with half that adoration, he's a lucky man. Tommy thought.

"They're getting awfully close, Rose." Tommy was dividing his time between watching the train and the zombies.

"The better to feel my bite. Fire in the hole!" The explosion was so loud it was deafening. Steel bearings blew through bodies, instantly disintegrating them into splintered fragments of themselves. A downwind breeze coated Tommy and Rose in a fine red mist. "Well, that was disgusting." Rose immediately replaced the discharged explosive. Fifteen zombies had been reduced to their component parts. Ten stayed near the train.

Tommy turned the hose on and blasted any in his path. Some were crushed against the unyielding steel of the train, the rest tumbled away like weeds in a gale. Winters waited until Tommy shut the sluice off before climbing up to open the sizeable cylindrical hopper door.

"Got a problem!" Gary said as he got his rifle up to his shoulder. Zombies had deboarded and were now climbing up the train. Tommy took care of those that were far enough away from Winters, sending them on painful flights, but he dared not get too close.

"Rose!" Tommy called.

"Almost finished."

"Staff Sergeant Winters needs help!"

She looked up from what she was doing. She hated leaving things half-finished, but their medic was in trouble as zombies clamored up and onto the top of the train and were moving for him.

"Is that water tank bulletproof?" she asked before firing.

"I don't know, just don't hit it," Tommy told her.

Rose fired three quick shots, all high above her targets.

"You're not going to be able to scare them away."

"Comedians are not welcome at the end of the world, Staff Sergeant," she retorted.

"Tell that to the captain."

Seventy yards wasn't an overly long distance for a rifle, but a fast-moving target with a friendly in the vicinity made it challenging. Plus, the crucial backdrop may or may not have been vulnerable to a bullet. That left her zone of shooting significantly diminished. Gary was killing zombies quickly but was yielding ground as he slowly backed up. Rose was doing her best to kill the ones in the middle of the pack. She was hitting nearly one in five. She grunted in satisfaction with each one that fell off and to the side.

There was enough room between Winters and those trying to kill him that Tommy felt it was safe enough to bring the water to bear. There was more shooting from the side away from the hydrant as Stenzel did her best to keep the zombies from ever climbing back aboard. As Winters backed up, his foot hit a slick spot and he slipped. His rifle hit him in the lip as he let go, trying to grab hold of anything to keep him from falling completely off. The descent looked like the speed had been slowed for dramatic effect. An astonished O was forming on his lips, his arms back peddling as he fought a losing battle against gravity, his legs swimming in a substance far too insubstantial for meaningful thrust. As his back slammed into the ground, there were loud, resounding snaps of bones.

"Man down!" Tommy called out.

Stenzel was immediately out of the engine room. She seemingly didn't even have enough time to aim before she pulled the trigger and shot the brains out of a zombie making a run for the downed man.

"Rose, put the box by my feet and go help her get him into the engine room!" Tommy shouted.

Kirby had limped out onto the catwalk. He was far from being in fighting condition, but this was an all-hands-on-deck emergency. "Is he alright?" he asked, doing his best to keep the attackers away. Between the pain and the pain killers, he was having difficulty acquiring and keeping his sights on target.

"We have more passengers than we thought. I don't know if I'm going to be able to keep them away!" Gary shouted breathlessly.

"Do not hesitate to get back into the engine room if you have to!" Tommy ordered. Each person was alone on an island at the moment, and there was no more help to send should any of them need it.

Winters was flat on his back unmoving, his forearms up in the air, his fists balled. Tommy hoped he'd only had the wind knocked out of him but was doubtful. Rose and Stenzel were both advancing on him, continually shooting and keeping the zombies away.

"Reloading," Stenzel said as she dropped the magazine and inserted another without taking her eyes off her sights.

Rose was not quite as practiced in the maneuver but was up and firing nearly as quickly. Tommy could hear Kirby's labored breathing in between shots, but every bullet he fired helped in the mission. Tommy was a handful of heartbeats away from letting the hose go and grabbing Winters.

"Uh, guys, we have more coming!" Gary shouted.

Stenzel was standing over Winters, shooting. The expended brass glittered in the sun as it arced away. She spared a glance down; Winters' eyes were glassy and unfocused.

"Still with us?" she asked.

"I'm in trouble."

"How bad?" She kept shooting.

"Can't feel my legs."

"Can you move your arms?"

"Not sure."

"And if I drag you back by your feet?"

"If I broke my back, it's not like we're anywhere near an emergency center, and time would be of the essence to keep me from being permanently paralyzed."

"What are you saying?" Stenzel asked as she pulled another magazine free making sure to drop the other one away from his body.

"I'm saying—" A series of coughs racked through his body. "Damage might be done that can't be undone. I don't want to be eaten."

"Staff Sergeant Talbot, come out this side, help Rose get Winters back to the engine room. I'll hold them off."

Once Rose was by Winters and clear of the water cannon, Tommy let loose another torrent. The zombies that had been relatively clustered broke up, making it much more difficult to blast them as a group. Some were circling to get a better angle on him. He stayed on those haranguing the rescue mission; he could not afford to pivot and keep his flank clear. Winters screamed out in pain as Rose began to pull on his legs. Gary came and lifted his torso. It was happening so agonizingly slow Tommy thought he could see individual water droplets flung up into the air after they battered the zombie bodies. He shoved down the urge to tell them to hurry. No one was out stopping to smell the roses, a flower so arrogant it pricked you for getting too close to observe its proffered beauty. His sister had been like that. She was beautiful from afar, but if you got close, she would draw blood. A silent tear ran down his face, lost in the deluge of the blast back, and for the first time on the mission, Tommy felt tired.

Kirby hopped out of the way as Gary had bent down and grabbed Winters in a bear hug to manhandle him up the small set of stairs. The engine room was beginning to look like a triage as the casualties mounted. Tommy could only hope Michael was faring better.

TOMMY DID the only thing he could. He was blasting zombies, sometimes peeling the skin clean off of them like a layer of dirt under a pressure washing. When the space was afforded him, he would direct as much water into the tank as possible before repeating the process. With everyone in the engine, the zombies had turned their attention toward him. Stenzel had come back out onto the small catwalk to lend what assistance she could. Zombies were battered and broken as they slammed up and against the train, legs twisted backward, arms broken in multiple places, skulls split open. Chests were caved in and pelvic bones pulverized. Their unquenchable numbers had finally begun to dwindle. Stenzel was relentless as she took them down. The only time she'd sworn was on a rare miss. The last zombie standing got the added bonus of being propelled into a bullet. Its head exploded like a cherry bomb placed in a rotten watermelon.

"Nice job," she told Tommy as she went into the engine to check her gauges. "Coming up on a half tank." Tommy had found his range and the appropriate stance to keep the water flowing. Most was now entering into the relatively small opening. He hoped it filled soon, not least of all was because he was quickly becoming exhausted.

"How's Winters?" he asked.

"Unfortunately, he's the only one qualified to give that answer," she replied. As she looked upon him, he didn't look good. His face had turned ashen, and his forehead felt cool and clammy. His chest was rising and falling much quicker than it should. "He's going into shock. Rose, cover him with whatever you can, we have to keep him warm."

"If he's not warm in here…" Gary trailed off.

"Aren't we supposed to raise his legs?" Rose asked.

Stenzel shook her head. That was only done if there was no chance of a back injury. She motioned for Rose to get Winters' headset off. Once she was done, she spoke to Tommy.

"He's going into shock; we can't do much for him. I'm not sure how much longer he has if we don't get him medical attention."

"What's the tank at?"

She looked over her shoulder. "Coming up on three-quarters."

"Who knows CPR in there?" he asked.

Rose, Gary, and Stenzel replied in the affirmative.

"That might become necessary. I should have enough water in the tank in about ten minutes. Keep him comfortable, loosen any restrictive clothing." Once the tank was full,

Tommy briefly debated letting the hose go but was fearful of being hit by the whipping metal end or being blasted by the stream.

"Rose, I need help with the water, the cut off is frozen open."

Once she'd turned the hydrant off, Tommy needed a moment to get his body under control. His back was spasming uncontrollably, his arms felt leaden.

"Are you okay?" she asked as she came back.

"I will be. How's Winters?"

Her lips closed tight, and she gave a quick shake of her head. Tommy groaned and stood tall before moving quickly to the engine compartment. He carefully picked up the fallen Staff Sergeant to bring him back to one of the passenger compartments where he'd have more room. Tommy knew fundamentally that souls were incontrovertibly unmeasurable, but the man felt lighter, as if the ghost he carried within him had already fled.

"Ready to roll," he told Stenzel as he knelt next to Winters. The rest of the squad had joined him there.

13

MIKE JOURNAL ENTRY 6

I LIKED the Segway marginally better than I like horses, and if you've not already picked that up, I'm not a fan of horses. The only thing better about the Segway, besides the fact that they, so far, had not tried to bite me, was there was less distance to fall when it happened. Because the when of it was inevitable. The ground was too cluttered with debris for it not to happen. The first time I almost dumped, I'd run over a two by four because I'd been busy watching BT. The man was so big he made the device look like a pogo stick, and then I went down the rabbit hole of imagining him hopping around like the village idiot, then I started laughing because that's what fucking insane people do in the middle of an apocalypse. Standard operating procedure, according to the voices in my head. Then I hit that piece of wood and bounced around like I'd hit a speed bump at seventy in a car with less than stellar shocks. That sobered me up pretty quickly.

"Whoa, that was close. Did you see how well I recovered?" I asked him.

"You do know the machine did most of that, right? There's a gyroscope inside designed with dipshit drivers like you in mind," BT responded.

"Don't take this from me. You realize this is the stupidest shit ever, right? Segwaying around like we're in the robotics club at MIT."

"Would you rather be walking?"

"Yes, no, maybe. There. I covered all my bases. Yes, because, like I said, this is ridiculous and I know someone is going to get hurt doing it. No, because we have to get back to the train and find out what is going on with the rest of the squad as fast as we can, and maybe, because what if someone takes a picture of us riding around, then the world rights itself and this gets posted to social media? We have no idea whether we'll turn into viral heroes or absolute laughingstocks. How are we ever going to live this down?"

"So you're worried about a Facebook post?"

"Aren't you?"

"Can't say the thought crossed my mind."

"Good thing you have me to remind you of that."

"Yeah, good thing," he replied.

Not sure how he made his go faster, but he pulled ahead.

"Sir, I'm seeing movement behind us," Grimm, who'd been bringing up the rear, said.

Anyone with any half-decent skills could easily turn their wheeled vehicle around. I brought mine to a complete stop as I stepped off to look back. The scientists and their cargoes passed by. I then manually turned the Segway around. "Coming," I told Grimm, who had also stopped. "Keep the column going, Top." I manually spun my ride again before I began looking where Grimm was pointing. There was an old home in the distance, slate roof and stucco siding that had faded to gray. All around were green fields of two-foot-tall growth.

"I don't see anything."

"Watch the grass."

That had not been what I was focused on, but now that I was looking, I saw slow, steady movement. Stalks moved to the side, independent of any breeze. One or two, and I might have been able to convince myself it was a couple of small animals foraging. But as I scanned the entire area, it became quite clear.

"Top, see how much quicker you can get them all moving."

"Problem?" he asked.

"Yeah, you could say that. Grimm, go take a leak or something."

"What?"

"I want it to look like we're not on to them yet. Maybe we can get out of here without a battle."

"You want me to take a piss while zombies are stalking us?"

"Yeah, that's the gist of it."

"Now I know why Kirby complains so much before going out on missions." He took a couple of steps away and turned his back to me.

"Any day," I told him as I got a little antsy.

"First off, you're watching, along with who knows how many zombies, and I just went at the last pitstop."

"Top, you noticing anything around you?"

"No."

"Mount up, let's get out of here," I told Grimm.

"Now I think I have to go."

"Hurrying up would be appreciated."

"That ought to help," he responded. A stream a chipmunk would be embarrassed about dripped to the ground. "Done."

"When we get back, Grimm, you should have the doc check out your prostate. Slow and steady, not quite ready for them to spring up. I want the column to get as much of a lead as we can offer."

"I don't like being bait, sir."

"Don't think of us as bait, but rather enticement."

"That's better?"

"No, not at all, just a different word."

"Can we outrun them, sir?" Grimm asked.

"Not a chance in hell, not on these. That's why we're trying to keep them focused on us."

"Top speed of this model of Segway is twenty kilometers per hour; a fast human can reach thirty, no problem."

"Thanks, Double D," I said, referring to Doctor David. I grabbed my rifle and placed it atop the handlebar. All great and fine if something came at me head-on, but there wasn't a chance in hell I'd be able to hit anything to the side or rear of us, not while continuing to drive anyway.

BT and the rest had opened up a half-mile lead, and I was warring with how much space did we put between us. Yeah, I wanted the mission to succeed; I also wanted to make sure Grimm and I came through the other side. I could feel it in my bones, the zombies were getting ready to spring.

"Let's pick up the pace."

He nodded. Would have been tough to miss the tension change in the air as we both let out a breath. The zombies must have heard the speed change of the tires on the roadway, that, or the coincidence was perfectly timed. Almost as one, dozens of them stood and charged, arms pumping, fierce expressions on their faces. Most were of the traditional speeder variety, but there were more than a couple of the strange melders, some hampered, some enhanced. It was clear they would be upon us in under a minute.

"They're coming," I said flatly. "Over fifty."

"Set up a defensive perimeter?" BT asked.

Fifty was a good-sized force, but it wasn't a horde, and seven skilled shooters should be able to take care of an unarmed force relatively easy. But zombies rarely did anything that didn't involve a stadium's worth of them.

"Sir, they're going to cut us off," Grimm stated flatly.

It would have been hard to miss the zombies up ahead. They weren't making a break for us but rather for the path we were about to cross. Doing anything besides driving straight forward was nearly beyond my skill set, dodging something trying to tackle me was going to be impossible.

"Shit."

"Talk to me," BT said.

"Got about fifteen seconds before we're in the thick of it."

"Walde, you're with me," he said.

I was going to order him not to come back, but he wouldn't listen, and besides, we were going to need the help.

"We stop here," I told Grimm. There was no sense in rushing up to greet our guests.

"Really?" he asked as he looked over. We were about to be attacked on three sides.

"Ammo?"

"Three mags," he replied.

We had a little over two hundred rounds between the two of us. That sounds like it should have been plenty, but with adrenaline pumping high-octane fear through constricted veins, it's amazing how many bullets never find their mark. And ammunition is like bubblegum, you want to make sure you're able to give all of your enemies a piece or two.

"Top, stay to your right when you come back, don't want you downrange. Grimm, I've got the front and half the side, you're covering the rest."

"On it, sir." He was using the handles of the Segway to brace his rifle. His first volley was a three-round burst.

I looked over.

"Sorry." He switched his selector lever.

Like I was saying. Three bullets brought one enemy down.

I was doing my best to keep the zombies from getting back on the roadway, which would only make a bad situation worse. Kind of like chewing on pebbles to fill a cavity. Maybe that fits, maybe it doesn't. My first two shots went wide; I was attempting to keep one eye out for the reinforcements.

"Clear your mind, Talbot." I closed my eyes, inhaled for a count of three, exhaled for a count of five, my heart slowed a few thuds per minute. I opened my eyes, then narrowed them before closing my right lid. "Fuck you," I breathed out softly. Not trying to piss anybody off, just a factual statement. "Boom," I mouthed as a flap of scalp flipped up and off, the zombie falling as if it had tried to catch a meteor. "Boom." Into the right cheek, a spray of brain and blood flew out the back. "Boom." A disintegrated Adam's apple. I didn't need to do headshots; I wanted to do headshots. The zombies were more intelligent, so maybe it would have some psychological effect. Maybe it wouldn't, but it was certainly helping me out. I used to wrestle with the fact that the zombies were people once, living, breathing, sisters, cousins with hopes, dreams, some were decent, some were assholes that parked in handicapped spots when they weren't supposed to. I'd gotten over that by necessity. To continue to think I was murdering people on that scale would have been a mind fuck I wouldn't be able to come back from. I literally snorted. I don't even know what possessed me to think I was ever going to get over the myriad issues I already had.

"Reloading," Grimm shouted out.

How long had we been fighting that he'd already gone through a magazine? I'd been so intensely focused I honestly didn't know.

"We can see you." BT and Walde were moving quickly.

"Your six, sir," Walde warned.

"Son of a bitch." I turned to see another dozen running and five more loping along in a strange amalgamation of arms and legs. Those disturbing monsters I shot first. One, because they were easier targets and two, just fucking because. Between Grimm and myself, we'd shot somewhere in the neighborhood of twenty zombies, and considering we'd started with a couple dozen, the fact that now we were dealing with thirty was some of the strangest math I'd ever come across. Must have been calculus, never understood that shit.

Grimm and I were now effectively surrounded. BT and

Walde were fighting through the zombies ahead of us, I didn't think them coming to join our circle jerk was necessarily the best idea. The zombies had tapped a seemingly endless supply. We were killing them in droves, but this time they didn't appear to be deterred. Some high muckety muck in the zombie hierarchy had done the numbers. We were going to lose the battle, victory was theirs for the taking, and damn the mounting casualties. I didn't have any magical cavalry that could extract us from this situation: no explosive Rose, fast-shooting Harley, or even a Van Gothic vampire.

"Top, it's Dallas, we've got zombies approaching!"

Our entire line was under attack. We were spread out, and we had already been as thin as fishing line to begin with.

"Get back to the scientists! That's an order, BT!" It went unsaid that if they didn't make it, then none of this was worth it. Of course, I didn't voice that if Grimm and I died, then it wasn't worth it for us, anyway.

I couldn't see him through the maelstrom, but his delay in answering was all I needed to know that he was contemplating disobeying my orders. In reality, any order I gave him was merely a suggestion, and if he was okay with it, he'd do it, otherwise, not so much.

"Fuck you, Talbot," he said as I figured him and Walde had turned around.

I didn't know if I was mad or not that this was the order he'd decided to follow.

"Sir?" Grimm asked.

"Looks like it's just you and me."

He didn't reply; what could he say? I'd just told the only help for miles that we were beyond helping. Well, not that so much, as that we weren't as crucial as another group. Semantics. What did it matter? Either way got us dead. I don't know exactly what was going on, but the zombies hadn't stopped advancing, just seemed to be taking their time on the approach. They were no longer running full tilt but rather coming at a leisurely jog like they were finishing up a Sunday morning outing. Then it dawned on me, and it wasn't a completely foreign notion. They didn't care. Let me rephrase that. The zombie leadership didn't care about the bullet catchers they sent our way. We'd kill as many of them as we could, then the alphas would come in to claim the conquest when we could no longer fight back.

Grimm sounded out of breath when he announced the need to reload. It occurred to me that it wasn't because he'd been jogging in place but rather he was amped under the stress of the situation that we were rapidly about to face. "Last," he added.

I'd just popped in my last magazine, expecting to get bowled over at any point, and when I looked up, the zombies had stopped. Just flat out stopped. We had about ten yards clearance all the way around. Dirty, gray faces with bright, eager eyes stared at us. Blackened tongues licked cracked teeth. Snot hung, and gore clung to beards and hair. Split, aged yellow nails clawed at the air.

"What are they doing?" Grimm asked.

I wasn't entirely sure until a zombie broke from the pack and ran for us. As near as I could tell, I'd hit it dead center in the sternum. There was roughly a minute's pause before the next zombie sprang with the same results, though this shot was off-center. They were playing with their food. They were going to keep coming until we'd exhausted our supply of bullets; a deadly game of Red Light, Green Light. If they kept at this pace, we had maybe an hour left before switching to blades, and by then, we'd be measuring the remainder of our lives with an egg timer.

"Train's moving," BT said. "The zombies attacking us seemed to be more of a chasing us off type of crowd; when we got far enough away, they stopped—"

That was a good piece of news; I just wasn't feeling charitable enough to care.

"—and headed back to you," he added. That didn't dampen my mood. First off because as far as moods go, mine was about as damp as one gets, moist even, and secondly, you could add in another thousand zombies to Grimm's and my predicament, and it changed nothing in terms of the outcome.

"How are you planning on getting out of this one?" he asked. It was our running joke how I always seemed to get out of the worst of situations. As I looked at the zombies around Grimm and me, I wasn't feeling any sudden bouts of inspiration. There was no drain under our feet we could escape down. No rolling tank coming to pick us up. No helicopter to drop a ladder and pick us up.

"Airstrike would be nice," I quipped.

I could hear some talking on his end, but it was muffled, like possibly he was covering his pick-up so that I couldn't hear. Wasn't like if he revealed a secret, I was going to be around much longer to spread the news. The next words from BT were unexpected to the point I didn't believe them.

"You're a fucking genius!" He sounded excited.

It should be noted I'd been called all manner of things during my time on this earth, most tended to range somewhere on the curse word spectrum; this may have been a first. Well, maybe not *first*, I'm sure when I was like two years old, and I'd somehow managed to, with blind luck, put the square peg in the square hole, I'd had an aunt say I was a genius, but that would about be it.

"Say that again?" I'd heard him just fine, but if those were close to the last words that were going to be spoken to me, I might as well go out on a high note.

"Bloody brilliant, Captain." That sounded like Doc Dave.

"BT, what's going on?" I asked. Grimm was picking up the slack of shooting the one-offs.

"Ferreira's drone," he said excitedly.

"What about it? Is it big enough to carry us off?"

"I just called you a genius, and you're already starting to use your toes to count."

"Top." I was agitated. If they were cooking something up, I wanted to be in on it.

"It has eight manipulator arms; it can carry and drop things."

"We need ammunition!" Grimm blurted out.

"I've been talking to Rose." I could about hear the smile as BT said this. "Ten minutes Mike, that's all."

Ten minutes felt like an eternity. If the zombies kept doing what they were doing, we'd make it, if they instead decided to make a full-fledged run at us, we had less than a tenth of that. Hope can be a bitch. Having none kept you in a dour state of mind, having a glimmer caused enormous amounts of anxiety. When you were tossed the merest of morsels, you clung to it no matter how far-fetched it seemed.

"Sir?" Grimm looked over at me. He was asking if I thought it might work.

Knowing Rose, we were in danger of becoming what? If bullets from our ranks are friendly fire, what are explosives? Sociable atomization?

"Should we get back on the scooters?" he asked.

"No. We do something different, they might too." There was a hiccup a couple of minutes later. Three of the zombies had been released from their leashes at the same time. We got rid of them handily enough, but if this was the new norm, our timer had picked up speed.

"Armed and heading back," Rose replied.

"What are we in for?" I asked.

"Any chance of taking cover?" she asked.

"We're in the middle of the roadway, surrounded," I told her.

"So that's a no?" Again the mic was muffled. "You should be fine." She gave directions to Doc Dave in terms of how close he should drop the payloads and which arms had what.

It would be a fine capping to the day if, instead of dropping us munitions, we caught a bomb instead.

"Walde, Dallas and I are coming back to help your escape," BT said, "the rest are heading to the train."

He was being mighty optimistic. The zombies heard the drone before I did, or they were receiving direction to look for it from an outside source. The sizeable flying machine, which I'd initially thought of as a waste of space, upon our initial departure, was now coming in as our aerial savior. The manipulator arms hung low like some flying metallic octopus.

"Those grenades?" Grimm asked.

I was looking at the small green bag, hoping that was our spare magazines. "As good a guess as any," I told him, just happy they weren't claymores.

"Got you in sight," Doc Dave said.

"Not that one!" I heard Jackie yell.

"That would have been bad," Dave said.

"Do I want to ask?" I asked.

"No," BT and Dallas replied simultaneously.

"Shit," Dave and I said, also at the same time, as we saw the baseball-sized object fall. I let my rifle drop as I caught the grenade in the air. I underhand lobbed it some twenty feet; it was noggin-high when it detonated. I'd never seen anything quite like it as a dozen or more heads were vaporized. The bag of magazines caught me in the shoulder before Grimm could grab them.

"Fuck, Doc, why are you trying to kill me!"

"I haven't flown this in a while," he begged off.

Grimm quickly opened the bag. The attention of the zombies was fixated on the drone; good thing, too, because I was shrugging off the pain while Grimm was busy getting the bag open and handing out the resupplies. We both now had three new magazines, maybe enough to get out with a one-shot one-kill mentality, but I had no desire to stay here for the ensuing firefight.

"Doc, if you're ready to drop your payload on the zees, we're ready to get out of here. Grimm, we get on the segs the second the next grenade drops, but we don't move until they've all gone off, clear?"

He nodded, a grim expression on his face. (Sorry, had to.) I wasn't sure if the doc was going to drop them all at once or….the first fell. The zombies moved toward it like it was beads being tossed at Mardi Gras. Festive colors erupted. When the next dropped, they began to push away. Wasn't much room, so the results were just as impressive.

"Sir, the bodies."

"We're not going to be able to drive out!" I had to shout over the subsequent explosion.

"We'll be ready," BT promised.

I was watching the zombies, looking for the opening we needed, and Grimm was tracking the grenades.

"Last one," he said as I looked on an opening a tractor-trailer would have been happy with—if the driver was all right with having to scrape clean the undercarriage afterward.

"Now!" I shouted as the grenade went off. We ran. Made it to the edge of the carnage. Most of the zombies were still watching the death dealer from above, and the doc did us a solid as he flew it to the far side of the circle. We were out and past the wreckage before they ever took note of us, then it was game on, and no Jumbotron to watch our pursuers, as we raced to the goal. You'll note I refrained from calling it an "endzone" for obvious reasons. With us running and no more explosions, we were suddenly the *it* thing. Seemed that they all wanted a piece of us. Do I need to add *literally* in there? Seems superfluous. I'm sure if you're reading this journal, you understood it. It was the zombies further away that understood the ploy and didn't fall for it, can't fault the ones that were in the line of fire. They were too busy trying to keep their parts attached. Word passed quickly about our escape attempt, though, as the zombies tried to close the circle back up. But by then, we had escaped the closing clamp.

I don't know when they'd switched it out, but BT's Segway was pulling a trailer. I needlessly pointed to where we were going; it was worse than telling a horny teenager where their girlfriend's boobs were. All I knew was Justin wasn't born in a vacuum. Is that too obscure, or should I be a more obvious captain?

"Shit!" Grimm slipped awkwardly on the top half of a hand that had made its way a fair distance from the blast zone. He was gimping, hopping, more like. "Hamstring!" His head thrown back, eyes closed, teeth clenched, and one hand behind him clutching at the damaged muscle. I grabbed his belt and yanked, making his pants ride up in an attempt to bisect his privates, thus giving him something else to focus on.

BT, Harmon, and Dallas were in a line to our left. For some reason, I was so hyper-focused on grabbing Grimm and dragging him to safety I didn't hear the shots, only watched the muzzle flashes. I might not have actively been hearing the shots, but I could feel the microburst of air they were pushing out of the way on their deathly travels.

"Hurry the fuck up!" BT growled.

"Seriously?" I asked, more hefting Grimm along than assisting. We were moving at a decent clip, considering only one of us was trying. I tossed Grimm up onto the small trailer like he was the sack of potatoes I'd been carrying for far too long, and I couldn't wait to drop my load. Dallas and Harmon mounted back up and were already moving as I hopped aboard next to Grimm. I was sitting with my legs trailing behind as I fired on the zombies chasing.

"Faster!" I yelled to BT. Fair's fair, if we're going to start stating the obvious. Walde and Hammer were a little further up. Hammer was on full auto, decimating the zombies even though he didn't have the wonder bullets.

"Go!" BT urged.

We couldn't outrun them, not on these things. The only distance we could make was by killing those closest, Space Invaders-style. Grimm was sweating profusely, though I think that had more to do with the pain than anything else. Not like this was the first battle we'd been in that hadn't gone smoothly. After a moment of finding a position he could somewhat deal with, he added his rifle fire into the mix.

"Where are the scientists?" I asked as I reloaded.

"Told them not to stop!" BT yelled back.

"How far?" was my next question as I sent the bolt home.

"About three miles!"

Zombies were all around, threatening to again cut us off. If that happened, I couldn't expect that their leaders would again show restraint. BT was also shooting, trying to keep the path ahead clear. I honestly didn't see how we could make it. It wouldn't stop me from trying; just making the observation. A zombie bumped into either the side of BT or the Segway itself. We fishtailed and Grimm had to grab me to keep me from falling out of the trailer. It was so damn bizarre; we were going so relatively slow it seemed inconceivable I could be pitched out. As I was being righted, I saw BT take his left hand off the controls, he punched the zombie's jaw hard enough I heard something crack, and no part of me believed it to be BT's hand. The zombie staggered away and was trampled by another pursuer. If zombies could get concussions, that one was going to be under the watch of a neurosurgeon for a while.

"How close?" Rose asked.

Going by everything that had happened so far, I was wondering how she couldn't see us yet. Hope, which can be a fleeting thing anyway, stood up, flipped me off, and galloped away on a giant unicorn as BT answered.

"Little under two and a half."

"I can work with that."

"What can you work with?" I shouted as I continued to

shoot. Luckily I could shoot and talk at the same time, wasn't like I needed to aim particularly well.

"Setting up some help."

"Need to come closer, Rose, no way in hell we're going to make that," I told her. Grimm may have hesitated when I said the words. Sucks when what you already know to be true is verbalized.

"I can work with that. A lot closer, but doable." I could hear her breathing heavier as she was double-timing to a new location. We had about a ten-foot cushion towards the sides and back. BT was doing an admirable job of keeping them from heading us off, though they did seem more set on attacking us directly as opposed to ensnaring. The zombies were packed tight in the chase, sometimes shooting one took three or more out of the immediate pursuit as they went down in a tangle. It was a postponement, but no matter how many extensions you file for on tax day, you're still going to have to pay, and that was how I felt.

"I see them," Rose stated. "Go, go!" she urged. I would imagine others had slowed to offer assistance.

"I'll help," that was Walde. "Sir, we're about two clicks from the train. I'm going to help Rose set up some claymores and drive her back."

"Roger that." I grimaced as a fragment of hot brass sizzled against my neck, I didn't even spare the half-second it would take to brush it away. Even that small measure of time was irreplaceable. Strange to give so much weight to the tiniest bit of a moment. How much time had I wasted sitting at traffic lights or watching a horrible movie, or eating at my in-laws? What I wouldn't do to get back that tedious hour and a half watching the *Eternal Sunshine of the Spotless Mind* and apply it here. I could have taken a leisurely stroll back to the train; hell, I could have taken a piss. That was just one instance. If that fantasy were a viable option, I'd take all those traffic light hours and apply them to bedtime with my wife—and not the sleeping kind, well maybe some would be sleeping time. Refractory and recovery is a real thing.

"BT," I said.

"Little over a mile," he said, doing the conversion for me. Slightly embarrassing as a military man, but deliberate. At this point, I'd actively decided not to understand some of the lingo. Command prerogative.

"We're running low on juice," BT said as if he were talking about nearly being out of spray cheese, and we still had two boxes of Triscuits. A tragedy in its own rights, but not overly comparable.

"How much?"

"I don't know, meter is in the red."

That meant nothing. A Hyundai on E might go another thirty miles, a Super Bee Charger in the same fix might get thirty feet. If this thing just up and died, we wouldn't make it out alive; we'd be swarmed before I could even stand, and they'd have Grimm where he lay.

"Is it flashing?" Jackie asked.

"No," BT answered immediately.

"You have about two kilometers."

"BT," I said again.

"Little over a mile."

So at a little less than two-and-a-half miles to the train, we had roughly half that left in power, and we were going to run out at or near to where Rose and Walde were facilitating a rescue. They say football is a game of inches; that exact phrase could be used for war, and sex. However, regardless of the historical jargon, war is no game. As I was tossing empty magazines, it was becoming increasingly difficult to find a holder that still had full ones. I don't know how much ammunition we had left, but I'm pretty sure it was about a mile's worth, give or take a life or two. There are differing theories on coincidence, but it was hard to argue that something strange wasn't going on here. Just too many things were coming to a head at exactly the same time.

"I can see them," BT said. That there wasn't even the slightest hint of relief in his voice was more telling than any words he could have spoken.

As I frantically patted my body looking for a magazine, a zombie snagged the heel of my boot. If it had reached a couple of inches up and grabbed my ankle, I'd be on the pavement under a pile of rotten corpses. Two fingernails snapped off its hands and spun in the air as it lost its grip and balance. Its chin smashed off the ground, and a slithering severed tongue jumped out ahead of it.

"I think this is my last magazine!" Grimm said as he fired.

"Of course it is." I was not jubilant as I finally grabbed my last magazine as well. Perhaps if I performed a cavity search upon myself, I'd find another tucked deeply away.

"Walde, Rose, you need to go!" BT shouted.

"The line is only so long," Rose responded.

BT mumbled a decent litany of swears. I felt like we were a carbonated bubble of air deep in a can of soda. (In this representation, the soda was Moxie because, well, that drink and zombies just plain suck.) The sheer number of unacceptable things that happened in quick succession felt like an overdone country song: a man, having found out his woman was cheating with his best friend, races home recklessly, and totals his truck into his favorite brewery. Upon finally getting home, he discovers his traitorous wife has left and, driving in the final nail, taken his dog with her.

"They're too close!" Rose warned.

No shit threatened to bubble forth from my mouth, I swallowed it back down.

"You need to make more room!" she beseeched.

"No sense in saving any," I said, more to myself, but Grimm took it to heart. He opened up a split second before I did. Fifty or so rounds in the grand scheme of things wasn't much, but it did push the night back, "night" being a metaphor for zombies. I'm never sure what's clear when I write this stuff down.

I caught sight of a claymore out of the corner of my eye just as the Segway came to a jarring jolt of a stop. As I was sliding forward, I was being pushed sideways, my back to the zombies. I saw BT pitch over the handlebars, and I lost sight of Grimm, but felt him smack into my lower legs. What might have happened next could be attributed to instinct; I'd like to think I reached down and pulled Grimm toward my chest to protect him from the explosives, but it may have also been a subconscious impulse to use him as a cushion for when I hit the ground. No sense in letting him know that part; he couldn't prove it anyway. The roar of Rose's detonation was deafening. The pain in my ears was substantial, but that was soon surpassed by the burning in my back. I cried out from the agony; we'd been too close to the backblast. I want to say fifty feet is what's required, we were half that.

"Jesus, this is going to hurt," he said, the words happening after the action. My spine was on fire. Godzilla would have been envious. BT was running with me cradled in his arms. Grimm had his arms and legs wrapped around BT as the big man ran.

"Stay with me, Talbot." My head was lolling, my eyes becoming unfocused. I was laid on another sled. Before my eyes closed, I wondered what had happened to BT, his arms were covered in blood. I wasn't conscious of this at the time, but I wanted to pass out. Possibly my body knew that if I did that, I wouldn't be so likely to come back around. My eyes were closed, and I wanted to venture off into realms that weren't shrouded in agony. I had no such luck. I felt every imperfection in the roadway as my body was jostled. I alternated between expecting to internally combust and teeth shattering cold. Gunfire was still happening, but I was about as aware of it as I was a distant bird cawing while having sex.

Sure your ears picked up the noise, but your brain had much more important things going on than to give two fucks about it. Maybe it got cataloged away, or more likely, it just slid along the surface of your gray matter and dissipated like water droplets on a hot pan.

14

MAC & WILKES

"*BUGGER ALL!* Wilkes shouted. You're going to stop there?!"

"Remember how you said you were going to read so I could take a break?"

"I never agreed to that." Wilkes was pacing about.

"I'm exhausted," he told her as he put the journal back in the plastic bag and sealed it up.

"I wasn't so sure about you in the beginning, but if I'd had any inclination to just how cruel you could be, I would have shot you."

Mac snorted.

"He thinks I'm kidding."

"Get some sleep, we've got a long day ahead of us."

"What if I were to sprain my ankle, and we had to stay here for a few nights, and you had to continue to read to me?"

"I'd make a sled and drag you each day, and then I'd be way too tired to read to you at night."

She hmphed and crossed her arms. She thought about stomping her foot but refrained; it seemed undignified somehow.

It was jokes and humor now, but the day had started off scary and had throttled up to terrifying rather quickly. Mac could not help but think upon it, and if his throat wasn't truly raspy and on the verge of croaking out, he might have decided to begin reading again. Anything to let go of his own worries and dwell upon the problems of others. Strange how that could offer comfort.

The beaters inside had been quiet for a good portion of the morning; even those outside had ceased their milling about. One had stopped not more than three meters from where they needed to climb down from. Wilkes had offered to shoot it, and he would have given the okay if it hadn't been partially blocked by a tree. The shot would have had to be perfect and, on top of that, noiseless, because another beater wasn't more than ten meters from the first. One miscalculation and there'd be a group of them, and he and Wilkes would be pinned there.

"Are you sure you don't want me to shoot it?" Wilkes asked again. She pointed to the sky off in the distance. A line of black clouds was making a steady march toward them, and with it a genuine threat of rain. The wind had begun to pick up, and the temperature dropped; the threat appeared to be moving into the fulfillment phase.

"We'll wait, the rain will conceal our getaway."

"I don't like getting wet," Wilkes told him.

"You part cat?" Mac tried to lighten the mood.

"Sorry?"

"Cats don't like water."

"It's always so difficult to get warm again." Wilkes had grown more serious as she watched the storm move closer; she pulled her outerwear tight around her chest. She made sure the journals were watertight and put on her backpack; she wanted to be ready to leave as soon as they were able.

They both sat as the sun was muted and the day quickly faded out. The drops felt like tiny ice daggers being thrown down by a petulant god. Wilkes began to shiver immediately. Mac wanted to wrap her up in his arms but wasn't entirely sure how she would react to that. Instead he moved closer to the edge of the roof to look down at the beater. The zombie had not moved and, strangely enough, seemed to be hunkering down against the inclement weather, something Mac couldn't ever recall seeing before. They generally didn't care about the elements.

"Weird," he muttered as he motioned for Wilkes to come over. "You ready to go?" he asked quietly, though, with how hard the rain was coming down, anything below a yell would have been difficult to hear.

Her teeth were chattering, and her lips were an unsightly blue. The rain was cold, but her reactions seemed extreme. She nodded her response. His original plan had been to send her down first, as she was a better climber and stealthier, but the way she was shivering, he was afraid she wouldn't be able to control her descent, and he wanted to be there to break her fall if need be.

"I'll go first." He got on his stomach, feet toward the edge, and slowly pushed down. Once his legs dangled over the ledge, he began to slip. Wilkes was slow to react, she moved to grab him but missed. He was able to capture the lip of the roof, but he'd been going so fast that he'd not been able to stop the momentum of his swinging legs from hitting the wall.

He looked up to a wild-eyed Wilkes. She had her finger to her lips and mouthed, *Don't move*. He knew the beater must have heard him. Rain was pouring torrentially, to the point he was having difficulty looking up, and holding on was becoming precarious.

"Don't. Move," Wilkes hissed, but he needed to find purchase for his feet quickly.

"Fuck." He breathed out, spittle caused by rainwater fell away and to the feet of the prowling beater. If the beater didn't move soon, Mac was going to fall on top of it. He was intently watching Wilkes for any sign that it would be okay to move, but her attention was stubbornly fixated on the beater, to the point he wanted to scream at her to look at him. Finally, she did, and with a nod, he swung his feet to the window frame. With one hand, he let go of the edge of the roof and placed it palm up against the soffit. He took a deep breath as his cold, stiff fingers got used to not being curled over. The pain was intense but short-lived. He stayed squat like that for another minute or two; there was a beater at the end of the hallway looking down the staircase as if it expected a person to come bounding up it. The one in the yard had quit walking around and was once again partially behind its tree. Mac was convinced it was indeed seeking shelter from the rain there; otherwise it would have stayed where it thought the sound had come from.

15

TOMMY

"WE'RE COMING IN. The captain is hurt…bad," BT said.

Tommy was the first to the Segway. He lifted Michael off of the trailer; the man's back was coated in blood like an iced cake.

"Help him," BT begged. "Get Winters."

Tommy shook his head regarding the medic. "I'll do what I can," Tommy said. "Get everyone on the train. I'll be in the second booth."

BT nodded in understanding as he directed everyone onto various parts of the train in preparation for its defense. The train finally began its journey back to Wales, but it was very much in doubt who exactly would still be alive once, or even if, they made it.

"Can you do anything?" BT asked.

Tommy was kneeling next to Mike. "Maybe." He briefly looked over at Winters.

"What?"

"Neither man is going to make it, not unless I intervene." Tommy spoke only to BT. "And I won't curse Winters like that, never again."

"Are you sure?"

"His breathing is shallow, he feels cold and clammy. He most likely has internal bleeding."

"Are you sure?" BT repeated.

"BT, I have personally witnessed the deaths of hundreds. There is not a doubt in my mind the man will not last another hour. I do not believe that if we wheeled him into a hospital this very instant, he would survive. Mr. T on the other hand." He left the statement open.

"Jesus." BT stood, wiped his hand across his face, and walked to the far end of the car. "Mike would never be able to live with himself if he knew he played a part in Winters' death."

"I can ask them."

"How?" BT turned; tears streaked his face. "Neither is conscious."

"There are ways."

"Do it. Hurry," he said as the blood bubbling from Mike's back began to slow.

Tommy relaxed his body as best he could and lay his head on the seat rest. When he entered the field, Winters was staring off into the distance at a brilliantly shining sun.

"Beautiful, isn't it?" Winters asked as Tommy approached.

"It is."

"I'm dying, aren't I?" Winters turned to see Tommy's reaction.

"Yes."

"I enjoyed my life. A lot of hardships...though, they made the good times that much sweeter. Do you know what awaits?" There was no fear in his voice; apprehension, perhaps, but mainly only curiosity.

"Your heaven will be made up of the best of your life."

"That sounds wonderful." Winters again stared off to the horizon then took a step forward.

"Before you go, I would like to ask a question."

It took Winters a long moment before he realized Tommy had spoken.

"Yes," he answered, not looking back.

"The captain is going to die if you are not there to help him."

"I am hardly of your plane anymore; what can I possibly do to help now?"

"Your blood."

Now Winters did turn, confusion furrowed his eyebrows. "The captain?"

"Michael."

Winters' eyes darted about as he sought to gather the information in his untethered mind. Tommy knew that cognitive thought was not easily accomplished outside the earthly realm.

"He's like you?"

"Yes," Tommy told him.

"I think I knew that. You can't pass over here, right?"

"Right."

"I feel sadness for you." He turned and began to walk.

"Winters."

"Of course. I no longer have a need for the vessel that housed me." He continued to walk.

"Goodbye." Tommy gave a small wave before wiping his eyes. A sob escaped his lips as he came awake.

BT was doing chest compressions on Winters' lifeless body.

"He's going." Tommy placed a hand upon BT's shoulder as the big man's head sagged.

"Save him," BT said as he switched his attention to Mike.

Tommy again took a breath and closed his eyes. This time, he found himself on a dirt pathway; Mike was up ahead dragging a stick against the ground. To his left were majestic peaks, on his right, a dark forest.

"Michael?"

"Tommy!" Mike turned, a smile upon his face.

"Where are we?"

"Damned if I know. Gotta stay out of the woods, though, that much I know, lot of scary stuff in there," Mike told him.

"You're dying."

"Figured as much. What happened?"

"Claymore."

"Did I not read that part about 'This side toward the enemy?'"

"Backblast."

"Well, ain't that a bitch." Mike continued to walk, kicking up dust as he did so. His stick made a small rut along the path. "You'll look after everyone?"

Tommy hesitated. Mike stopped and peered at him. Unlike Winters, Mike appeared to have all his faculties, such as they were.

"You didn't just come to say bye. What is it?"

"I can save you."

"But?"

"You need blood."

Disgust swept across Mike's features.

"A lot of blood."

"Tomas, you know me; I will not kill another to save myself."

"What if they are already dying?"

Both men paused, watching as the forest began to creep out onto the pathway, invading the border.

"Got a feeling if I take so much as one step into that forest, I'll get stuck, and there'd be no way out. What do you think the mountains are all about?"

"Unobtainability," Tommy answered.

"Figured as much, thought I'd ask. Who's dying?"

"Winters."

"Ah, shit. He was a good man." Mike shuddered; up ahead, the path was entering into the forest. A cliff had formed to his left, making it impossible to skirt the woods. He didn't turn around; instinctively he knew the path behind him had ceased to exist the moment he stepped past. Even in a world he knew had very different rules from what he was used to, he didn't think he could handle seeing an all black void behind him. "Looks like it's decision time."

"It would appear that way," Tommy told him.

"What do you think I should do?"

"I don't think I'm the best person to give advice; my answer would purely be selfish. There's still so much to do, so many people counting on you."

The corners of Mike's eyes crinkled as he smiled. "That's not all that subtle of a push."

"You asked. Subtlety is not our way," Tommy answered.

"Fuck. What are the repercussions?"

"Besides you living and continuing to protect all those you love?"

"Wow, any thicker, and you're going to bury me in it."

Tommy looked down, avoiding his friend's gaze. "You've already paid the highest price."

"In for a dime in for a dollar," Mike told him.

16

MIKE JOURNAL ENTRY 7

WHEN I AWOKE, my belly was full, and I had a strong taste of iron in my mouth like I'd been gnawing on a rifle. BT was in a seat to my right, watching me intently. The small boat we were in was bobbing about in choppy water. I was suddenly nauseous, either from seasickness or what was sloshing about inside of me, I grabbed the lip of the boat, pulled myself to the edge and leaned my head out to the ocean, where I proceeded to throw up a thick column of blood. Through the corner of my vision, I could see the young oarsman's eyes grow huge.

"I'm fine," I told him right before I repeated the process. Pretty sure if the blood had been mine, I would have shriveled up like a grape in the desert sun. Nothing more came up, but I kept my head hanging overboard the rest of the trip.

We'd lost a team member, and Grimm and Kirby would be on light duty for a while. I was a mess, physically, mentally, and spiritually. I like to hit all cylinders when I spiral down. If the scientists didn't come through, I was going to enjoy exacting a measure of revenge.

"I'm so sorry." Rose was hopping about on her feet as she watched me placed on a gurney and wheeled away.

I told her it wasn't her fault, but whether she heard me through her suffering, I wasn't sure.

"Mike, how bad off are you?" BT was walking next to me; he'd grabbed my hand and leaned down.

"I can't feel anything below my waist," I told him.

He winced.

"No one needs to know that."

He didn't seem too keen about keeping that a secret.

"BT." I gripped his hand harder.

"Fuck, okay." He turned away, wiping his eyes.

Tracy came running down the hallway as I was being wheeled into the hospital section. She grabbed my hand.

"Oh, Michael." She had tears streaking down her face. "I heard about Winters."

I browbeat back my own that threatened to fall. It wasn't so much that I was ashamed to cry but I wanted to avoid the pain that would come with the wracking sobs once I opened up those gates.

"This is far as you can go," the orderly told BT and Tracy. I looked back and directly at my friend, making sure he kept the promise.

There was a team of doctors and nurses scrubbed and ready to go. Eastman was up in the observation room.

"Good to have you back," he said over the speaker.

I managed to give him the finger. It's what Winters would have wanted. The doctors said nothing as they cut away my clothing and makeshift bandages. Someone gave me a shot of something, and before I could count back from ten, I was out.

I HAVE no idea how long I was out. I was still in the hospital, so not long enough. My head was foggy, my throat hurt, and my stomach still roiled. "Recovery," I groaned.

"You're awake." It was a nurse. I knew his name; damned if I didn't with all the times I'd been in the hospital area for myself or one of my squad, he was damn near family.

"Hey," I croaked. "Can I get something to drink?"

"We've got to wait until the doc clears you from recovery, don't want you aspirating."

"What if I ordered you, Astrez?" His name had come to me in a flash.

He laughed. "Major Trellon outranks you."

"Trellon did my surgery?"

"You're lucky he did, too. He's the best spinal surgeon alive."

"Astrez, that's like saying I'm the best tuba player alive."

"I would have missed our talks if you hadn't made it, Captain." He was smiling, but I could see the seriousness in his gaze right below the surface. "I'll go see if they'll authorize some ice chips."

"It would be better if those ice chips were floating in some vodka."

He shook his head in mock displeasure and walked out the door. Astrez was back a few minutes later with a cup of chips sans the liquor.

"How much longer in here?" I asked as I savored the frozen water on my tongue.

"Ask him." Astrez motioned to the door as Major Trellon entered.

"Ah, Captain." The major was looking at a medical folder open in his hand, in fact, he never looked away from it as he spoke. "You're fortunate to be alive."

"Is that because you were my surgeon?"

Astrez sputtered out a laugh and covered it up with a small coughing fit.

Trellon continued as if he'd never heard me talk. His bedside manner was so shitty I wondered if he'd been an undertaker before he was thrust into the front lines of operating on the living.

"You suffered massive trauma to…" I started drifting out when he began to talk about individual muscles and the sections of my spine that had sustained damage. He may have droned on for four or five minutes. He'd never once bothered to look up and read the room. By now, Astrez was standing behind the doc, watching with punched lips, his hands clasped firmly behind his back. I came out of my words-induced stupor when he began to talk about physical therapy. "…possible with a lot of hard work that eventually you will get to the point of walking with braces and a walker. Okay, I'll leave you to it." Trellon left before I could ask any questions.

"Astrez?"

"Captain," he started sympathetically. "We're still trying to figure out how you're still alive, but as far as regaining your mobility?" He shook his head. "Our best prognosis is twenty percent."

"Twenty percent chance I can walk again? I can work with that."

"No, you've misunderstood; there's a chance you might, with time, regain twenty percent of your previous capacity."

"That…that's not going to work for me."

"With a motorized chair, you'll get around just fine, hardly even know the difference. Wait, I'm sorry for that last part, I'm not good with relaying bad news."

"I would think you'd have a lot of practice, working for Trellon." Neither of us smiled. "Could I be alone for a moment?"

"Of course." He nodded and headed out.

I wanted to cry; it seemed the appropriate reaction to the news I'd just received. Instead, I finished off the ice chips, my mind nearly as numb as my frozen tongue.

An hour later.

"You ready for this?" Astrez asked as he undid the lock on my gurney wheels and headed out of the recovery room.

I was going to ask him, *ready for what?* A life of getting my ass wiped by someone else? Yeah, the pity party had started; unfortunately, I was the only one in attendance.

"I think half the boat is in the waiting area trying to visit, and the other half is waiting until they get off duty."

"Astrez, I'm not ready for that. I...I need some time to process this."

"I understand, but seeing family and friends is good for the healing process."

"Am I ever going to walk again?"

He was tight-lipped.

"Then what needs to heal?" I pressed.

"It's not only your body that took damage. I know this sucks, Captain Talbot, but you can still lead a very fulfilling life; you have to get to the point of acceptance. Embrace the change."

"Embrace it? I'd rather fuck a porcupine."

He snorted. "See, that's what I'm talking about. Humor in the face of adversity."

"Oh, you've got it wrong, my friend. That's my coping mechanism, a way to shun the truth, not face it."

"You'll make it; I know how tough you are." He wheeled me into my room, pushed the bed into place, and locked the wheels. "I'm going to get your wife."

I wished he wouldn't. I didn't say anything, and I knew Tracy wouldn't take no for an answer, so why bother. My wife's steps faltered as she came through the door, her complexion paled, which, given its natural color, was a feat. I had no idea how I looked, but gauging her reaction, I'm going to say it wasn't stellar. I'm smart and intuitive like that.

"What can I touch?" she asked hesitantly as she approached. "I don't want to hurt you."

"Not sure you can do any more damage." I'd meant it as a joke, it came out sourer than I'd intended. She was keeping a brave face, but I could see how close to losing it she was. My kids funneled in next. Travis was having a hard time looking me in the eye, but I was confident it had more to do with him attempting to maintain his stiff upper lip. We talked for a while, or, more precisely, they spoke for a while. I was in and out as the cocktail of drugs working through my system did their thing. Astrez checked in a few times under the pretense of adjusting my pillow or topping off my water, but mostly he was watching how I was interacting. Eventually, and thankfully, he told them I needed some rest and that they should come back tomorrow. The kids all told me they loved me, and Tracy gave me a tender kiss on the lips. Tears leaked from the corner of my eyes before the door could close all the way.

I was asleep or unconscious, tough to tell, when I saw light spilling in from the hallway as the door opened. Didn't know who it was and didn't care. With any luck, it was an angel of mercy come to release me from my earthly shackles.

"Hey, Mr. T." Tommy had what looked like an enormous Pop-Tart in his hands. Maybe it was the drugs.

"Tommy? Are you here?"

"Want some?" He held out the pastry wannabe that was the size of a hardcover book. I saw large crumbs fall from the edge. Knowing the strange flavor profiles the boy enjoyed, I was thankful none fell toward my mouth.

I either shook my head or told him to fuck off.

"Are you with it enough to understand what I'm saying?"

I nodded, but only because it seemed like what he wanted.

"You took an enormous amount of damage to your body. By all accounts, as a human, you shouldn't be alive. You've got the entire medical team wondering how you survived. Over the next few days, you will continue to heal, and, yes, you will regain control of your legs, but this part is important, Mr. T, you're going to have to pretend that you have not."

I didn't understand, or I stopped listening after hearing I would walk again, or maybe I slipped into a fugue state, who knows?

"You're going to have to suffer through rehab, make slight gains over time, otherwise the suspicion they have now will go into full-blown frenzy. You will become the poster child for medical testing. I'm doing all I can to keep your secret."

If he had more to say or had even said more, I didn't know, I'd joined the nether realms. When Astrez woke me up the following day, I had a vague memory of a visitor the previous night, though I was half-convinced it had been a dream until Astrez frowned down at my chest and grabbed up the large crumbs. He looked at me questioningly but didn't say anything.

"How are you doing today?" He adjusted the bed and my pillow.

"I'm in pain."

He checked the IV bag, spun the dial on the line to shoot me up with some juice. He lifted the cover from my feet and, with his rubber hammer, tapped under my right knee. My leg twitched ever so slightly. What Tommy had told me flooded into my head, but I wasn't entirely sure how I was supposed to stop a reflexive action. Astrez's head popped up like I'd just farted out the entirety of a *White Christmas* in perfect pitch.

"Did you feel that?"

I shook my head. That was the truth. He did the same thing to my left knee, I tried not to react, but again it was a reflex, and besides, I still hadn't felt it and didn't know what to stop.

"I, uh." He stood and scratched the top of his head. "I've got to get the doctor."

I don't know how Tommy and Astrez didn't bump into each other at the doorway. The boy was inside and apologizing before I could ask what for. He pulled a needle out and injected it into each of my knees. I want to say I felt a prick of pain, but it could have been a lie. "Bye." He melted out before I could say anything.

A couple of minutes later, a very animated and excited Astrez had a harried and doubting Doctor Trellon in tow.

"I'm telling you, Major, I did the knee-jerk reflex, and there was movement."

"And as I told you when you interrupted me, that's impossible." He went into a lengthy discussion of why that couldn't be the case, oblivious to the fact that he was giving his grim prognosis in front of his patient. I wanted to punch him in the nose, but that little nugget of hope prevented it, that, plus I would have had to get out of the bed to do it, and Tommy would be pissed. Although I never really promised him I wouldn't show my hand.

"Watch!" Astrez grabbed his handy dandy red rubber mallet and struck my knee. Nothing. He tried again, a bead of sweat forming on his brow, same results.

"Are we done here?" Major Trellon asked, but he was already heading for the door.

Astrez looked at me with pleading eyes like he was asking why I was doing this to him. "I saw them move, didn't you?" He didn't sound so sure.

"I'm on drugs." I hated to lie outright; avoidance seemed the best course of action.

Tracy came in later that day, she appeared better. Tommy must have got to her because she didn't look on the verge of breaking down. We talked for a good bit, but my legs and back were beginning to hurt to the point I couldn't think of anything else. Or maybe they'd always been hurting, but now I was starting to *feel* it. Astrez bumped my IV a couple of times. When he stopped, I tried juicing that bag like I was making homemade lemonade.

BT was in later in the day holding a six-pack. He didn't even try to hide it, and no one attempted to stop him. He twisted the cap off of one and held it out. I gladly took it. We clinked bottles before he settled down into a chair.

"I'm getting too old for this shit." That was all either of us said as we killed the beers. "Good seeing you." We fist-bumped before he left. Like I've said before, guys can have a year's worth of conversation without a word spoken. It was a comfort just having him there. The rest of the squad came in during the day, but Tommy had not clued them in, and they were all apologetic. Stenzel seemed to take it the hardest.

"I'm so sorry, sir." She had grabbed my hand, her head hanging down. "I feel like this was all my fault, if I could have kept the train running or something, this wouldn't have happened."

"Sergeant, none of this is your fault. There's nothing you could have done. Stop beating yourself up about the impossible."

"You're the best commander a Marine could ever ask for, sir. It's been an honor to serve with you."

"Same, Stenzel. You've made my job significantly easier and better, and for that, I thank you, and I still may surprise you."

"Okay." She wiped her eyes before heading out.

"This is a fucking blast," I said to no one in particular.

17

MAC & WILKES

MAC CLIMBED down the house and jumped the last few feet onto the spongey grass. The beater heard nothing as he slammed his knife into the side of its head. It stilled and fell over. He was turning to tell Wilkes to join him, but she was already nearly down. When her feet hit the ground, they took off wordlessly. They'd traveled a few kilometers away from the beaters, but Wilkes had yet to warm up. Her teeth were chattering, and she had her arms wrapped around her midsection. Mac knew she was in trouble and had to find her some shelter soon. He wasn't confident that they were far enough away yet, but the more pressing problem needed to be dealt with first. They crossed through a small area of trees and came out onto a secluded cul-de-sac. A solitary stone cottage sat at the end. Mac led them toward it. The rain intensified, as if proving the point that getting out of it would be for the best. He could take a hint. He pushed open the door; all the furniture had been covered in white sheets that had long ago yellowed.

Mac pulled one free. "Get your clothes off, cover up in this." He handed her the sheet. "I'll see if they have anything you can wear in the meantime, then I'll see about a fire." He was looking at the wide fireplace. The steep staircase led to a narrow, short hallway not designed so much for habitation as for storage. There were more than a dozen large blue plastic bins. When he went to pull the lid off the first, it broke apart in his hands. "Dry rot," he said, looking at the contents inside. It was kitchenware, plates and utensils with the occasional mug. By the fourth one, he found what he was looking for. It was full of oversized sweaters, socks, and sweatpants. By the time he got downstairs, he could smell the smoke of a burgeoning fire. The only way Wilkes could have been any closer was if she had climbed in with the logs.

"Got you these," he said, handing her a pile.

"You…you get anything for…for yourself?"

"Going back up. Get changed, I'll be right down."

"Th…thanks."

He didn't like that he could see her breath. He changed and brought down as many of the clothes as he could carry and made a makeshift bed out of them. Wilkes was asleep immediately; he'd wanted to stay up and stand guard until he realized he was freezing as well.

"I'll just sleep for a minute," he lied. He awoke hours later, the fire had burned down to embers, and he needed some water. As his stomach grumbled, he figured he wouldn't mind taking care of that issue either. He was warm and dry, though. It was still raining, and the day was dark because of it. It was unlikely any of McGowan's hunter-scouts would be out in the inclement weather. The beaters couldn't care less about the temperature, but without a reason to look, they wouldn't do so. For now, they were safe.

"Hey," Mac said when he turned and saw that Wilkes was pulling some logs from a cabinet.

"You ever seen anything like this?" she asked as she placed the wrapped wood into the fire.

"I've never used one, but I saw them in the store when I

was a kid. Fake wood. I think it's wax and sawdust or something like that."

"Sure does make it easier to start a fire. It doesn't look like we're going anywhere today." She smiled.

"I'm not doing any reading until I drink a bunch of water. Speaking of which, where is your canteen?"

"Outside, filling up."

Mac opened the door. The canteen was on the front porch, a wide funnel sticking out of the top. He brought it in and they both took a large swallow, hoping to push back the hunger, then he replaced it.

"I don't understand what's happening with Talbot," Wilkes asked as Mac sat down. She fished in her backpack to pull out the journals. "He gets hurt, can't move his legs, then can move his legs, and Tommy makes it seem like he can't move them? Why? Won't everyone be happy that he's getting well?"

"Remember, Wilkes, as far as we know, this is still just a story. Something that could very easily be made up. Perhaps this person was alone and scared and wrote things down, just so they weren't quite as afraid."

"So then, writing can kind of do the same thing reading can?"

Mac hadn't honestly thought about it in that way, but she was right. "Yeah, I guess so."

"But if he's living in the time of the beaters and was afraid of them, why would he write about them if he was trying to forget? Unless it's all true."

"Yeah, I guess so." Mac didn't know how else to respond to her. She was right, as near as he could tell.

"Then I'm going back to my original question. Is he a vampire too?"

"Vampires aren't real. They were fictional characters in books and movies."

"So Tommy lied to Rose? Why would he do that?"

"Your guess is good as mine." Mac's stomach twisted into a knot from hunger, the water doing little to curb the sensation. "I can start reading, or you can listen to my belly sing."

"Read, definitely read. It sounds like we have a bear in here."

18

MIKE JOURNAL ENTRY 8

IF THIS WERE some strange 80's movie, this is where the scriptwriter would insert a montage scene. Personally, I'd like the song to be Queen's *Under Pressure,* but I have a feeling I'd end up with Tina Turner's *We Don't Need Another Hero.* I'd be doing all of this rehab stuff, assisted walking on dual bars, falling over, angrily pounding the floor, getting back up. I'd have folks gripping both my arms, urging me on while my wife clasped her hands under her chin and watched. There'd be a point where I would take a tentative step on my own like a baby finally getting to two-legged locomotion. Eventually, the triumphant scene would end with me running up the seventy-two stairs that led to the top of the Philadelphia Museum of Art, a la *Rocky,* arms upraised and all.

This was all made much more difficult by the fact that two days after Tommy's announcement, my legs were fine. Oh, there was still some mind-numbing pain, but they worked. I'd never imagined how difficult it was going to be to pretend they didn't. Can't tell how many times I nearly got busted just scooting up on my bed. I finally convinced Trellon that I should go home, that my recovery would happen quicker there. He assured me in his best bedside manner voice that "recovery" wasn't an option. What a D-bag. No wonder he was a military surgeon; I'm guessing he got fired from every civilian hospital he'd ever worked for. I am of the belief that a fair percentage of getting well resides within a person's mind. Hope is a powerful tool, and to have it quashed by a small-minded doctor is detrimental. Had I not already regained the use of my limbs, there's no telling what his words may have done to my psyche and thus my recovery, but since I had, fuck him. She'd no sooner walked through the door when I told my wife. There was no way I would be able to keep it from her, and why would I want to?

"I've got to tell you something," I told her once she'd wheeled me into our quarters and closed the door.

"What?"

"Come in front." I'd grabbed her hands and, while looking up into her eyes, stood. Oh, you can bet there was a romp in the park after that reveal. I'd like to go into detail about what this romp entailed and what went where, I mean, since it's my journal, I should be able to, but I'm always afraid one of my kids will come across this, and I've already done enough damage to them, no need to finish it off. I told her she had to continue to play along with the charade and wheel my ass to rehab every morning so that, four months later when I was walking around slowly with the assistance of a cane, it could be considered a miracle. How I was going to convince Eastman I was duty-ready the next time my squad was needed was going to be difficult. I had a timeline in mind to lose the cane and start walking around the ship without it. I wanted to normalize that fact, make people forget I'd ever been injured, if possible. This was very easy with the vast majority of those on the ship because my interactions with them were minimal, if at all. It was with those closest that it was going to be diffi-cult. My family, BT, and Tommy were easy enough, but my squad and my superior were a whole other can of worms. Although Rose, for some strange reason, seemed nonplussed about the whole thing. I got the feeling she knew, or suspected she knew.

When Eastman called me to his office some five months after the incident, I was deciding how I wanted to play it, although, going in there with a cane, shuffling along, or even with just a limp would be overplaying, as I'd already rejoined my squad for physical training.

Eastman's attaché led me to an empty conference room. "The major will be right with you." "Right with you" ended up being forty-two minutes. If I hadn't been busy playing Tetris on an old Game Boy, I would have been angry.

"Captain." The major entered the room quickly. I damn near knocked myself out as I stood and saluted, dinging the Game Boy off my forehead. He didn't see any of it as he had his nose buried in a manilla folder. I gave God a slight nod for small favors and gently put the game down on the table. He did look over when he heard the handheld give a digitalized chime. Eastman raised his eyes to look upon the intrusion. With as much military bearing as I could muster, I reached out and shut the game down.

"Why are you wearing a duty belt?" he asked, finally looking over at me.

"Guard duty, sir," I told him.

"I would imagine, as a captain, you have heard of the concept of delegation, correct?"

"Leadership by example...and I'd rather be out walking around. After my umm scare, I very much like using my legs."

A hawk gazing upon a mouse would have received less scrutiny.

"Major Trellon is still in denial about your condition. He had me in his office and we went over some very graphic photographs of your injury. He had charts and diagrams and took pains to explain to me in layman's terms everything that was wrong with you."

"I would think he'd be more interested in patting himself

on the back for a job well done than trying to disprove something that is so obviously fact."

"Perhaps. But he was very demonstrative in his demonstration. He had even assembled a PowerPoint display of how you shouldn't be walking. Captain Talbot, without him actually coming out and saying it, he wants me to order you to report to the medical bay so he can do exploratory surgery and figure out what is going on inside of you."

"I don't like the sound of that. Is this why I'm here?"

"Consider this a warning. If I were you, I wouldn't go there unless you absolutely needed to. Follow me." We went back to his office. "Sit." He swept his hand toward a chair.

"Thank you," I told him. I let out a louder sigh than I'd meant to.

"I don't know how you were able to bounce back, and I'm not concerned with the why of it anyway. I am genuinely happy to have you back. As much of a pain in the ass as you are, I've never come across a Marine more likely to get a mission completed than yourself, an asset that would have been sorely missed."

"And here I thought you cared."

Eastman reached into his desk and pulled out a bottle of Scotch. If the bottle was any indication, it looked expensive, in the time when money mattered. He didn't ask whether I did or didn't as he grabbed two glasses and poured both of us a couple of fingers' worth and pushed the amber fluid toward me. I wanted to tell him I'd rather snort lines of dry Kool-Aid and chase it down with shots of hot sauce than drink the Scotch.

"Bottoms up." He raised his glass and held it there until I followed suit.

"I'm on duty, sir," I answered, hoping that would get me out of quaffing the poison.

He continued to hold the glass up. When the highest-ranking officer implies that's it's okay, then it is.

"Fuck, that's gross." I wiped my mouth as I put the empty glass down.

"That's thirty-five-year-old Scotch!" Eastman seemed genuinely surprised by my reaction.

"Oh, that's the problem; it's old. Probably would have been better if it were fresh. Do you have any beer or something I could wash that down with?"

"I could always use a new officer in charge of waste and disposal." Thankfully, he put the bottle back in the desk and closed the drawer; it would have been better if he locked it as well. "I notice that you don't have much trouble speaking your mind when you feel as if you or yours have been wronged, but when it comes to personal issues, you are as close-mouthed an individual as I have ever come across. I suppose a lot of that has to do with my being your superior, but not all. I talked to your therapist. Relax." Eastman placed a hand out, palm facing me when my mouth opened and I was about to protest. "He didn't say anything specific to your case. Even if HIPAA didn't exist, he is entirely too honor-bound to his patients to divulge information. I merely asked him if you spoke at all about any of your problems or if you merely sat there in silence for your mandatory hour."

"And?"

"And, like I thought, he said if I had any questions regarding your care, I should ask you."

"If you think one shot of that liquid fire is going to make me open up and spill my guts, followed by a whole bunch of 'I love you mans,' then you are sadly mistaken. I am no cheap date, sir."

"You are five months removed from a catastrophic injury which, by all accounts, should have put you in the ground or at the very minimum in a wheelchair for the rest of your life. I need to know, mentally and physically, where you are at, Captain, before I can allow you to rejoin your squad on missions."

"If I was a smart man, this would be where I would tell you that I'm in no shape to rejoin. That my back could give out at any moment and my mind is one bitter cup of coffee away from making me want to punch random people in the nose."

"How close to reality is that statement?" Eastman asked.

"If I substituted out 'stupid' for 'random,' it'd be spot on."

"So, business as usual?" he asked.

I shrugged.

"And your back?"

"Hurts so bad sometimes that, at the end of the day, I go back to my quarters and shove my face into a pillow and cry."

"And would any of this prevent you from leading a mission?"

"No," I told him, maybe a tad too quickly.

He eyed me speculatively. "I want to believe you; I need to believe you. I just don't know whether I do. I need to be convinced, and I'm not sure how to get there."

"Come watch us train, then make up your mind."

"Much like your family, Talbot, I don't think there isn't anything you wouldn't do to ensure the safety of your squad."

"Fair statement," I replied. "I'll go one further; I consider my squad my family. Even Kirby. Kirby's the dopey cousin that eats worms on a dare, even if he's the one that dared it."

"Is this your attempt to obfuscate my question?"

"My wife calls it deflection."

"She's had more practice than me," Eastman mused. "I will take you up on your offer. We'll talk next week."

"Can I ask you to give me an idea about this proposed mission?"

"You can."

"I, umm, feel like I just did, sir."

"Sure did. You're dismissed, Captain."

"Ah, fair play, I suppose." I stood, saluted, and saw myself out the door.

I was surprised to see my entire squad sitting in the waiting room outside the major's office.

"Corporal Gantry, please send in Top Tynes," Eastman said over the interoffice system.

"What gives?" BT asked as he got abreast of me.

"He's interviewing my replacement," I told him. "Good luck." I gave a nod to my squad before heading out. I didn't like it at all that he was interrogating them. It angered me for reasons I couldn't thoroughly explain. They were my family; he didn't have the right to pry into our inside jokes and, even though he did, fuck him. What specifically was he looking for and why?

I finished my patrol, stewing in my thoughts as I walked the entire perimeter of the ship. A giant squid could have been attempting to pull the bow into the depths of the ocean, and, in all likelihood, I would have blindly stepped around the tentacles. BT was waiting at the guard station when I turned my duty belt in.

"Want to go grab a beer?"

He asked the question in the same manner Eastman had offered the scotch, meaning, I had little chance to refuse. Although, all things considered, I'd take a beer over that other caustic toxin any day.

"What's on tap, Vern?" BT asked as we walked up to the makeshift brewery. Eastman wasn't overly keen on the beer bar, but he hadn't nixed it. The only caveats were that if you were on duty you couldn't drink, and he imposed a strict three beer maximum, which was fine because Vern, the proprietor of this fine establishment, was about as anti-establishment as they came.

He'd been a survivalist living off the grid for years when an unfortunate instance of timing had caused him to be in town when the z-poc hit. Before he could get back to his homestead and his considerable array of weaponry, he'd been rounded up and deposited into Etna station. He took every opportunity he could, and to whomever he could, to bitch about that very fact. He would say that Russia would be jealous of his stockpile, and not even their piece of junk nuclear weapons would be able to hurt his bunker with a direct strike. On a few occasions, I'd tried to pry the location of the place out of him, but he wouldn't budge. Kept saying I was a cog in the machine trying to grind him down. I can't say he was completely looney tunes, as we did agree on a bunch of things, and the crazy goat could brew a decent beer, which instantly made him one of my favorite humans. Except for today.

"IPA," Vern replied, pouring a glass before BT could tell him yay or nay.

"The bitter shit?" I asked. "Vern, I keep telling you, lagers, pilsners, ales, even a pale lager, but not that IPA shit."

"IPAs brew faster, and the way you people drink, I can barely keep up with the demand as it is. Have you ever had to tell a Marine there's no more beer? You guys are dicks when I tell you there's none left. Drink slower, and I'll make lagers."

"Hey! Hey!" I pointed my finger at him. "Don't get crazy, man! Drink slower. You might be dipping a little too often into your own well, buddy." I pointed a finger at him. "And give me a boot."

Vern looked around before reaching under the bar and grabbing a mug that looked suspiciously like a boot and was easily three times the size of the pint BT was drinking. As I said, Vern was anti-establishment and was always finding ways to skirt around the letter of the law.

"Give me a list of the materials you need to build another brewing barrel," I told him after I finished unscrewing my face from the bitterness of the beer. "Fuck, Vern, this shit is either over or undercooked, but it ain't right," I told him as I took another large draught.

"Yeah, they all say the same thing and still drink it and pay for it." Vern was smiling; I think he was very much into watching, or possibly even causing, the minor suffering of others.

"Do you think maybe we can talk now?" BT asked as he led me over to a small table in the corner of the cafeteria. On a ship this big and the amount of personnel that normally have staffed it, the place should have been busy at any time of the day, but for a few tables on the far side, we were alone.

"I'm listening. Gawd, this stuff is horrible." I stared at the beer, wondering how it could look so similar to my beloved beverage and be so awful.

"Eastman's no dummy. He knows something is up, and he's aware your tests have been tampered with."

"What did you tell him?"

"The truth, obviously. That Tommy is a centuries-old vampire, and he turned you into one as well."

"How'd that go?"

"Well, you're supposed to walk me down to my psych eval appointment."

"He can suspect all he wants; he can't prove anything."

"I'm not thinking you completely understand. We're in the military; he doesn't have to abide by the same laws he would if we were citizens. Shit, with the way the world is now, he doesn't have to follow any rules or regulations he doesn't want to. He could lock you up and have every test imaginable administered to you."

"He won't. Eastman is much too honor-bound."

"You might have a little more faith in him than I do. The replacement part, I thought you were kidding."

"I was."

"Eastman isn't. I'm up for the position, and you're not going to like this, but so is Hammer and Malton. He wants to promote me to lieutenant no matter who he ultimately chooses."

"Hammer? He's much too egotistical for the job."

"Have you met you?"

"But my ego is endearing."

"Says you," BT answered.

"And Malton? Can you imagine?" I stood up.

"Where are you going?"

"I'm going to Eastman's office to tell him he's an idiot. Or that I'm fine. Maybe both."

BT looked alarmed. "You can't do that! I'm not supposed to be saying anything to you. He recited some lines from the manual about the punishment I could receive."

"Why's he being such a hardass?"

"Have you met you?"

I gave a slight nod of my head sat down and pursed my lips as I picked my beer up. "Makes sense though. If I had a chance to get rid of a major irritation in my life, who knows what lengths I would go to do so. Funny, a part of me is beyond pissed, and another part is sighing in relief that I won't have to go out and do these insane missions anymore."

BT harrumphed in agreement, took a drink of his beer. He appeared to enjoy it much more than I did.

"Why do you think he's interviewing the rest of the squad? You think maybe he's contemplating putting Kirby in charge?" I asked.

"If that's the case, I'll wait until I receive my commission, then I'll resign. He shouldn't be in charge of a squad of GI Joes."

"That's funny. Vern!" I raised my empty boot up.

BT looked at his still half-full pint. "Jesus, Mike, no wonder he's always out."

It was a week later when Eastman showed up for a training session. We'd already been going at it for a couple of hours, and myself, like the rest of the squad, were bathed in sweat.

I'd just called for a fifteen-minute break. My back was on fire. Tommy had assured me the residual pain would fade, but I was having a hard time believing him at that moment. I sat slowly, finding the optimal way to get comfortable and not cause more discomfort.

"Captain," Eastman said as he came down the corridor. We'd been doing room clearing exercises, and I had to force myself to descend a few levels on the ship to get this done. "Don't stand." He had his hand up. "I saw how long it took you to sit."

Anger immediately bubbled to the surface; where the fuck had he been while I was running around like a ninja for the last two hours? He must have been a cop in another life. The sweat had to be proof of how hard I'd been working, but if he was genuinely looking for a way to push me out, then he'd never see my hard work.

"Top, can I talk to the captain alone?"

BT looked at me, and I nodded. The big man stood and headed over to another area.

"I've come to a decision."

"Okay," I replied. What I wanted to say was something like *good for you. I came to a decision as well, in fact, I come to a bunch of decisions every day, fuckwad.*

"I've talked to Second Lieutenant Malton, I am giving him the commission of first lieutenant; he will be taking over your squad effective immediately."

I stood quickly, hiding the wince to the best of my ability. I was going to murder Eastman, even pictured how I would get it done, grab his head in my arms, and instead of a quick snap to the side, breaking his neck, I was going to make a savage power move and rip it free from his body. Tommy and BT must have sensed something was off because they both had stood immediately and were drifting closer.

"Malton? Skinny guy, cheesy mustache, and extremely well-pressed uniforms?"

Eastman didn't say anything. The only reason I noticed Malton's uniforms was that you could cut a steak on the crease lines.

"Not that there's anything wrong with it, sir, but isn't he an intel boy wonder? Has he ever been out in the field?"

"We all have to do our part, and he is willing to step up and lead a squad." I noticed he never directly answered my question.

"No," I said flatly. "Go get him a box of Army men if he wants to play squad commander, pretty sure Kirby has some under his bunk."

"I don't think you have much say in this, Captain."

"No say? You're going to send a desk jockey out there with my crew. What's he going to do if he's in trouble? Give forms to the zombies to fill out in triplicate?"

"As I've told you before, Captain, it's *my* squad to do with as I see fit. You are not mission-ready, and I will not risk you or our squad because of it."

"Fuck you very much, sir." I turned and was heading back down the hallway.

"I haven't dismissed you, Captain."

"Dismiss this." I tossed him a bird over my shoulder.

"We'll go on strike!" Kirby announced. My entire squad was at the beer garden.

"Marines can't go on strike," BT told him.

"I'll quit then." Kirby smiled, thinking he'd found the answer.

"He'll throw you in jail if you try," Stenzel told him.

"This is horseshit, sir," Rose lamented.

"It's just Talbot, now," I reminded her. I'd gone back to Eastman's office after our meeting and had handed in my uniform. I think I told him he could choke on it, not sure, there were so many expletives it was challenging to get in a coherent sentence. Not from Eastman; he'd been quiet throughout the majority of my tirade. Though, he did finally call for an armed escort to get me out of his office; they didn't get there before I overturned his desk. My next stop had been to Malton's quarters. He was standing in his open doorway.

"I was wondering when you were going to show up here."

"Did you do this?" I had a finger so close to his face he could have bit it off at the knuckle without moving more than an inch.

"I realize you're pissed, Captain."

I didn't correct him. Much like I had with Eastman I was too busy debating killing the man. "I asked you a question," I growled.

"I did not do this. I did not get you injured, I did not undermine you. I did, however, seek to take over your squad —once it was realized how severe your injuries were. In fact, I actively lobbied to take this commission. Specifically told the Major that I thought it would be for the best if I took control of the unit, that no matter how unlikely your recovery, you could not possibly be in any shape to go out on a mission this soon after your grievous injuries. Your squad approaches near mythical status, and I could think of no higher honor than to be a part of that. I have been hoping, and training, for months to be your replacement. Your injuries only provided an honorable opportunity."

I didn't know what to do with that. I'd been working up my anger to the point where I was genuinely contemplating murder. I'd expected denial on the lieutenant's part; when someone flat out tells you yeah, they're actively trying to fuck you over, it's a shock. I don't know if I'd ever said more than a half dozen words to Malton, and to suddenly be faced with the knowledge that he'd been plotting ways to have me removed was a betrayal I couldn't fathom in my present state of fury. It's difficult to just let that type of frothy energy dissipate. I looked at my finger still hovering in his face and pulled it down. Especially since it hadn't been his fault. Dumbass kept piling it on, though. "If you ask me, Captain, Eastman has been looking for a reason and a way to have you removed. I get the feeling he doesn't like you much. The problem was he couldn't replace you with anyone you know or work with closely; any candidates in your immediate sphere are either too scared or too respectful of you or a combination of both. Fortunately, I don't have either of those problems."

"Figure this out all on your own?" I was not quite ready to simmer down. My blood had been boiling; it wouldn't cool to simmer for quite some time.

"I'm an intelligence officer with a lot of downtime, and I'm far from the first person approached for the position."

"Intelligence? Yeah, I don't think so. This might singularly be the dumbest thing you've ever done. And as far as my job goes, you could have said no."

"I could have."

"But…"

"But I didn't. Listen, Captain, what were the options? The major was planning on putting Lieutenant Oswald in charge."

"My socks are older than him." Oswald was a good kid, but he was jumpy. I didn't know his backstory, whether something had happened since the zombies came or he'd always been the nervous type. He was constantly glancing around expecting trouble, and any noise louder than a shoe squeaking on a floor sent him into a near panic. I was surprised that Eastman hadn't given him a psych discharge. It just showed how short on personnel we were.

"He's a skinny admin kid that has zero experience in the field. The most action he's seen is in his video games. I have two combat tours under my belt. Whatever you think of me, I'm your best chance of your personnel surviving whatever missions we're placed on. I haven't been sitting in my quarters celebrating his decision. I've been studying your people's strengths and weaknesses, figuring out the best ways to keep them safe while also being successful."

(I didn't know it then, and I had to use a contact in the admin department, Oswald, as a matter of fact, to discover that Malton's two combat tours, while technically correct, were not exactly useful experience. Malton had been assigned to the rear echelon.)

"Fuck." I rubbed my hand through my hair. He was right. If Eastman wasn't going to allow me to be with my squad, Malton was their best chance, no matter how I felt about it. Oswald couldn't fight his way out of a wet paper bag. But the way he looked at me, like a used car salesman that had somehow convinced me to buy the worthless extended warranty.... "This is horseshit."

"On that, we agree," he lied.

I wasn't sure how I was going to let this go. My brother, my best friend, a squad of people I considered family would be led by this cretin. How could I possibly sit here on the ship while they did God knows what and faced unimaginable enemies? "I uh…" I was at a loss. I did the only thing available and made a tactical withdrawal.

"Good talking to you, Captain."

I flipped him off and stormed a lap or two around the ship. I contemplated telling Eastman I wanted my commission back, that he could promote Malton to major and that I would be his subordinate and take his orders. At least that way, when things went pear-shaped, which they would, I could be there. I even went so far as to head to his office, until I saw the two, armed guards standing outside his office.

"You sure about this?" Sergeant Griffith asked as I came closer.

"No," I told him.

"We're supposed to arrest you on sight, sir," Griffith said, he'd put up a hand to halt my progress, his next move would be to place his hand on his holstered weapon. "I don't want to do that. I respect the hell out of you, sir, and what you've done, but I have my orders. I'm asking you not to make me enforce them."

I thought about telling him *as if he could*, but that would definitely be an escalation and would do little to improve my chances of getting my squad back. I stood there for long seconds, thinking about my next move. Tracy would have been proud as I debated my actions and the consequences that each would render. The corporal with him looked as if he wanted to be anywhere but where he was. I wasn't known for my cool, calm demeanor. Our collective attentions shifted when the door they were guarding opened. Eastman came through; he was holding a folder and reading from it, he looked up to see the détente in progress.

"I thought I was clear, Michael," he said evenly. "Sergeant Griffith, civilians have no reason to be in this part of the ship."

The sergeant snapped to attention. "Yes, sir."

"Are you going to remove him, or should I find someone who will?"

"Sir, it's Captain Talbot," he offered as if that explained everything, and to a degree, it did. It was like Michael Jordan had shown up for a pick-up game of basketball and was being told by the playground administrator he wasn't allowed to play.

"Not anymore. Mr. Talbot has resigned his commission and as such has no reason to be here. I do not like repeating my orders, Sergeant."

"Understood, sir. Captain, I mean, Mr. Talbot, I'm requesting that you remove yourself from the premises before I have to place you in the brig," Sergeant Griffith said, with visible difficulty.

Eastman pressed the issue. "No, Sergeant, the moment he walked down that hallway, he was in violation of my order."

Griffith's head bowed. "Sir, I'm going to have to ask you to come with me." He pointed down the hallway the way I'd come.

I let out a short laugh that came across more as a bark. "What are you scared of, Major? Do you figure I'm gunning for your job? What is it with people in power and doing all they can to hold on to it? How do you think this is going to look when it's found out you've placed me in jail for coming to see you? Arguably your most successful field officer?"

"I believe you think entirely too highly of yourself, Michael," Eastman responded.

The way he said my name and was looking down his nose at me, I felt like I was looking at a male reincarnation of Deneaux. It had me wondering if that were somehow possible. From what I understood, demons could possess a person, so why couldn't they jump from one to another. Then I saw the hesitation in the major. Had to admit, it was nice to have someone else have to think upon their actions. Going to the brig was going to absolutely suck, but no doubt about it, there was going to be pressure put upon him for it. Would it matter? I don't know. How important were the opinions of our population to him? It wasn't like he was an elected official that had to be concerned with his constituency. Major Eastman, in all reality, was a supreme dictator. I'm not saying he was an evil, megalomaniacal *dictator* in the typical negative historical connotation, but his word was law and was upheld without question; to do otherwise meant suffering the consequences. He answered to no one but his moral compass, and if that got skewed, who was going to be there to stop him?

"Let's go, Sergeant. I'm ready for a little R&R." I held up my arms in the traditional handcuff pose.

"I don't think that's necessary," the sergeant said, approaching.

"Leave now, Talbot, and we can forget that this entire incident ever took place," Eastman said.

"I wouldn't forget." I hadn't moved my arms.

"In honor of your long service, I was planning on allowing you and your family to stay within the military section of the ship; I can see now that it would be for the best if they were moved to the civilian portion."

It was a threat. It wasn't like the civilian area was the slums, actually pretty nice, but it was communal living; we would no longer have the privacy of individual quarters.

"That is, unless you were to go about your business now."

He was scared, about what I wasn't entirely sure. "Poor decision after poor decision." I shook my head. "You keep this shit up you're likely to have a mutiny on your hands."

Sergeant Griffith let out an audible gasp.

"Are you threatening me, Talbot?" Eastman was on the ragged edge of rage.

"Me? Certainly not. As I've said before, I have no desire to be in charge. And besides, I'll be in jail, remember?"

"Sergeant, take him away. I want a twenty-four-hour guard posted, and he is allowed no visitors."

"For how long?" he asked.

"For as fucking long as I say!" It was a shriek.

I sometimes amaze myself at how well I am at eliciting those reactions from others. His next move was going to be concocting a mission for my squad as soon as possible to get them off the ship. Would it be something inane where they were merely off-ship for a bit until things calmed down, or would he put them in the worst situation possible, hoping that events would take care of his problems? If it was the latter, he had brought more misery on himself than he could begin to imagine. Who's to say Deneaux hadn't been a perfectly happy spinster who attended church every Sunday and her knitting circle on Thursday nights punctuated with some local gossip and a couple of goblets of wine? Perhaps it was the insertion of me into her life that had changed her entire trajectory? One garbage can mishap too many. Who the fuck am I kidding? The only events that bitch attended were funerals for fun and ritual sacrifices at an altar, probably for more fun.

I cooled down some as I went toward the brig, as I realized I was going to be spending the foreseeable future in a ten-by-ten cell. Yeah, this was going to be fun. The only good to come out of it was I was supposed to go to BT's for dinner in a couple of nights. Had a pretty good excuse to get out of that social engagement.

"I'm sorry about this," Sergeant Griffith said as he opened the door to my new digs. I stood outside for a moment; I was contemplating making a run for it, he could probably see that. I didn't deal well with enclosed spaces, and with little to do in the way of distraction, I was very much going to be trapped in my mind as well. Not a great recipe for my mental health. I took a deep breath and stepped in, but just one step in.

"Can I get you anything, Captain Talbot?"

"I'm no longer—"

"—You'll always be a captain, sir."

"Sergeant Griffith, I've seen you around a few times, we've maybe nodded acknowledgment of each other's presence half those times, yet I feel as though you have a connection to me of which I am unaware."

"You saved my sister, sir. For that, I will always owe a debt of gratitude."

I couldn't place what he was talking about, but luckily, he continued.

"One of the first supply runs you did was for medical supplies."

That I remembered. The sheer number of zombies we'd had to deal with had made it a harrowing experience.

"Three teams before yours had tried that very same run. Each time they had cited overwhelming numbers of the enemy as to why they'd had to unsuccessfully withdraw. My sister is diabetic she needs an insulin injection every day or she will go into diabetic shock. The base stores were down to the last few days, and I was so worried, I was prepared to go out on my own. When you came back and had secured it, along with dozens of other much-needed medicines, I cried with relief. I thought I was going to have to bury my little sister; what was I going to tell her kids? I tried to get to you to express my thanks, but your group holed up for a bit, and then, well, the whole Deneaux thing went down, and I never got a chance. For that, I will always owe you a debt."

"Sergeant, I appreciate that, and it's a great story, but you don't owe me anything. My team and I did it for the betterment of everyone."

"I don't know why you would think that would temper how I feel. If you need *anything*," he stressed, "do not hesitate to ask."

I left it alone. I didn't want him to get in trouble, and when people tell me they'll get me *anything*, well, I'm human, my thoughts tend to run...fuck it, I'm not even writing it down. Just let it be known there's cream cheese, Thai hookers, a kangaroo, and bean bag chairs involved. It's a fucking glorious mess.

"Thank you, Griffith."

He got on his radio and got a private down here to start the first shift. Kind of jacked up when you're the first person to christen the brig. I'm sure it was used during the ship's regular floats, but as far as I knew, this was the inaugural opening post apoc.

"Would you like a book?" he asked once he'd finalized the plans for a rotation.

"Beer would be better," I told him. I was kidding, mostly. Sure it seemed like the perfect opportunity for a beer, but there are times that you can't expect one.

"I'll see what I can do." He left before I could give him a meager protest just as Private Wilson came bustling through the doorway. He gave the kid some instructions and then was gone.

"Hey, private," I called out. He was a skinny kid; I think his acne weighed more than he did. Something that desperately wanted to be called a mustache clung to his face. His uniform looked as if it were hung on a hangar. With a bit of string and a stiff breeze, I didn't see any reason he couldn't be flown like a kite.

"Can I help you, sir?" He didn't leave the desk, as he was working on adjusting his duty belt.

"Are you prepared to ensure my safety from the other prisoners?"

"Sir?" he asked, looking around at the empty holding cells.

"When I take my showers, I tend to drop my soap. I'm afraid of any unlawful entries. Know what I'm saying?"

"I'm sorry, sir, I don't." He was clearly confused.

"You know, Bubba time? Bum-rushing, up the river, kicking the bobo, probing the prison pocket, parking in the rear... that is the type of thing I'd like to avoid."

"I'll uh, make sure none of that happens, sir."

"Much appreciated. I have a delicate constitution, you know."

"Okay. Are you going to keep talking, sir?"

"Oh, without a doubt."

I felt somewhat bad for the kid; I rambled on for a solid hour. I tend to do that when I'm pissed or scared, of which I was both in varying degrees. Pissed about my situation and scared for my squad. I would have kept going, but Sergeant Griffith came back. "Wilson take fifteen," the sergeant told him. Wilson couldn't get out of there fast enough, looked like a high-strung chihuahua on a freshly waxed linoleum floor, running from a loud banging noise.

"Is this where you get rid of any witnesses and rough me up a little bit to show you're the top dog of this jail?"

"That's funny. I couldn't get any beer, but I scored you this." He handed over a flask. "If you get caught with that I'd appreciate it if you say you smuggled it in."

"Of course, boss, I'm no snitch."

"I don't think you've been in long enough, Captain, to start using prison lingo."

"Probably right."

"What are you planning on doing?" he asked.

I looked around my not so spacious accommodations. "Thinking I'll sleep some, take a piss eventually, start scratching out the days with my ragged fingernails."

"Are you planning on escaping?"

"What prison flicks have you watched, Sergeant? Pretty sure even if I was, I'm not supposed to tell you. Then even if I got out, where am I going to go? Safe bet the first place they check is my wife's quarters, where there's not even enough room to hide under the bed."

"I think what the major is doing is wrong."

"You're going to want to keep that to yourself," I told him. I unscrewed the top and took a sniff of the liquid inside. "Fuck, Griffith, this smells like gasoline." I took a sip. For something that smelled like it could strip paint, it went down relatively smooth.

"Homemade moonshine. Good, right?" He was smiling.

"Why is this not on the black market?"

"Small batches. I'm not trying to end up in the cell next to you."

"You'd better hope I don't end up in here for long, I'll kill your stash."

"The least I could do. I'll talk with you tomorrow, Captain."

Wilson came back in as Griffith headed out. The kid was relieved when I went and sat on my cot. I had a date with a flask I wasn't planning on being late for. I drank half, submerging any errant thoughts as they crept forward in a stalking manner, ready to pounce. Then I kept drinking, in an effort to drown the bastards once and for all. Didn't work. It never works. But the booze, faithfully, has the benefit of dropping me into a restless, fitful sleep. I didn't have the foggiest clue as to how long I slept, but I felt like warmed-over badger shit. From my understanding, they have among some of the smelliest fecal matter out there.

"Having fun?" BT asked.

I sat up in my cot and pinched the bridge of my nose.

"I raided bars that smelled less like alcohol than this." BT's nose wrinkled. "Did you piss yourself?"

"Shit, I don't think so, but if you could stop screaming at me, I would greatly appreciate it. What are you doing here? I was under the assumption I couldn't have visitors. Is Eastman letting me go?" I went to stand, swayed for a good three seconds before deciding I liked sitting better.

"The squad is being deployed tomorrow."

I stood so fast it took vertigo a good half-minute to catch up. "What?"

"We're circling England again. We're looking for a plant."

"*What?*" I understood each individual word, but, taken as one missive, I hadn't made any meaningful connections. "The major is going to risk lives for what? A shrubbery? I figured he'd want you all out of the way for a while, but this seems like a stretch."

"The scientists need some plant that's native to the region to finalize the vaccine."

"A vaccine to fix a vaccine. Nothing to see here, move along." Safe to say, anger was building up inside of me, and making my head throb. "BT, if Malton does some stupid shit or puts any of you at unnecessary risk…"

"Are you hinting at fragging him?"

"Oh, there's no hinting at all. No beating around the bush, no incognito winking, no code words, no reading between the lines. If he needs to go then he needs to go."

"He seems like a decent enough guy."

"It's not him necessarily I don't trust."

"Eastman? For what reason?"

"I don't know, but doesn't this seem a little extreme?" I flourished my hands to the interior of my cell.

"For you? Knowing your penchant for colorful rhetoric and thinly veiled threats, I think he probably went easy on you. Don't worry too much about us. The briefing said this thing is native to the coast. We hit the beach, hike out a mile, grab what we need and head back. Shouldn't be out more than a couple of hours."

"You believe that's what commanders send their entire A-Team out to do? Pick flowers on the beach?"

"Look, I'm packing out enough ammunition that there are weight concerns within our landing craft, and I gave Rose free reign. Make you feel better?"

I grabbed the bars and let my head hang low. "I shouldn't be in here."

"We both know you probably should be, but for the reason you are? Probably not. Don't do anything stupid, Mike, and make your incarceration justifiable. We'll be back before you know it. Okay?"

"I'm not going to promise to do nothing."

"I know. I'll come here straight away when we get back."

"Be safe," I told him.

He gave a slight nod. He had misgivings as well but said nothing. Our unit had suffered last time out, and every member was still feeling the effects from the loss of Winters. Morale was not quite where it needed to be. Sending them out so soon, on a mission with a different commander, showed bafflingly poor judgement, especially since we weren't even up in the rotation. My squad shouldn't be punished for any transgression the major felt I'd committed. BT rapped his fist on the bars, lightly pursed his lips, and headed out.

Not long after, Sergeant Griffith came in and opened my cell. "Going to need you back in two hours."

"Huh?" I asked.

"I don't have the personnel to watch you all the time.

You've got two hours. Go home, please take a shower, eat some food, then report back here."

"The major sanctioned this? I don't want to be out on deck and get shot for attempting to escape."

"I shared my concerns earlier today; you can imagine he wasn't too pleased. I need your assurance you won't try to contact him or try to escape—or cause any other trouble."

"My assurance?"

Griffith nodded.

"I'm not entirely sure I can do that."

"I already told your wife to expect you home within the next..." he looked at his watch, "three minutes ago, shit. you're already late. Sorry about that, there were tacos at the chow hall, I ate more than I should have. I suggest you get home, sir. Mrs. Talbot didn't seem like the type of woman to be trifled with."

"You have no idea."

"See you back here at fifteen hundred or thereabouts." He stepped aside and let me through.

TRACY GAVE me a hug when I walked through the door. "Take a shower. I'm making some food."

I showered, ate, we talked for a bit then I headed back to jail. The whole thing seemed unreal and surreal, not sure if they're the same thing, I've seen real things that were surreal. Like BT, my wife had advised against me doing something stupid.

"Shit." Griffith let his feet slip off the desk. "Didn't expect you to come back."

"You didn't seem overly worried when I left."

"Brought you some more hooch." He held out the flask.

My stomach roiled in protest, the back of my throat

preemptively coated itself in spittle-based lubricant, and my ego begged my id not to take it. Did it anyway. So much for not doing something stupid. I sat down at the desk opposite the sergeant before taking the lid off and taking the first of many sips that night. The sergeant and I talked for a while, played a few games of backgammon and checkers before I announced in some slurred speech that I needed to go nightie night. I think I told the sergeant he could tuck me in if he wanted to, I'm truly hoping that part didn't happen. Good chance he might not remember it anyway, as he was in his chair, feet back up on the desk, head lolled back and snoring lightly. I closed my cell door behind me. As far as jail went, this wasn't the worst one I'd ever been in. When I awoke, I knew without a shadow of a doubt I'd not slept enough and that it was five a.m., the time BT told me they would be heading out on this run. I was still drunk as a skunk, for whatever the hell that meant. I'd never once seen a drunk skunk. As far as I knew, they didn't even drink, abstaining little stinkers. It's the fucking monkeys you gotta watch. Sergeant Griffith was still asleep, although he had moved to the floor, and my cell was still unlocked. I could make a run for it, join my team on this mission.... And then what? Was this all a setup? Was Griffith pretending to be asleep? I sat up, my head and stomach in some strange synchronized, sickening swim. If I did somehow manage to get to the launch and insert myself onto the team, there was no next move. Eastman would know, and either I'd spend the rest of my time on float in jail, or I'd be given the option to disembark. Probably nowhere good, either. My guess is China, where even the zombies would have adopted some form of communism. There'd be huge lines at the morgue as they waited for their brain loaves.

I had the lives of two families I had to weigh here. Yes, my immediate family and I had been through some unimaginable horrors and come through, though not completely unscathed. The psychological horrors would be something we all carried through the remainder of our years. My squad were highly trained Marines with an abundance of weaponry at their disposal. I would have to trust that Malton brought them all home. That was about as easy as telling a helicopter mom that she couldn't smack the shit out of the playground bully who was using her son as a step stool. I stewed for a bit, waited until it was guaranteed they were gone. I thought about waking Griffith up; my stomach demanded something besides alcohol and bile. I decided to let him sleep because if he felt anything like I did, he was much better off snoozing. I let myself out and headed to the chow hall to grab a couple of trays of food. When I returned, Griffith was at the edge of panic, up at his desk, phone in hand.

"Never mind." He hung up quickly.

"Got you what's passing for food these days."

He didn't say anything, just started shoveling the powdered eggs and bacon substitute into his pie hole. "What?" he asked, his mouth full. "The only chance of salvaging the day after that rotgut is to coat, absorb, then evacuate it as quickly as possible. If you catch my meaning."

"It wasn't that difficult a concept," I answered as I began to eat as well.

He sat back when he was done. "I thought you might have taken off."

"Thought about it." I'd never before eaten toast that had substituted out dirt for flour, not something I'd recommend, and still, I finished it.

"What stopped you?"

"Your life."

"Sorry?" He was clearly confused.

"If I'd left, you'd have to drink your swill by yourself, and the likelihood you could survive another week of it would be...unlikely."

"Right now, I think you're right. I wish I'd taken up a different hobby, maybe knitting."

I walked back to my cell. "I had no idea when I came here the cruel and unusual punishment I was going to receive. I'm going back to sleep. If you hear anything, Sergeant..."

"Of course, Captain."

I lay down on my cot, made several horizontal revolutions around the room, and then was asleep.

19

MALTON

"Everyone ready to go, Top?" Lieutenant Malton asked, looking over his map.

"They are, LT."

Malton stopped what he was doing. "It's Lieutenant Malton or sir, Tynes. I won't tolerate any other way of being addressed. We're Marines, understood?"

"Understood," BT paused. "Sir."

He held his eye longer before saying, "Good. All geared up?"

BT knew Mike would have a field day with that question. However, he answered with a yes and an again delayed sir.

"Are we going to have a problem, Top?"

"No problem, sir, and I would prefer to be called by my rank as well."

"Very well, Sergeant Major."

"Been a while since you've seen so many stripes on a uniform, sir? There's an eagle, globe, and anchor housed within. That makes me a Sergeant Major of the Marines Corps."

"If I have to use that title every time I need something, we are going to lose precious seconds."

"I will not answer to anything else."

"I would hate to start this day off placing you in the brig for insubordination."

"When we get out on that beach, sir, who do you think these people are going to follow into battle? We are all very protective of our own and will dispatch of *any* threat to our continued existence."

"That sounded almost like a threat, Marine."

"A threat? Heavens no, sir. It's just that, in the heat of battle, who's to say what happens out there? But I'm sure you'll be fine." BT slammed a heavy hand down upon the lieutenant's shoulder. "Kirby, you shamming shit, your leg is fine. Pick up that pack, and let's go!" BT bellowed.

Malton was pissed. He hadn't had a dressing down in ages and never from someone that was supposed to be a subordinate. He was glowering at the large man when his visage shifted; he saw that Sergeants Stenzel and Rose were watching him. As scary as the Top was, those two might be the deadliest of the bunch; they'd never follow him if he didn't stand up to his Top now, but it wasn't in him to fight for command. Not up front, anyway. "Off to a great start," Malton muttered as he moved to watch the launch boats get loaded.

"All ready to go, LT," Private Reed said as he loaded the last of it.

Malton looked over to BT, who could only shrug as if to say he'd not said anything. Malton decided on the spot this wasn't a fight worth fighting and let it go. The boats were pushed out the carrier's side, and the sailors assigned to them began to row.

"Mush!" Kirby ribbed them until he saw his Top looking over at him. He didn't even wait for BT to say anything as he grabbed an oar.

"My wife's attempts at banana bread are less dense than you, Kirby, and I've used those as mallets."

"It's okay, that's part of the reason I love you," Rose told him. One of the sailors snickered at her. "Perkins, I know where you bunk. I'd hate to see your underwear explode. Wouldn't take much of a charge, considering what I'm attempting to blow up, although, I'm sure you'd be devastated with the loss, no matter how small."

Perkins gulped, his face blanched. Rose was not to be trifled with, ever.

"That's what I'm talking about." Kirby stuck out his tongue and let go of his oar long enough to make a set of devil's horns.

"Rose, there will be no undergarment explosions, no matter how miniscule."

"Aye, Top." She smiled.

"Stow the banter, we're on a mission," Malton said.

"We're a mile from shore, and this is our pre-mission ritual," BT told him.

"Not during my missions or in my squad," he clarified.

"Your squad?" Stenzel asked.

"My squad. You have a problem with that, Sergeant?"

"As a matter of fact, sir." That last word dripped with enough derision it could have been a swear. "I do. I don't remember seeing your face anywhere near our drills, training, or PT sessions since we've been on board. If you've been busy catching up on your beauty sleep, you might want to think about a new regimen."

"I need all of you to acknowledge and remember that I am now in command of this unit. I wasn't secretly out to remove Captain Talbot. He was seriously injured during combat to the point where command has deemed he is no longer fit for duty. Major Eastman asked me to take control of this squad."

"You could have refused," Stenzel pressed.

"I could have, and then what? Someone less qualified takes my place? You could have done far worse than me. Whatever you think of me, I do have combat experience, and

I'm very good at what I do. It is my goal to have a successful mission and bring all of you back safely."

"I find it telling, Lieutenant, the order you stated your goals. Captain Talbot has always been personnel first," Stenzel told him.

"Then he was wrong. There are times when the sacrifice of the few is needed in order to ensure that the needs of the many are met. Is my stance clear enough?"

"Crystal, sir." Stenzel checked over her rifle and cleaned the lens of her scope. Lieutenant Malton took that as a sign that she understood and was no longer willing to verbally spar with him. BT saw it entirely differently. Stenzel was an absolute beast with the weapon; he would talk to her privately when they reached shore, make sure she wasn't planning anything truly inconvenient. He couldn't even begin to imagine the questions he would have to answer if they came back without Malton.

The ritualistic dispelling of pre-mission anxiety had been quelled, and a pall settled over the group. No one talked or laughed, and even Rose, who would generally dote over her boyfriend, was dour. BT could not remember seeing so many scowls. This was not the optimal way to head into battle, but he was unsure how to turn it around. That was Talbot's territory through and through.

Malton had them repeat the mission plan incessantly, which only further solidified the discord. The unit was unconventional in a lot of ways, and their look of unprofessionalism was one. But that's all it was, a look. He'd never been part of a group more focused, ready, willing, and able to complete anything thrown their way, and a large part of that was preparation. They knew the mission inside and out, and this mindless parroting of Malton's was not helping anyone.

"I think they've got it," BT said as they were getting ready to go into round five.

"They've got it when I say they've got it."

266

"Yeah, we're done here. Perkins turn this rig around."

"Umm, excuse me?" Perkins asked.

"I'm not going anywhere with this dipshit leading, and I'm not letting him take my people anywhere either."

Malton pulled out his sidearm and leveled it on BT's face. BT didn't think he'd ever seen his personnel react so quickly. Stenzel, Rose, and Kirby all had their rifles trained on the lieutenant.

"Put it away," BT said calmly.

"This is a fucking mutiny," Malton spat.

"You call it what you will, I'll not allow you to risk the lives of my people to appease your ego."

"We get back on that ship, you'll face a Court-martial and a potential firing squad."

"I'll take my chances. I figure I have better odds there than with you in the field."

"I don't know what to do," Perkins said as the boat was bobbing in the ocean, drifting slowly with the current.

"What's going on?" Walde asked. "We can see a lot of firearms."

"The Top has decided he will not go on this mission, and I am charging him with dereliction of duty," the lieutenant informed her.

"Top?" Walde asked.

"I am not giving you permission to talk to him, Staff Sergeant!" he fairly screeched.

"I didn't ask for your permission," she replied coolly.

"This is Major Eastman. Apparently something is happening out there. I would like an update as to why you have halted the mission."

"The lieutenant has lost control of his squad, and I have lost confidence in his ability to lead this mission competently," BT replied. "And I will not allow his inability to lead to jeopardize the safety of the squad."

"That's a serious accusation, Top. Are you sure this has

nothing to do with the status of your previous commander?" Eastman asked.

"I think you already know the answer to that question, Major," BT told him.

"Fine, we'll do this your way. Lieutenant, continue on. Top, you will stay with the return boat where you will be remanded to a cell next to your previous commander."

"Sir, this is Sergeant Stenzel. I think I speak for the entire squad, here...none of us will be stepping out on that beach with him."

"Is this true? I need to hear it from every member of the squad and remember—this will be used as evidence at each of your tribunals."

"Fuck your tribunal, oh yeah, this is Sergeant Talbot, sir."

Eleven dissenting voices later, Eastman ordered the Navy to turn the two landing craft back to the carrier.

Rose shut down her comms. "Top, I have enough explosives. I could take that ship down."

"You mean...? What? No, Rose. Do not blow up the aircraft carrier," BT exclaimed. He noticed that she hadn't paid much attention to his words and appeared to be studying the great ship for weaknesses she could exploit.

Stenzel had her rifle up and was looking through her scope. "Looks like the major has rolled out the welcome mat, Top."

"What do you have?" he asked, looking over.

"A dozen armed personnel and a hastily put together machinegun nest."

"That seems a bit excessive," he replied.

"And this is somehow better than me leading a mission?" Malton sneered.

"Yup," Kirby answered.

"The major looks pissed." Stenzel quickly opted to stop using her rifle scope. She didn't want it to be interpreted as an act of aggression and have the armed guards open fire. Perkins offered up a pair of binoculars.

"Oh, I'm sure he doesn't just look pissed." BT was concerned about his group. Where he led, they would follow; he could only hope he'd not led them into a mess they couldn't get out of.

Malton was the first to exit the craft once they'd been hauled back up onto the landing area. "I want all of them arrested!" his voice cracked. "Even the Navy personnel!"

"They had nothing to do with this." BT stepped out of the boat. He noticed that three of the guards pointing rifles at him had taken a step backward. He thought if he shouted *boo* that they might go running into the bowels of the ship.

"Weapons on the floor," Eastman said as the entire squad stepped onto the deck.

BT did not hesitate; he was not going to get into a firefight with their own.

"You sure?" Kirby asked.

"Put it down," BT told him.

"Sergeant Major, do I need all of you in handcuffs, or will you go willingly?" Eastman appeared disappointed in the day's outcome.

"We don't need the cuffs, but a muzzle on Kirby might be warranted." BT shouldered past the guards and began walking toward the brig.

20

MIKE JOURNAL ENTRY 9

"Is it my birthday?" I asked as I saw BT walk in, followed by the rest of my squad. Then I saw the rifles. "What the hell did you guys do?"

"We didn't want you to have all the fun, sir." Stenzel was smiling.

"Malton was power tripping before we could make it to shore. I thought I'd be able to reel him in, but he was pretty high on himself. You know the kind that's more into awards, accolades, and ribbons and screw the consequences. I was not going to allow him to trade lives for medals," BT said as Griffith led him into my cell.

"Sorry, we're above capacity, going to have to double up," the sergeant said.

"Why do I get the largest man in mine? I feel like a cat in a milk bottle. All smushed up to the side."

"Oh, I've seen those pictures. Funny," Griffith said, still placing BT in my cell.

"Sergeant do not put Sergeant Rose and Lance Corporal Kirby in the same cell. None of us want to be kept up all night from the sounds that will be made at all hours," BT said.

"Good call, didn't even think of that," I told him. "And

don't put Tommy next to us, most of the Pop-Tarts he eats make me want to gag."

BT fist-bumped me.

"Any other accommodations I should be made aware of?" Griffith asked.

"That should be it for now. And Sergeant, I like to eat my dinner at seventeen hundred sharp, don't be late." BT sat on the cot.

"Hey, that's mine," I told him.

"Was," he said before lying down.

"No shortage of cots on an aircraft carrier; I'll have more brought down," Griffith said.

True to his word, we were all settled-in less than a half-hour later. Rose let me know she had a small brick of C-4 and could take a door off lickety-split; I told her in no uncertain terms absolutely not. Had a feeling at some point while I was asleep I would be awakened to an explosion. An hour later, a grim Griffith came to visit me.

"The major wants to see you." He opened up my cell. "And he wants me to put these on you." He held up a pair of handcuffs. "I'm sorry about this," he said as he ratcheted them on.

"Don't be, this is his way of showing who's in charge."

Griffith knocked on the door.

"Enter," Eastman said. It was easy to hear how miffed he was.

Griffith opened the door, and I walked through. I suppose I shouldn't have been surprised to see a red-faced Malton sitting there.

"I'd salute, but." I raised my hands.

"What the good goddamned fuck, Talbot!" Eastman shouted as he stood. Griffith had barely got the door closed before the tirade started. I feel like it went on for a solid five minutes; I'd tuned out a good long while ago. I don't know if you'd call it a self-defense mechanism, but I'd completely stopped listening, didn't hear a word. This was a skill I'd honed with my mother. Was she a tad overly severe in her doling out of words? Yeah, most likely, but more to the point, I was a curious teen with a penchant for trouble. On those occasions when I was caught and brought to the mat, she would rail on me for close to an hour. Not hard for a kid with ADD to lose focus relatively quickly. Sure, the first couple of minutes would be terrifying, but after that, her yelling would become a sort of annoying background droning as I would replay the hijinks that had got me there in the first place. Eventually, I got to the point that I could shut down after the opening line, just like now. It was an invaluable tool, though it was a work in progress, still needed practice recognizing the cues for when to come back into focus.

"Well? What do you have to say for yourself?!"

I got the impression this wasn't the first time he'd asked the question.

"Mind if I sit?" I asked, stalling for time.

"NO!" He made that clear enough.

"I'd say that I've been treated fairly within the correctional facilities aboard this ship."

"Why you insubordinate piece of sh—"

"Lieutenant!" Eastman turned to Malton.

"Yeah, you don't want him being this pissed at you. Why don't you be a good lieutenant and get me a cup of coffee. My cell was a little cooler than normal, and I didn't get a great night's sleep."

Malton stood and got in my face. The man was shaking with rage and, I'd imagine, the desire to smash me in the face.

"Go for it," I whispered. "If you think these cuffs would in any way prevent me from giving you a thorough ass-whooping, you're sadly mistaken." Got to admit he surprised the living shit out of me when he launched the haymaker. I saw the thing coming for days and easily ducked under, but still, that he'd thrown it all told me all I needed to know. When I came back up, I made sure to bring my forehead into his nose. Blood sprayed out in a concentric circle. He flopped back down into his chair, covering his broken and bleeding proboscis.

"Captain!" Eastman shouted, forgetting that I was no longer part of his army.

"Just defending myself, he swung on a handcuffed person. What kind of asshole does that?" I placed my foot against the side of Malton's chair and pushed it to the wall. "Do that again, and the next thing I break will take a lot longer to heal."

Sergeant Griffith, get in here!" Eastman shouted.

Apparently the sergeant had never moved away, as the door opened immediately. He'd heard everything, but seeing everything was different. Eastman's face was redder than a candied apple. Malton was bleeding profusely, blood sloshing through his hands and pooling in his lap, and I was standing there, trying to look as if I'd been minding my own business all along. I figured this was where Eastman ordered Griffith to begin batoning the back of my head until such time as I welcomed the floor up close and personal. Yes, I realize I made a noun into a verb. Did you understand what I meant? You're welcome. The sergeant was reaching for me; there was no reason to think I wasn't being hauled back to jail.

"Please take the lieutenant to medical." Eastman sat with a sigh, like a balloon that had been rapidly depleted of air.

"Um yeah, yes, sir." Griffith switched gears. "Would you like me to get another guard up here first, sir?"

"Are you planning on attacking me, Mr. Talbot?" Eastman asked.

"Planning on it? Not at all, but clearly the first question should be are you planning on attacking me?"

"We'll be fine here, Sergeant." Eastman watched as Griffith led the injured lieutenant away. "What the fuck is wrong with you?"

"I'm sure you've got a file on me that rivals *War and Peace*, you tell me," I said.

"Your entire squad has mutinied. They are facing extreme punishment."

"I will lead an open rebellion if you attempt to harm them in any way." I sat without prompting. It was no idle threat. In all likelihood, Eastman had the numbers, but the battle would be bloody, and by the time it was quelled, the damage would be done and most likely irrevocable.

"Options?"

"You could drop us off at a port of our choosing. You save face by kicking us all off, including family members. I'm not a huge fan because, once again, we're in the thick of it. As much as I hate being on a ship, the safety it affords my family is something well worth my discomfort. And it doesn't work for you, because you only have four squads available for onshore missions, and everyone knows we are leagues above the other three. Our success rate is unparalleled. I guess you haven't noticed, but two of your squads aren't even trying anymore. They camp out for a couple of days close to where they're dropped off then they radio in with some bullshit emergency and request immediate extraction. They do that because they know you'll just send us in; why should they risk themselves? This is happening because you're actively turning a blind eye. You don't care that it's always my squad that has to go in and clean up the messes."

Eastman was seething, though I couldn't tell if it was because I'd called him out or that two of his squads were run by incompetent officers. "What's my second option?"

"I get my commission and command back, and you find new officers to lead your two useless squads. Hell, give one to that asshat Malton."

"And how does that instill confidence in my ability to command? If my personnel see that my people can do whatever they wish and get away with it, we move one step closer to anarchy."

"How do you think this looks already? You took a command away from arguably your most successful team after we lost an irreplaceable member on a fucked up mission, which we completed, by the way. Then you slammed me in jail because I dared to question you about it."

"I'll have to...I've got to think about this. You can escort yourself back to jail."

"Don't take too long, Major. If I get enough time to dwell on it, I just might choose to take my ball and my players and go home." I left.

"Wasn't sure when you'd be home. Just like you to wander back in without telling anyone. Had I known, I could have prepared dinner," BT said as the guard on duty let me in.

I rubbed my wrists once the cuffs were off. "Sorry, you know how work is. I never know when they're going to let me loose."

"Is that blood?" BT was examining my face and shirt.

"Malton's."

"Jesus, you cannot play nice for even a day. What happened?"

"Jackass took a swing at me so I head-butted him. Laid his nose flat against his face. He's going to have a tough time getting modeling gigs, unless he has a good plastic surgeon do some work."

"Malton took a swing? I wouldn't have thought he had it in him."

"To be fair, I did goad him a bit, and I have to figure he thought he had a huge advantage with my hands cuffed."

"So now what?"

"Three possibilities. Eastman sends some goons in the middle of the night and they force us overboard, or, second, he pulls up to the nearest country, gives us a crate of

Ramen, and tells us to fuck off; or, three, we're back in business."

"And the odds?"

"I figure it's fifty-fifty between goons and missions."

"And the Ramen?"

"Pipe dream. He's either going to want to end his misery or extend ours. Probably thinks we'd be on perpetual shore leave if he dropped us off, and then they'd be short on Ramen."

"Can't have that," BT answered sarcastically.

"Exactly. Now if you'll excuse me, I stayed awake nearly an extra half hour with worry about you and the team; I'm exhausted. Gonna catch up on a little shut-eye."

"A whole half hour?"

"It was brutal."

21

MIKE JOURNAL ENTRY 10

I HADN'T BEEN EXPECTING to sleep and definitely didn't expect the weird dreams I had, either. Something about a big-horned ram trying to kill me. Not sure what that was supposed to signify. Even within the confines of the dream, I was trying to figure out what he had against me. Who knows, maybe the thing was supposed to represent Eastman. No matter how hard the thing attempted to slam into me, it always felt like a push from an impatient three-year-old ready to leave the housewares section of the department store and get to the toys.

"Captain Talbot." I awoke to Sergeant Griffith tapping my shoulder.

"This better revolve around dinner," I told him.

"You and your team are free to go." Griffith was beaming.

"You're only that happy because it gets you off guard duty," I told him.

"Have you seen my wife? Of course I want to spend more time at home."

I clapped him on the shoulder. "Thank you, Sergeant."

"The cells are open; your squad is asleep." With that, he

turned and headed to the stairs that led up and out of the holding area.

I roused BT. "Time to go. Eastman has instituted capital punishment."

"Huh?" BT asked, rubbing his eyes.

"He's sending you home where you'll be exposed to my sister's cooking. Man, I had no idea he had it in for you so bad."

"Screw you, Mike, she's getting better. I had a piece of toast just the other day that could be salvaged after only a minimum of scraping. Although, the apple butter jelly she gave me tasted suspiciously like cold medicine."

"Let's get the rest of the squad and get out of here."

"Where are the guards?" BT had a hand on my shoulder.

"Griffith let me out then took off."

"What time is it?"

"Why?"

BT stepped out and looked at the wall clock above the duty station desk.

"It's three in the morning. Doesn't that seem like a weird time to release prisoners?"

"It didn't, but it does now."

"What if this is a setup? An escaping prisoner scenario. We leave the jail only to be faced with a platoon of armed personnel?"

"I hate your paranoia. Reminds me of my own. Where's Kirby? We'll send him out first," I suggested.

I spent a few seconds debating how I wanted to proceed when the door above the stairs opened, and Eastman strode through.

"I trust everyone got some sleep?" he asked like he was the concierge at a fancy hotel. "Not that I care all that much. Your actions have delayed an important mission, one which is about to recommence now."

Lieutenant Malton came through the door with a look of smug satisfaction on his face.

"Not this again," BT hissed.

"I've rethought my strategy," Eastman was looking at me when he said this. Both were wearing sidearms, and myself and my squad were conspicuously without. They had the high ground and weapons; I didn't get the sense this was going sideways, but it is wise to not be lulled into feeling safe.

I moved to the forefront. If bullets started flying, I would be the first to catch some. Out of the corner of my eye, I could see Tommy moving into a position where he could inflict some damage, should it come to that.

"I'm listening," I told him.

"It's obvious your squad won't act without you leading. I may have acted hastily by removing you from your command."

"Umm, okay." I wasn't expecting that, not many officers were willing to admit when they'd made a mistake, but there was still a chance this was all a ruse. He confesses and then gets rid of all the witnesses was not above human actions. As a species, we are a deceitful lot.

"And as you pointed out, your squad is highly successful at what they do. I thought incorrectly that parts would be inter-changeable, like they are in almost all military units. But again, as you pointed out, your squad is family, and you can't change out a patriarchal figure and expect everything to be the same."

I wished he would just get on with it. I felt like I was being buttered up for a good old metaphorical fucking, and he didn't disappoint.

"That is why I've decided to leave you in place while also adding to your unit. After the regrettable loss of your medic, I'm offering a replacement for a new assignment."

It dawned on me what was going on. Malton wore a stupid grin under his swollen blackeyes. He looked like a kid who had ratted out his older sibling and was watching a measure of justice being served, although it wasn't quite up to the punishment he felt was warranted. Happiness mixed with some disappointment.

"No way," I told him before he could finish.

"You and the rest could finish off the duration of this float in those cells, if that would be better," Eastman said.

I looked back to my cell. I loved BT; didn't mean I wanted to spend a significant amount of my life crammed in a box with him. "He's still a lieutenant?"

"He is."

"I'm still a captain?" I asked.

"You are."

"Wait, so does this mean mustache is coming with us?" Kirby asked.

"Oh sweetie, it's Lieutenant Mustache," Rose told him.

"Seriously?" I turned to them. "Busted nose with tape across his face, and it's the pencil-thin mustache that gets the nickname?" I asked.

Kirby shrugged. "The nose will heal."

"Yeah, and he can shave, too," I added.

Malton had streaks of red rising up his neck and splashing on the sides of his face. Eastman laid a hand across his chest in an effort to quell what was most assuredly going to be an outburst.

"He's unproven in battle. I don't like not knowing the limitations of my people," I said.

"How is he possibly going to get experience if not out in the field?" Eastman asked. "And who better to train him?"

"Oooh, flattery. I'm getting all flush with excitement. If we weren't in this particular predicament, I'd have no problem explicitly telling you how I feel."

"This isn't explicit?" Eastman asked.

"Fairly tame," BT responded, and a bunch of my squad

nodded in agreement. I wasn't entirely sure how I felt about that.

"You should have seen what he did when my mother grounded him from going to a party; it was stupefying."

"Gary."

"Yup, sorry."

"It's settled then. Your gear and your transportation are waiting." With that, Eastman turned and left. Malton didn't look at all comfortable as dad left and he became the focal point.

"Let's go." I went up the stairs and brushed past the lieutenant; the rest of my squad followed.

"It gets better." Dallas offered him words of encouragement. "I was the outsider once as well." She told me afterward that the look he gave her resembled that of someone that had just taken a bite from a lemon.

I had to give Eastman props where they were due. My wife and kids were waiting for me by the boats.

"Back in uniform, I see?" Tracy said. She was worried and relieved at the same time. I realized just how much of a pain in the ass it was being human; oftentimes there were directly opposed, competing feelings. We had to be the only creatures that walked the planet that could somehow be happy and sad at the same time.

"No Henry?" I asked after I'd hugged and kissed each of them in turn.

"If I got him up, Ben Ben would have heard." Tracy smiled.

I loved the little dog, but I wasn't sure I was up for his unbridled enthusiasm, not at this ungodly hour.

"Do you know when you'll be back?" she asked.

I couldn't answer that because I wasn't even aware of what the mission entailed. "BT?" He was busy engulfing my sister.

"Little busy over here."

"Fuck...Malton?"

"Yes...sir." It took him longer than it should have for that to come out.

"How long will we be away?"

"Mission parameters say ten days."

I sighed, not because he hadn't shown his respect, but because that was two hundred and forty hours I would be away. I plucked a sleeping Wesley from my daughter's arms and gave him a light kiss on his button nose before handing him back.

"Be back soon, love," I told Tracy as I kissed her.

"I know," she told me.

22

MIKE JOURNAL ENTRY 11

"Captain, are you aware your corporal is using his rifle as a fishing pole?" Malton asked.

I looked over his shoulder. "What are you using as bait?"

"Beef Stroganoff noodles," Kirby responded.

"And?" I asked the lieutenant. "Maybe now's a good time to break out Eastman's orders and tell me what we're doing here, wherever here is."

"You don't know where here is?" Malton raised his eyebrows.

"All I see is a shit ton of saltwater and some land over yonder."

"Did you just say yonder?" BT had been kicked back with his hat over his face, getting some sleep.

"It's sailor-speak," I told him.

"It's a wonder you don't stink, you're always so full of shit." He placed his hat back over his eyes.

"Are you going to allow him that insubordination?"

"Fuck, Malton, is it difficult to walk with that stick jammed so far up your ass? I've got to figure you have splinters in your ass cheeks from clenching so tightly." I asked.

283

Stenzel had spit out an entire mouthful of water she'd been drinking. "Sorry, sir." She laughed, wiping her chin.

Malton gave Stenzel a look he hoped would impart fear; it didn't. The woman had stared down death countless times; a mean-mugging by a boot lieutenant wasn't even going to scratch the surface.

"Can we get back to where we are?" I asked.

"We're back in England." Malton had finally pulled his gaze away. I vaguely wondered how long it was going to take until he wrote her up.

"Seriously? Not a big fan of the British Isles." The price to come ashore here had already been too high. The sting of losing Winters had only begun to lessen and morph into the deep grief where his memory would reside, along with the countless others along the way. I often equated this accumulated despair with the chain Jacob Marley had forged. Always dragging that heavy iron around was a burden, one which could never be lessened. "Okay, out with the rest of it."

"The major told me that the rest of it was on a need-to-know basis only," Malton said as he patted his pocket.

"This is going to be painful." I lightly rubbed my forehead, hoping to prevent the headache that was surely waiting in the wings to hammer the walls of my skull. "Lieutenant, this is a need-to-know basis. We're less than fifteen minutes from landing."

"The major was very specific."

"And what happens to the mission if, the moment we land on that beach, a group of zombies hauls your ass away for breakfast?" I asked.

He sputtered. "That…that can't happen."

"Oh, I assure you it can." BT had sat up. "Happens all the time. Now either you can hand over those orders, or I'm going to lift you by your feet and shake you until they fall out of your pocket. Are we clear?"

Malton gulped. "Did you hear that, sailor? An NCO just

threatened me. The code of military justice is unambiguous on this. You'll be back in jail before noon!"

"Perkins, did you hear anything?" Rose asked. She made a slight explosion sound and spread her hands apart, mimicking her words.

"Gosh no. With all this splashing and the seagulls going crazy, I can't even hear my own thoughts," Perkins said.

"Good boy." Perkins flinched as Rose patted his shoulder.

Surprisingly, Malton handed over the single page document but held on to the accompanying pictures.

"Kind of figured," I said. After I read it, I handed it over to BT.

"What's it say, sir?" Stenzel asked.

"The enlisted don't have any reason to know," Malton said.

"Normally, I want all my personnel to feel free to speak freely. You, however, it would be best if you didn't talk at all. Consider yourself an outside observer that is doing their best to be unobtrusive."

"You can't silence me. I am an officer in the United States Navy."

He wasn't going to shut up, and Eastman would frown on me shooting him. I was going to do the next thing available and ignore him. "It says we're heading in to pick up Chris Wren."

"The other scientist?" Dallas asked.

"Says here he's crucial to the work of the ones we did pick up," I said. "But if you ask me, it's all a crock of shit."

"Well? Let's hear why," BT stated.

"If you'd given me half a sec, I would have already told you. The docs haven't had any major breakthrough since they've been on board, and to save their skin, they say we need to go and save this other guy whom we haven't heard from in weeks and is most likely dead. Then, when we come back empty-handed, the docs will be able to say: 'Oh no. Without him, we can't complete our work.' It absolves them of their inability to deliver on what they promised."

"Little cynical, even for you, Mike," BT said.

"Remember what I told them if they failed to deliver?"

BT nodded.

"And we lost a team member saving them. Lies have a price, and I'll make sure they pay what's due."

"They're civilians, you have no authority over them."

"Malton, when we land and the sailors head back to the boat, who's going to be your witnesses?" BT asked. "So do as the Captain said and shut the fuck up, or I'm going to bend you so far forward you'll be able to visually check how well you wipe."

"Eww," this from Rose.

Malton gulped. Not sure how worried he was about the anal observation, but it was true he was about to be dropped off in hostile territory with a group of hostiles. It made sense to tread lightly, and BT's threat gave meaning to the whole shitting where you eat scenario.

"No train this time. How far from where we land to where this guy is?" BT asked.

"We'll be landing in Weymouth, traveling through Dorchester and then off to Salisbury, where we last heard from him. He was hiding inside the Salisbury Cathedral."

"Whoa," Gary said, "those are all places in Massachusetts, except for the cathedral, I don't think there's one of those there."

"Why would they name places after cities in the US?" Kirby asked.

"If we were on land, I'd have you drop and give me twenty," BT said.

"I don't get it," he said to his girlfriend. "What'd I say wrong?"

"Let him be," I told BT, "there aren't geography questions on the ASVAB."

"It's basic knowledge," BT pleaded.

"You'd think. I once read a report where a hundred people were asked where the Berlin Wall was, forty got it wrong. Forty. One even went so far as to say Kentucky. The *Berlin Wall*, the answer is in the question, and they still got it wrong."

"That doesn't make this right," BT said to me.

"I know, man, I know, but it doesn't matter."

"Hey!" I had a meaty finger in my face. "You have your hang-ups; I have mine."

I raised my hands. "Fair enough. And it's about a hundred miles round trip."

"What?"

"You asked how far, and I'm telling you."

"Ten days seem excessive? It seems like we could hike in and out in half that. Unless…." He left that thought there.

"Big unless."

"How many are we talking about?"

"Well, it looks like they scoured the country for the largest concentration of zombies and then magically placed our objective in the middle. We should have stayed in jail." I handed over the glossy images.

"Does Eastman have a daughter?" BT asked me, though he was looking at Malton.

"I don't think so," I answered, not knowing where this was going.

"Why's he so desperate to get rid of this one, then?" He motioned with his chin to the lieutenant. "Figured he must be dating her or something; no way any father would approve."

"Makes sense. So, Malton, you saw these pics and still lobbied to come on this mission?" I asked. He didn't respond. BT handed him back the stack of photographs.

"Do you know what's in Salisbury?" BT asked.

"Not the Berlin Wall," I told him.

"You're not incorrect."

"Stonehenge," Stenzel piped up.

"I was going to make him squirm a bit more." BT looked ang-gravated. (I just made that up. Perfect blend of angry and aggravated. Where's Webster when you need him?)

"Can I see that, Lieutenant?" Stenzel had her hand out for the pictures.

Malton appeared frozen, his gaze stuck on the images like he was seeing them for the first time. Amazing how anger can cloud your judgment. He'd been fighting so hard to lead this expedition he'd not spent the time wondering if he should. "You're enlisted," he said absently.

BT snatched them and handed them over, Malton didn't protest. That was the smartest thing he'd done so far today. I hoped the trend continued.

"This is weird." Stenzel nearly had the photo pressed to her face. "The zees, they're not surrounding Salisbury, they're surrounding Stonehenge." She handed them back.

Stonehenge was a mile or so away from where we needed to go. It was subtle, but she was right; the storm's eye was the strange rock formation, not our target. That was a wee bit of good news, but not hugely significant. It was like saying the driver's side blinker still worked though the car was totaled. Big fucking deal. Although, maybe it was. If they were fixated on elsewhere, it was possible we could sneak in and sneak out. "Anyone have a theory as to why this might be?" I asked the group, though it was Tommy I was specifically asking.

He shrugged, which didn't give me a bunch of hope that anyone else would come up with something viable.

"No." I held out a finger to Rose, who was about to speak. "You cannot blow up Stonehenge. I can't believe I even need to say that."

She mumbled something, I wasn't quite sure what it was, but it sounded suspiciously like "Wet blanket."

We were approaching the shore, and it was time to start acting like I was in the military. "Headsets on. Minimum noise, I want a radio check." I motioned to the other boat. Walde gave me a thumbs up and proceeded to get everyone geared and ready. We had thirteen people about to make shore, I didn't have triskaidekaphobia, but that didn't mean I liked the number. We were going to have to trim the fat. I looked over to Malton; he must have sensed something because his expression looked troubled. Like maybe he just realized the fart he'd let slide out had been a little more substantial.

The sun had yet to make its return, though it was beginning to lighten up, a promise that no matter who lived or died today, there would be a sunrise. Celestial events gave little thought to terrestrial ones.

"Nothing on the beach." Walde was scanning the area with her NVGs.

That didn't mean a whole bunch; the beach was a tiny strip of sand with huge buildings directly behind it. Plenty of places for any number of enemies to lie in wait. I didn't like it at all in terms of an insertion point. Three and four-story structures surrounded the entirety of it. One person with a rifle and a desire to cause mayhem could inflict severe casualties on our group as there was little cover. It didn't make sense for people to attack us, I had to be content with the odds that it was unlikely, not impossible, just unlikely. As monstrous as humans had proved to be, there just weren't enough of us around anymore to be considered the main threat. Zombies had knocked us off the perch. Sure, they were human derivatives, but not technically humans.

"Any light whatsoever from those buildings?" I asked Walde. If people were hiding in the buildings, there was zero reason to believe they had even the slightest notion we were coming. Unless, in the whopper of conspiracy theories, Eastman had set up an ambush. Being paranoid sucks. Could also save your life. If they didn't know we were coming, there was a chance they'd give themselves away with a small lantern or candle.

"Nothing, sir." Walde took off her night vision gear.

Our boat had bottomed out, and I stepped onto firm ground. "Thanks for the lift," I told Perkins, who nodded.

"We'll be back in ten days, sir. Good luck."

"Don't forget about us."

"Already have you penciled in, sir," Perkins said.

"Much appreciated." Within two minutes of us being on the beach, the sailors were making their return voyage to the carrier. One of the few times I was jealous I'd not decided to be a sailor instead of a Marine. The infantile part of me couldn't reconcile being called a Seaman, though. How many problems could one person have? Was it limitless? It felt that way sometimes.

Kirby began fumbling with his belt, to the point I was wondering what had crawled up his leg. "Need to shit." He was dancing around and heading for the nearest building to take care of some personal business.

"Are you kidding me right now? Tommy, could you watch his six please?" I asked.

"How closely do I have to watch it?" I could tell he was smiling even if I couldn't see his face as he followed after.

"You're going to let him do that?" Malton asked.

"What would you have me do, Lieutenant?"

"I…I don't know, but not nothing."

"Can't stop nature." We began to follow in Kirby's hurried footsteps.

"I told him not to eat all those dried bananas," Rose tutted.

None of us had the good fortune of Kirby remembering to shut his mic off. What followed were a series of grunts, squelching sounds, and a litany of *oh gods*. I didn't know exactly what being ear raped meant up until that very moment in time. He must have found a stall because there was an echoing quality to his words. I don't know that my squad had ever been so silent, I attribute it to shock.

"Tommy could you see when he might be done, and please make sure his colon is still in place," I said.

"Marine, have some decorum! Shut off your headset!" Malton yelled. Mid-ass bleating Kirby went dark.

"Should be good to go in five," Tommy replied.

"Appreciate you taking one for the team," I told him.

Kirby wasn't the least bit embarrassed when he exited the three-story brick building. Relieved, yes; proud, possibly. Embarrassed? Not even a little bit. The water was beginning to sparkle as sunshine kissed the surface. I wanted us completely off the beach where there was absolutely no place to hide. Just because we had desert camouflage on didn't mean we weren't going to be seen.

We were staying to the side of the highway, the under-growth thick enough that it made walking difficult, and it didn't help in the least that Malton was constantly grousing. I finally had to pull him aside, shutting down both our headsets.

"You need to shut the fuck up about the conditions. No one likes this shit, but you're an officer, act like one because where you go, the troops will follow. If you piss and moan, so will they."

He was perturbed. I'd called him out but not enough to stop the whining, at least not to me. "Why can't we walk on the road?"

I turned. "Anyone want to tell the good lieutenant why we're not making our journey much easier by walking on the roadway?"

"Oooh, ooh, I know this one!" Kirby had his hand raised. "Anyone?"

Kirby was dancing in my field of vision. "I know this!"

"You fuck this up, and I'm going to sit on your back while you do pushups," BT told him.

"Maybe let someone else explain," I said as Kirby lowered his arm.

Dallas picked up the torch. "The roads will be watched. It's been discovered that zombies will now place sentries dead center in them, waiting for unsuspecting meals to come their way."

"Ding ding. Give that Marine a prize," I said.

"Aw man, I knew that." Kirby looked genuinely pissed, as if he'd missed out on some grand set of gifts.

"So this is why we stay off the road, near it, but not quite visible. With me?"

Malton nodded.

I got close so only he could hear me. "So shut up about the traveling conditions. Remember, this is Britain; it's probably going to rain soon, and nobody wants to constantly hear about how wet they are." As if on cue, a fat drop of rain splashed off my visor. "Son of a bitch." I looked up. We'd been traveling in ideal conditions; I couldn't remember when the storm clouds had rolled in. "Grimm, find us some digs."

We hadn't gone far, just about the outskirts of Dorchester, which put us less than eight miles into our journey. But just because I'd told Malton not to complain about something didn't mean I wanted to deal with it; we could make up the shortage tomorrow. Walking down the main street in Dorchester looked like something out of a Medieval movie. Not going to lie, something in the back of my mind kept expecting to see jousting knights and fair maidens strolling along the sidewalk. Grimm reported back that he'd found suitable accommodations, it ended up being a pub. The Borough Arms Pub, to be exact. It was a two-story Tudor that looked as if it had rooms above the bar. This was one of those times I hoped that the rain continued for more than one day.

"Might be a promotion in this for you," I told Grimm as I walked in. The windows were intact, and as far as ransacking went, this place had mostly been passed by. When you're trying to survive, Vodka isn't necessarily high up on the priority list.

"No." BT Scotch blocked me as I gazed longingly at the rows of liquor on the wall. "We're on a mission, remember?"

"Yeah, I do; that's what I'm going to try and forget," I told him as I went around his rather substantial mass.

"Kirby, you're on guard duty." BT was looking at some special bottle of cognac, I heard him quietly oohing and aahing as he found himself a snifter glass.

"You changed your tune," I told him.

"This is Remy Martin, this bottle is worth more than you."

"Ouch." I opted for a bottle of beer, didn't quite have the pop of carbonation I appreciate, but there was still some fizz, and it was relatively cool. "Always nice to have a beer after a hard day at work." I smacked my lips.

"Hard day at work? We went for a hike," Walde said, grabbing herself one.

We clinked our bottles together.

"What are you doing?" It's bad enough you're drinking, but your enlisted personnel? I'll have no choice but to report this."

There was a quick flash in my mind of me, smiling, cracking the bottle against the side of his skull. What's life without a bit of fantasy?

"Malton make yourself useful. Why don't you go upstairs and make sure this location is secure," I told him after taking a swig large enough to drain half the bottle. I thought I'd done reasonably well until Walde slammed her empty on the bar top. "Nobody likes a show-off," I told her.

"Private Reed, Lance Corporal Grimm, Corporal Dallas, Staff Sergeant Talbot, Staff Sergeant Van Goth, Lance Corporal Harmon, Sergeant Stenzel, Sergeant Rose, you're with me," Malton said.

"Fuck me," I muttered. "So the nine of you are going to go upstairs?"

"You want the place secure, am I correct, sir?"

"Going to be difficult to maneuver in narrow hallways with that many people traipsing about. More liable to shoot each other than any threat you may encounter. Now I realize that you're more likely using eight human shields to protect your ass, but that's not the way we do it around here. Tommy, could you take the lieutenant upstairs and have a good look around?"

"Can do," he said.

"Only the two of us?" Malton asked with disbelief in his eyes.

I chose to ignore him; I'd given my orders.

"Why should I be sent to do this when we have enlisted?"

"Leadership by example. Either go and do this, or I'll report you for disobeying orders, and as unfit for command. Then you'll never get to feel self-important. Any of you that would like a beer, you can have one now and after your guard shift, another if you're so inclined." I made a sweeping motion with my hand for Malton to head up the stairs. He looked as reluctant as a kid that was told to head outside and find a suitable switch to get his hindquarters swatted. BT sidled over as I watched Tommy move quickly up and Malton tentatively follow.

"Is this where you tell me I should take it easy on him? I feel like this is that time."

"Malton? Hell no," BT said. "That kid has no place out in the field."

"You don't think he can get there with some experience?"

"I don't." BT was thinking. "Too nervous, high-strung, and willing to put others' lives in danger before his own."

"Yeah, the thing is we're running low on able-bodied people to run these shit shows."

"He's not going to make that sad statistic any better." BT went to the bar to grab a beer.

For whatever reason, Malton was Eastman's pet project. I

have no idea what he saw in him other than another body to throw at a growing problem.

"Sir, are you coming?" Tommy asked over the radio.

I walked over so I could see up the stairs. Malton had frozen two steps from the top. He looked to be shivering, and I didn't believe it had anything to do with the weather. I didn't know what to do; I should feel ashamed that one of the choices running through my head was a bullet. The man was dangerous, but only in the fact that he was going to get others killed.

Leadership by example, I thought as I headed up the stairs making enough noise that he would hear me and not get startled. "Need to move, Lieutenant," I said with a calmness I was not feeling. "You can't leave your point man twisting in the breeze like this."

"I know that," he snapped.

I could add *not great at being under pressure* to his budding resume.

"Now, Lieutenant."

I suspected he was waiting for me to pass him by, and then he'd follow. A sloth would have been envious with how slowly he moved, could even see the moss begin to form on his uniform. I wanted to nudge him with my rifle, instead, I got close enough to have my hot breath on his neck, he liked that sensation slightly less than entering the second-floor hallway.

"Entering." Tommy was at the first doorway; it was already open. He stepped in, I kept creeping up on Malton, making sure my beer-smelling self was constantly on his heels. Clearing the upstairs had taken fifteen minutes longer than it should have, and what was worse was I didn't think Malton had at any point got better at the task. If he didn't show improvement, he was going to be more of a liability.

When we came back down, Malton was sulking and did so in the far corner. He made sure there were plenty of us between him and whatever could possibly come through the door.

"Sir, I'm setting up guard rotation. What would you like me to do about Malton?" Stenzel asked.

"He wants to be here; he pulls a shift like everyone else. Give him an early one so I can keep an eye on him."

"On it," she replied. Malton gave her an indignant look when she told him, then he looked over her shoulder and to me. When he realized I was watching, his expression changed. He even smiled, though it was far too toothy to be considered anything friendly. It looked more like a frightened dog about to lash out. He didn't protest, so that was an improvement. Baby steps. The rain picked up in intensity as night descended. The best a guard was going to be able to do was tell us when the enemy had walked inside. I sent the majority of the squad upstairs to get some rest. It was just Malton, Kirby, and myself downstairs, although the lance corporal had long ago fallen asleep.

"I'm a good officer," Malton said unprompted.

"Okay." I briefly looked up from my journal scribblings.

"I was near the top of my class at Annapolis when this started."

"Okay," I repeated. I had a fleeting thought running through my head, and I was doing my best to get it onto paper before it fled, and he wouldn't shut up.

"Major Eastman has the utmost respect for my abilities."

"I guess it wasn't that important." I sighed, putting my pen down, the words lost. "Are you looking for my stamp of approval, Malton?" There was a flash of anger from him that was perfectly timed with a flash of lightning, it was impressive at the moment. He couldn't stand that I wouldn't use his rank as way of addressing him.

"This is supposed to be my command."

"Why are you in such a lather to do the wet work? Maybe you are good at what you do, being out in the field is different;

it's not for everybody. It's for the best when people know their limitations. It's when you overextend that bad things tend to happen."

"You just want all the glory for yourself."

"Glory? You think I do this for glory?"

"Why else?"

"That what they teach you at Annapolis? I hope you had a scholarship, otherwise you wasted your money. Glory would be the last reason I do any of this. I do it because these missions are vital to our continued survival. I do it so I can, to the best of my abilities, make sure that every one of these people here makes it back. They count on me, and I count on them. Glory? You fucking dolt."

"People idolize you."

"That's what you want, idolation?"

Malton stared at me intently but did not answer. Maybe he felt as if he'd said too much. It wasn't a good thing to show another your heart's desire, especially if it was a small, dark thing. There had been a tiny piece of me that wanted to believe that, with some time and training, Malton could be half decent. But that wasn't going to be the case. Even if he overcame his petty cowardice, his ambition was going to get in the way. As the room got darker, so did my thoughts. It would not be the worst thing in the world if Malton never made it back; how to facilitate that without it looking like murder was my next mental exercise.

"I shouldn't be on guard duty."

"Fuck, you're a wanker." As far as British swears go, I like that one. And why not? "You shouldn't ask of your people anything you're not willing to do."

"I bet you cook and clean when you're back at home, don't you?" he asked derisively. He smiled as if he'd wounded me deeply with his jeer.

"Why the fuck wouldn't I? I live there. I wear the clothes. I eat. A marriage is a partnership, not an indentured servant arrangement. I don't feel like I need to go out on a limb here, but you're not married, are you? My guess is never even been in a long-term relationship with that set of mores. Ah, okay. Some of this is starting to make a bit of sense, now. You figure if you're successful out here, it will have the women flocking to you back there. Is that it? Wouldn't be the first time men have done stupid shit to impress women. That right there is half the reason why the average life expectancy of a woman is greater than a man's."

If Malton pressed his lips together any tighter, it was likely they would burst. I wasn't sure what ruptured lips would look like, only that I didn't want to find out. Thankfully he turned around and stared out the window, for all the good that did. Couldn't see more than a few feet out through the gloom.

"Are you going to light a lantern?" he asked after a while.

"How willing are you to make a visible silhouette to any passersby?"

He shut up again. I had my red lens covered flashlight out as I attempted to recapture my escaped reflections. Elusive bastards were skittering around the periphery of my thoughts. The storm had reached a crescendo; I didn't think there was any way it could keep this pace up, and I was right to a degree as we traded out one storm for another. Malton's shift was nearly over, if the way he kept telling his watch to hurry up was any indication. He looked up triumphantly as if he'd just broken his personal record in a half marathon. "Done."

The word was no sooner out of his mouth when I heard a far-off tinkle of glass being broken. By the way Malton went stock still, it was safe to assume he'd heard it as well.

"Get away from the window. Slowly," I added. He moved like a slowly deflating whoopie cushion collapsing down. Once he was on the floor, he low crawled away, heading back to the far corner. I turned my headset on. "We've got company," I said quietly." I could hear movement upstairs as my squad got up.

"What's going on?" BT asked hardly above a whisper.

"Heard glass breaking outside. Not sure where." I was moving toward the window Malton had vacated.

"You'll be seen." Malton reached a hand out as if he were going to be able to stop me from his hiding spot some twenty feet away.

"We're on our radios now, Lieutenant."

"I...I left it on the table."

"Then shut up," I hissed as I took a glance out the window. Like I thought, there wasn't much to see. A flash of lightning damn near froze my heart mid-beat. Out in the middle of the street, two columns of bulkers were ambling. If I dreaded them, what they were following was a fucking nightmare. I hoped the image had more to do with my milli-second of illumination than any basis in reality. The thing in front was walking on eight legs, its black body glistening like it was bathed in crude oil. The hairless head was bulbous, but instead of being like a multi-eyed spider, the entirety of it was covered in broad, single nostriled noses.

"Mike?" BT asked tremulously.

He'd seen it too. If this wasn't some random chance encounter and that thing had led them here, it would be foolish to think it wouldn't find us within the pub. I sensed movement behind us, figured it was Malton getting ready to pull up some floorboards so he could hide beneath them. It was Kirby. The fright had been intense enough I'd forgotten he was there. This zombie melding thing was horrific; there might be no limit to what they could come up with. And then, because being appropriate is not ever my default method of communication, I wondered if the Army would commission them. You know, to make a zombie that was multiple penises, this way, it could fuck you over in a multitude of ways.

"We'll be coming to you." Staying on the bottom floor with bulkers about to breach was tantamount to throwing in the towel. "Rose, we're going to need your expertise sooner rather than later." I tapped Kirby on the shoulder and motioned for him to head up. Malton looked away as I moved closer, as if he believed if we didn't make eye contact, I would just leave him alone, or maybe even that none of this was real. "I'm not carrying you up, let's go." I tapped him on the shoulder; he flinched. "For the love of God. Malton! We need to go upstairs."

When he shrieked that he wasn't going anywhere with me, I punched him hard enough to knock his stupid ass out. "Did they hear us?" I grunted as I climbed the steps, carrying Malton's deadweight.

"It's raining, not hailing," BT gave as way of an answer.

"They coming?"

"Not yet."

I thought about depositing Malton nicely on a bed; instead, I let him thump off the ground. Fuck him. Rose rushed past the door; she was setting something up. I was going to do my best to stay as far away from it as possible this time. My back twinged in agreement. I moved up next to BT to watch what he could see. The storm was moving away, and the lightning was more intermittent but we caught sight of the bulkers that had turned and were facing the pub, their broad faces a blank mask of apathy. I couldn't tell if I liked this better than the twisted expression of hatred they generally wore. I wanted to ask BT what they were doing; social norms dictated that neither of us could have possibly known. Twelve bulkers and Nose-stradamus. I had to imagine Rose had enough boom to deal with them, but zombies were like rodents, where there was one, there were dozens, where there were dozens, there were hundreds.

"Stenzel, need you in the first bedroom, bring the suppressed Ruger." Our resident sniper had stumbled upon a Ruger 10/22 rifle, probably the most popular rifle ever in terms of something to teach someone how to shoot with. It was reliable, accurate, and had zero kick. An armorer had threaded the barrel for her, and with the suppressor on, it was quieter than when Malton was dumped on the floor. The bullets she carried were hollow points filled with a zombie-killing compound; the question was whether they would penetrate the bulkers at all to deliver their lethal payload. "See what you can do about our infestation before I have Rose try to kill a spider with a flamethrower, please."

She noiselessly opened the window and placed the rifle against the sill. "Can't see anything, sir." By now, what few flashes of lightning were still happening were far off in the distance and doing nothing to penetrate the darkness around us.

I couldn't believe the words I was about to utter. "Pop a few rounds where you think they are."

She must have felt the same way about what I said because she turned to look at me.

"They're bulkers, Stenzel, packed tightly together in the roadway, not fifty feet from where you are. I promise there are no innocent civilians in between."

"Goes against everything I learned."

I winced after the first shot whined off from a ricochet. The second was a solid thunk of lead on mass, as were the next half dozen—still nothing—no reaction from the zombies. Two more zinging sounds as bullets bounded away after striking the ground, Stenzel pulled her rifle from the sill and sat with her back against the wall.

"They've withdrawn."

I didn't question her on it.

Rose came back a few minutes later, appearing as if she'd just finished an intensive PT session. Knowing Rose and her fireworks displays, that was very likely the case. I yelled for her before she could disappear completely down the hallway.

"Yes, sir?" she asked, peeking in.

"Need to know that this building is going to continue standing once you've detonated your charges."

"Should be fine, sir." She headed back down the corridor.

"Goddamnit." I'd planned on calling her back and getting some clarification, but sounds and smells from outside began to assail my senses.

"Start shooting again, sir?" Stenzel asked.

"No sense now, smells like the reinforcements have arrived." You'd think that with all the time we'd been exposed to zombies that we'd have gained some immunity to the stink. This was not the case. It was such a sharp, eye-watering, disturbing odor, it made the unconscious taking of a breath a dreaded event. Death had a uniquely pungent, earthy scent, surely nothing anyone with a modicum of civility would choose to smell with any repeated occurrence, but zombies somehow took that and amped it up. Diseased flesh mixed with offal and rotting meat was a combination that could bring the strongest to their wretched knees, and tonight, for some troubling reason, it was worse. It was a damn fucking shame that the sun was going to come up and we were going to discover why this was.

The night yielded little of anything, little trouble, and, unfortunately, little sleep. Dealing with zombies was one thing, but fearing that the pub was going to be obliterated at any moment was quite another. Maybe it was time I sat Rose down and had the talk with her. The bombs and explosions one.

Three things happened at once, conspiring to lift me from my less than perfect sleep. The storm had cleared, and a stream of muted sunlight was pouring through the window, depositing its rays across my face. The second thing was the groans of Malton nearby as he sat up. The third was the sound of my brother retching some two doors down.

"Everything good?" I groggily sat up then realized that, besides the lieutenant, I was alone in the room.

Rapidly approaching footsteps garnered my attention as I swung my legs off the bed.

"Staff Sergeant Talbot says you're going to want to look out the window," Kirby said.

"Do I?" I asked in all seriousness.

"No." He shook his head as he said this. The kid was the prototypical Marine. Fuck it or shoot it, the general credo. That something had him disturbed to this extent didn't bode well for how my day was going to start. I looked anyway. Wasn't quite sure what I was looking at. As expected, the numbers had swelled, but what exactly was down there, my mind couldn't quite grasp. But by the twisting and churning of the juices within my stomach, it had figured out the scene before my brain could.

"Melders?" I asked quietly, but that wasn't quite right, and in some strange twist, that would have been preferred. More than half the zombies standing on the street carried various types of weapons, axes, farm implements, cricket bats. Some hadn't quite grasped the concept of what it was for or even what constituted a weapon, as evidenced by the individuals wielding lengths of limp rope, bent plastic Wiffle ball bats; one had what looked like a femur. Still, though, that they were an armed mob, waiting for us, using their hands for more than grasping at food. It was terrifying.

"They're wearing skins, Mike." BT had turned away.

That's when it clicked. The reasoning part of my brain had finally caught up with the images being imprinted upon it. I didn't know how to feel, how to react; I had no point of reference, no prior knowledge upon which to draw a conclusion. It was a well-established fact that the infected people we called zombies ate the uninfected, it was what they did. But now it appeared we were more than food, we were clothing and adornment, maybe even weaponry. Their victims had been partially skinned and draped over shoulders and tied around waists like pre-button-down man may have done with a bison hide, though with far less skill. In some cases, rib cages were still attached or parts of a head would be draped down a back, a slack face looking forlornly to a future it no longer possessed.

Nearly all of the zombies on the roadway had shed their clothes, and most but not all had various versions of loincloths covering their genitalia. The absolutely disgusting part about it was that the coverings had been stripped free from the same place. Rotting and blackened penises flopped uselessly like misshapen sporrans as the zombies milled about. In a Freudian twist, most of the female zombies wore the same appendage across their loins. A time would invariably come when I was a doddering old man, in the depths of my winter, and still, I would remember this sight—the undead covering themselves with the dead. Hell was going to be envious that it had not come up with this before the zombies had. If something ever deserved to be nuked into non-existence, I was staring at it.

"Rose, fucking do something!" I hoped I didn't shriek, but if I had, it was white noise to my squad. I had a pretty good feeling no one was paying attention to how close I was to losing my shit.

"Fire in the hole!" she shouted.

Ducking down and turning away are both intelligent things to do when dealing with an impending explosion, but I did neither. I watched as zombies were shredded by the force of the blast. Legs were blown free from bodies, arms ripped clean from sockets, blankets of skin the size of ponchos went flying like sickening kites. Errant cocks rained down onto the ground.

How does one come back from something like that? I'm not writing this down as a rhetorical question. I would genuinely like to know the answer.

The blast was the trigger point for the zombies. The skin-wearing zombies still intact cleared the street on the far side, their backs against the stores; a line of bulkers began their thunderous approach.

"Fire!" I ordered. The bulkers weren't attempting to break through the doors to storm the entrance; they planned to make the structure collapse by taking out an entire support wall. I wasn't sure if that was something they could accomplish, but it was a damned good plan, and not something I was willing to let play out to see what happened. Seven tons of dense bone and thick flesh pounding against the building was certain to have some severe repercussions. I watched as one of my bullets dug a groove into the side of a bulker's head; it twisted slightly before looking up at me, displaying its cracked, black and jagged teeth as it pulled its lips back in anger.

Rose tossed out another bomb; the windows downstairs were blown in, and a super-heated blast of air rushed past me. For a moment, I could see nothing but the spreading after-image burned into my retinas. Didn't need sight to realize some of the bulkers had met their goal. I fell to the side from the jarring impact. A crack raced up along a cement joint line. Wood splintered and glass was smashed. More than one had breeched the property and were downstairs doing some massive renovations. There was a vein of fear streaking through my body, and still, I felt regret for all that liquor spilling needlessly, forever undrunk. And my wife says I have a hard time getting my priorities straight? What does she know?

The massive zombies that had not found a way in defaulted to what they knew best, and that was to pull back and get another running charge at their target. Of the fourteen original, only four were running back to their starting points, and none made it back. But that did little to stop the ones already in. Dust and plaster were raining down upon our heads as the zombies in the bar were slamming their weight against the support beams. The splintering of a pole was louder than the report of a rifle. I didn't know how many of the thick oaken columns there were or how many would need to be broken before the upstairs fell away, but the inevitability of it was, well, inevitable unless we did something. Rose had set up her wares in the belief that the zombies would come to us, having no idea that they were going to make us go to them.

"Rose, I'm going downstairs. I'm assuming that's enough direction not to set anything off."

"Got it, sir."

"Stenzel, Tommy, with me. The rest of you make sure nothing else makes it in."

I didn't know where Tommy had been, but he beat me to the top of the stairs. Stenzel was fast approaching, slamming a new magazine into her rifle. Tommy took the lead as I was scanning the stairs for tripwires, as they were liberally peppered with explosives, and I had no desire to see how well they worked. I was halfway down when Tommy started shooting. A team of galloping Clydesdales wearing tap shoes on a marble floor in a closed sound stage could not have been louder than the five bulkers bouncing around like pinballs hitting juiced up bumpers. The destruction was so complete on this level, I think Rose would have been impressed, and possibly regret that it hadn't been done by her expertise. Tables and chairs had been reduced to fragments in some cases not much larger than toothpicks. The deep burgundy, mahogany bar had been completely unearthed; the intact parts had been pushed up and into the wall of bottles. None had survived the initial impact or subsequent rattling of the bar.

Stenzel and I stood on the bottommost step, shooting at zombies. Acquiring a target and hitting it was not much of a problem within the confined area. Tommy was in the bar proper, a few feet to our side. There wasn't much that scared the boy, unless it had to do with the safety of those around him, but when a bulker made him its personal mission to flatten, there was a register of fear within his expression. Without a word spoken, Stenzel and I both trained our field of fire on the zombie making a run for Tommy. He was backing away, attempting to give himself enough room to dodge the bone-crunching collision. I put over ten rounds into the bulker, and it had yet to drop. Receive damage, yes. Die, no. By the time it got close to Tommy, it was staggering wearily, and he pulled a pistol free and placed it against the forehead of the zombie, who could do nothing more than wait for the impact. The last bulker had fallen to the ground; the problem was I didn't think the building was going to be far behind. We were literally on tremulous footing.

"Someone get Malton up, we're going to have to leave soon." I was looking at the ceiling, which had begun to sag in a few places. Now that the bulkers were no longer making enough noise to drown out a heavy metal concert, it would have been impossible not to hear the squeal of nails as they were pulling free of their moorings. We could hear floorboards upstairs popping loose. The building was coming down, perhaps in slow motion but coming down all the same.

BT had Malton propped up and was walking him down the stairs. I winced and froze, waiting for my face to melt as the semi-coherent man knocked a bomb down. I figured if I hadn't smelled burning flesh after a second, I should be fine. I ran up to help, to make sure it didn't happen again. Reed and Walde had gone outside and were setting up our potential escape. We all filtered out, expanding our sphere. The cloaked zombies were watching our every move, intelligence clearly displayed in their eyes. They were looking at our weapons as much as they were looking at us. That did not bode well for us in terms of their future development. The only reason they might not be similarly armed was England's general lack of firearms.

"Cap?" Reed's one word question revolved around whether he should open fire, and I didn't know how to respond; there was something to be said about a preemptive strike. Maybe we could get them to retreat, give us a chance to get away. The street was narrow, and there was not much room between us and them; if we started shooting, it was just as likely that we would hasten their attack. We were going to have to do something soon. Debris was falling behind us, so to stay where we were was to risk getting hit by some of it. The zombies, however, were not yielding ground. When we as a group shifted to the right, they stayed pat. They looked to be a little fewer than one hundred, a number we should have been able to deal with. It was the effing proximity that had me being cautious. I should have known it was going to be Malton that would fuck this up. He took this most inopportune of times to become fully cognizant of himself and his surroundings.

"Zombies!" he screamed as if we weren't all abundantly aware. He pulled his sidearm free and placed a shot high up in a building across the street. One of the zombies turned to see where it had impacted. Malton's gun hand was waving around violently. "I'll kill you!"

"Malton...Lieutenant, put your gun down," I told him in as even a voice as I could muster.

"Are you out of your mind!?" he shrieked.

"Debatable." I gave him an honest answer. "They're not attacking, and we need to keep it that way."

"Natives are getting restless, sir." Reed had his short barrel rifle up against his shoulder, his green laser pinging off a greasy forehead not fifteen feet from him. In any other setting, I would have howled with mad laughter at what happened next. One of the zombies, having seen something moving upon the face of one of his compadres, decided to take action. He swung his cricket bat with enough force to crack the skull of the mate he was attempting to save. The struck zombie's eyes crossed, blood poured down its face as it fell to its knees. Reed, also spellbound by the slapstick, kept the dot firmly attached to the stricken one. The cricket player, feeling like he needed to score another run, brought the bat down upon the top of the other's head, finishing the job of destroying bone and brain. The zombie crumpled to the ground, and blood began flowing down the slight incline of the road.

Malton was shaking violently, as if he were shivering from the cold. He was no more able to stop the grip of fear than he would have inclement weather. I'd seen fear paralysis before, even suffered from some degree of it myself. But this was different; a person with epilepsy having a grand mal would have been less violent. My squad was in as much danger from the flailing gun as the zombies. I'd seen movies where Malton's tremors would immediately be followed by something exploding out of his chest. And if I had to wager, I'd say the zombies had seen the same science-fiction fare as I had, because where they had the ability to, they had backed up.

I had no idea why. Was it *fear? Confusion?* Did it matter? On one side of the coin, that was a good thing for us. The zombies gaining in intelligence meant they got to deal with all the uncertainties we humans did: self-doubt, anxiety, grave existentialism, and a host of other less than pleasant experiences.

"Tommy, grab Malton. Grimm, grab his gun. Let's see if we can use this to our advantage."

Grimm, thankfully, got the weapon away without incident. Tommy had a rough hold upon Malton's shoulders. The lieutenant looked like a severely inebriated Russian sailor on shore leave attempting to learn how to twerk to an up-tempo song, and the zombies wanted nothing to do with it. How he was jerking around didn't seem like it was anything he would be able to do for long, not without exhaustion setting in, or until he did damage to ligaments. Malton was beginning to fold in on himself like an inflatable tube man. Tommy hefted him up. His feet no longer touching the ground, Malton's spastic movements became eerier. When the front and back of his uniform became stained, it was easy enough to guess why. No one said anything and probably wouldn't for the entirety of this mission. But if we survived and made it back, word of this would spread to the entire ship. Malton would never be seen as fit for command again, and as far as I was concerned, that was a bonus. He had no place out here, as he'd so eloquently proved.

To whomever may read this journal: I hope that doesn't come across as mean or uncaring, but if the actions of a commander needlessly put their people in danger, I'm not overly sympathetic to their plight. Although, in this strangest and rarest of events, he was somehow helping.

"Kirby, what are you doing?" BT asked.

I could see that he had a cell phone in his hand.

"Recording this. Can you imagine how many followers I could have got if I posted this?"

"Do cell phones work again?" Stenzel's question was hopeful in nature. The potential to ring up a loved one or a friend, however unlikely, was something that would be game-changing; unfortunately, it wasn't so.

"Enough chatter. Kirby put that phone away. Tommy, see how long you can keep them backing up."

At first, it was working perfectly. For every step we advanced, the zombies backed up one. But the further we went and nothing adverse happened, the less retreat the enemy offered. After less than fifty feet, we were once again at a standstill, though we did gain two tactical advantages. The first being we were away from the trembling pub, the second, we were at the mouth of an alley. Rock walls lined the immediate half we could see, the other appeared to open up onto yards or other businesses. Malton's face was contorted into a grimace of pain as Tommy placed him back upon the ground.

"Lieutenant, you need to take control of yourself," he whispered.

"C...c...can't." Malton hunched forward before popping back up. Now, all we needed was a lot filled with used cars behind us, and this would be perfect. Maybe disregard my earlier comment. I very well could be mean.

"Stand the fuck up!" I shouted. I was embarrassed for the man and hoped the yell would be as effective as a slap to the side of the head. It wasn't.

"Zombies are inching." Reed was swiveling about, keeping his rifle trained on as many as he could.

"Grimm, Kirby, go make sure no surprises are waiting for us. The rest of us will pull back. I want you to keep your eyes on the front. If we show our backs, we'll trigger their chase response." We were in the mouth of the alley. Grimm let me know the way was clear. All was going reasonably well before it went to shit, as these types of things are wont to do. To add to Malton's uncontrollable movements, he started an ear-splitting, hiccupping shriek. I had no idea how he could get that level of volume as he was intermittently crying out. I wondered if he had some undocumented case of Tourette's that had been brought out by the overwhelming stress, not that it mattered much at the moment. We had worse things to deal with. Whether it was the pitch or the sheer strangeness of the sound that did it, we'll never know, but that shrieking was the last straw for the zombies. Without any discernible order that I saw or heard, they attacked as one. Reed being in front, he was the first to fire his rifle, chirping loudly in his hands to devastating effect.

He was slowly backing up until there was a line of us, five across: myself, my brother, BT, Walde, and Reed. The lead, steel, and poisonous sheet of bullets we laid down were too much firepower for the zombies to overcome. In less than three minutes, we had halved their numbers. Those remaining pulled back some, hiding in buildings across the street. We'd bought some time, but we'd also alerted the National Horde to our existence, and it was highly likely they were on their way to quell the insurrection with a mass mobilization.

The following passage will date me, and it's highly unlikely that anyone who stumbles across this not of a certain age is going to have any idea what I'm talking about. But since I'm writing this first and foremost for myself, that's a chance I'm willing to take. Kirby's video notwithstanding, I want to keep a mental image of what I saw in my head. There was a skit on *Saturday Night Live* years ago—*lifetimes* ago. Dan Ackroyd and Steve Martin played two brothers from Czechoslovakia who moved to the United States. They dressed far too loudly and had not the slightest clue on how to act around women. Their catchphrase was, *"We are two wild and crazy guys,"* but beyond and above that were their signature movements. Whether congratulating themselves on their phenomenal cool or out on the floor dancing, they made this vibratory shimmy with their entire bodies, jerking themselves in the most seemingly awkward way possible, in what they believed to be a display attractive to the opposite sex. It was as if Malton was emulating the two comedians, but, perhaps in an effort to prove how much he admired their genius, he was overacting the bit, and it was going on far too long. As he stepped, he would bend forward and then back, his shoulders continually rocking as he did so. His legs were wobbling but out of synch to the rest. If I didn't know better, I would have assumed Malton was an alien trying to fit in with the locals, moving about as he assumed those around him did. The bit was hilarious on television, especially after taking a couple of prerequisite tokes off a joint. However, in the flesh, when that very substance was on the line, not so much. Not even close.

"Tommy get him and go. We'll cover you." Malton may have protested, didn't know for sure, and didn't care at all.

"Where to, sir?" Grimm asked.

I moved to where he was. Far off through a yard, I could see zombies running. My guess was to keep us encircled, which meant they were probably running the other way as well, but I couldn't see them. I couldn't see anything but dollars to donuts we were being watched. I swear I could feel the slithering eyes of zombies upon us.

"Hole up again?" Grimm was looking at either a very

stout home or a bank. If we needed a place to wait until relief or an evac came, it would have been perfect, but we had a mission. Being stuck in one location was not a part of it. The brief firefight had not dug much into our stores of ammunition. My squad was well-versed in the necessity of taking much more than was reasonably expected. But if we were harried by zombies, the entirety of this errand, even our somewhat vast stores, would be tested.

"We need to double-time, get past the zombie cordon, if possible." I heard some groans, mostly Grimm, although he had been working on his cardio. Still, running in boots with full gear was never going to be on anyone's list of fun things to do on a Saturday. At least, I think it was Saturday, would've made more sense if it was Monday, though. Had a job once where I had Monday and Tuesday off. I could never reconcile that Friday was mid-week and Sunday was my Friday and that I should thoroughly be enjoying Mondays. While the rest of my friends were out partying, I was working, and when I was ready to go out, they were going to bed early for their work-week. It was a relatively lonely period of my existence, and now I wonder how productive my life could have been had I not had a proclivity to diverging off into tangents.

I didn't let Rose lead because she had no problem double-timing us into the dirt. Not Grimm either because, although he was getting better, he would stay on the slower side.

"Harmon, you're point. Get us out of here. Cut to the left, get us on the road. Kirby, you're the rear guard. Tommy, you're going to have to help the lieutenant." And by *help*, I meant toss him over his shoulder. Malton didn't protest, I don't think he had the energy to do so. We got to the road without incident. I had Harmon move to the shoulder when I noticed just how loud it was to have twelve sets of boots pounding pavement.

"They're here." Kirby did in his best Carol Anne impression, and it skeeved the hell out of me.

"Kirby cut that shit out," BT growled. Gonna say it did the same to the big man.

I took a peek over my shoulder. There was a half dozen, and they were keeping a respectable distance. To come closer meant we'd shoot. Smart bastards, they were tailing us until such time as they knew we'd have to stop, and they'd have beefed up their forces. That wasn't going to work.

"Stenzel, got some wet work for you, to the rear."

She immediately stepped out of the column, came to a stop, and did a once over on her weapon. I slowed as I caught up to her and stopped.

"Don't miss," Kirby told her as he jogged by.

She flipped him off as she got down into a kneeling position. I was her cover, making sure nothing came at us from the side or tried to cut us off from the front. Six kills was a tall order. The zombies were still running toward us, making the prospect easier, but the moment she opened fire, it was likely they were going to scatter and seek cover. A hundred yards melted to seventy-five, and still, she was in the midst of her breathing regimen, her eyes closed. Seventy-five evaporated to fifty.

"Umm." I had my rifle up, waiting on her cue.

At twenty-five yards, I would be shooting, regardless of my sergeant's actions or lack of.

"Stenzel?"

Her eyes opened, and I swear I watched her pupils dilate like a lens on a scope. In one blink of my eyes, she'd done two skull shots and one to the neck, nearly severing the head. I put two center mass, and when I realized that wasn't going to be enough, the third entered an orbital socket and shot out the side of its head. The two left broke in opposite directions; mine stayed on the road. One to the spine broke the connection from mind to legs, and it fell over, its upper half still moving. Something was wrong with our golden bullets. Stenzel's target had made it into the woods and was sprinting away. She was tracking it with her rifle, but the sheer number of trees and the increasing distance made the shot go from unlikely to impossible. I was itching to finish off the crawler, but I watched the zombie in the woods; he was lost from view behind a particularly large oak tree. Before I saw him again, I heard the report from Stenzel's rifle and then the zombie came out from behind the tree only to have his head vaporized. A mist of blood surrounded it like a cloud of gnats on a hot summer night. The zombie took its last step, slammed off a tree, and fell backward, dead. My mouth hung open. I turned back to Stenzel, who was standing and checking her gear, getting ready to resume our hasty departure; she'd thought no more of it than if she'd hit a barn wall from ten feet.

"Fuck me," I said as I got a couple of steps closer to the downed zombie and put one to the back of his skull, his reaching fingers stopping their search for purchase. I'd seen her shoot some incredible shots before, but that in no way tempered my amazement in the next. I was a good shot, better than average, but Stenzel was in a league of her own. It was like watching a world-class athlete at the peak of their game performing something us mere mortals could only marvel at. Poor turn of words on my part, but I meant it more figuratively than literally. Once we caught up, I had us go another mile, just to ensure we'd not been followed, before I called a halt.

"Blisters?" I asked as I walked up and down the column. By now, my squad was well versed in the placement of moleskin, a thick adhesive that acted as a protective barrier between the feet and footwear. I always thought this should be taught during boot camp and not something that needed to be learned through experience. I suppose DIs had to get their thrills somehow.

Dallas was sitting and had taken her left boot off and the sock as well, although when I walked up on her, I wouldn't have known it. She had so much of the brown protectant on that I thought it was her sock. "Had a corner roll up, been driving me nuts for the last half a mile." She smiled sheepishly as she attempted to force the errant piece to lay back down, but like Alfalfa's cowlick, it kept popping up.

"You're going to need to cut that flap off, and maybe next time take it a little easy on the stuff. We're leaving in five."

Once Tommy had put Malton down, the lieutenant walked a bit away from the squad. My guess was from embarrassment, although he had a strange way of masking it.

"How are you doing?" I asked. Does it make me an asshole if I didn't care? It was just a way to break the ice and have him run on his own.

"Why are you talking to me?" The words were neither hesitant nor tentative, they were anger-fueled. He had curled his fists and puffed out his chest. In terms of intimidation, a sleeping Rose had more thorns. "When we get back, I am going to have you Court-martialed!" This came out in a high-pitched squeal.

I put my hands out, palms up, hoping that would get him to quiet down. We finally had some distance between the enemy and us; I didn't want him blowing that.

"You struck an officer!!"

"I'm going to do it again if you don't take a civil tone. You can be as pissed as you want, report what you want, but stop fucking endangering my squad." I'd taken a step closer, definitely breaking into his sphere of influence. I needed him to shut up, but I hoped I hadn't pushed him toward the funky chicken dance again. He stared into my eyes for a moment longer; I could see the muscles in his arms twitching, preparing to strike out. Finally, he relaxed his shoulders let them roll down while he unfurled his hands.

"You cannot punch me." He defended his actions.

"Are you alive?"

"That's beside the point!"

"Is it? Because if I hadn't knocked you out, you'd be halfway through a zombie's colon by now. That doesn't seem like a great ending to the day."

"Why?"

"Why? You're asking why did I save you? Weird, a thank you would have been cool, but I guess I'll take what's offered. Why would I want you dead? Sure, you're kind of a dick, and you wanted to force me out from my command in your little power grab, but that's hardly a death sentence-worthy infraction. I don't know you or what you do on the ship, but you must be fairly decent at your position for Eastman to entrust you to take over my squad. Whatever it is you do, Malton, I think we both can agree you're better at that than you are out here. And that's alright. Not everyone should be out doing this shit. I'm not going to lie; most of us here have a few screws loose, the inner workings of our minds bouncing around a bit when we move. Look at Kirby and Grimm over there, playing cards in an active warzone without a care in the world. The humming fool? That's my brother. My guess is he's listening to some Lita Ford on his Reagan-era tape machine. Reed is squirting tubes of peanut butter into his mouth to see how many he can fit because Walde bet him a dollar. Her record is eight and he needs to beat her. Dallas is making moleskin moccasins. Tommy just choked down a Pop-Tart that smelled like steamed cabbage and baloney."

"Crose," Tommy spewed out, his mouth full.

"Harmon is counting her bullets because that's what she does every time we stop, and Rose, well, I figure she's wondering how many sticks of dynamite it would take to rig the Eiffel Tower to come down. My Top...I mean, what can I say about him that won't cause the man to kill me? We'll leave it at that. Of us all, it may be Stenzel who's got it the most together, but that may only be because she's somehow able to still all the demons in her mind so she can focus on taking a shot that the rest of us would consider impossible."

"What's your point?" Malton asked.

"Huh. I figured that was fairly obvious. You're not wired wrong enough for this job." He turned away to rub at his eyes, I left him to his own devices.

"Hell of a pep talk," BT said as an aside.

"Did it work?" I didn't want to look back.

"Maybe. It looks like he's getting ready to rejoin the group."

"You think he's still going to bring me up on charges?"

"Without a doubt."

"I guess that's okay. I haven't had a reason to wear my dress blues in a while."

"I noticed you didn't mention yourself when you were giving the freak report on the squad."

I smiled at him. "All right, ladies and gents, finish up what you're doing, we're leaving in one."

I was surprised at the lieutenant; he had no problems keeping up or staying there. I again kept Harmon at the front; she kept a decent pace. After a few miles, I watched as Gary and Grimm began to lose their places in the column and slowly drift back. I was the last in the column proper, Kirby was about fifty yards behind. We couldn't jog the whole fucking way to where we needed to go. When I called a halt, Grimm flopped to the ground like a melodramatic soccer player looking for a foul. Gary took much longer fumbling around for his music than was customary.

"Anything?" I asked Kirby as he caught up.

"Shit, sir, nothing. Haven't even seen a bird. Little bit eerie, if you ask me."

"Dallas, Rose, perimeter duty. We're going to stay here for a few minutes."

BT was looking to the sky.

"Yeah, I know, we're going to need shelter in a few hours. No sense in running everyone into the ground. I want to scope the area out, look for some alternate means of transportation. I'd even think about a horse right now."

"Really?" BT arched a brow.

"Not really, but that I even said it should show you how desperate I am."

"Sir, might have something," Dallas said. "You're going to want to see this." She was motioning to me to come over. It didn't seem to be an emergency of any kind, so that she was messing with my downtime was slightly irritating. I quickly got over it when I saw what she was pointing at. A large green sign proclaimed *Gillicuddy's Sweetheart Bicycle Rentals*.

"Might as well check it out. Top, Dallas and I are going to check out a storefront."

"Need back up?" he asked.

"Not yet. If that changes, we're close enough you'll be able to hear our screams."

"Super comforting, sir," Dallas said.

All of the lower windows to the two-story establishment were broken. What was strange was the glass was on the outside. Vandals didn't generally enter to do something like that. I poked my head in to get a look; there was a fair amount of destruction, but not the kind one would equate to a battle. I was no crime scene investigator, but if I had to bet money, my guess was this was staged. Maybe the owner, having had a downturn in business, used the zombie apocalypse as a way to make an insurance claim. Obviously, they had not known the extent of the event or they wouldn't have bothered.

"I have a confession, sir," Dallas stated tentatively.

"Do I want to hear this?" I asked.

"I don't know how to ride a bike."

A broad grin appeared on my face. "Then this is your lucky day! For the rest of us, not so much. Top, get everyone over here."

"Tandem bikes? Are you serious?" Reed looked absolutely appalled. "I'm a highly trained military man, and you want us gallivanting around the country on bicycles built for two? This can't be happening."

I wasn't thrilled about the prospect, but he seemed mortified. I was thankful that Jodi Gillicuddy, according to the strewn business cards, hadn't deemed it necessary to slash the tires on the bikes. Probably couldn't bring himself to do it. Within ten minutes, we had seven operating cycles. The bigger problem was getting six alpha Marines to agree to ride in the backseat. Rose made it abundantly clear that Kirby was going to be her bitch; he fell in line easily enough. Dallas had to ride in the back as no one was going to trust a person that didn't know how to ride a bike to steer the ship. Gary thought it was a hoot to get on the back, okay, so maybe not *too* difficult. Top ordered Grimm, and Walde ordered Reed.

"Maybe you shouldn't have been such a malcontent, and you wouldn't have to stare at my backside," Walde told him. I didn't know if anything was going on between the two, but he could have done worse. He played at reluctantly taking his position, but it would have been difficult to miss where his eyes tracked.

"I'll take the lone bike," Tommy offered. We were odd-numbered, and someone was going to have to go solo. The bikes were heavy, heavier than they should have been, and he was going to have to work doubly hard to pedal his. It wasn't much of a burden to him, but I was still thankful he was sparing someone else the hardship.

"Ha, ha!" Grimm pointed at Kirby's plight.

"You make my job so easy sometimes," BT told him, pointing to the back of the bike he was holding.

"Dammit," Grimm muttered.

I shook my head when Malton went for the head of the bike. I didn't trust him. Stenzel picked up my movements and took the lead. The lieutenant, surprisingly, got on the back without protesting. That left Harmon and Gary, and my brother had already made his choice.

"You ready?" I told Dallas.

"You're not going to crash, are you?"

"Wasn't planning on it, but one never knows."

"Great." She grabbed a helmet.

While she was adjusting the straps, I found a screwdriver and removed the small bell attached to the handlebars. It would have been entirely too tempting to ring the little fucking thing no matter how much unwanted attention it would draw. I know my limitations. Without prompting, BT went over to Kirby's handlebars and ripped his bell off.

Within five minutes, we were cruising along. It was far from the most comfortable experience. The seat felt like it was made from wood. I think Gillicuddy took his cue from some fast-food joints that made their seats deliberately uncomfortable to prompt their patrons to leave as soon as they had finished their meal. I couldn't blame them for this somewhat underhanded tactic. When I was a little kid, my mother would drag me out to lunch with her and her sisters; they would sit there for what seemed like hours. Drinking cup after cup of coffee, smoking cigarettes, and discussing all manner of adult stuff I had no desire to join in about. Besides the seat feeling like it was trying to sandpaper my ass away, the abundance of shifting weight from my gear added to the overall discomfort. Then, just because I felt like bitching, the muscles in my thighs were burning from the unusual effort. Riding a bike was something I hadn't done since I'd got my learner's permit.

"Are you pedaling back there?" I asked Dallas.

"I was going to ask the same thing of you," she replied.

I had a feeling if I cut through the frame of the bike, it would be filled with cement—just another way for Gillicuddy to ensure no one pedaled off with his wares. No one in their right mind would want a four-hundred-pound bicycle. If, at some point, I stumbled across Gillicuddy on this adventure, I was going to fatten his lip. Went for a couple of hours until I called a halt. It took me over a dozen steps before I could stand correctly. My back was protesting, and I did my best not to let the rest know I was in sheer agony. There were two reasons I'd stopped where I had, first was to figure out how far we were from our destination; the other was the Apothecary door I was staring at.

"No," BT said as he watched me looking over.

I motioned for him to turn off his headset and come over. "I'm in some trouble, man. My back is seizing up, and I'm afraid it's going to lock. I need muscles relaxers or something along those lines. Could probably use a half dozen aspirin as well."

"How is this possible? I thought…you know, because of your…" He made a circular gesture around his top teeth.

"I should be dead, so this is an improvement, but Tommy said it's going to take time. A couple more months at float, and I probably would have been just fine, but right now, bud, I'm fucking hurting so bad that if it was just you and me, I'd be crying."

"Jesus, Mike, I didn't know."

"Can you help me in there without it making it look like you're helping?"

BT turned back to the squad. "What the fuck are you looking at? Set up a guard rotation and get some food."

"Great. If they weren't watching, they are now. Just follow me close, so they don't see me shuffling along." I paused at the door; reaching out with my arm to open it seemed like it might be enough to set off a cascade of issues resulting with me being paralyzed on the ground. Instead, I just got the weight of my body to force it open. A part of me was concerned that zombies might be inside, but, one thing at a time. The place was ransacked, but in an English way, if that makes sense. In the States, when we went in to scavenge an establishment, most times it looked as if Rose had preceded us. Meaning a bomb had gone off. Stuff ripped to shreds, trash everywhere, and usually a fair amount of blood to go along with it. This place appeared to have been looted in an orderly manner, shopped, if you will, people only taking what they needed. I had my doubts that the pharmacy portion would have anything worthwhile unless I wanted to get my hemorrhoids under control; should probably knock on wood after that. I rested with my hand against a bare shelf.

"I'll go look," BT said.

"I figured that was assumed," I told him as my head sagged.

"Do you know what I'm looking for?" he asked once he got behind the counter.

My head perked. "There are options?"

"Surprisingly, yes, and no, I'm not looking for any hard pain killers."

"You don't have to be a dick about it."

"You're loony enough without drugs."

I was racking my brain for names of drugs, but who remembers that shit? The doc prescribes me something, I take it and toss the bottle. Most times, I don't even spend the time going over the extensive list of side effects. (Besides, the anal leakage only happened once, and, sadly, the devil horns receded after a week.)

"I have no idea."

"Lot of insulin here. Pregnancy vitamins. Prozac types of drugs. It looks like they left the stuff that other people would need."

"Shit like that makes me believe that people are worth saving." I was making my way over.

"You serious?" BT looked over.

"Nah, not really; we're all shit. Hopefully when all of this is over, the dolphins will learn how to walk on land and take over; they seem much more playful."

"Fuck, sometimes I forget just how strange you are." BT was busy looking through the meds.

"I truly figure the problem is that the surviving species will end up either being crocodiles or rats because they already have legs. I can't imagine things will work out too well with either of them in charge."

"Hah!" He held up a large white bottle. "Norflex."

I held out my hand.

"Don't you want to know the side-effects?"

"Are they worse than not being able to function in a hot zone?"

"I…I don't think so."

"Then gimme." I dry swallowed three.

"Normal dose is once every twenty-four hours."

"Looks like I just took care of three days then."

"I don't think that's how it works."

"Sure, man, if one is good, three is better," I told him.

A little bell above the door let us know we had company.

"Hey," Tommy said. "Everything okay?"

"Besides Talbot taking enough meds to relax a cow? Sure."

"My back," I explained when Tommy looked over. "I can feel everything tightening up, and my legs are getting tingly and numb, not sure how long it's going to be until I can't move them."

"You didn't tell me that part!" BT was alarmed.

"I didn't want to worry you."

"What's changed? Because now you have," he said.

"Shit. I suppose I should have waited until you went out then."

Tommy came over. "I should be able to stretch you out." Without warning, he wrapped his arms around my waist and leaned back.

"I feel like Baby."

"From *Dirty Dancing*?" BT asked.

I would have outstretched my arms for effect, but that was a hard no at the moment. Tommy leaned back further.

Between the pressure on my lower back and being pulled out of position like that, I was in agony, eyes closed, teeth clenched tight. I wanted to tap out, let him know that he'd bested me in this MMA bout, but my arms hung limply by my side.

"Please," I begged weakly. I felt like a rag doll as he shook me up and down. Then came a loud popping noise, a flood of heat expanded from my lower back all the way to the tips of my extremities. Tommy gently put me down, making sure to keep me standing, as it was not something I could do on my own. My legs felt rubbery, but the pain had faded—not gone, but in the background. Kind of like the issues in my head, in the background, at least during the day. They tend to creep to the fore at night.

The bell rang again, this time, it was Stenzel. She quickly took in what was happening. I was leaning against the counter, Tommy half holding me and BT watching intently, didn't take a whole bunch of deduction to reason out something was wrong with me.

"Umm, sir, we have a possible sighting of zees, and Lieutenant Malton looks like he might go running off."

"Coming," BT told her. "You good?" he asked me. I nodded. "Turn your headset on, I'll let you know if we need to leave." I nodded again.

Riding a bike at that very moment was out of the question. Even if all I had to do was sit and hold the handlebars, it seemed an impossible task. I got nauseous thinking about having my feet on the pedals and the pain it would cause to have my legs rise and fall.

"Did that help? I could do it again," Tommy said

"God no," was my reply. "Maybe I could just stay here, and you guys could swing by on your way back."

"You're okay with leaving the lieutenant in charge?"

"You're right; you're going to have to shoot him." I turned my headset on.

"...albot." BT had said my name with a decidedly cockney accent.

"Repeat that last, Top."

"We're going to have to get moving." I could hear the concern in his voice.

"I could drive you," Tommy whispered.

I shook my head. I didn't want to show weakness. Don't know what my problem was; it wasn't like this was a baboon troop and my rule would be challenged if I was in anything but prime form. I took a shaky step, then another. Either what Tommy had done or the relaxants were beginning to kick in or a combination of both, but I felt marginally better. Can't say mission-ready-better, but enough. Stenzel gave me a surreptitious glance then quickly looked away. No one else did, which was good. She was keeping her concerns to herself.

"What's going on?" I asked. I may have moved my head too quickly; I got a tracer effect, like my eyes weren't tracking properly. In hindsight, maybe taking three pills wasn't the wisest decision.

Grimm came over with a pair of binoculars and pointed to a field off to our left.

"Reavers, fuck." I would have let my head sag if I wasn't worried that I wouldn't have the muscle strength left to lift it back up.

"We can stay and fight; the drug store is a fairly secure location," BT offered.

"We push on. Mount up everyone."

Not quite the charge of the Light Brigade," Gary said as he got on his bike.

"We can't outrun those!" Malton's legs were twitching wouldn't be long until he had another episode, and we didn't have the time.

"Can't if we stay here. Let's go." I hoped everyone was busy getting on their rides instead of watching me struggle to get on mine.

"Sir?" Would have been impossible for Dallas to miss it, though. I gave her a thumbs up. I stood on my up pedal, using my entire weight to get the behemoth moving. The compression of nerves felt like I'd placed them in a vise and tightened down to the point of making them explode—that or maybe a cattle prod to the general area. Agony is a good word to describe how I was feeling. Dallas didn't waste any time lending her efforts, so my next pedaling foray wasn't quite as painful. Any subsiding was good, no matter how minute. Once we were up to cruising speed, the pain lessened, or the pills strengthened; either way, I was good with that.

"We're going to need to move faster," Tommy was in the back. I didn't bother to look, but I could feel the shift in our bike, meaning Dallas had.

"He's very much right, sir," she informed me.

Moving at a good clip on a decent bike was roughly thirty miles per hour; on the clunkers we had, even with an extra person pedaling, reaching twenty-five seemed out of the question. Twenty on the downhill seemed doable.

"How many?" I asked. The looser my back got, the more my eyes wanted to roll around inside my head. It was not a great sensation. I almost told Dallas to take over the steering until I remembered her handlebars were nothing more than a static grip. There was still a chance she'd be able to steer better than me.

"Ten," he answered with confidence.

Reavers were basically hunting dogs. If they were on the prowl, so were their overlords. We stop to kill them, and the much larger force behind would have an opportunity to catch up. For now, our best course of action was to keep going. It was likely we wouldn't be able to outpace the reavers, the vast majority of the zombies, though, would not be able to keep up. Just because they were tireless didn't necessarily make them fast. *A few more miles*, I told myself, *then we'll take care of the immediate problem and keep on going.* What's that old saying about plans? Even the best-laid ones can suck a scab encrusted dick? Something like that, right?

We rounded a corner and were now staring up at Mount Everest. I mean, not really, but the hill was fairly steep, as far as hills go. We'd never keep up our speed, trying to push our heavy metal bikes up the mountain.

"BT, somewhere defendable, now," I told him.

I saw his rider's head swiveling around for a place that didn't suck. Considering I'd made my request on a two-lane country road, his options were severely limited.

"Culvert or hedges?" Grimm asked.

"That'll work," I answered without doing any such thing.

BT pulled over to the edge of the road.

"Should we use the bikes as a wall?" I think Stenzel thought she was joking, but considering the construction of the damn things, there was a good chance we could make an impregnable cage from them. My muscle had gone from taut as a tow strap in use to billowy as seaweed in a gentle current. BT came over under the pretense to talk about defense options when in reality, it was to help me off the bike. By now, it didn't appear to be much of a secret that I was less than a hundred percent. I don't know how or when that happened. We'd been biking along, and we were all on the same frequency, so no one was talking about it. The reavers were a lot closer than I'd anticipated. Safe bet we wouldn't have made it halfway up the hill before they started dragging us down from the rear. We, in fact, did use the bikes as a barricade, making a semi-circle barrier out of them with our backs to a thick hedgerow. We now had a breezy fort.

"There has to be a better place." Malton's eyes opened so wide he looked perpetually surprised. He kept looking at the shrubbery for a place he could escape into, but without a chainsaw and a half-hour, he wasn't going anywhere. Once he started to pace back and forth, I nodded at BT to calm him down.

"Stenzel, set up your super sniper shop," I said.

"Sir?" She looked back.

"Might be the muscle relaxants making me loopy; the alliteration sounded better in my head. Kill some reavers."

"Why is the cap telling Stenzel she can't read?" Kirby asked.

"If you weren't so damn pretty." Rose gently stroked the side of his face.

"What?"

"He didn't say she was illiterate," Rose answered.

Stenzel placed the barrel of her rifle upon a bike seat. "Open for business." The thing about my sniper was not only was she an incredible shot but her ability to acquire a target and make a lethal shot quickly was an enviable quality. I knew I was a decent shot, but on my best day with targets moving half as fast and much closer, I would not have been able to shoot with her efficiency. She was doing so well I thought about taking a seat before my back started waving hello at me. I didn't think it was a good idea to be that cavalier about the entire situation, that, and I wasn't so sure I'd be able to stand up on my own. The rest of the squad was ready for mop-up duty; two reavers had made it through Stenzel's ring of death only to be met with a barrage of bullets. From start to finish, the minor skirmish had only lasted a few minutes. Enough for Malton to have a mini-meltdown and long enough for my back to begin tightening. I wasn't sure how I was going to make it up the hill.

It would have been better if I'd switched up rides and had either Tommy or BT drive me, but you know, stupid, sinful pride. The bikes came efficiently equipped with only one gear, so mechanical physics couldn't help. There would be no throwing it into high gear, easy-pedaling like mad without going anywhere. The first third wasn't horrible; we'd built enough speed to cruise up with barely a change, then it abruptly altered as I had to stand, using all of my weight to assist in the process, Dallas was doing all she could, if her grunts of exertion were any indication, and still, we were losing ground on the pack. Tommy was bringing up the rear, making sure to stay behind us.

"Mr. T."

"If you tell me zombies are coming, I'm going to ground you," I said as I was breathing heavily.

He remained silent. Whoever made up the saying that ignorance is bliss nailed it. That is, until you realize that just because you remain oblivious to the facts doesn't make them disappear. We were halfway up, and our speed was hardly above a vigorous walking speed. I wasn't even sure how we were keeping the bike upright. BT, who was in the lead, was cresting the hill. The idea of sitting back and coasting down the other side was about the only thing keeping me going, I mean, that and not getting eaten.

"Umm," Tommy cleared his throat.

"What did I say?" I asked.

"Talbot, get your ass moving and don't pull that grounding shit on me! We're not related!" BT shouted. "Wait, I guess we are. Shit. But you can't put me in time out."

"Dallas, I'm spent. We need to run." That was our best option; we'd be moving faster than this glacial pace.

"Sir, I can bring you up to the top," Tommy offered.

As awesome as that sounded, I was not going to leave Dallas to make it on her own. "Fucking Eastman," I muttered. He was an easy scapegoat. Another couple of weeks, month maybe, and I would have been close to a hundred percent; now I was placing my people in jeopardy because I couldn't perform at my optimum. I brought the bike to a halt and nearly tipped as I wasn't able to move my leg fast enough to keep us upright. It was Tommy's hand grabbing my handlebar and Dallas picking up the slack that kept that from happening.

"Go." I urged Dallas. She was hesitant. "Don't make me order you," I told her.

I started walking the bike up; we still needed the torture device.

"Don't think that's a good idea," Tommy interceded.

I had still not turned around to check on the pursuit. I was not at all expecting to hear a gunshot, followed by a bunch more. Like always in life, this was both good and bad. Good because zombies were getting shot, and our withdrawal was being covered, bad because the zombies were close enough to necessitate being shot.

Tommy had dismounted. He urged me to run while he grabbed my bike and ran alongside me, pushing both our rides. For right or wrong, I am a prideful man, and it'd been a long time since I'd felt that useless. He was easily keeping pace as I struggled. Whenever I felt as if I'd struck a plateau with my pain, I was not so pleasantly reminded it could still climb higher. At some point, I was able to cut through my misery to note that Tommy had glanced from me to the bikes. I knew what he was thinking.

"No," I told him flatly. Just because my pride had taken a severe ding didn't mean I was going to consider it totaled, sell it for scrap. There was a part of me that would rather get eaten than be carried—pride goeth before the fall and all that shit. I could hear the zombies' footfalls over my tortured breathing. I wondered if it was time to fight. BT didn't think so; he was waving me on like he'd bet his last ten spot on me to finish the race.

I focused on my squad up ahead. All of them were shooting except for Malton, who had not gotten off his bike. He was waiting like the getaway driver for a bank heist, nervous and sweaty. All he needed was a bunch of snuffed-out cigarette stubs by his foot, and he'd be all set. His blackened eyes shone wetly as they watched everything. Fifty feet from the top, BT came down to meet me and mostly dragged me the rest of the way. For some reason, this was acceptable in my pride versus humility equation. He said something, but the meaning got lost in the buzzing disruptor of pain, blanketing my neurons. I was dimly aware of Rose sending a few rounds with her grenade launcher. It seemed exceedingly close, and the rifle fire became one unbroken snapping sound of bullets tearing into combatants. I wanted to bend over and suck in some air but fundamentally knew that if I did so, the gears in my back would lock up, and I'd forever be bent over at a forty-five-degree angle, suitable for a continuous fucking by the universe. I may have earned that, but I had no such desire. I already felt as if the bitch had had her way with me and not even sprung for a suitable meal.

I shambled over to the only bike still standing. Dimly I noted that Malton had switched from the back to the front. Later I would speculate that he'd been about to take off. It wasn't going to happen while I was propping myself up against it. If he knew I couldn't have even waved at him as he sped away, there was a good chance he would have done it anyway. He was about as trustworthy as a politician at a PAC meeting.

"You ready, sir?" Dallas's eyes were wide as she came over with our bike.

"I…"

"I'll drive," she said.

The last time I'd been so scared when I heard those words was when I was teaching Justin how to drive. The kid could do a lot of things at a high level, that just wasn't one of them. Our first venture had been with a stick shift, my thought process being, once you know how to drive one of those, the rest was gravy. Yeah not sure what I was thinking there. It was like each part of him was operated by independent and opposing entities, the left leg having no clue what the right was up to. When he stared out the passenger side window to make a turn, I'd seen enough. I told him that, whatever driving video games he had been learning his technique from, he needed to request a refund.

"What?"

"I'll lead the bike. I think I can do it."

I think I can is fine when it's in regard to homework, for example, I think I can solve this algebraic equation. Flying down a hill on a two-wheeled mode of transportation with zombies in tow was different. Then there was the problem of me raising my leg high enough to get on. That was solved easily enough. Tommy finally got his wish, lifting me up and dropping me unceremoniously onto the bike seat. The bolt of torment wiped all else away. The next thing I registered was the feeling of wind in my face. The bike was wobbling slightly. Dallas, instead of going with the flow, was fighting the bike, attempting to correct every slight deviation. She was going to overcorrect us into a major spill, one that was likely going to cost me a medical evac. If I was confident that there would be one of those, I would have leaned far enough to one side just to get it over with.

"Easy," I told her. "Your grip is too tight. Your whole body."

"I'm terrified!" she yelled.

"Just let the bike do the heavy lifting." I had to shout to be heard, making what I hoped was soothing sound anything but. Stenzel and Malton passed us by on the right. The lieutenant was pedaling like mad; Stenzel had taken her legs entirely up and off. She gave a slight shake of her head as she went. I saw her mouth the word *dipshit*. The hill was long and winding, but at some point, it was going to become necessary for me to help move the thing, and I didn't think I was up for it. The stretch we were on now was in a state of disrepair; my eyes were jiggling so violently I didn't even bother trying to focus. To Dallas's credit, we never did face plant onto the pavement, and for that, I was thankful. BT brought us to a halt, and, invariably, all eyes went to the top of the hill. I could tell by the reactions of my squad that nothing had yet crested the top. That was a good sign. The bad one was up ahead. Stenzel and Malton both had their hands in the air, and not in any "I don't care" aspect.

"Sir, we have a situation here," Stenzel said calmly. Malton, on the other hand, sounded like an overconfident Chihuahua telling the mailman he's going to rip his ankles to shreds. They were close to a bend in the road; whoever had got the drop on them had strategically placed themselves in a position where I couldn't see them.

"What's going on?" I managed to dismount. Took a few stumbling steps but luckily didn't fall.

"Got a kid…"

"Man!" I heard the shout over Stenzel's mic and through the air.

"Got a…" she paused, "man here with what looks like an antique Winchester 1887 breech-loading ten-gauge shotgun pointed at us."

"Loaded?"

"Not sure how you would want me to find that out, sir. He says if anyone comes close, he'll make sure we die, and considering it looks like I'm staring at a cannon, I'm ready to believe him."

"It's a kid, Stenzel. Can you get the drop on him?"

She hesitated. "It's a kid, sir," she said softly.

Meaning she could, but that would potentially mean putting a bullet in him before he had a chance to cut her in half.

"What's he want?" I was moving into a position where I could see what was going on.

"What do you want?" Stenzel asked.

"I want you to fuck off." I didn't need my sergeant to repeat it to hear, though she did.

"That's helpful." A couple of steps later, I had him. Kid couldn't have been more than eight. He was leaning back as a counterbalance to the much too large weapon he was holding.

If it was loaded and he shot, he would end up on his ass. I didn't like sighting in on zombie kids; this was far worse.

"Put the weapon down!" I shouted, moving closer. He looked over, but the muzzle of the rifle never wavered.

"No." He gave a simple enough answer; the repercussions were anything but.

"I don't want to shoot you, but I will, to save my personnel."

"You move any closer, and you won't have to worry about it."

For an eight-year-old, he sounded like a hardened criminal that had served decades in the joint and was not going back. By now I had back up; I wasn't concerned for myself, though.

"What's your name?" I asked, hoping to break through what I figured was merely a candy-coated shell hiding the goodness within.

Instead, he ratcheted the lever. Not sure I'd ever known a shotgun to have a ratchet, but there it was.

"I'm Captain Talbot."

"Good for you." This time he didn't bother looking.

I couldn't even fathom how someone so young could be so jaded until I remembered that his formative years were spent surviving an apocalypse; that he was alive meant he'd already bucked the odds. It was likely he'd had to do all manner of mind-twisting actions to get to this point. It was also likely he'd never be able to fit into a traditional society, should one appear. Not any more. Not with the neural pathways he'd been forced to create.

"You kill them, you won't live to regret it," I told him.

"L...l...listen to the captain," Malton pleaded.

The kid smiled, I think. It was among the creepiest things I'd ever seen. It never touched his cold, pitiless eyes. The lips pulled straight back to reveal his yellow stained teeth.

"This one here your weak link? I could be doing you a

favor." The smile, or whatever it was, remained even as he spoke, like it was some sort of strange ventriloquism act.

"Jesus," BT muttered next to me. He must have shut his mic off because what I heard thankfully didn't go out to the rest of the squad. "He's going to shoot."

"You sure?" I needed him to be.

"Without a doubt."

We were close, but not so close that what I was about to try wasn't without risks. If I missed, this was going to be a bloodbath. A kill shot would have been easier. I fired, aiming for the meatiest part of the rifle. I mostly succeeded. There was a deafening boom before the shotgun fell to the ground. I'd amputated the ring finger on the kid's left hand; blood poured from the wound. The little bastard had still managed to get a shot off, destroying the front wheel of Stenzel's bike. The kid had the nuts to reach for the gun, but by that time, Stenzel had her rifle trained on him. Malton still had his hands in the air.

"Harmon, can you get him checked out," I said as I went and moved the rifle and any temptation to retrieve it. The kid glared at me even as he protectively cradled his wounded hand.

"Don't touch me." He pulled away from Harmon as she came closer with the small first aid kit.

On the surface, I felt bad that I'd hurt the kid. But, hidden in a dark corner that was becoming larger all the time, the thought was there. Perhaps the wiser thing to do would have been to put this one down. I knew there was evil in the world, just figured it didn't show itself in people until after puberty. Maybe I should have paid more attention to the *Damien* movie franchise.

"Comply or die!" Malton was a half octave away from shattering crystal as he pointed his pistol at the kid's face.

I thought about telling the lieutenant to take it down a notch, but something instinctual said not to, to see how this played out. There was more at play here than I could see. A battle for good and evil that didn't necessarily have anything to do with me, other than I could change the course of some distant far-off war. The problem was I didn't know in which way I would alter it. Still, we were dealing with a kid here. I could not judge him for something he had not done and may never do.

"Lieutenant, put it away." I had my hand out and was slowly approaching. Malton didn't look good; he'd been pushed to his breaking point.

MAC & WILKES

Mac TIGHTLY GRIPPED the pages he was reading, nearly bending the journal in half. "It can't be!" He peered at the pages, willing them to give up their secrets.

"What's the matter?" Wilkes asked, never having seen her traveling partner act like this. He had become more vested in the story as he'd continued to read, but this was different.

"They had him! Wilkes, they had him!" He looked over at her, his eyes wild with an emotion she couldn't identify, desperation, despair, maybe some hope.

"I don't know what you're talking about."

He stood, the journal now balled up in his fist. "They fucking had him! Why didn't they kill him?"

"What?" She instinctively backed up.

"McGowan! It's McGowan, as a kid! He has a missing finger—he never said how it happened but…"

"That's not much to go on."

Fundamentally Mac knew Wilkes was right. Most times, with the lack of health care, the best way to deal with an injury was amputation. It was common to see people with missing appendages. But he couldn't shake the nagging suspicion. Talbot had known, had felt something off about the boy. "Why didn't he do something?" he begged.

"You said you weren't even sure if these stories were real," Wilkes offered. "And…and even if they are, what are the chances it's him? Just think of all that happened. You try to kill him and run away, you find me, I find the journals, and they just so happen to be written about the very same person?"

"I know….I know, it sounds strange…too coincidental, but maybe…" he paused, opening the journal back up and trying to smooth it out. "Maybe there's something in here, something I can use to stop him."

"What about Scotland?" Wilkes asked hopefully.

"You don't understand. He's a monster; he's killed so many people, people like you just trying to do their best to survive. They either become slaves for his war machine, or they become victims. I owe it to them. I was given this chance for a reason." He shook the pages in her face.

Wilkes didn't like what she was seeing. She'd seen more than a few people get lost in religious fervor as they attempted to make sense of an increasingly harsh world. Mac had that same crazed look.

"What are you going to do?" she asked as he sat and started reading again.

"I don't know yet, but when it happens, it'll be epic!"

TALBOTSODE 1

My wife and I used to have a routine, long before this shit storm started. It revolved around going to sleep. I had a set bedtime that gave me just enough downtime to start the next morning of work. Now that I'm writing this down, maybe the routine was just mine and she followed suit? Weird how you gain clarification upon examination. Losing track here. Eleven. Eleven o'clock was when I liked to go to bed. I got up at six, got ready for work and then my commute. I worked fine on seven hours of sleep; six was a different story. (Won't go there now, suffice it to say that one hour made everyone around me an asshole.) Yup, clarification upon examination; perhaps it was my perspective that changed.

Tracy used to work for the airlines, so her schedule was much more fluid than mine. I was the more traditional eight to five, Monday through Friday guy, but she could work the swing shift occasionally, the dreaded overnight, or Dracula shift, as I liked to call it, and even sometimes the more standard fare. All of that was fine until it came to her sleep time, which could vary wildly. I was the creature of habit, and she was the fly by the seat of her pants monster. It would have made more sense if we slept in different rooms during this time in our lives, but we were a relatively newly married couple with kids, and I don't think the option ever truly presented itself. Even if we had considered it, there were no free rooms available, and our couch was as comfortable as burlap covered sandbags.

Did I say eleven? Right? I mean, that's when I went to bed, not ten fifty-nine not two past. But Tracy, I mean, I don't think it was conscious thing, but just as I'm getting ready to turn the light out, she would get up. Like, every time. Or check her iPad for the book she was listening to, or realizing she'd completed the book and needed to get the next one, would spend time shopping for another. It was like bedtime had snuck up on her, and she panicked, trying to finish her evening. Looking back, I don't think it was a passive-aggressive thing, sort of tracks that way, though, doesn't it? I used to roll with it because, well, I'm a somewhat smart man, and I knew that going to sleep after being punched would take a while, all that throbbing around the impact area and half-meant apologizing. The delay on her part was generally a standard four minutes. Yes, an anger would build in me for those two hundred and forty seconds. Sure, I realize it sounds like a small amount of time, but it was the inconsideration of the gesture. It was as if she were saying "Yes, I know you have a routine, it's just that I don't give a shit about it."

Then came this confluence of events. She got up to use the facilities, came back to realize her book was done and she'd need to purchase another. Okay, so far standard fare and then the biggie.

"Oh, the battery is low. I need to charge it for a few minutes."

Then I hit her with this line. "*What?* You can't even be late on time!" It was delivered with a dose of irritation, but we ended up laughing our asses off, I mean, until the next night when we repeated the whole thing. The woman had the memory of a goldfish, not that I'm telling *her* that because *that* she would remember as if it had been etched onto her hippocampus.

25

MAC & WILKES

"Mac."

"Yeah," he answered.

"I understand what you said about the journals, that they're his record of the events that transpired, part homage, part remembrance. A way to ensure that the apocalypse isn't forgotten."

"That's what I believe."

"These small stories at the end, though, that have nothing to do with the rest of the pages. Why?"

Mac thought for a moment, his hand cupping his chin. Wilkes liked when he did that, it meant he was truly considering the question. "I think that he writes these asides as a way to remember more than the worst of what the world had to offer during his time. That once, there was a life worth living, that it didn't always revolve around tragedy and heartache. Does that make sense?"

"It does. I feel bad for him; how horrible it must have been." Wilkes shuddered.

It was long years since their protagonist's struggles had come to a violent end, but life now was not easy, either. They barely scraped out an existence, fighting for every morsel of food that could be scavenged, harvested or hunted. At least Talbot had, at one time, been able to go to a grocery store and pick up all manner of food products. Yes, Wilkes knew what they were, but before Mike had filled in the details, they were merely dilapidated shelters with faded signs, the barest indicators of the multitude of products that long ago resided on the now mostly collapsed shelving. Freezers and refrigerators that promised frozen dinners and the meat of animals already slaughtered, cleaned and neatly arranged for easy consuming. He could hardly remember, and he wondered if Wilkes could even imagine the concept. One place to get fruits, vegetables, breads; it made his head swim to think how easy living had been. Even after the zombies had come, packaged food had been plentiful. It was rare now, that they didn't go to sleep hungry.

"Do we have time for one more?" She looked over at him with pleading eyes. The sun had set an hour ago and the fire was kept low so as not to alert any nearby predators to their presence. Unlike in Mike's world, man was no longer at the top of the food chain.

26

TALBOTSODE 2

BT and I were sitting on the deck, not doing much of anything besides enjoying the silence. But we all know how I do with that.

"Hey, did I ever tell you about—"

"Yes," BT cut me off at the pass.

"How about—"

"Just the other day."

"You're seriously going to be able to sit here and have no noise except the occasional seagull?"

"Yes. Actually looking forward to it. You do realize your nephew has colic and has yet to sleep through an entire night, right?"

"I do and I can't tell you how sorry I am about that."

"Bullshit."

"Yeah. I know. It is fun to see someone else besides myself go through it."

"Ghosts?"

"What?" I asked.

"Is the story about ghosts? This is the time you generally do ghost stories."

"It can be, if you want."

"Maybe not. Already got enough of those running through my head," he replied after a few moments to think on it. I agreed. "Girls, then? You always feel the need to tell me about your exploits."

"It's locker room talk, and you're my best friend. You're supposed to eat that stuff up."

"Generally I do. Maybe it's the exhaustion." BT continued to look at me, kept eye contact to the point where it was uncomfortable. "Seriously, Talbot, that wasn't a big enough hint?"

"Oh I got it," I told him. "But I can't, man, I can't sit here in the quiet. There is no peace for me there."

BT's look softened. "Yeah, I get it, go on."

"Shit...where do I go." I looked up for inspiration.

"What? So all of this preamble and you don't even have a story to tell? You are truly a pain in the ass."

"Okay, okay. It was a dark and stormy night."

"You're plagiarizing Snoopy?"

"Fine. It was a clear and bright day, that better?"

"The stormy night thing has more pop."

"Got one!" I think I poked my tongue through my teeth.

"Go on with your bad self."

"I was laying in bed."

"Lying."

"No I'm not; I was definitely in bed."

"No, it's *lying* as opposed to *laying*."

"Are you seriously correcting my grammar while I'm trying to relate a story?"

"It would appear so." He clasped his hands behind his head, smiling. "You have your cheap thrills, I have mine. And considering a baby platypus has a better grip on the English language than you do, it's pretty easy to exploit."

"I was *lying* on the bed."

"See, you can teach an old dog new tricks."

"You're ruining this for me."

"Like you ruined my downtime?"

"That's like comparing apples to giraffes."

"Just go on. The sooner you're done, the sooner I get my nap."

"There's this guy."

"What's his name?"

"Shit, man, it's just a weird thought I had, I didn't get that far. But if it's that important we'll call him Brewer. That cool?"

"Like a beer maker?"

"I suppose," I told him.

BT nodded his approval.

"No more interruptions."

He again nodded.

"So Brewer, his wife, their two kids and a dog, just bought a house in New Hampshire, see? It's on a big plot of land. Sixty-four acres, to be exact."

"Arbitrary, but sure."

"You promised."

BT shrugged.

"It's a beautiful fall day. Brewer tells his wife, er, Sophie, that he's going to walk around the land a bit. It's New Hampshire, so it's foresty."

"Come on, Mike, foresty?"

I plowed on. It was a made-up word but it conveyed the meaning well enough. "Brewer is breaking through some dense brush, thorns, burrs, brambles, he was honestly thinking about heading back, he didn't want to tear his jacket. Just as he made up his mind that this jaunt wasn't worth it, he stepped onto a thin game trail, not much more than a foot and a half wide. He was enjoying himself now. He couldn't believe how lucky he was, being able to buy the home of his dreams with a huge chunk of land within his price range. Thinking something had to be wrong with the house, he'd sprung for two separate home inspections, but besides a couple of minor cosmetic issues, the home had a clean bill of health."

"A ghost coming now? This seems like ghost time."

"There's no damn ghost, now shut up. He's walking for fifteen minutes on this path, convinced by now that he can't still be on his land, but he doesn't think about it again. Beautiful fall day, no one is going to be angry about someone hiking in the woods."

"Except the ghost."

I decided to ignore him, that was the best strategy. "The path begins to get wider, not a bunch, but enough that the trees are no longer crowding him until finally he comes upon a clearing. It's circular, maybe fifty feet across, but it's not empty. In the middle is a pile of stacked stones some ten feet high, by ten wide and length."

"Like the New Hampshire Stonehenge?"

"You saw that documentary, too?"

BT nodded. "Weird thing. Still not sure if I believe it's an ancient artifact or a modern hoax."

"So Brewer is looking at this thing, walks around to the other side. The rocks are arranged in such a way that there's a kind of entry, not much more than four feet high, but enough he can duck down and take a look. But when he does, he can't see in more than an inch or two, it's just way too dark. He pulls out his phone, turns on the flashlight, but inside is like a black hole, it sucks the light away before it can illuminate anything."

"Tell me he left." BT was leaning forward. I had him now. I thought about ending the story with something about dirty diapers littering the floor of the cavern. I'm an ass, but generally not that big of one.

"What fun would that be?"

"Oh, so he's white." BT nodded. "Don't know what it is with your kind and doing stupid shit. Hey scary chain rattling noise in the basement? I think I'll go check it out. Power's out?

No big deal, I have this pen flashlight that illuminates eleven square inches. What? The crazed Disemboweler has escaped the nearby asylum, you say? Why would he possibly be in my basement of antique farm implements? If this was a movie, I'd be yelling at the screen right about now."

"Not me. I always wanted to see how stupid the actors were going to get."

"Why? Does it make you feel better to know there are people more senseless than you?"

"Words hurt, man, but yeah, that's one of the reasons. You're going to love this part. Brewer ducks down and steps in. Weirdest thing though, as his foot makes contact with the ground past the entry and his head clears the low threshold, he can see perfectly inside. A small tingle at the base of his skull shouts out a warning, which he completely crushes with the excitement of the discovery. He takes another step in and completely stands. When he looks back at the opening, it appears to be shimmering, sort of like one of those bathroom shower doors. You know the ones, they have that rippled glass, only the images he's looking at outside aren't nearly as distorted."

"This isn't enough for him to leave?"

"What would you do?" I asked.

BT mulled it over. "I don't know, man. I guess I'd be curious, too."

"I'm pretty sure I would have left," I told him.

"You couldn't be any more full of shit. You'd probably have a party inside there."

"Anyway, back to it. So Brewer takes another step then another. The weird thing is though, the back wall never gets any closer. Perspective-wise, he's always near dead center inside."

"Whoa this is crazy." BT had his hands clasped together and was listening intently.

"I know, right?"

"So you're in bed just thinking this crazy stuff?"

"Yeah, it gets weirder. Brewer decides that this is indeed strange, and he's going to head back out to see if he can find some information about this place on the internet, or maybe from the previous owner. He absolutely cannot wait to tell his wife about it. He heads quickly home but he forgets completely about the formation when he sees the large U-Haul in the driveway, and his wife Josie on the ramp, muscling down a box clearly labeled 'bedroom.'"

"Sophie."

"What?"

"Her name is Sophie, not Josie."

"You realize I'm making this up on the fly, right?"

"Fine, but try and stay consistent, and yeah, it makes sense. They did just move, but a dickish thing to do on his part, leaving her to unpack while he goes frolicking through the woods."

"That's the thing, man. He helped her unpack that truck three nights ago. They busted their asses to get it done so they wouldn't have to pay for an extra day of rental."

"'That was a hell of a bathroom break.' His wife looks over, sweat glistening on her forehead. 'If I didn't know any better, I would say you're trying to get out of work.'

"Brewer is confused as hell right now, that was the exact same line she delivered at the exact same time, only like I said, three days before."

"Is this a joke?" he asked.

"But she didn't hang around; the box wasn't getting any lighter and she had to go up a flight of stairs. He did the only thing he could think to do and that was help unload the truck *again*. Then not half an hour after it was emptied, right on cue, her parents show up and drop the kids off, same as before. Brewer is racking his brain trying to figure out what's going on. He takes the truck back and leaves it at the rental facility."

"'Everything all right?' Josie's, or Sophie's father Matt had followed him so he could give Brewer a ride home.

"I uh, yeah, I think. Long day," is all he can figure to say.

"They snag pizza from a place down the street. Brewer is thinking to himself that the order is screwed up."

"Jalapenos. He points to the pizza that's supposed to be pepperoni; Josie gives him a sidelong glance."

"Sophie. This is weird, keep going," BT prompts.

"JoSophina covers all my bases, cool?"

BT nodded.

"Brewer realizes that something happened in that rock formation, that he somehow went back in time three days. Has no clue how or why, but that's a fact, he can't deny it. If this were a practical joke, it's too involved, too in-depth to be pulled off so successfully, and to what purpose? He realizes in the next couple of minutes, his youngest, Brewer Junior, is going to try and flush an old stuffed animal down the toilet. There'll be a little flooding, and a much larger resultant fight. Brewer remembers being tired and suffering from indigestion, and he'd reacted a little stronger to the transgression than was merited. Damn near screamed at Junior. He got in a big row with Josie over it."

"Row?" BT asked.

"It means fight," I told him.

"Then why didn't you just say that?"

"I'm trying to expand my vocabulary."

"Right, right, I forgot about foresty."

"Done?" BT motioned that he was. "So, this time, Brewer decides to head Brewer Junior off at the pass."

"The poor kid's initials are BJ? His friends are going to ride him mercilessly over that," BT said.

I ignored him.

"Where are you going with Puffer?" Brewer asks little BJ; he's walking with his head down, dragging his stuffed bear along the hallway."

"Puffer needs to be washed; he's dirty from the move," BJ tells his father.

"How about we give him a bath." Brewer smiles. He and his kid use the tub and some baby shampoo to clean Puffer off.

"That night, instead of Brewer and Josie—Sophie, shit, got to remember that. So, instead of going to bed mad at each other, they make passionate love like they haven't since before the kids were born. Brewer still has no idea what the stone thing is all about, but it's fantastic. He lives out the next couple of days more or less the way it played out originally, but then he decides he wants to go back to the cavern and relive that wild night. I mean, who wouldn't, right? I would imagine having small kids just curtails the living hell out of any love life." Mike ribbed his friend. "Am I right?"

"The story is going good, don't screw it up," BT threatened.

"Fine fine. So on the same day he'd originally gone on the hike, he does the same thing, figuring it was all some sort of weird dream, and it's not going to be there."

"Was it?" BT was on the edge of his seat, any further and he would be able to play catcher.

"Dude, it was!"

"Hot damn." He clapped his hands. "I knew it would be. So what happens?"

"So Brewer, he goes through the brambles again, jogs down the path and bam! there it is. He cannot believe his luck. The past three days have been among some of the best in his life; reliving them again sounds like a dream. Plus, he knows how tonight is going to turn out, and that one thing he's always wanted to do, gets done."

"Okay, man, you don't need to go into that much detail, some of us don't have magic portals."

"Sorry," I told him with a smile that definitely told him I wasn't. "Brewer approached the formation; he had the briefest hesitation before he ducked down and went in. He did his best to replicate the same number of steps, figuring that had something to do with how far he had leapt back in time. The weird thing this time is, when he steps outside of the formation, he's no longer in New Hampshire. He's at a rest stop in Iowa. You can imagine how confused he is as he heads from the main building toward his U-Haul. Sophie is on her phone; he knows exactly what she's doing: shopping for curtains on Amazon."

"That was a hell of a bathroom break," she says as she looks up from the screen.

"I like the flannel ones better," Brewer says before she asks the question, her eyebrows furrow in confusion.

"Me too," she answers, not knowing how he'd known what she was about to ask. "Your turn to drive."

"You can imagine he's not overly thrilled to have to get behind the wheel again. The only decent part about this move was that his parents had flown out and flew back with the kids. He couldn't imagine a cross country trek with them."

"Too many steps into the structure?" BT asked.

TO BE CONTINUED!

ABOUT THE AUTHOR

Visit Mark at **www.marktufo.com**

Zombie Fallout TV Trailer
  https://youtu.be/FUQEUWy-v5o

For the most current updates join Mark's newsletter
  http://www.marktufo.com/contact.html
  I love hearing from readers, you can reach me at:

email
  mark@marktufo.com

website

www.marktufo.com

Facebook
https://www.facebook.com/pages/Mark-Tufo/
133954330009843?ref=hl

Twitter
@zombiefallout

For information on upcoming releases please join my newsletter at:
newsletter sign up

Zombie Fallout book Trailer
https://youtu.be/FUQEUWy-v5o

All books are available in audio version at iTunes Audible and Barnes and Noble.

DevilDog Press LLC

If you enjoyed the story please take a moment to leave a review. Thank you.

ALSO BY MARK TUFO

Zombie Fallout Series

Lycan Fallout Series

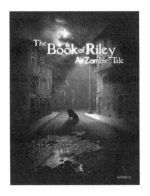

The Book Of Riley Series

Timothy Series

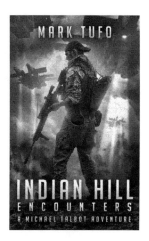

Indian Hill Series

Dystance Series

The Spirit Clearing

Callis Rose

Demon Fallout

Devils Desk

CUSTOMERS ALSO PURCHASED

CUSTOMERS ALSO PURCHASED:

SHAWN CHESSER
SURVIVING THE
ZOMBIE APOCALYPSE

WILLIAM MASSA
OCCULT ASSASSIN
SERIES

JOHN O'BRIEN
A NEW WORLD
SERIES

ERIC A. SHELMAN
DEAD HUNGER
SERIES

HEATH STALLCUP
MONSTER SQUAD
SERIES

MARK TUFO
ZOMBIE FALLOUT
SERIES